S.L. SCOTT

Print ISBN: 978-1-940071-36-7

Interior design: Angela McLaurin – Fictional Formats

Cover design: Kari March Designs

Front Cover Photographer: Samuel Ramirez

Featured on the Front Cover: Elliott Law

Editing:
Marion Archer of Making Manuscripts
Marla Esposito of Proofing Style
Nicole Strauss – Perfectly Publishable

*For the first cheerleader in my life
and the woman who gave me someone
to look up to. I love you, Mom.*

A PERSONAL NOTE

I'm so grateful to be surrounded by such love and talent. My greatest loves are my husband and children – I've said this before, but it still stands eternally true.

I am because of you.

To my mom, sister, and niece, and all of my family – I love you. You are brave and strong, beautiful and giving. Thank you for always sharing your love with me.

I am so fortunate to have friends who have stood by me for years. Some from the age of fourteen and some from before I earned a high school or college degree. You are my constants and I love you dearly – Jennifer, Kerri, and Kirsten.

My readers and the bloggers who have shared, reviewed, bought, loved my books – You are Amazing and I'll be forever thankful.

The book world has brought me some of the most wonderful souls into my life. You make this journey fun and exciting. You cheer me on daily and celebrate my successes as well as comfort me in times of need. Thank you Adriana, Danielle, Flavia, Heather, Irene, Kandace, Kellie, Laura, Lisa, Lynsey, Marla, Mary, Ruth and Sonia.

And I couldn't do what I do without the support and help of these amazing women. Some I've met and some I'm determined to meet soon, but they all hold a special place in my heart – Amy B., Andrea J., Serena M., Annette P., Kristen J., and Tiana, J. and to my amazing Kiss & Tells.

Thank you so my #PartyWhores. You make me smile and laugh. You are amazing and a highlight of my day.

Angela M. – Thank you for designing beautiful books that I'm so proud to share.

A Huge Thank You to Marla, Marion, and Nichole for your keen eyes and speedy skills.

Sweet TALK

DANNY WESTON

Height 6'3"

Waist 33.5"

Chest 41.5"

Suit 42 L

Inseam 34"

Shoes 13

Eyes Light Brown

Hair Medium Brown

Editorial Note: Most sought after male model in the industry. Hollywood calling. Best known for his body—underwear modeling, fitness, runway, print ads. Needs extra room in the inseam. Easy to work with.

Flirts. *A lot.*

Follows through. *Even more.*

CHAPTER 1

Danny

"GOD, I WANT you, Danny," Simone whispers into my ear. She licks just below it before sliding down over my jaw and biting me.

My hold tightens around her hips, steadying her. I should have seen the bite coming. They all do it, assuming they have to do something extreme to be sexy, to get my attention. Like every other time it happens, I pull back and run my fingers into her hair at the nape of her neck, then tighten my grip.

She gasps and digs her nails into my shoulders while the innocence she's trying to portray in her eyes fails under the skepticism found in mine. Our bodies are pressed together and heated, the fan not strong enough to cool us down.

Tilting her head back, I kiss the divot at the bottom of her neck, then lick from base to chin, taking my sweet time. Simone's back arches, pushing her breasts against my chest and she moans in pleasure.

"That is so hot. Keep it up," a voice intrudes.

Simone sighs, irritated, and pulls away. I turn to the photographer's assistant standing at the edge of the set just as Simone reveals her frustration by leaning back and swinging her

1

leg over me to stand up. Leisurely, my gaze slides up her lean legs. She's taller than most women and the heels she's wearing add another good five inches. Appreciating her physique, I smile and recline back with my hands behind my head while watching her adjust the strings at her hips. Her head snaps up and her eyes narrow on the assistant off set. "If you want us to *keep it up*, then shut up next time." She storms off, her shoes clacking loudly against the gray cement floor.

Knowing an angry model needs time, I sit up, and ask, "How much time do we have?"

Everyone is well aware that the mood has changed on the set. Worry creases the assistant's brow when he answers, "I think, umm... five or ten minutes."

The guy's anxiety rolls like waves crashing around me. Feeling bad for him, I reassure, "Don't worry about her. She'll be fine. Just give her a few minutes to cool down."

"Thanks." He smiles though it's weak. "Are you doing all right?"

I smile genuinely while standing up. "Yeah, I'm good. Thanks." When I start to walk, the knit boxer briefs I'm wearing for the shoot tighten uncomfortably, so I stop to adjust. They're a size too small, so I grab my cock and shift. "Actually, I could use a larger size. These are cutting off my blood circulation down here."

Before the assistant can respond, two women suddenly appear from the darkened side of the large loft. A cute, petite blonde offers, "Let me take a look. Maybe I can help." She's bold, not shy like I would have guessed from the librarian look she's chosen.

The other lady—taller with some gray strands running through her dark hair—seems new to the modeling world. She stands there staring below my waist, and by the way she's ogling me, I'm guessing she might be new to naked men in general. Maybe she's never worked on an underwear campaign before. She clears her throat and finds her voice. "They fit around the waist so I can add more material, if you'd like? But I'll need them to do that."

Bypassing the first offer, I accept the second. This is my job. I'm a pro, a model, and used to being naked in front of strangers, so I drop my drawers. I bend down to get them, and when I stand back up I'm greeted with two mouths hanging wide open. "Ladies, you're gonna make me feel shy," I tease. *I'm not shy at all.*

Lifting their chins until both their mouths are closed, I chuckle as they continue to stare unabashedly. The taller woman says, "Oh you have nothing to be shy about."

"Absolutely nothing," the blonde adds insistently.

"Thanks," I reply, my voice it's usual charm. I hand the boxers to the lady and walk off set to grab my robe. When I slip it on, Becs from wardrobe approaches and says, "I can add some room in there for you. I'll have them back in ten minutes."

"I already gave them to the seamstress."

"What seamstress?" she asks.

"The one over there." When I turn to the set, they've vanished. Scanning the loft from one side to the other, the two women are nowhere to be found. "She was just here with a blonde lady." Perplexed I scan again. "I have no idea where they went."

Becs rolls her eyes, shakes her head, and sighs loudly. "Good grief. Not again." Turning on her heels, she yells out, "Security. We've had another breach." With her eyes narrowed on my waist, she adds, "Tighten the belt. You don't want anyone selling a photo of your frank 'n beans to the highest bidder." Her mood lightening, she smiles and shrugs. "Or maybe you do. I'll get your next wardrobe change—"

I laugh but point to my privates. "Extra roomy."

Becs waves her hand in the air while walking off. "Yeah. Yeah. I got it."

I make my way to craft services where I find Simone eating what appears to be her third Snickers by the wrappers littering the table next to her. "Do they have fruit today?"

She speaks with a full mouth. "Down at the other end of the table."

The photographer's assistant announces, "Five minutes."

Eyeing her as she shoves the last of the candy bar into her mouth, then makes what I guess is the universal sign for vomiting with her finger, I try to hold my lecture for another time. When she disappears down the hall, I understand the stress she's under. The modeling world is competitive. One pound over the other girl and a model can lose the job. Simone desires to keep working, to stay on top of her game, but I've never found gaunt sexy. When the camera adds ten pounds, I get why they do it.

Grabbing an apple, I eat while walking back to the set. Becs is there and hands me a pair of customized black briefs, extra fabric finely sewn into the middle. "Let's get these on and see how they look."

I pull them on under my robe before untying the belt to let her take a closer look. She bends and eyes my dick, making me smile. When she stands up, she clasps her hands together. "Yep, looks good."

"Thanks," I reply smugly. *What?* I'm human. "You're not so bad yourself."

Becs's attempts at playing it cool are undermined when her cheeks pink. "I don't date models, Danny."

"Who said anything about dating?" I wink playfully.

"That's *exactly* why I don't date models," she replies, not able to hide the cute blush. Watching her walk away, I notice the pep in her step and hope I made her day a little more enjoyable.

After three-pointing the apple core into the wastebasket, I mentally celebrate scoring with a self-satisfied smile while returning to the bed and waiting.

When Simone returns, she sits next to me. Her body is tense, her hands have a slight shake, and she's paler than before. As makeup rushes over and starts touching her up, I whisper, "You okay?"

She stares down at the floor while they apply more powder. "Fine."

I've known Simone for a few years. Not quite twenty-four, her career is going strong, but sometimes she's moody. I think it's the constant lack of food, so I offer, "Wanna grab a bite after?"

The makeup lady leaves and Simone looks up. Touching my cheeks, she says, "You're always so sweet, but you know I don't really eat, much less out at restaurants in front of others."

"I was hoping you'd break your rule for me."

She smiles, and sounds hopeful. "I'll break mine if you break yours. Why won't you sleep with models?"

"I've slept with many models."

"Then why haven't we ever slept together?"

With a cocked eyebrow, I point out, "You were too young." Taking advantage of young girls isn't my thing. A lot of male models go through these girls with abandon, but by the time I hit my upper twenties, there was no appeal in dating a girl barely legal to drink just because she was hot. Now that I'm in my early thirties, I don't want a girl. I want a woman. "And as you pointed out, we're friends."

A gleam enters her eyes when she laughs, leaning back on the bed. "That's right. You were the first to ever turn me down. The only, in fact. Why are you so good, Danny Weston, when being bad is so much more fun?"

Memories flash through my mind like a spinning Rolodex. "I've done a lot of bad, and nothing worked out. Maybe a little good will suit me better."

Maneuvering her body, she wraps her legs around me, and drags her nails very lightly down my chest, careful to not leave a mark. Moving close enough to kiss, she whispers, "Well, if good doesn't work out for you, come find me."

The photographer shows up and without noticing the intimacy, starts filling us in on the angles he wants to complete the shoot. "We're not going to use the bra in this set. You two will be blurred in the background, but I want side breast and shadows. Covered nipples, but that's all I want hidden. Intimate, desire, like in pre-sex. Give me foreplay. I want kissing but no tongues showing. Simone, his scent is driving you wild and you can't keep your hands off him." He turns around and shouts, "Prepare for the close-up of the cologne bottle. Whoever has been spraying my studio with that shit is fired."

When he leaves, Simone's lips quirk into mischievousness, ignoring his rant. "Foreplay. Pre-sex." She reaches around, her breasts pushed out, and unclasps her bra. Bare before me, she directs her eyes on mine. "We can do that, right, Danny?"

Keeping my eyes on hers, I don't deviate lower. "I think I'll manage."

From the sidelines, the photographer instructs, "Touch her breasts." When I do, he adds, "So hot. Keep going."

Two hours later, Simone lies on the bed, her gaze is lowered, her body exposed without care. I try to stand, but she stops me by grabbing my waistband and tugging. "Maybe I'll see you again soon."

"Yeah, maybe we'll be booked together again. See you around, Simone."

"See you around."

Fifteen minutes later, I walk out pulling my T-shirt down over my head. "Hey, Becs, I'm late meeting the guys. Got anything I can snag from the shoot to wear?"

"I've spoiled you in the past, but you know you're not supposed to take anything. We have to turn in our expenses and return all of the clothes." She takes a navy blue button-down shirt from the rack and hands it to me. "So don't get caught. Wear it like you already own it."

I tug the shirt off and swiftly slip on the other. "Thanks." I kiss her on the cheek as I button up.

Good-humoredly, she shoves me away. "Go, handsome. Get out of here and have some fun."

Shining my million-dollar smile, I reply, "You're the best."

"Always the charmer, Danny."

"You know it."

"I think I see you on a shoot next week anyway, so go."

"If you miss me in the meantime, you've got my number." While heading for the door, I waggle my eyebrows.

"Oh, I have your number all right. Go, ya big flirt. Go find someone who will fall for that line."

"What about these abs and my sparkling personality?" I rub my abs to tease. "No love for these?"

With her hand on her hip, she continues to play along. "Those abs are easy to fall for."

"Ouch. Nothing for my personality?"

"Go!"

Laughing, I sneak out before I get caught with the shirt. "See you next week."

"See you then, playboy."

Checking the time, it's just gone ten. I jog to my Jeep, which is parked down the block. Dinner with the friends has long passed. I'll catch hell for missing it... like I always do. I rev the engine to life and take off so I can catch them for the second half of tonight's festivities.

Tempted to drive home instead, I turn on the radio to

mentally amp up for the night. I have a feeling tonight will be the same as Wednesday and the Sunday before that. I'm ready for something different, a change in scenery, a change in company, something or someone that makes me excited to go out.

Silver lining: every night is a new opportunity, every day, a second chance to make things right.

I arrive at the club and toss my keys to the valet, who gives me a welcoming nod. "Dan Man."

"When did you start working here, James?"

"Last week. The hotel canned me for taking a lady for a ride in a Ferrari."

"Did you at least score points with the lady?"

The valet smiles and purses his lips. "You know it."

"Way to go, but I imagine the owner of the Ferrari wasn't too happy."

"He was more upset about me borrowing his car than his wife blowing me. My boss didn't like that either."

Bursting out laughing, I fist bump him. "Oh shit. Well, take care of the Jeep. No joyrides."

"You got it, bro." Just before he hops in, he calls to me, "Good luck and have fun."

"I intend to."

CHAPTER 2

DANNY

THE LARGE METALLIC Illustrious sign gleams in the LA mid-morning sun. Illustrious is the most prestigious modeling agency on the West Coast, and my name carries weight there. Star power. It's not arrogance that allows me to acknowledge this fact. It's my hourly fee. I don't come cheap. Some call me a supermodel, though personally, I hate that term.

The elevator opens on the fifth floor and I push through the glass doors, greeting the new and very cute blonde receptionist when I pass. I hear the chatter before I round the corner into The Pit—the area where all the agents work—no walls, but rows of desks, ringing phones, and trendy California agents. I take the corner and am met with a glare from my agent, seen through the clear glass of the conference room wall that separates him from me.

Joining me as I walk toward the meeting being held on the other side of The Pit, Mark's assistant, Jody warns, "You're late and he's in a foul mood. Tread lightly."

"I had a late night." I smile. Nah, I give her a full-on smirk. "When isn't he in a foul mood? Oh, that's right. Payday."

Checking her out, I say, "Looking good, Jods. Working out?"

Adding a little ass wiggle while she walks to show off her hard work, she says, "Spinning down at Hollywood Cycle."

"It's paying off."

"You should join me sometime. Those women would eat you up."

"That's what I'm afraid of." I send her a wink and push open the conference room doors. She veers off in the opposite direction, leaving me to deal with Mark's bad mood on my own. *Shit.*

Mark stops speaking and greets me like his long-lost son, adding a few pats on my back for good measure. "Ah, here he is. The man of the campaign."

"My apologies for being late. Traffic sucks in this city. I'm sure you under—"

Blood rushes through my ears; my heart's pounding hard enough to make me worry my chest has been split open by the dagger that just hit me.

Soft waves of brown hair flecked with gold frame her face. Starry-blue eyes stare straight into my browns.

The one that got away.

The only one who ever could have brought me to my knee— my left to be precise—is sitting in front of me. A gentle smile that always melted my heart settles into her expression. I haven't seen Reese Carmichael in ten years, but looking at her now, my heart's forgotten the pain it once endured. *Stupid heart.*

Mark interrupts our moment by making introductions. "Danny Weston, I'm pleased to say you're now the face of Vittori. They have a new campaign to shoot for fall and you've landed it."

Another man wearing a deep-purple pinstriped suit stands and reaches for my hand. "It's such a pleasure to meet you." His smile is wide, all blinding white teeth against his too tanned skin.

Yikes. Sunscreen never hurt anyone.

"Nice to meet you..." I leave it open for him, though there's a vague familiarity about him.

"Vittori. Tonio Vittori."

Fashion Designer—best known for art-inspired designs on the runway and high-end dresses. I've seen him at Fashion Week, but never met him. "This is quite the honor. It's very nice to meet you."

"*Felicissimo.* Delighted, and the honor is all mine." The short man with slicked-back black hair ogles my midsection, then lifts my hand as if he's about to kiss it. I pull back and steal a glimpse of Reese, who's snickering under her breath.

"Mr. Vittori," Mark cuts in. "I know I speak for Danny, myself, and the Illustrious staff when I say, we are truly excited to be launching your new line of menswear."

I stand to the side and listen to him speak, but my gaze keeps drifting to the brunette with eyes so blue the skies are envious. Stunning. She's absolutely beautiful. My memory didn't serve her well, but that might've been the heartbreak clouding them.

Just as I let my gaze slide down to her left hand, Mark elbows me. "Mr. Vittori and his team will be in town for two days. We'll be taking them out tomorrow night. I hope you'll be able to join us."

My eyes shift to Reese again. "I wouldn't miss it."

I finally turn to her, but before I can say anything, she says, "It's a pleasure to meet you."

Her blues hold a secret message only meant for me, and I pick up on it, though I don't understand yet why we're pretending. "Believe me, it's all mine, *Mrs.*?"

A smile spreads across her lips and a light blush colors her cheeks. "Carmichael. *Ms.* Carmichael."

"Very nice to meet you, *Ms.* Carmichael. I look forward to

working with you."

A throat is cleared and I'm well aware it's Mark before I even turn around, so when I do, I get the added bonus of a hard glare, one he quickly covers after delivering his silent warning. "Ms. Carmichael is the lead on the campaign. She works for Klein, an advertising agency out of New York, and will be the main contact."

Joining in, she says, "This campaign is going to be amazing. I'll make sure of it."

Mark says, "All of my information is in the file Jody emailed you. If you need anything, please don't hesitate to contact me."

"Thank you. I'm thrilled to be working with Illustrious. We've worked with the Manhattan and Paris offices. But Danny," she says, stopping to look my way, "he's something special. I knew he'd be the perfect man to represent Vittori's new collection." When she turns back to Mark and the others, a charming smile curves her lips. I remember how different the one she used to give me was—reaching her eyes, relaxed, happy, sincere—not just congenial.

Shaking Mr. Vittori's hand, Mark turns and does the same to Reese, and says, "We'll see you tomorrow night and if you need anything, please don't hesitate to contact me personally." He hands her a business card and then heads for the door. "Your car has arrived. I'll walk you out."

When Vittori leaves the room, Reese stays a beat or three longer, remaining next to me. She looks up and whispers, "It's good to see you again."

She double-steps to catch up with the group and I'm left here watching her sweet little ass in a tight black skirt leave me completely stunned in a different way. Six words in that melodic voice I could never forget. She sounds even better than in my memories and I want her to stay and say more, anything to me.

Taking a seat at the large table, I run my hands through my hair while staring down at my reflection in the shiny black surface.

When I woke up this morning, I didn't expect to be blindsided by the one woman who broke my heart. I sound like such a pussy for admitting that, much less, twice now, even if only to myself. What stage of grief is that anyway?

Shit.

Am I still grieving the loss of her ten years later?

Six words. *It's good to see you again.*

Oh shit, my heart still hurts. Fuck.

I pull my phone from my pocket and text the second number on speed dial.

Me: *Free tonight?*

You asking me out, pretty boy?

Me: *My place at 4?*

Make it mine at 3:30.

Me: *Done.*

Mark walks back in and sits down across from me. With his fingers laced together in front of him, he says, "Don't fuck this up. This account is not only huge for you and your career, but my career as well, and for Illustrious."

What the fuck? When have I ever let him down? Sitting back, I sigh. "Thanks for the vote of confidence."

"I have no doubt you just saw something you'd be willing to put this whole deal on the line for. *She's a client.* You know the Illustrious policy. No sex with the clients."

Feeling like a smartass, I say, "I don't think that's the verbiage in the handbook."

"You know what I'm saying. Don't screw this, or her, up. Are we clear?"

"Crystal."

He stands and exhales a loud breath, big victorious smile on his face. "Glad to hear it. You need to hit the gym and be in top shape for this campaign. It's their new menswear line that will include undergarments—underwear, under tanks, and more... or less. Whatever they want. Be prepared."

"Where are we shooting?"

"They're out of New York. I know there will most likely be a shoot there. I'm trying to convince them of one here. We'll find out more over dinner. Mr. Vittori said he'll have a better idea by then."

Following him to his office, I remain in the doorway while he sits behind the large desk in the corner. He's earned his title of Director as well as his corner office. I like to take a lot of the credit for that. He'd agree when he's in a good mood. As long as I'm landing the good jobs and the big paychecks keep rolling in, I don't need the glory when he's in a bad mood. "When and where's dinner?"

"Spago at eight."

"Spago? For real?" Shaking my head, I know what Spago means. It means celebrity stalkers, paparazzi, gawkers, and schmoozing. Yep, that's right up Vittori's alley from his over-the-top appearance. I mean, what's the point of putting that much effort into your clothes if no one sees them? I look down at my jeans and old, worn black Adidas.

When I look up, Mark is now shaking his head at me. "At least you showered for the meeting." He grabs papers on his desk, pushing through them, looking for something. Holding up a photo of a small bottle, he adds, "Vittori International has a new cologne coming out at the same time as the menswear line. If shooting goes well, the job will be yours. You want this job, Danny. Make sure that happens."

I salute him, then nod. "Will do. See you tomorrow."

As I'm walking away, I hear him yell for Jody to get me the

updated schedule for the next two weeks. She comes running up next to me and matches my pace step for step. Handing me two sheets of paper, she says, "I emailed the schedule to you, programmed it into your online calendar with added alerts. Here's the hard copy. You have a fitting right now down the street at Vargo. They're waiting on you."

"Got it, doll. Thanks."

She stops at the glass door while I keep walking. When I press the elevator button, she says, "Congrats on the new campaign and let me know if you need anything."

"I've got your number. Have a good one."

She's already heading back to the big boss's corner office before the elevator arrives. She's a good girl. I'm lucky to have her on my side.

As soon as the elevator doors close, my back hits the mirrored wall. Sideswiped by the one and only, *Ms.* Carmichael. I smile; glad to hear she's a *Ms.* over *Mrs.* Through the double doors and down the sidewalk, I make my way to where I parked down the street.

The sun is out with no clouds in the sky. This is a perfect Thursday. A day I'd normally drive to the beach and catch a few waves, I'm now comparing the sky above to the color in her eyes. I wasn't close enough to see if those flecks of gold still encircle the soulful blue and black of her pupils. I wish I had been...

The drive to Vargo isn't long enough for me to get lost in any visions of our past, but I know I'm not looking forward to any downtime I have ahead.

After an hour of being pinned and tucked, and not in a good way, I'm done. The clothes for next week will fit like a glove. "We'll see you next week, Danny," says the stylist as I head out.

"See you next week."

Two fifty. I stop into a convenience store and grab a six-pack of beer before heading into the Hollywood Hills. No gates in this community. No barriers or tall fences. No celebrities, but a few moguls who like to play the part happily live here until they can move to Los Feliz or some other hot neighborhood a few income brackets higher than their current one.

The door is open, music playing loudly through the speakers. I walk in like I own the joint. I once did. That gives me some residual claim over the place if you ask me. "Luke?"

"Be down in a minute," he calls.

I look toward the stairs, to where I heard his voice trail down. "I'm drinking."

"Go ahead."

Pulling a beer from the box, I go to the kitchen and set the rest down. As I stare out the back, through the large windows of the modern home, I twist the top and start drinking. In the distance, there's a slight view of downtown. It's gotten smaller since I owned the place and the trees have gotten taller. I'm glad he kept the trees.

"I'll see you later."

Turning back around, Luke is walking a girl to the door. She looks familiar but I can't place her. There is this little wave with her fingers she does as she says, "Hi, Danny. Coming back to yoga?"

Yoga. The hot teacher. Ah. It's all coming back to me now. "I'm more of a hiker or weights guy these days."

"It shows. Looking good." She lifts up and kisses Luke on the cheek. "Bye, handsome. Call me soon."

"I will."

The door shuts and when he looks at me, he says, "Or won't."

"Ass."

"She's got a nice one if that's what you're referring to."

"I wasn't."

He walks by me, holds up his hand, and we bump knuckles. Grabbing a beer, he opens it and joins me at the window. "You miss the old digs?"

"I prefer the beach."

We walk outside onto the deck and settle into our usual spots. Mine is a faded green patio chair. His is the wood bench against the railing so he can stretch his arms out, which he's doing now. With his beanie in place even on this warm day, he pulls his sunglasses from his pocket and puts them on.

"So you're fucking Janet now?"

"Jenna."

"Jenna, Janet, Mary Sue Elizabeth. Does it matter?"

"No," he replies looking away from me.

"Then why are you still doing this? What point are you trying to prove?"

"No point. Just trying to move on."

Eyeing him, I say, "Why try so hard?"

Leaning forward, he looks uncomfortable, but he shouldn't or I'd be more worried. He picks at the label on the bottle, and says, "What if the prick asks her to marry him?"

"He won't. He's an ass. Unfortunately, you have to wait for her to figure that out on her own."

"I've loved her since I was sixteen. Half my life."

"Then why'd you wait for her to find someone else before telling her?"

Sitting back up, he rests against the wood and crosses his ankle over his knee. "I thought it was understood that we'd be together when the timing was right."

"Man, it sucks. It does. Jane's a good girl."

"But? I hear the but already."

I sigh, blowing out the reality he's now faced with. "You waited too long. She's a smart girl, but sometimes even smart girls make bad decisions. You blew it for now. With that said, I don't believe she'll marry that dick."

"I hope you're right, but in the meantime?"

"Stop fucking around with girls that don't matter and focus on the woman who does."

We both take a minute to absorb the advice and ponder the possibility. My beer is emptied and when I go to get another, an extra is grabbed for Luke.

"Thanks," he says. "And let me know when you're ready to tell me why you're here. I know it's not about my shitty love life, so it must be about yours."

Honesty. I can be myself, the real Danny Weston when I'm with my best friend. We've been through a hell of a lot—career highs and lows—women, and more over the last ten years. I can tell him anything and he'll always have my back. Even if he acts like he won't. That's just part of the game we play. My palms press into the railing as I stare ahead. "I saw a ghost from my past today."

"A ghost? Care to elaborate?"

"It's the one I never mention."

In my peripheral vision, I see the sudden jerk of his head in my direction. "Reese?"

My glare should say it all, but just in case, I remind him, "Don't say her name."

An exasperated sigh is his response. He stands and turns to face in the same direction as I am, mimicking my stance and staring at the trees in the distance. "Where'd you see her?"

"Work."

"Shit. That's not good. And stop making me ask for every fucking detail. Either tell me or don't, but let's skip all the leading questions."

Like I said, honesty. "I had a meeting at the agency this

morning. It was a stealth attack in the conference room by my agent, an Italian designer, and *her*."

"You're standing. You're in one piece. It couldn't have gone that badly."

"I landed a big campaign today. The deal was closed."

"Congrats. Why do you sound like you lost the job? What am I missing?"

"*She's* the lead exec on the campaign."

"Shit."

"Yeah, shit."

"Can you work with her?"

"What do you think?"

Looking at the beer bottle in his hands, he turns to me. "I think we're gonna need something stronger."

CHAPTER 3

Reese
Eleven Years Earlier

THE GLASS SCREAMS when the pebble hits it, causing me to jump. I look over, making sure it didn't shatter. Knowing who it is, I throw the covers from my body and peek over at my roommate who is sleeping soundly as I get out of bed. Tiptoeing to the window, I dread letting the cold in, but open it anyway. *How can I not?* My boyfriend of one year is standing beneath the window. Under his feet, a light layer of snow covers the grass, new since I returned to my apartment after my evening class had ended.

Snow is falling and the winter scent of pine fills the air. My favorite season always makes me happy, but nothing compares to his smile, which warms my soul every time I see it.

Danny Weston is the most handsome man I have ever seen. He's popular with girls *and* guys, and never lacks attention on campus. But he only has eyes for me. He's great about making me feel like the most beautiful woman he's ever seen. I lean out the window opening, already smiling. "Hey there, stranger."

"Come down," he whisper-yells. "It's snowing. First snow this winter."

One year has flown by, but we already have a tradition. One of them is being together during the first snow of the season. We met the night of the first snow our junior year at a party down on Frat Row. Then, we woke up together in his off-campus apartment and walked together to get coffee.

I nod. "Coming down." I rush to close the window. When I turn, I freeze in place when my roommate rolls over, mumbling something about a test, but she doesn't wake. I grab a Huskers sweatshirt and slip it over my head and pajamas. Then I pull my sleep pants off and put on a pair of my tightest jeans. Thick woolly socks and snow boots follow. A coat. A hat. Gloves complete the ensemble.

Running out the door and down one flight, I make my way around the corner to find Danny scraping together a very pathetic snowman. "I think you're gonna need more snow for that little guy."

Danny stands up, dusts the snow from his gloves, and comes to me. Excited to see him, I jump up on him. He catches me as I wrap my arms around his body. I kiss him, wanting him to know how much I love him—deep and hard. When our lips part, my legs come down and my feet touch the ground again. He smiles, still holding my hand, and says, "Maybe."

"It's a valiant effort though, I must say." I look at the miniature snowman, then back into Danny's eyes that remind me of melted chocolate that you dip sweet treats into.

I only just notice the snow that falls around us. It's easy to get caught up in Danny—his magnetic personality, his caring side, and that face. Yep, super easy to get lost in him. I force my eyes to the sky and open my mouth wide, hoping to catch a snowflake on my tongue.

"I'll show you a valiant effort." He swoops me up into his arms and walks to his old Jeep Cherokee. The evergreen color shines under the nearby street lamp. He always keeps his car clean despite taking it off-road whenever he has a chance. He's such an outdoorsy guy, but he treats me special and never wants me to get dirty—unless I want to—which is more than I ever thought I would.

I release one last squeal as he tickles me and then sets me down, my back pressed against the door and his arms caging me in. The light reflects in his eyes as he gazes down into mine. A gloved hand touches my cheek, and he says, "I love you, Reese. I'll always love you."

"I love you, too," I reply readily, as if by habit though the feeling is felt deep within my soul. But the intensity of his expression makes me question what's really happening. "What's wrong?"

He kisses me instead of answering. I kiss him back, but my heart is flipping into panic mode as worry covers the lightness from seconds earlier. Pulling back, I push against his chest and repeat the question, "What's wrong, Danny?"

"I got a contract."

It dawns on me quickly. He'd been trying to get a modeling contract for months. "You got signed?"

His happiness is contagious, his eyes bright with hope, waiting for my reaction to match his own. Jumping up, I wrap my arms around him and hug him. "Oh my God. You got it! This is it, Danny. Everything you wanted."

When his arms wrap around my waist, his hands move tenderly up and down a few times. The movement is slow as if he's savoring every centimeter. Then he pulls me closer. He rests his head down on the top of mine, and replies, "Yeah." His voice is somber, surprising me considering the great news. "Everything I wanted."

Confused, I look back up at him and ask, "I thought this was what you wanted?"

"It was. I mean, *it is*." The intimacy of his closeness leaves my body when he takes a step back and tucks his hands into his coat pockets. "I thought it was. But now that it's real, I'm having doubts."

"No," I instantly reassure him, "don't. This is good. This is amazing. You said modeling for catalogs and inserts was boring. Think of the new adventures ahead of you. You may end up flying all over the world and finally make decent money." I can't hide the excitement I feel for him. What an opportunity. "Paris. Madrid." I shake my booty. "Exotic islands..."

I carry on as the snow continues to fall around us until he interrupts, "I leave tomorrow."

The distraction of the snow surely caused me to mishear, so I ask, "What?"

"I leave tomorrow, Reese. I signed the contract with the agency and they booked me on a job."

"Wow, that was fast." My tone reflects my sudden concern, but I want to be positive for him, so I flip back to the awesomeness of this opportunity. "Where are you going?"

"The Maldives." Every answer from him is presented as if he's testing the waters. It feels like there's more to the story than I'm privy to, and I don't like this sinking feeling in my gut.

Then it dawns on me, and I can't hide beyond a fake smile. "You have finals in less than two weeks. You can't miss them or you'll fail. How long will you be gone?"

"Probably close to that, but I'll study on the flights. The Maldives are a long way from Nebraska."

This is all so fast, so much out of the blue, and it continues to plague me. It's what he wants. I just need to support him, but we've always been honest with each other. Considering the bad feeling spinning in my stomach, now should be no exception. "What does this mean?"

"What does what mean?"

"For us?" He's so unaware of the attention he gets without trying. Even with me on his arm, I see the stares, the glares, and hear the murmurs. Women are ruthless when it comes to a man they want. *Will I lose him when I don't even know how to hold on to him?*

He grabs my hands and pulls me close. After a kiss on the forehead, he says, "You're mine and I'll always be yours. I love you, Reese. I'm in love with you. I'll be back. It's just eight days or so. I'll be back for the tests, and for you. I'll always come back to you."

His words, his voice, the sincerity in his eyes make me feel better, easing my mind and worries. Embracing again, this time feels more like a goodbye than just a short parting. When I shiver in his arms, he suggests, "Let's get in the car and warm up."

A soft smile sneaks onto my cheeks. "I know how we can warm up."

"Great minds think alike, pretty." The door is opened and I'm ushered into the back seat. Danny quickly hops in after and the door is shut just as fast. "It's freezing tonight."

"But we got snow and I love when it snows."

He smiles while reaching forward and starting the car. Danny turns on the heat and sits back. Our eyes meet in the darkened car, our breaths coming in puffs of white, quickening as seconds speed past. I touch his cheek and lean my head forward until his lips touch my forehead. When he looks at me, I feel helpless against the desires he draws out in me. I close my eyes and fist his coat just as our lips come together.

Within minutes, the windows are fogged. Coats, hats, gloves, and scarves have come off. Warm hands caress my body under the sweatshirt while our lips find comfort against each others. My fingers run along his neck and into his hair, keeping him close. He never feels close enough... not until our bodies are bonded again.

My shirt comes off as does his. Despite winter in full flurry outside, inside the car our skin is heated, warmed by each other as we press together, sliding farther down into the seat. My breathing gets rougher as our need for each other grows. He pops the top button and zips down my jeans. The confined space adds to the challenge of our striptease, but we laugh, enjoying the fun in the moment. My legs are in the air as he tugs the jeans from my ankles. Hovering over me, as we get more comfortable, his head hits the window to help him balance as he removes his own jeans.

He stays above me then lowers down, his mouth finding my shoulder while I scrape my nails lightly down his back. I love the feel of his body. I take his boxer shorts down lower while lifting for him so he can remove the remainder of what separates us. Bared to each other, the heat from our passion penetrates the cold air, warming us.

His desire for me is felt, his body hard to my body's soft. "I love you," he whispers before lowering his mouth to my neck and adorning me with kisses as his body settles between my legs. "I want you. Always."

"I want you too. Always." Squirming beneath him, I add, "Make love to me, Dann—" His lips capture my words and fill my body with small moans and whimpers when he pushes inside me, slowly, carefully, lovingly.

His body stills, his breath halts, seeming to get stuck in his chest. I know him well. He does this every time we make love. Opening my eyes, I touch his face, cradling his jaw in my hands until he opens his eyes and sees me. "Breathe," I gently remind him.

A harsh breath is released along with the tension in his shoulders. He smiles, adjusts, then starts to move again, each roll of his hips hitting deep at this cramped angle, causing us both to moan. There's not enough room to tilt back or forward, so I remain still, but spread my arms out to hold on to anything I can reach—the back of the driver's seat and the back seat.

It never takes us long to peak and collapse, our love and lust for each other is both emotional and physical. Although I know he must be uncomfortable, Danny stays on top of me for minutes longer just because he knows I like it.

I stroke his back, not wanting to lose this, to lose him, and whisper, "I'm going to miss you."

"I'll miss you, too." We rearrange until we're sitting upright again. He leans forward, resting his head against the seat. Though his hands are relaxed at his side, the position of his body reminds me of The Thinker, his muscles defined as if for only me in this moment.

I hold my sweatshirt against my chest until he turns and looks at me. Reaching over, he lowers it. With anyone else, I'd feel embarrassed with them looking at me so unabashedly. But not with him. His expressive eyes don't ogle, they caress, making me feel beautiful, making me hope he always looks at me like this. "Are you cold?"

"No."

His voice lowers, befitting the mood inside the car. "Don't hide yourself from me, not yet."

I gulp. "Okay."

Angling his body toward mine, he leans back. "Come here." I fit between his legs, leaning my back against his chest. When he wraps his arms around me, he says, "You'll always be home to me. No matter where we are in life, we will always find our way back to each other."

"Promise?"

"Your heart has the map. You just have to follow it. It will lead you right back to me." He kisses the back of my head and his arms tighten around me.

Staring out the back of the window, even through the foggy glass, I see stars in the sky and smile. Despite the dark, I see the light. My heart will always belong to him. My faith is completely wrapped up in him. His faith in us is unwavering, his heart beating steadily like mine.

When I turn my head, I close my eyes because even though the space is confined, emotionally I've never felt closer to this man.

We rest, but then he rubs my arms. "We should go. It's starting to snow harder."

"I like it here with you."

His chest rises and falls when he chuckles softly behind me. "I like it here with you, but I don't want you to freeze."

"Good point." Working my clothes on, I move to the front seat to give him more room to get dressed.

Peeking back at him, I feel my love growing inside, my heart expanding for the man. Our love is the same in so many ways—passionate, loyal, honest. We're also different in some ways. I'm a planner and ambitious where he's more laid-back with a carpe diem attitude.

I've always had to work hard for everything despite my looks. Not many people, especially men, have taken my determination for success seriously because I'm considered "pretty." I've never been comfortable with that word to describe me, not until Danny. He says I'm pretty, but I see something more meaningful in his eyes. The word so simple to say, but packed with so much more than what the six letters represent. He makes me feel beautiful.

While I sit in the front seat of the Jeep, the quiet of the outdoors—of the night between us—weighs me down. Things are happening. Changing. For him. For us. I told him they would sign him. I believed it. He's gorgeous and personable. He's the full package.

Danny had run out of patience with the modeling industry a year ago. He had been at this since he was seventeen. It had paid for his school, his rent, and all of his expenses, but it wasn't going where he had hoped. That was before he did a local catalog campaign that led to a meeting with a big-time agent who loved to discover "fresh faces." Danny doubted it was only about his face considering almost every shot he took for the agency had him in his underwear. He wouldn't argue though. The agent said he could get him work and he's done just that. When I look back at him, I think about all the repercussions from the decision he's made. I won't voice them. This is his hard work paying off. He deserves all the success he finds. I just hope it's as good as it sounds.

SHE THINKS I don't see her. *I do.*

When Reese moves to the front of the Jeep, my eyes are on her until she catches me. A small smile appears, but she looks away shyly as if I've never seen her naked, as if I've never been inside her. As if she's not inside me, consuming my soul. *I love her.* More than she knows. I need to show her. I want her to feel how much she means to me.

Her blue eyes pierce my heart when she glances back at me, her cheeks still flushed and heated though it's freezing outside. Lowering my gaze to the jeans I'm fighting to get on in the cramped space, guilt takes over. I haven't told her I'll be spending the holiday break in Europe. Withholding information from her has made me feel like a liar. I'll be on a plane headed for Asia tomorrow, and detouring to Europe on the way back to have fittings for Paris, London, and New York fashion week. I haven't told her because I don't want to break the promise I made her. She hasn't said it but I know she wants a ring, a commitment I'm more than willing to give her because I want the same. *But how can I?* Christmas was going to be when I did it, but I won't even be with her now.

Maybe I can pop the question on New Year's Eve?

She asks, "You're somewhere else. What are you thinking about?"

I smile for her. "Just thinking about tomorrow. I need to go home and pack."

"Can I come over?" she asks, as if she doesn't know the answer already.

"Of course. You're always welcome over." She has the basics at my place, so I hop into the front seat and drive to my apartment.

Thirty minutes later, she sits in the corner of my room at my desk, and sips coffee. A suitcase is open on the bed with a few items of clothing folded neatly inside. She's much better at folding than I am. If it was up to me, I'd throw it in there and deal with it after I get to the final destination. I fold it, trying to follow the way she showed me. "You can stay here, you know."

"I am here."

"I mean when I'm not here. You can stay here." Giving up, I drop the sweater into the case. "You don't have any privacy at your dorm. Here, you'll have the place to yourself."

She ponders my offer, and then says, "It would be good timing since I need to study for finals."

I'd feel better, less guilty, if I can give her something. I can't give her peace of mind. She's going to be worried about me. But peace and quiet from her noisy roommate, this I can give her.

"See? It works out."

"Thanks." Relaxed with her head leaning back, she swivels back and forth in the chair. Suddenly, she stops, sits straight up, and asks, "Why do I have a bad feeling in my gut?"

I stop, our eyes meeting. Lying isn't second nature but I'm not unfamiliar with a white lie either. But with Reese, I hate lying. I don't do it. I trust her. She trusts me. Don't get me wrong. I've had to tell a white lie before. Like the time she wore those hideous leggings with the cats smoking pipes on them. But I love her enough to let her wear what makes her happy and those damn ugly leggings made her so happy, so I lied and told her she looked great.

But this? Our future is being pulled right out from under us. Instead of feeling happy about the opportunity I've been given, I'm unsettled by what I'm sacrificing in the process.

Walking around the mattress, I sit down on the edge and swivel her to face me. Leaning forward, I say, "This is good. All good. I'll make some money and this job could lead to bigger jobs and more money. It could lead to amazing opportunities."

"That's what I'm afraid of."

The smile I save for only her covers my mouth and I take hold of her hands. "We're going to be fine."

"Promise?"

"I promise."

CHAPTER 4

Reese
Eleven Years Earlier

TEN DAYS, FIVE hours, and I check my watch. Thirty-three minutes. I should be working on the test in front of me, but I can't wait to see Danny. He should be home any minute.

It's been torture with no viable out-of-country cell service and his phone card ran out of minutes on our last call, almost five days ago.

The door slams open and I sit up, startled from the loud noise, but when I see Danny, I relax as if home has been found.

Danny walks into the auditorium and stops to look up. When he sees me, he turns to the teaching assistant coming toward him and smirks. She nods and waves him on. He takes the steps by two and rushes down my row apologizing to everyone he bumps and bothers along the way.

Sitting down next to me, his beautiful smile appears when I look up. "Danny," I whisper, but I'm loud enough to get the attention of the test takers surrounding us. "You're here."

A girl sitting on my left is loud in her demand, "Shhhh."

He cups my face and kisses me and all the lonely nights we spent apart fade away. When our lips part, clapping ensues, the

33

auditorium of Communications 3.0 students hooting and hollering. Always the showman, Danny Weston never disappoints—me nor them. He stands up and takes a proud bow before kissing me again.

The teaching assistant shushes everyone, but her smile remains. "You have thirty-five minutes left. I suggest you get back to the test."

Everyone settles down and he takes my hand to kiss it. "There's more where that came from later."

"Hopefully not so public next time," I tease.

"I can't make that promise. I do love to show off my girlfriend," he whispers after getting a harsh glare from the girl on the other side of me again.

I tap my pencil against the small desktop in front of him that has the exam waiting on it. "We only have thirty-five minutes."

He grabs the pencil I set before him and starts on the test. When I'm done, I leave quietly, giving him the last few minutes to finish up.

Ten minutes later, the doors are pushed open and Danny walks out. He looks left, then right and when he sees me, he comes to me. It's winter, but the sun is bright outside. His gaze slides down over my curves—in at the waist, rounder over the hips. He loves the dip and takes hold. An unspoken bond, an unshakeable connection binds us together.

"Hey there, handsome. How'd you do?" I smile when I'm welcomed by his.

"I finished. I think I did okay."

"Luckily you had an A going into the exam. I didn't think you'd make it."

Danny takes my backpack and swings it onto his shoulder before taking my hand. We walk outside together, and he says, "I'd say I made it just in time."

I stop before we reach the corner of the building. Lifting up on my toes, I hug him, tucking my face into the base of his neck. "I missed you."

His warm embrace is what I missed. His sweet smile and the way he looks at me—it's a look envied by others, one that I read about in romance novels, and one that often appears in my dreams. So to see it again today after two weeks, I feel the need, an urge to touch him, to attach myself to him in ways that could end in heartbreak if I'm not careful.

We've been together for over a year, but these two weeks away has shaken our foundation. Unlike the short breaks prior when I went home or he did for a weekend, this was the first extended time apart, the lack of communication every day during that time—the long distance, different time zones, and the unknown hasn't helped. I've been studying day and night, attending classes, and been here in his apartment by myself while he is hanging out on the beach with scantily clad women doing who knows what. My imagination always gets the best of me if I let it.

When we walk into his apartment, he asks, "Wanna go out tonight?"

"I have two finals tomorrow. When are yours?"

He sighs and drops my backpack just inside the door. "Tomorrow and Thursday. Then I'm done."

"Me too." Rushing to the dining table I start gathering my papers and books together. Looking around at the apartment, I suddenly feel awkward. "I kind of made myself at home."

I follow him out of the corner of my eyes as he walks into the kitchen. "I'm glad. I like your stuff here." When I walk into the small galley kitchen, I'm grabbed and pulled close. Brushing some hair away from my eyes, he asks, "What do you think about moving in here next semester?"

Peppered kisses to my neck are used as persuasive weapons.

He knows I'm weak to them, but I love the onslaught too much to stop him. Closing my eyes, I reply weakly, "I can't."

"You can," is whispered against my neck as he continues to kiss and suck, tugging my shirt collar to the side for more access to my bare skin.

His magic is working, but unless I want to be a puddle of happy goo on the floor, I need to stop so we can talk. I push back gently. "You're evil with your sweet kisses. You know how weak I am to them."

As he stalks toward me again, he grins. "I do." I scurry out of the kitchen and straight into his trap—the bedroom. Standing on the other side of the bed opposite from him, he chased me in here, but stops with the mattress between us. "I missed you a lot."

"What did you miss about me?"

"I missed your breath when we kiss. I missed your hands on me, when you touch me with the sole purpose to please me." He takes his shirt off and tosses it behind him. My eyes lower, awakening other parts of his body. As he works on his belt and jeans, he says, "I missed being inside you and how when we're like that, I never want to be anywhere else."

My lips part as my expression surely must reveal my heart. I was never good at hiding my deepest emotions from him. He wants me as much as I want him. He slips off his jeans, then his boxer shorts and climbs under the covers. Lifting the covers on the side where I'm standing, he pats the bed. "Come here." Then he says, "I miss you when you're not here with me. I miss the way your eyes form two half-moons when you smile and a small dimple appears at the top of your left cheek when you're laughing." While I undress, he watches me, letting his gaze roam freely over my body. "I miss spooning you at night."

I slip under the covers next to him. As we lie there in the room, naked in each other's arms, we don't move. We listen—with each of our breaths becoming shallower, harsher, and unsteady.

I turn to the side, our eyes meeting. With my finger tracing imaginary swirls across his chest, I say, "I missed kissing you and touching you. I missed you being inside me and feel half of a whole when we're apart." Reaching up, I touch his cheek. "I missed the way you watch me when you think I don't see. I missed laughing. No one makes me laugh like you do. And I missed you spooning me. I just missed you." I kiss him. "I'm so glad you're home." Moving even closer, our bodies become entangled together.

REESE CARMICHAEL FEELS like my future wrapped in my arms. The girls I posed with during the shoot in the Maldives were gorgeous, but superficial. Reese has depth and beauty, the kind of beauty that I, despite my popularity, feel I would never have. And she loves me. She loves me as much as I love her. Yes, Reese is mine, but more importantly, she will be mine forever.

Thinking about the ring I saved up for, New Year's couldn't come fast enough.

Positioned between her legs, I push in. A breath is pushed out and I drink her in. While I kiss the underside of her chin, she says, "I'm so glad you're not leaving again anytime soon."

I still. Not wanting to ruin this moment for her, or me, I start moving again, ignoring the inevitable conversation I'll be having with her soon.

A few hours later, the heat is on, but Reese is cold. She's wearing pajama bottoms and my sweatshirt, fluffy socks and she's drinking coffee as she studies at the table.

I watch her from the sofa, burning my burdens into her back. Honesty has never been an issue between us, but it suddenly feels like an insurmountable obstacle to me. I can tell her the truth and risk her wrath or worse, a breakup. I can lie to keep the peace.

But dishonesty isn't a part of my makeup, especially when it comes to Reese. I would want to know, so I feel she will as well. "I kissed a girl."

Reese's head jerks around until her gaze lands heavy on mine. "What?"

"It didn't mean anything. I had to do it for the campaign I was shooting."

She sits there, stunned into silence, so I continue, releasing all the truths as my shoulders sag down. "We had to make out on the beach, in the water... in a bed. It had to look real."

A line forms between her eyes as she turns her body to the side to face me. "Was it? Real?"

Standing up, I shake my head. "No. No, it wasn't. I thought about you the whole time."

"Is that supposed to make me feel better, because right now I feel sick to my stomach."

Hurrying over, I kneel next to her and put my hands on her legs. "It wasn't real. It was all on set. Nothing more, but I did it. I did it because I had to for the job. But that's all it was—a job."

"Did you like it?"

"No." Kind of. No. Fuck! I feel sick over that lie no matter how tiny it is. That *kind of* makes me reevaluate what I'm becoming after only one job. "I felt nothing for her." That is true. She wasn't my Reese. The model in the Maldives was a chain-smoking narcissist. No one was worth losing Reese over, especially not that model.

Present Day

I WAKE UP from the sun burning the back of my lids. Last night "something stronger" led me to do bad things... bad things like drinking tequila and tequila never leads to anything good from my experience. Okay, that one time in Ibiza was pretty damn good—*Ouch!*

My body hurts and my head is pounding. I roll over and right off the edge of the couch. When I hit hard, bright white tiles, I realize I'm at Luke's. *Fuckin' tequila!* Rolling onto my back, I lie there and close my eyes again. An image of how good Reese looked in that tight black skirt competes with the pounding in my brain. Shit. The whole reason I was drinking tequila in the first place was so I wouldn't think about her and here she is the first thought I have in the morning. I thought I had successfully tucked her away with the other heartache she caused, but just one face to face and all those old emotions resurface. *Fuck!*

I sit up and rub my temples. When I see Luke passed out in a lounge chair on the patio, I start laughing, until that hurts my head, so I stop. Grabbing a pillow from the couch, I toss it as hard as I can and hit him in the head. He doesn't budge.

After rolling my eyes, I stand up slowly and put on my sunglasses that are conveniently located on the coffee table next to me, and make my way into the kitchen. I grab two bottles of water from the fridge and search through the cabinets until I find Ibuprofen. Armed with what I hope is quick relief, I go back into the living room, pick up the pillow again and hit Luke over the head. "Wake up, princess."

One eye, then the other opens and one side of his face scrunches together. "What are you doing here?"

"I was asking myself that same question." Right after I was thinking about Reese's hot little ass. I leave that part out of the conversation. Luke will never let me live it down if I don't. I set down the pills and water, but remain standing. "What happened last night?"

"Beers. Shots. The pub. More beers. Tequila. Pancakes, I think. Janet—"

"Don't you mean, Jenna?"

"Nope."

"I've got one word for you—Jane."

"If I could have Jane, I wouldn't need Janet or Jenna."

"Are you listening to yourself?" I ask, walking toward the door. "Maybe Janet and Jenna are the reason you don't have Jane."

"You've got all the advice in the world except when it comes to yourself. I've got one word for you—"

"Don't say it."

"Reese." He laughs. "Hey look. I said it and nothing happened. The Earth didn't open beneath your feet and swallow you whole. The apocalypse didn't happen. The sun is still shining. Too brightly I might add, and guess what?"

"You're an asshole?"

"We all know I'm an asshole. Guess again, Dan Man."

Checking my watch, I realize I need to go if I want to get some Zs before the dreaded dinner tonight. Done with this conversation, I turn around and ask, "What? Just say it."

"You survived hearing her name."

"Whatever. I've got to go."

"Hey, Danny?"

"What?" I shout over my shoulder as I open the door.

"You also talk in your sleep."

With my hand on the handle, my gaze lands hard on the wood

of the door and I glare straight ahead, freezing in place. He doesn't need any encouragement from me. I just gave him plenty of ammo, and like the best friend he is, he's not afraid to use it. "You won't let me say her name, but you'll mumble it all night long. How does that work when you have a lady friend staying the night?"

"You were right about one thing." He doesn't say anything, so I do. "You are an asshole." I walk out to my Jeep. Sitting there I pop the pills and down the water. I start my engine and drive home, annoyed the whole way back. What the fuck ever with her and my so-called best friend? I don't need that bullshit spewed back at me. I can take advice, even my own occasionally. It's just not wise to do so. I learned that the hard way ten years earlier.

Move on.

Yep. That's what I'll do. Once again. Just like she did so easily from me.

So tonight is only business. I'll lay it on thick, wine and dine them, seduce them with charm and make them never regret hiring me. I park at the curb out in front of my house and with a firm plan in place, I go inside and crash for a few hours.

My dreams are heavy, my past back to haunt me.

CHAPTER 5

Reese

THE GARDENS AROUND the hotel are lush, the room brightly decorated in florals, evoking the Southern Californian vibe. The French doors are wide open letting the sunshine in while I stand in front of the minibar debating if the rosé or the pinot grigio complements the swarm of butterflies that have invaded my stomach.

I was prepared. Hell, I planned the meeting. As soon as he entered that room earlier today, I discovered I wasn't prepared at all.

Tall. *So tall.* I'd almost forgotten how he eclipsed the average man, burying them in his shadow. His smile brightens any room. Two small—and incredibly sexy—dimples that captured more than my imagination, they caught my heart. My thoughts were fuzzy under the warming gaze I hadn't been privy to for far too long. His eyes were never just one shade of brown, but twenty shades from molasses to maple syrup. Even all these years later I discover in an LA office that caramel plays a part, instantly throwing all my insides into a complete tizzy as if I were still my twenty-year-old self.

With an enviable jawline covered with more than a night's dusting of beard, he's sexy in spades, and regret immediately fills my chest for thinking I ever stood a chance getting over that man. But his looks were never the issue.

It's not right for him to look so damn good after all these years. *Doesn't he age like the rest of us?* Surely whatever he's doing to stay young, that hot, just like he did so long ago has to be black market. Me in my corporate black suit—*Ugh! I'm so embarrassed.*

The blue dress. I should have worn the blue dress. We're in LA, not Manhattan. A glass of rosé is poured and I stand on the balcony, sipping, and looking out over the pool. The peace and serenity of the hotel doesn't ease my regrets or whatever else this feeling that has invaded is—*mortification?* No, too strong. *Shyness?* No, too weak. I down another sip to douse the doubts creeping in. I'm caught in the middle of an emotional landslide when there's a knock on my door. The glass has been emptied, so I set it down on my way to answer the door.

As soon as I open it, Vittori rushes in. "You've got to tell me everything. Everything. Every. Last. Detail." His accent seems to have slipped away and a New York dialect has replaced it.

"C'mon in," I say, waving my arm like I'm rolling out the red carpet, though he's already passed me.

He walks right for the balcony and looks out. When he turns around, he looks satisfied, and says, "Nice view." He shrugs. "Mine's better. I'm over the garden and apparently some nearby neighbors have decided to have a pool party. The guests are naked and playing with their balls."

"What?" The door slams shut behind me and I stand there with wide eyes staring at him.

"Beach balls, dear Reese. My, your innocence is charming."

Rolling my eyes, I walk to the bed and sit on the edge. "Did you want to discuss the campaign?" I have no idea why he's here.

"No," he replies sitting down next to me. With his hand patting my leg, he looks at me like I'm being ridiculous. "I want to discuss that hunk of man that couldn't take his eyes off you."

"So you're not really Italian?"

"No." He swooshes his hand in the air. "Pfft. Of course not. As an Italian from Brooklyn I couldn't get the internships I wanted at the big fashion houses in Manhattan. They have stereotypes in the industry and I didn't fit what they were looking for back then, so I created it." Standing in flourish, he spins around before landing heavily back down next to me. "But keep that our secret."

"If it's a secret, why are you telling me?"

Another shrug is followed by his arm cradling me to him. "Because I like you. I think you're wonderful."

"You don't really know me."

"I know you enough to see we're cut from the same cloth."

"Nice fashion reference there," I say sitting up. "But I don't know what you mean."

"I think you do." Standing he walks to the minibar and looks in. "We need champagne."

He's a whirling dervish of frivolity. I love his energy, but I'm shocked by this whole new side of him. "Go on. Order the champers."

"Okay, fancy pants. Settle down." I pick up the phone and order a bottle of Veuve from room service, then join him on the balcony. "Ordered. I think your view sounded more interesting."

Perking up, his smile grows. "Yes, send the champagne to my room." He hooks his arm in mine and says, "Lots of good eye-candy there. Let's go."

I call and have the champagne sent there instead and we head to his room. The champagne arrives when we do. I watch Vittori eyeing the cute delivery guy who is popping the bottle open and pouring it for us. He tips the guy big lingering his hand in his until the guy smiles and thanks him. The delivery guy is obviously straight since he seems completely clueless to the major come on, but it is amusing to watch.

His room is larger than mine and has a balcony with lounge chairs. We take up our positions, pretending to get some rays when we are both enjoying watching the pool party over the large hedge and brick wall.

Vittori clinks his glass to mine and says, "My real name is Vincent. My mom calls me Vinnie. You don't have to call me Mr. Vittori."

"Can I call you Vinnie?"

He nods. "Vinnie it is. Now that I've let my hair down for you, I want to hear about Model Danny."

Bubbles clog in my throat and I spew the champagne. Hacking. Coughing. Grabbing my throat, I cough again to clear it. My voice is jagged, not sounding like me at all when I try to speak, "Excuse me?" I cough again and try taking a deep breath to relax my throat to get control of my breathing.

He's laughing. *At me.* "I rest my case." Sipping his champagne, I see one perfectly styled eyebrow rise in a clear, *I told you so* arch.

When my breathing evens out, I say, "I don't know what you mean."

"You sure about that, Candy?"

"Candy?"

"I see beneath that hard sugar coating of yours. I get vibes from people and yours are good. A little damaged, but whose aren't, so let's drop the deep and dive into the shallow. The sparks flew between you two. I stepped back to make sure I didn't get burned."

I scoff and turn so I'm facing forward, unable to hold eye

contact with him. Anyway, he'll see right through me if I don't. "We barely said two words to each other."

"No words would have sufficed. Fire I'm telling you. On fire! So this whole campaign is just a ruse? You know, to get the man?"

"No," comes rushing from my mouth. "I would never do that."

"Oh, calm down, Candy." He waves me off. "I'm teasing about the set up. I've seen you in action for months now working on this project. I know how dedicated you are to the finished product." Eyeing me devilishly, he smacks my arm playfully and leans in. "But he was hot, right?"

"So hot." *Fine. I admit it. Danny Weston is hot.*

Refilling my glass, he looks up. "Super hot. Now I understand why he's a supermodel."

"I think he's going to make the menswear line look amazing. Not that it's not amazing on its own, but on his body…" I swoon a little inside. *Damn him and his incredible body.* My mouth dries as I try to remember if his shoulders were that broad in college, but I struggle to push down the pain that comes with the memories.

"You can keep trying to change the subject, but I'm really great at dragging us right back to Danny and your connection. You felt one, right? It looked like you did."

The speed of his words, mixed with thoughts of Danny, make my head spin. Maybe it's my emotions that feel like they're spinning out of control. The story of us… "Not all fairy tales end with a happily ever after."

"Tell me more."

Drunk.

This is what drunk feels like, though I've only had the two glasses. "I'm not feeling well." I put one foot down to ground me and then level my eyes on something still—my Fitbit.

Hooting and hollering distracts him and Vinnie rushes to the railing to get a better look at the men at the party next door. As he fans himself, he proclaims, "Good Lord, have mercy on my soul, this is what fantasies are made of."

"Maybe you should join the party," I suggest, enjoying his reaction to the buff men. Until I sit up and get a better gander. "Whoa!" I stand and join him at the railing. "I guess I wasn't paying close enough attention. My oh my."

"My oh my is right."

Another minute passes, then he turns to look at me, lifts his sunglasses to the top of his head, and really looks at me. "You're really pretty."

A blush floods my cheeks from the unexpected compliment. "Thank you."

"What are you wearing to dinner?"

Ten minutes later I walk out of the bathroom and into the bedroom, and then twirl for him. "I only have this dress with me."

"I love it. Fits you perfectly. But I don't want you dressing for me."

"What do you mean?"

"This dress is great for functions—business, cocktail parties even, the theater," he says, switching his accent to mimic upper social circles of Manhattan. "I want you to dress to knock socks off."

With a hand to my hip and a look that backs my attitude, I say, "And let me guess. You have just the someone in mind that you want me to knock the socks off of?"

He nods enthusiastically, and answers with a huge grin, "Danny."

"I don't think that's in the cards."

"Sparks. Fireworks. You two have them. The chemistry between you is so combustible it's hot."

Combustible—a truer word never spoken. But deep down, I

can't help but want to look amazing in front of him. Make him regret what he let go. "Help me look my best?"

"You got it, babe. Meet me tomorrow at four sharp."

Standing there a minute longer, a debate rages inside. As much as I find Danny attractive, still find him attractive, we were never meant to be or we would be together now. Damn those broad shoulders and the strong hands that used to hold me.

There is so much to handle back in New York, *him* to deal with. I'm in no position to even think about a relationship, much less one with Danny Weston.

Vinnie pushes me playfully toward the bathroom, and demands, "Go change out of that dress and let's go back to my room with the hot boy view."

The next day it's T-minus two hours to dinner and I'm standing on a pedestal in the middle of the Vittori on Rodeo showroom with no less than four salesclerks critiquing me in an over-the-top design. I shift uncomfortably under the stiff satin and knock the large flower on my shoulder to the side so it doesn't hit my face. "I'm thinking this might be a little much for dinner."

"Oh darling," a tall woman with jet-black hair slicked back into a tight bun says, "it's Spago. You only go to Spago to be seen, so if you're going to be seen, you might as well look fabulous."

Vinnie agrees, his Italian accent back in play while he rubs his chin. "It is divine on you. But it's not right for you tonight. Try on the black skirt and shirt ensemble."

All five of them relax and start drinking their champagne as I step down and disappear into the dressing room. A shorter, but super tiny salesclerk shows up just as I slip the skirt on and adjust it into place. She zips the back up and smiles. "Yes, this is the outfit. Whoever this outfit is intended for doesn't stand a chance."

"It's for me," I quickly correct, refusing to acknowledge that Danny has anything to do with my choice of attire.

One side of her lips rises. "Okay."

There's no point arguing, so I walk out and the voyeurs of the showroom break into applause.

Vinnie runs over and hands me a pair of black strappy heels. "Try these."

As I sit and slip on the shoes, buckling them at the ankle, he says, "You have legs forever. Why do you hide all this? Your assets sell, Candy."

"I'm not trying to sell myself. I'm all about selling other products, like yours. My assets don't come into play."

"I beg to differ, but now I understand why Keaton is all over you. Or should I say *not* over you?"

When I look up, my eyes meet his. "What do you *not* know about me?"

"I'm just observant." He offers me a hand up and I'm a good three inches taller than him now, even with his bouffant reaching full height. "He's all wrong for you, you know?"

"I don't want to talk about him."

"Yes, wise. Let's focus on Model Danny instead," he merrily chirps.

Rolling my eyes, I add, "How about we don't talk about either? Tonight is technically a business meeting and you're treating it like it's a double date."

"Mark's cute," he says offhandedly, "but not my type. Now Danny on the other hand."

"Then you go for him and leave me out of your matchmaking scheme."

"Fine. I'll stop pestering you, but promise me you'll wear this Vittori stunner. It was made for your body and it's my gift to you."

Smiling, I walk to the mirror among a sales team of oohs and ahs. I can't deny his talents. The outfit is amazing. And with a little tilt of my head, I have to give it to him. I look incredible in it.

Leaning forward, I kiss him on each cheek. "It's amazing."

"You're amazing."

And just like that I have a most unexpected ally, a new friend who wants the best for me when I was beginning to believe I didn't deserve it. "Thank you."

"Don't thank me yet. We need to go. You have a hair appointment for a blow out with a good friend of mine a few blocks from here and I don't want to be late."

"My hair too?"

"Well of course, darling. Whether you like it or not, I'm going to have everyone drooling over you." His natural accent reappears and he whispers, "And besides that, you're with me. I can't have stick-straight hair when you're in one of my creations. My clothes ooze sex and you've already got the appeal, so let's put them together. And make sex appeal happen."

"You're lucky this outfit is so stunning or I'd argue my hair is fine."

"Yes, your hair is great, but it's so New York. Let's be LA. LA is all about body," he states, pointing to my head and then down my body to make his point. "Now get that ass in gear."

Feeling sassy, I shake my ass just for him. "Oh, it's in gear. C'mon, let's go. I have hot dates tonight and don't want to be late."

"That's my girl."

"Hey, Vinnie, don't let me drink too much. I don't do yellow. I go straight from green to red in an instant. It's weird. I've never been able to hold my liquor." I lose control of my better judgment, especially around sexy Danny Weston. "Four drinks and I'm done. Okay?"

"Four it is."

CHAPTER 6

"HOLY FUCK," I mutter under my breath and turn around the second I see Reese standing at the bar. My hands are shaking and I quickstep outside. I need distance. She shouldn't look that good. *Fuck.* Age has only benefitted her. *How is that possible? Everybody else is aging, some not so gracefully, then comes Reese to blow that up in my face.*

"Sir, do you have your valet ticket?"

I look up at the kid standing there in a valet uniform. "Huh?"

"Are you leaving?"

"No, I'm staying. I just need a minute." I step to the side to make myself feel less awkward.

"*Ahhh,*" he says like he knows what I'm thinking. "Woman trouble?"

Fuck. Maybe he does know. "No. I don't have trouble with women."

He nods. "Cool. Hey, did you see that brunette in the black skirt? Man oh man, is she something."

Narrowing my eyes at the kid, the guy who is way too young to even look at Reese, I ask, "The *woman* at the bar?"

He looks over my shoulder and through the glass doors. When he turns back to me, he says, "Yep, that's the one. Hottie, right?"

"Aren't you a little young for her?"

"LA is the land of cougars. They love the young ones." He tucks his hands in his pockets like we're chums who'll be here for a while. "I think she's single. I might try to get her number when she leaves."

"The fuck you won't. She's with me. Keep your eyes and your hands off, punk."

Stiffening, the kid's spine jets upright under the scolding and his eyes go wide. "I'm so sorry, sir. I had no idea. My apologies." He rushes off to wherever valets go to hide when you don't need them.

I march back inside, pissed, and right up to her. She's alone. Vittori has disappeared, giving me the perfect opportunity to confront her. She sees me and now her eyes go wide. As soon as I reach her, she asks, "Are you okay?"

"No, I'm not okay," I whisper so only she can hear, taking her by the arm and pulling us closer.

"What happened?" she asks worried, like she doesn't know what she's doing. *Pfft. I call BS.*

"You. This. What the fuck is going on?"

Her whole stance softens under my hands as well as her expression. "I shouldn't have presented you to Vittori. I knew he'd love you. I... I hoped we were past our past, our history, but I can see I've upset you. I'm sorry, Danny."

As I stare at her, listen to her words as they float out in shame, I realize she's misunderstood what I meant. "No, the job's good. It's great actually. Thanks for that, but I'm talking about what you're wearing."

Her head jerks back, then her hands run down her skirt, an innocence appearing in her blue eyes—almost like she doesn't know how hot she looks. "My outfit?"

"Yes, the outfit." I run my hand through my hair. "Damn, Reese. How am I supposed to act professional with you dressed like this?" Shaking my head at myself, I realize what an ass I sound like. A jealous ass at that.

A smile instantly covers her face. Her gaze drags over my body, lingering on certain parts, before reaching my eyes again and flirting. "Thanks. You look good, too."

She laughs and it's like the sound never left, stayed with me all of these years, recalling the fondest of memories. Her hand covers mine that has remained on her arm. "I'm thinking we need to catch up soon."

"I'm thinking the same. In the meantime, we don't know each other?"

Sighing, she says, "I don't know. I wasn't sure what to do. It seemed easier to pretend we didn't at the time. What do you think?"

I'd like to answer her, but her hand is still on mine, almost holding me there. The heat is getting to me, making me want to touch her in other ways. I reluctantly pull my hand back and tug at my collar. She's distracting. Too distracting. The close proximity. The short black leather skirt. The valet making comments about her. Tonight I need to think with my head, not my dick. I'm not her boyfriend. I'm working with her, which I remind myself, puts her in the "no hit-on" category.

I step back, putting distance between us. "I think we should stick to business."

Her head moves the slightest and her tone lowers, sounding disappointed. "You're right."

I'm disappointed too. I feel the twist in my stomach. "Can I get you a drink?" *I sure as hell need one.*

"I have a glass of wine. Thanks." She picks it up from the bar and takes a long swallow. I can't help but stare at her throat as she does. *Fuck, that's hot.* I need that drink. I ramble up to the bar, bumping a guy by accident. "A bourbon. On the rocks." Just as the bartender catches the order, I catch a glimpse of Reese adjusting the strap around her ankle. Seeing that ass, that body, those legs... I clear my throat, and anxiously add, "Make it a double."

"Scotch on the rocks," I hear called over my shoulder.

I drop my head down, recognizing Mark's voice. I swallow down my ridiculous emotions and turn to him composed. "You're late."

"You're one to talk." We shake hands. "How's..." He glances over at Reese. Vittori has rejoined her and they're talking away. "Ms. Carmichael and Vittori?"

"Distracting." *Shit. I shouldn't have said that.*

"Distracting? Don't lose this gig for us, Weston."

I hand his drink to him and take mine, tapping the thick lowball glasses together. "Don't worry. My eyes are on the prize," I say, eyeing the brunette that looks dangerously delectable tonight.

"That's what I'm worried about." He steps away, and host of the year kicks in with his greeting. "Mr. Vittori. Ms. Carmichael. So good to see you both again. Seems our table is ready if you are."

We drop into two pairs as Mark's hand rests on Reese's lower back guiding her forward as we walk. Jealousy begins to brew when I realize he's allowed to do that and I'm not, and never will be.

"Beautiful. Don't you think?"

Who am I kidding? I'll never be able to keep it professional between us. Checking out Reese's ass, I easily admit, "Sure is."

"I meant the ensemble. It's from my new line. But she's

quite the beauty too."

I glance down at him. A glint of something is caught in his eyes and we exchange a brief, knowing look. We're led to a table for four and I pull out Reese's chair for her before sitting directly across from her. "Thank you, Danny."

"You're welcome."

"This is cozy," Mark says, scanning the room.

Briefly looking around, I spot a few A-listers scattered about the room, C-listers near the window, and three Lakers. At tables too close for comfort to the one we're led to are two women I would prefer not to catch up with. I've slept with both—one actress when she was just a starlet before the fame hit big, and one model. I regret both, but don't dwell on regrets, except one and that would include the woman sitting at the table across from me. I lower my head, hoping they don't see me.

Wine is ordered for the table. I order another bourbon, having finished my first one before we left the bar. As soon as the waiter leaves, Reese says, "We've confirmed the studio and two locations for the New York photo shoot. We're still waiting on foreign. We visited Paris four days ago, but the photographer wasn't sold on the early scouted sites."

Vittori interjects, "I read that Danny does shoot scouting."

"I do. I have. I've even done some professional photography. Just in case this whole modeling thing doesn't work out."

Reese says, "Was there ever any doubt?" Her tone is more serious than it has been, a heaviness coating her words.

Mark says, "I think it's working out just fine, better than ever. Danny, here, has always been a working model, but his name, good reputation, place in the industry has grown exponentially over the last five years."

"As has his paycheck." Vittori smiles as the wine is poured.

Mark adds, "His return in value well exceeds his pay."

"I have no doubt. I'm more than happy to pay his fee. My clothes are the best, and so it's only natural to team with the best." Holding up his glass, he says, "Here's to a fruitful relationship."

After we toast, Reese adds, "We've hired Rebecca Lange to handle wardrobe and to hire makeup. We've worked with her before and we know she has worked with you several times. We thought it might make the photo shoots more comfortable with familiar faces."

"I just wrapped a job with her," I say. "She's great to work with."

Reese and Vittori look pleased, and she replies, "That's good to hear."

We go through three courses and I struggle to keep my gaze off her. Her lips. I remember kissing them like it was this morning. Her hair. Shades of auburn and gold were highlighted in the sunlight when she would walk across campus just to see me. Her breasts. They're larger. I remember how good they felt in my hands. When she excuses herself to the ladies' room, I watch her walk away. Her legs were great back when we were together. She was a runner. By the look of them now, she's stayed fit.

When I catch her eyes on me, I don't smile. I can't. I don't understand what this unsettling feeling is inside. It's unnerving and throwing me off my game.

"Danny Weston."

My attention is drawn to the right, following my name. Shit. This could go very badly. "Cherry Menger." I stand and we do the fake-kiss Hollywood thing, or so I thought until her signature cherry-red lips press hard to mine. I'd prefer the fake to those lips touching me again. "It's been a while."

"Restraining orders tend to do that."

"I dropped it," replying; I keep my tone light and friendly. I don't want a scene, especially not in the middle of Spago. That would go viral before we're served dessert.

Her hands hold on to me. Her grip tightens, trapping me in place. When she zeroes in on my dinner guests, she says, "Sorry for interrupting. I just had to come say hello to Danny. It really has been too long. We should get together?" She looks hopeful, but her eyes glance to Reese when she returns to the table, and then back to me. Her tone lowers. "Are you going to introduce me to your friends?" Recognition dawns on her face and she squeals. "Oh my God. You're Mr. Vittori. I adore your clothes and I wear your perfume."

She starts to lean down, but he stands up and they fake kiss. I catch Reese's eyes on Cherry before she looks down rearranging her napkin in her lap. The whole scenario reminds me of why we broke up.

Dessert is served and I use it as an opportunity. "If you'll excuse us, this is a business dinner."

Dramatically, her hand flies to her chest. "Oh yes, I'm so sorry. Mr. Vittori I would love to wear one of your gowns to the Oscars this year."

"If you're invited, please contact me. It would be an honor."

Ouch!

Taken aback, she replies, "Of course I will be. I have three new films coming out."

"Fantastic. Please have your people call my people."

She thanks him, though I can see the irritation on her face when she turns toward me. Kissing me on the cheek again, she says, "It was good to see you again. Call me sometime."

I sit when she walks away after not agreeing to have anything to do with her. I'm not that crazy. Overemotional actresses aren't my bag. Glancing up, Reese has eaten half of the slice of chocolate cake in front of her before I've taken my first bite. "How is it?"

"Good," she replies flatly, not looking up.

I take a bite, but I know I shouldn't eat it. Not with the Vargo shoot in two days. Pushing it away, I choose the bourbon instead. I know this woman. Well, I knew the girl. Her jealousy is showing. And I'm absolutely fascinated by her reaction considering she's the one who left. She moved on with no problem, so I need to play this right. I can move on myself now or figure out why I'm so damn attracted to her still.

Looking back at Reese, she seems to be searching for answers of her own by the way she's digging into her dessert. "Reese?"

She looks up, fork in hand, almost to her mouth. "Yes?"

I need to think fast. My need to make her feel better, to ease her stress over the Cherry situation made me open my big mouth and draw unwanted attention from Mark and Vittori. As all three of them stare at me, I blurt, "Your glass is empty and Mark mentioned wanting to speak to Mr. Vittori about something... umm... to do with the thing." I cough and stand up abruptly. "Would you like to join me at the bar?"

Her shoulders straighten and she sets her fork down gently. "Oh, okay. Yes, we can give them some privacy." Looking to Vittori, she says, "And then you can join us at the bar."

Vittori smiles. "Yes, we'll be here... to talk. You two run along now."

Mark is scowling at me until Vittori and Reese look his way. That frown turns upside down, and a half-smile replaces it. "Sure. Give us a few. We'll be right over."

I help Reese up by pulling out her chair, and remark, "Great."

As we walk away, Reese whispers to me over her shoulder, "I don't know what you're up to, but it better be good, Weston."

"It was always good. You've just forgotten."

"Please remind me then," she challenges.

With my hand on her back, I lean down, really close to her ear and whisper, "Believe me, I intend to."

CHAPTER 7

Reese

HE'S A PERFECT gentleman, maybe even more so than when he was in college. Danny helps me onto my barstool and then sits on the one next to me. After we place our order, an awkward silence creeps in.

Then he goes first, trying for casual chitchat like we don't have a huge pink elephant of ten years sitting right between us. "How are you liking your visit to LA?"

I volley back with a polite and boring answer. "I've been several times over the years, and every time it's a breath of fresh air from my gray Manhattan life." When my eyes meet his, I see a concern that he must mean to hide. There's no mistaking how he let Cherry Menger mark him with her red lips despite how flirty he's been with me. His dislike of me will likely overpower all other emotions he's capable of. Revenge is sweet and apparently he's got a sweet tooth tonight. Sitting up straighter, I add, "I don't mean to sound sullen. I think I'm tired from the travel. Europe, New York, and Los Angeles in four days wore me down."

I watch him as he speaks, the way his lips form the words, and remember how they used to feel against mine. "That's a lot of travel. I'm still not used to it and I travel all the time."

Taking a sip of my drink, I let it hold my attention long enough to rethink what I'm doing, what we're doing. I can't pretend when we're alone. Too much truth—of everything—exists between us to pretend it doesn't. Is he trying to torture me by his hot and cold attitude? His eyes veer to my cleavage, then back up, and suddenly I'm very aware of every little innuendo between us. I touch the fabric, and now wonder if deep down, I wore it for him. *Do I want his attention?* God, am I that desperate to think I could get it even if I did? He's got millions of female fans. *What would he want with the girl who walked away?* But he's staring at me again like he might have forgiven me. I'm so confused. I shake my head and say, "You've done well, Danny. Congratulations on your success. It's what you always wanted."

"I wanted other things too."

I can't hold his gaze when it's ingrained with his emotions. He always did reveal everything in his warm brown eyes. Looking away from him, I say, "I guess we can't have it all." I immediately regret the sarcasm. "I'm sorry. That was rude and uncalled for."

"It's different."

"What is?"

"*Us.* We're different. We're learning how to navigate this new relationship. The one where we don't know each other, don't love each other any longer, don't... One where *we*... where there was no *us*... where we never existed."

The words slice through my heart, baring the feelings that I've held, but had buried. My chest feels cold. The exposure hurts more than I expected. "This is more difficult than I thought it would be."

He nods, drinking the water he ordered instead of responding. I hope I didn't offend him. Logically, I shouldn't care... but I do. *Ugh! Why do I care? I left for a reason. Don't soften now.* "We can do this. It will benefit us both if we do. You score a multi-million-dollar deal and launch a huge line. I land the promotion I've fought to earn for two years. It's win-win."

"If we can do it."

Stealing a glance at him, I take my wine in hand. "We're both professionals and I have no doubt we'll be able to convince them." After a shot of liquid courage, I try to tamp down these foolish notions I once held so tightly to. I'm not the girl who once fawned over him. I'm a professional ad exec and have worked hard to get where I am, to be able to handle accounts of this size and budget. My goals aren't going to be pushed aside for a handsome face and a size thirteen shoe.

Glancing down, I can't help but be a little in awe of the nice Italian shoes and the size. Were his feet that big back in college? My memories never underestimated... I cough. His size. He's definitely a man now, not the boy I once loved.

His eyes meet mine, a determination filling them. "But can we convince ourselves?"

"I'm sure you'll have no problem carrying on. You've always been very good at moving forward."

He stares at me. Unabashedly stares directly into my eyes. My breath catches in my throat and I swallow hard. When I exhale, the air deepens, my body heating as my chest rises and falls. I turn to see Vinnie and Mark coming toward us.

His deep, dulcet tone draws me back in. "You can set down your weapons, Reese."

"I hope so." Putting a smile in place, I get up and walk to meet the others, not able to be the center of his gaze any longer. His eyes were always so alive, vibrant, filled with possibility, and so focused... on me. I once flourished under his adoring gazes, but now I feel small, weaker somehow. When I reach the others, I breathe easier under the reprieve and ask, "Are we ready to go?"

Vinnie smiles, a happy alcohol glaze covering his eyes. "We're going back to the hotel for a nightcap." He looks over my shoulder and I know who he's looking at, so I don't bother to turn. When he looks at me again, he wraps his arm through mine and we walk to the door. "Mark and I have a little more we'd like to discuss. I'm going to ride with him back to the hotel, so we'll be done by the time we arrive."

My arm tightens around his wrist in panic. "I don't mind if you talk business in front of us. I'm sure Danny won't mind. We should all ride together. It's more economical that way too."

"Oh honey, money is the least of my worries."

"It's killing the planet. It makes no sense to put those extra emissions out, destroying our Mother Earth. We should really save the gas."

He finally stops, allowing Danny and Mark to walk ahead of us and out the door. "What's wrong with you? Are you really worried about the gas emissions?"

"I am. I mean, yes, I am. I care about the planet, but please. I can't be alone with him right now."

"C'mon," he says comfortingly. We walk outside and two Priuses are waiting for us. "See? No need to be worried. Electric cars on demand. How fantastic is that?"

"I thought—"

"I know what you thought, but trust me," he whispers. "This is for the best." Releasing me, he waves as he rushes to get in the first car. "See you back at the hotel."

"It was a valiant effort," Danny says, waving at the car driving Mark and Vinnie away. "I actually believed you cared about the Earth."

"I do care about the Earth."

He smiles. "*Okaaaay.*"

I give Danny a dirty look. "Don't condescendingly 'okay' me."

"Okay." He chuckles. "Oops. That one just slipped out."

I want to glare at him longer, but seeing him smile and hearing him laugh breaks me. Those things always did. "You're ridiculous."

"But cute."

Teasing, I say, "Cute isn't the word I ever used to describe you."

"Was it sexy? Handsome? Hot? Great in bed? Virile?"

"Virile? Really? Who uses that word?"

"I do. You just did. To describe me, I might add."

"Ugh. You're incorrigible."

"So there's hope after all."

"Hope for what?"

"Hope that maybe we can be friends again."

"I was always too in love with you to be friends."

That silences him. The smile disappears from his face, the fun sucked right out of the Prius. He looks out the window while my mind races, running through what I said and what I meant and—

"I was also *too* in love with you," he says, keeping his eyes averted, distracted by everything and anything outside this car.

"We were having a good time, civil even, and I go and ruin it. Danny, I'm so—"

"You're worrying. Don't. It's fine."

I sit back, feeling deflated and emotionally exhausted from the night. I'm glad the hotel isn't too far. Leaning my head back, I close my eyes, resting them, and ready for this ride to be over.

But then something happens. Something I didn't see coming.

His hand slides over my wrist and with our palms pressed together, our fingers entwine. I don't open my eyes. I don't know why, other than I don't want his hand to leave mine. My gulp sounds loud to my ears. I hope he can't hear how nervous I am. Then I hear him gulp and it makes me smile.

Lifting my head, I open my eyes and turn to look down at our joined hands. I don't take this lightly. The heaviness is felt through our touch, the pressure, and the heat of our palms together.

Keeping his voice low, intimate between us, he says, "It's okay. We're going to be okay."

"Sexy."

He looks at me, puzzled by my response.

I continue, "Handsome. Hot. Great in bed. I've used them all to describe you." I give him a small smile that feels good to share. "I might have even used virile once or twice."

When a small smile appears on his lips, I feel okay again, just like he promised.

The driver speaks too soon. "We're here."

Danny's eyes meet mine, a look exchanged, an understanding that everything might actually be okay. The door is opened and I reluctantly turn to get out. Vinnie and Mark are walking inside and Vinnie holds the door open for me. As I pass, he says, "All better?"

I poke him in the arm. "Revenge is sweet, my friend."

He laughs. "You're welcome."

Turning back, I wink, and meaning it, I mouth, "Thank you."

As we walk through the lobby, I kind of wish Danny would touch my back again. I don't know why I found that so incredibly sexy, but I did. Makes me wonder if I should feel bad about liking it as much as I did. I wipe away the guilt that develops and decide one more drink will help me forget a lot quicker.

We reach the bar and find a round booth in the corner. I slip inside, following Vinnie, and Danny slides in right next to me. Mark settles in on the end after Danny. When the waitress takes our orders, Mark gives her a card to cover it all. "I want to settle this now. The drinks are on me."

Vinnie covered dinner, which was *very* generous considering the insane bill, so it's kind Mark is taking care of the rest. Perks of the business. Before I get too lost in my thoughts, Danny's foot bumps against mine, catching my attention. I don't say anything, but I also don't move my foot away.

The night is easy, relaxed, something I never thought would happen with us. Vinnie and Mark take the edge off, making us behave, and keeping the conversation light. When asked what his favorite city is, Danny says, "Lincoln," as if there is no doubt. Maybe for him, there isn't.

As for me... I've not settled on my favorite city.

Mark asks, "Nebraska?"

"Yep."

Vinnie squints in disbelief. "I've never been to Nebraska, but you have me intrigued. What is it about the city that makes it so special?"

The glass is spun slowly under his fingertips as he ponders his answer before speaking. "Maybe it's not the city, but the people that are special."

"Anyone in particular?" Mark asks, not understanding the Pandora's box he's opening.

With rapt attention I can't take my eyes off him. His leg shifts under the table, his knee knocking into mine. He looks at me before turning back to Mark and replying, "No one in particular."

I exhale a long held breath.

Loudly.

Everyone looks at me, but Vinnie takes the honors. "Are you all right?"

Hating the attention, I brush my hair behind my ear and smile. "Yes, fine." I shift. "Tonight's been fun, but it might be time for me to go to bed. The wine has gone to my head and the jetlag has caught up with me."

Just as I'm about to faux-yawn, Danny stands allowing me enough room to escape. "I should escort you to the elevators."

"Thank you, but you don't have to do that."

"I want to. For safety."

If Mark's glare came with a sound effect, I think it would be the buzzer from Family Feud. Although it's silent, I feel its intended effect loud and clear.

Danny ignores him and offers his arm to me. "Really," I say. "This is too much. I'll be fine."

He doesn't budge, so I give in and take his arm, wrapping mine around his, and glance to Vinnie who is practically clapping in excitement from this spectacle. After a short goodnight to the men, we walk through the bar and through the lobby. My heart is thudding so hard I'm afraid he'll hear it over the clack of my heels echoing on the marble.

We don't say anything. I don't because I have no idea what to say. He doesn't either until we reach the elevator. "You're leaving tomorrow?"

"Yes, I have an afternoon flight back to New York."

"Do you want to have a lunch?"

"With you?" I ask surprised, but realize that could be offensive. "I don't mean it that way. I just... you just caught me off guard."

"Maybe I shouldn't have asked." He pulls his arm back slowly when we stop in front of the elevators.

"It might be good to catch up." Too good, I sigh quietly. When I look at him, look into his gentle gaze, I'm more than attracted to him. It's then I realize how easily I could fall for him. *Again.* I can't go through that heartbreak twice. I shouldn't even put myself in that kind of situation. "I'd love to catch up." *Wait what? Shoot!*

"Good. I'll pick you up at eleven. I can take you to the airport after."

"Danny?" I sway, reaching for something solid. That just happens to be his bicep. My head may be spinning but damn, he's rock hard... my mind goes to other rock hard places.

Grabbing my shoulders, he steadies me. "You okay?"

Touching my cheek, I shake my head free from the thoughts of his hard places and try to stabilize my mind, focusing on his face instead—his oh so handsome face. "I need to go to bed. I'm a little tipsy and these shoes are really high. Probably not a good combination for me." The elevator door opens.

"How about I help you upstairs?"

Puffing out a big breath, hoping to miraculously sober up, I say, "I don't think that's safe. Not a good idea."

"Safe?" He chuckles. "I'll be a good boy."

"That's the thing, Mr. Weston." I point at him, attempting to prove I'm not drunk, though my mouth seems to have a mind of its own. "I don't think I can be a good girl around you." I poke him in the chest, which makes me sway again.

With a firm hold on me, he backs me into the elevator and right into a corner. Usually I'd protest from the metaphor, but he leans forward to press the button and I'm flooded with naughty memories of when we were together in college. And curious to what we'd be like now... *in bed.*

"What floor?"

My ass is propped against the brass bar I'm holding on to. I give up the fake protests and start going with the flow, his sexy flow to be precise. "Four."

He presses the button and leans back, our bodies pressed to each other's sides. I'm smarter than this, but just like years ago, we've slipped into this level of comfort that makes me relax. "I should be mad at you."

The back of his hand brushes against mine. "And why is that?"

"You know when I drink it sneaks up on me and then hits me hard." I lean my head against his shoulder. "Or have you forgotten?"

He laughs again, quieter, fitting of the small space. The elevator door opens and he takes my hand as if he owns it... something I'll have to think about once I'm sober. For now, it feels too good. He feels too good for me to let go. As we walk, his strength steadies me. It always did. "I'm 404."

"You were always a ten to me," he replies casually and sends me a wink.

"Haha! Clever."

"You still are, Reese."

I elbow him. "Awww, and you, my friend, were always the charmer." We stop in front of my door and I lean my back against the floral-papered wall behind me, feeling too at ease. I should really put some kind of guard up, but I'm too tired to try.

We stand there a minute before he glances back down the hall at the elevator. When his eyes land on mine again, he says, "I think we should get you inside."

Reaching up, I touch the bridge of his nose and drag my finger down and tap the end when I reach it. "Should. Could. Would."

His smile, the way the left side is raised slightly higher, is very sexy. His lips are sexy. I want to kiss them. I want them to kiss me. My finger runs across the plushness as I admire the way they look, move, and pucker. He's so damn tempting. "I always loved your lips."

"Your key, Reese. Is it in your purse?"

"My key?" He nods, and I realize he means my room key. "Oh! Yes, my key." I reach down and open my clutch, pulling out the card. He takes it from me and slips it in the slot, making even the small action seem so much naughtier and sexier than it should, or

I even thought possible.

The door is opened and he escorts me inside. I go for the bed, needing to lie down. As soon as I do, his fingertips slide down my shins, igniting my legs with a sexual energy, making me forget all about the shin splints I had the other day. Farther, farther. I barely breathe in anticipation of what he's about to do to me.

Ah.

Aww. My feet feel so good, free from the spiked confines of the platforms.

He takes one heel off and then the other and I push up, moving myself into a sleeping position. "Thank you," I murmur, my head melting into the comfy pillow.

He sits on the bed next to me as my body eases onto the mattress. Reaching forward, he pushes my hair back away from my face. If I knew better, I wouldn't have allowed him inside my room. The way he's looking at me, the feel of his skin touching mine—it's all too dangerous for my heart, for my body in such a vulnerable state. He leans down and kisses my cheek and I let him because I like him near, even more this close. I shouldn't, but I do. How can I not? I've always been attracted to this man, to Danny. *My Danny.* Then, he whispers, "For the record, I remember everything about you."

I'm tired. My eyes close on their own as the dream world starts sweeping me away, but I manage to say, "You forgot me, Danny. *You forgot me.*"

CHAPTER 8

WITH MY BACK against the door, I remain for a few minutes. A housekeeper eyes me as she walks down the hall. When she passes, she greets me, "Good evening, Sir."

"Good evening," I reply, pushing off and walking away from Reese's room reluctantly. I want to stay. I want to do much more than stay, but my fate was sealed with her last cocktail. Despite her state, she knew how to hit me hard, hit me when I couldn't argue back.

"You forgot me" plays on a loop through my mind as I trudge down the stairs back to the bar. I was dropped from the high I was riding as soon as she muttered those three words, affecting her enough for her to repeat them as she fell asleep. When I reach the first floor, I swipe my hands through my hair before I turn the corner. Mark and Vittori are standing near the entrance talking when I join them.

Vittori gives me a look like we're in on some secret together. He says, "You've been gone a while. Did you get Ms. Carmichael in bed?"

What? "Excuse me?"

"She was tired. I take it you made sure she made it back to her room?"

"Yes, don't worry," I say, shorter than I should be with him considering he's my new boss. I'm still thrown off from being with Reese upstairs, but take a deep breath and exhale, trying to find the balance I had prior to seeing her this morning. "She's sound asleep." Vittori looks over the moon from this news. Mark is glaring at me. I bypass him and focus on the one practically squealing in delight. Vittori asks, "I take it she has your number if she needs anything?"

"She does," I respond, finding him easy to please.

Mark's stare is icy at best. I'll thaw him out tomorrow by reminding him nothing happened.

Mark replies, "Hopefully she'll get a good night's rest and be ready for the flight home tomorrow. If there's anything I can do during the rest of your stay, you have my card. Feel free to call me." He shakes Vittori's hand and wishes him a good night.

Vittori winks at me and heads for the elevator after saying goodbye. When Mark and I walk outside, he stops and asks, "Be straight with me. You didn't fuck her, did you?"

While feigning offense, I remember the many times I did fuck her. But since he's acting like an ass and referring to tonight, I respond sarcastically, "Nope. She fell asleep before I could."

"Are you messing with me? You better be fucking with me."

Hitting him on the chest, I laugh. "Calm down. I didn't make any moves on her. When she wakes up in the morning, she will only remember what a perfect gentleman I was... If she remembers anything at all."

His stance eases and he smiles. Well, as much as Mark can manage to smile, which isn't much. "She is hot."

I lower my defenses. She's not mine to feel possessive over

any longer. "She is."

"She could have modeled."

"Could have?"

"She's too old to be starting out in this business now."

"I can't have this conversation." *Not about her. Not tonight.* The lightness that we had is gone. "I need to get home. I'm too tired."

By the way his eyes are squinting, has one cheek lifted, and his eyebrows tilting downward, he's clearly baffled. So am I. By my own behavior. That's why I need to go. A cab pulls up and I rush for it, needing to get out of here before I tell secrets that shouldn't be shared. "We'll talk soon."

"Don't forget Vargo."

"I won't," I reply and slam the door shut with me tucked inside. I give the driver directions to my place and lean my head back. Staring outside the window, the lights of businesses flash by until we hit the freeway. The dark is wanted. Needed in fact. I feel exposed. My heart is on my fucking sleeve and I don't want anyone to witness it.

At home, I empty my pockets, dumping everything on the kitchen counter and reach for a glass. I would bother with the shot glass if someone else was here, but since I'm alone, I don't lie to myself.

With half a glass of bourbon in hand, I make my way into the bedroom and strip down after a few hard swigs of the amber liquid. The sheets are cold. I fucking hate cold sheets. I climb in anyway since I have no choice but to warm them up myself. Grabbing the remote, I open the curtains. There's no view from here, but staring at the few stars I can see in the sky is better than drinking in the dark. The stars are better company than my thoughts tonight.

The glass balances on my chest as I lie there. I lift to take a sip and fall back, letting the alcohol heat my throat and lower into my chest. Closing my eyes, I remember too much... too much...

My body pins her against the wall. Her door is the next obstacle on this ride home from the party. I just want her. I've wanted her for so long. I bend forward and kiss Reese. Her hands tighten on my shoulders, pulling me closer. She tilts her head back and says, "My roommate is gone."

This is it. Months of buildup have led us here. I feel like I'm about to explode. "God, I want you so much."

"Me too." She spins around and sticks her key in the lock. The room is dark, but we know it by heart. We've fumbled our way around this dorm room many times while making out. But tonight's the night. I don't want fumbling. I want it to be perfect for her, and since my roommate is scoring with a Tri-Delt, her room is our only option.

She leads me to her twin-sized bed. Our breathing can be heard to a distracting level. "Should we put some music on?"

"Sure." She walks to her nightstand and starts a song.

My head tilts to the side. "Is this a boy band?"

"Yeah. I like this song."

"I can't have sex with you the first time while they're singing about lollipops and puppy love." I look down. "I'm already going soft listening to them."

She laughs. "How about classical?"

"Okay, but no Beethoven. No man can live up to those crescendos."

"I didn't know you knew so much about music."

"A little. Not much."

"Okay," she asks, "how about Maroon 5?"

"No. I don't want to compete with Adam Levine."

"Amy Winehouse?"

"Too depressing."

"Barry White?"

"You have Barry White?"

She shakes her head. "No, but I heard it's supposed to be sexy music."

Taking her hand I tug her back to bed. She lands next to me, all smiles and smelling beautiful. "We don't need music. We'll make our own."

She kisses my cheek and then sits up to take her shirt off. The room goes quiet again while I watch her. I've seen her breasts many times, felt them, kissed them, but knowing this is only the beginning and not the end changes everything. Lifting up on my elbows, I angle to get a better view.

Her snow boots, socks, and jeans come off next. I take the cue and take off my shirt and jeans after flipping off my boots and socks. She doesn't bother keeping her underwear on, so I don't either. She settles back down, but this time on top of me.

My hands roam her sides. She's little compared to me. Lean, but has great curves. I turn over, wanting her underneath me the first time. We start kissing and our bodies move against each other until my knee slips between her legs. She's wet and fucking my leg. Fuck. I readjust, needing to be inside her.

Reaching over, I grab a condom from my jeans pocket. She slides up and down my thigh, her breathing erratic until her eyes are squeezed closed and her mouth opens. "Danny, please. I need you."

"I'm not gonna last."

"Neither will I," she whispers.

When she spreads wider, I angle, then reposition and put the condom on. I cover her mouth with mine again, my hips pressing between her legs. Just the feel of her sends waves of sexual cravings racing through my body. Fuck.

I've got to calm down.

Her hand touches my cheek and she says, "Go slow, at first. Okay?"

I nod, words seeming impossible. Kissing her again, I slowly push into her welcoming heat.

My thoughts are floating, my body engulfed by the most amazing feeling. I want to tell her I love her, but I'm aware enough to know now's not the time. I pull back and push in again. Opening my eyes, I see her pretty face, flush with emotion. She says, "It's better than I thought."

I stop. "Better than you thought? Ummm."

Laughing, she corrects, "No. No. That's not what I meant. I just always knew it would be amazing with you. It's even better than amazing." I relax and start moving again. She adds, "Like so much better. God, that feels so good. You feel so good."

"You do too. You feel incredible." I kiss her neck. "This makes you mine."

"I was always yours, Danny."

...I'm not sure what time I finish the bourbon or what time I finally fall asleep, but I wake up when the sun rises. Hard. Uncomfortably hard. *I was always yours, Danny.* Except she wasn't. She hasn't been mine for over ten fucking years. Closing the curtains, I try to go back to bed, not bothering to check the time, and ignoring the urge I have to masturbate to the memory of the first time we had sex.

Fuck it!

I take care of business and go back to bed.

9:37 stares back at me from the clock on my nightstand. Eleven. I told Reese I'd pick her up at eleven. While I lie there a minute longer, last night weighs down on me. My eyes burn, my body heavy. A few more hours of sleep would help, but I won't miss this chance to spend some time with her. Too many questions still remain unanswered.

How is she still single?

Why pick me for this job?

Does she have a boyfriend?

How attached to New York is she?

How does she look that fucking incredible?

And, the one question that has burned inside me for over a decade. The one question I was too damaged to confront her about before... before now.

Why didn't she show up?

I get in the shower, letting the water run down over my head. With my face under the spray I realize I've thought more about her, about our past in the last twenty-four hours than I have since I saw her back in Nebraska.

We were different people back then. Clearly I didn't know her at all. In this life, the one I created after her, I don't utter her name. I don't dwell on our history. I don't look at the photos I've got in that Nike shoebox buried in the back of my closet. She doesn't exist in my life, in this world that was born from our breakup.

But now I have to. She's come back into my life demanding me to see her because of this campaign, to smell her, to think about her, to touch her because I can't be that close to her and not do any of those things.

The scale feels suspiciously balanced in her favor. How long was she planning this reintroduction into my life? And if she plotted this all along, why was she so distant during the meeting? Why are we pretending we don't know each other—for her benefit, mine, or both?

She had time to prepare, to plan for this reunion, but I got no heads-up or warning at all. What does she really want from me?

What does she hope to gain beyond using my name and reputation I've built in this industry?

I'm so fucking confused. Maybe I don't want to play this game. Or, maybe it's time I take the control back. Maybe I'll start making demands of my own.

CHAPTER 9

FUCK, SHE LOOKS hot!

Damn, look at her.

I push off the Jeep and go to her. Her eyes are down as she pulls her suitcase behind her. When they lift up to meet mine, a small smile, one that reveals more than she probably wants appears. That girl likes what she sees and I like that she likes it... that she *likes me,* even if it is just the package she likes—my package.

Chuckling when I reach her, she asks, "What are you laughing about?"

"You don't even want to know." I cover her hand over the handle of her suitcase and don't move.

Concern colors her eyes as she looks into mine. "What?"

I lean forward and kiss her cheek. She doesn't see me close my eyes, or notice that I stay longer than I should. She stands there with my forehead touching her temple. When I straighten back up, I confess, "It's good to see you."

A softer side seeps into her tone, the emotion reaching her eyes. "It's good to see you too." She starts to move again, but when I don't budge, she stops. Her voice is softer this time. "Danny?"

"Say it again."

"It's good to see you?"

"No."

"Danny?"

I don't know what's come over me... or maybe I'm not ready to admit what has. "Yes. One more time."

"Danny," she says with a smirk.

"I missed hearing you say it."

She rocks back. "You're being silly."

"I'm being serious, Reese."

A glance in my direction reveals my charms are working on her. When her cheeks pink, I know they are. The ridiculous part is I'm being honest with her. I'll play it safe and keep under the guise of flirting to protect the innocent—Reese.

She slips her hand out from under mine and nods toward the Jeep. "We should go." When she looks back at me, she looks like she's up to no good. When she adds, "Danny," I know she is.

I walk to the vehicle and watch her climb in as I load her suitcase into the back. When I get in, she says, "Did you put the top on for me?"

"I sure did." I start the engine and we pull away from the hotel.

Leaning her head back, she watches me. I see her in my peripheral, and I can feel her gaze on me. "Where are you taking me for lunch?"

"The beach."

She sits up. "The beach? Are you serious?"

"I am," I say, looking over and catching her wide grin.

The rest of the ride is filled with talk of the bad traffic, the LA scene, and apparently there are too many tanned people in her opinion. I volley back that Manhattan has too many gray days. She rests her case by saying, "Maybe it's good we live where we live then."

"Ah, don't judge us so fast. If I got a chance to show you the real LA, I bet you'd enjoy the city more."

"What if I gave you that chance?"

"When you say stuff like that I'm not sure how to reply."

"It's better if you don't. Sometimes I speak before thinking."

"That's your heart speaking for you."

"When you say stuff like that I'm not sure how to reply." She rests her head on her hand, elbow firmly set on the door. After exhaling a deep breath, she says, "We're going to be working together. I think we should keep it as easy as we can."

"Easy? I don't believe anything worth having comes easy. My mission is to make you miss me by the time you land in New York." She stares, her dark-pink lips parted, her blues in awe as she sits next to me. I pull into the beach lot and put the car in park. "You hungry?"

"Danny," she starts.

Here it comes...

"We need to talk."

I step out of the Jeep, but stand there. "That's why we're here."

The door shuts and I walk around and help her out. She walks toward the sand, stops, takes off her shoes and carries them in her hand. I grab the box lunches, the blanket, and two bottles of water, and follow her toward the water. While she stands letting the water coat her feet, I set up and sit down.

She stands there a minute longer, the skirt of her dress blowing in the breeze, her hair whirling around her head. When she turns to come back, her happiness is contagious. "I didn't think I'd get to come to the beach on this trip. I love it here so much."

"So maybe you're a little more LA than you thought."

"Maybe," she replies sitting down and then lying back. With her hand cupped above her eyes to block the sun, she looks at me. "Can we do this?"

"By *this*, you mean make out? Sure," I say, shrugging and smiling. "If you insist." I roll over and pretend I'm about to kiss her.

And I kind of want to.

More than I probably should.

She sits up and huffs, but I can tell by her own smile that she's entertained. Until she's not and something else comes over her, flattening the joy that was in her eyes. She doesn't push me away, her hands doing the opposite. The tips of her fingers touch the hem of my shirt. "You make this hard." I think she knows what I'm going to say, so she playfully warns, "Don't."

"Don't what, pretty?"

Laughing, she relents. "Fine. Say it."

"You make this hard," I reply, eyeing lower than my abs that are now exposed from her toying with my shirt.

"You never could resist."

"One of the many reasons you loved me."

This time she doesn't respond. She just agrees nodding silently. I don't kiss her. This time. And unless I'm reading her all wrong, she's disappointed. I sit up, both of us wrapping our arms around our knees as we stare ahead. Keeping my attention on the distant horizon, I ask, "Were you married?"

Resting her head on her knees, she faces me. "No. You?"

"No."

"Why is that?"

"Didn't meet the one, I guess. You?" Her pause is too long, so

I look at her. She's facing forward, this time with her chin on her knees. I ask, "Have I crossed a line by asking?"

"No." She doesn't look at me. "I'm just not sure how to answer that."

That's when I realize what I said. "I wasn't talking about you."

She straightens up, stretching her legs in front of her. "Be careful, Danny, or I might think you're saying you would have married me," she jokes.

"I would have."

The laughter stops. While her eyes search mine I can see panic rising. "What are you saying?"

She doesn't know. How can she not know? I told her I loved her, that I was coming back for her, to her, that I had something special to tell her. I had the ring. The scenario was all planned out. But she didn't show. She broke my heart and then never talked to me again. How can she really not know? "I'm saying I would've married you. So when I said I hadn't met the one, I was referring to *after* you. No one since then that I would have married." Tears fill her eyes. I didn't expect that reaction and suddenly my hurt heart doesn't matter. I just want to make her feel better. "I'm sorry. I didn't mean to upset you."

She takes the box of food next to her and opens it. "You didn't." When she stops messing with the box, she looks me in the eyes. "I am, but I shouldn't be. I have no right to be upset about anything regarding us." She laughs. "This is heavy, not easy at all."

"It used to be. We used to be easy."

"Many years have passed—"

"Water under the bridge?"

"Oceans"

I nod, but I don't know why. Oceans. She's right. Maybe I need to just ask the questions I want to ask and stop all the other

BS I've gotten caught up in with her. But as I sit next to her, I realize I'm doing what feels right. I like flirting with her. I like hearing her laugh and seeing her smile. I like that perfect pink that covers her face when I do push her sexual buttons. I like it all. I like her—sober and tipsy.

"Can we set work aside, and I ask you something personal?"

She bursts out laughing. "Everything has been personal, so why stop now?"

"What's in New York?"

"Are you really asking what or who?"

"You know me well."

"My job is based in New York."

I wait to see if she'll add to that. When she doesn't, I ask, "Why rush back?"

"What do you suggest? That I stay an extra day or two?"

"Is that idea so crazy?"

"Your campaign is the biggest of my career. I don't want to screw it up and lose this account. I have a lot of details to oversee. We're thinking two cities at least, maybe one more. There's planning involved that can be done from New York easier than from a hotel room."

"I understand the logistics, but what do you want to do?"

"Danny, my job is a sixty-hour-a-week job. It's not frivolous. I can't just take off spontaneously. My boss has been breathing down my neck. He *really* doesn't want to lose this account."

I've heard the word frivolous thrown around about models many times. It's a misnomer, but it's not worth fighting with her. Appearances can be deceiving. We just make it look carefree. "We should eat. We'll need to leave soon."

We're eating strawberries when she says, "I'm sorry."

"For what?"

"I don't think what you do is frivolous. I envy your freedom of choice and your ability to travel like you do."

"Don't envy it. It's lonely. I'm always leaving." I hear the catch in her breath and look into her eyes. Words from years earlier still haunt my memories. *"You're always leaving me, Danny."* She hated being left behind, but never realized how hard it was for me.

Looking back out to the ocean, a thoughtful expression softens her features. "You make it look exciting." She says this so quietly, I feel as though I need to repair unseen damage.

"It is, and isn't. It's hard to explain." Sounding much like a rehearsed pageant response. "I'm grateful for the opportunities I'm given. But I also work my ass off to get them. I'm lucky I don't have a sweet tooth and like to exercise."

"So are we," she deadpans, pushing against me playfully.

"A-ha! I knew you liked the view."

"I do and I'm not talking about the beach."

"Be careful or you might make me kiss you for real this time."

"Would that be so bad?" She licks her lips and suddenly all I want to do is follow in her tongue's tracks. I lean over, but my lips land on her cheek. She's looking down. "I'm sorry."

"No, I am," I reply, sitting back and losing my appetite. Looking at my watch, I pack the lunch back into the box. "We should go. LAX is a nightmare. You'll need the time if you're gonna make your flight."

She doesn't argue. It's going to take us hours to fight traffic and get her up to the terminal. I think we talk about everything other than what happened back there or even what happened in our past.

Avoidance.

We both seem to be masters at it.

As we get closer, I say, "Thanks for Vittori."

"You were my choice from the beginning. I knew he'd love you."

"What about you? Any soft spots still in there for me?"

"Danny." Her response is a warning mixed with resolve. "Please don't make this harder than it is."

I nod. We had all the time in the world and now time's run out. "How does this between us go from here?"

"We've met," she replies, looking at me. "Here, this week. So we know each other, but I think that's as far as it goes for us."

The button has been located. "You sure about that, pretty?" *And now pushed.*

"Please don't call me that."

"Why?"

"Because you know what it does to me."

"What does it do to you, pretty? Tell me."

She crosses her arms over her chest. "I refuse to fall in love with you, so you can just turn those eyes on someone else. I'm not falling for it. Again."

"Who said anything about falling? I'm not here to make you fall."

"Then why are you here?"

"To help you remember."

She looks out at the curb. "Professional," she whispers as if she's now reminding herself.

I keep my expression neutral and my emotions in check. The ignorance I've been living in for the last ten years is working. There's no point in changing what's good. If only this beating organ in my chest agreed with me. "Got it."

She picks right back up like most of our conversation never happened. "Most of our communication will be through Mark, but if you need anything, you can call me." She's holding out a business card.

I take it and drop it into the cup holder. "Don't worry, we'll be purely professional around each other. If that's what you want."

"Thank you," she says, her chin raising a bit; her stiff upper lip in place. "I think it's best."

When I pull over to drop her off, she stays in the Jeep until I have her luggage on the sidewalk. With the door open, I lean against the top. To make it easier on her, I'll take the blow to the heart again. "I think of you often."

She doesn't pause this time, giving me this one thing easily. "I do too."

As I back up, she gets out, coming face to neck with me. "If I didn't have a meeting with potential clients in the morning, I would stay an extra day."

I smile. I know just what she means. The storm brewing in her eyes gives her away. The emotional turmoil I feel inside, she feels it too. Pushing professional out the window, I slide my arms around her and she embraces me. With her head tucked into my shoulder, she whispers, "I look forward to seeing you again. Already, and I haven't left yet."

"I feel the same about you." I take one deep breath, inhaling her into my system and memorizing the notes that make up her perfume, that make up her, and how she still fits so perfectly in my arms after all of these years.

We part and suddenly a lump forms in my throat. By how quiet she is, I'm thinking she's at a loss as well. She takes hold of her suitcase and walks away from me. I shove my hands into my pockets and watch her leave... me.

Other than the lump and the sappy feeling I've got from her leaving me, Reese Carmichael is amazing. It didn't take long for me to see what I've been missing.

A few days. Maybe it's not about the past, but the future.

A second chance at love... *is that what this is?*

I look back once more as she disappears inside.

That's exactly what this is.

I'm going to have a hard time keeping things professional when she is so incredibly clever, beautiful, and driven... a woman I can easily fall for, just like I did with the girl. A girl who was once wholly mine. It only took a few days for me to see what I've been missing all these years. I admire the woman she's become.

Fuck!

I more than admire her. I already want her to be mine again. *You'll always be mine, Reese. Mine.* Just like I was hers.

Walking around the Jeep, I get in and glance back again. Reese Carmichael is back. Destiny has a funny way of working. I smile to myself as I start the engine. And by the looks of her, she's back better than ever.

Her strength is one to envy, but her heart is what I'm after.

CHAPTER 10

DAYS PASS AND I think of Reese, too much. With no word from Mark, I'm not sure what's happening with the campaign. Things sometimes move fast and I'm on a flight that night. Others crawl until the actual gig. Vittori is a multi-million dollar ad campaign, hence why I was hired, so it being slow to progress doesn't surprise me.

This might be the first time I've felt anxious, and it's not the shoot that's done this to me. I have the Vargo shoot in two days, so I've been putting my nervous energy into working out.

Running back home, uphill, I try to maintain the same hard pace I ran the last four miles. A distracting little blonde is up ahead—ass sticking out of her car, ponytail high on her head, a crap load of bags around her ankles. I suddenly feel a little more motivated to finish up strong.

Who am I kidding? I always finish strong.

"Hey there, stranger."

She ducks out of the car and a big smile slides across that beautiful face when she sees me. With her hand on her hip, my part-time neighbor—successful entrepreneur, one of the hottest bods in Hollywood, and very taken, Holli Hughes, says "Hey there, back at ya."

Even though my breath hasn't caught up, I ask, "What brings you around?"

"I'm around."

"Not nearly enough." I land the line with a smirk.

She pushes off me. "You are too much and yes, I missed you too if that's what you're saying."

"I am." Reaching down, I pick up the bags. "C'mon. Let's get these inside."

"I could get used to this kind of greeting."

Laughing as I walk up the path, I reply, "Don't tell me the rock star doesn't greet you like this."

"When he's home, he greets me in a totally different, X-rated way. There are no complaints there, Romeo." She laughs, patting me on the chest. Her laugh is genuine, from the heart.

Sometimes I miss it, miss her, hanging out on her balcony, shooting the shit. She's fuckhot sexy, but that ship sailed a long time ago. It all worked out how it was supposed to. I believe that deep down. And I got a great friend out of it. When I glance behind me, I see the happiness in her eyes. "That's good to hear. I'd hate to kick his ass again."

After a loud laugh, she says, "I'm sure he'd happily debate that fight."

"The great Johnny Outlaw can debate it all he wants, but that night, I got the girl."

She rolls her eyes when she passes me and unlocks the door. "How about I just tell him you called him 'great' and call it a day?"

"Yeah, probably best. We're on good terms. No need messing that all up again."

She sets her purse and laptop down on the kitchen counter and looks my way. "Wise man." Pointing toward the coffee table, she directs, "You can set those down there. Thanks for the helping hand."

"Anytime."

Coming into the living room, she sits down on the couch. "It's been a while. Fill me in on all the things."

"I'd say not much, but—"

"I'd know you were lying."

We laugh together; our friendship is one of the easiest relationships I've ever had, especially surprising since it's with a woman. I haven't felt this comfortable with another woman since... since...

Reese comes to mind, but I don't think it's wise for me to keep dwelling on our past. The problem is our past won't seem to let me go, or I can't seem to let it go now that she's invaded my present.

"I booked the Vittori menswear line."

"Impressive," she says, sinking back into the cushions. "Billboards, commercials, and the whole shebang?"

"I'm not sure what they have planned yet."

"Are you home much?" she asks, kicking her feet up onto the coffee table. "Or still traveling all the time?"

"I'm not home as much as I like, but you aren't either."

She waves me off. "Don't be silly. I'd only cramp your playboy lifestyle."

"It cramps my lifestyle that I'm not bothering my neighbors with women screaming my name in the middle of the night and loud parties full of beautiful people only looking to hook up."

"Yeah, it's just not as fun when you're not disturbing the neighbors." She laughs. "But all is not lost. I'm thinking about throwing a party when Dalton comes home from touring."

"Rebel."

"You know it." She stands abruptly and takes two of the bags in hand. "I brought this over for filing, but I really don't want to do it. Want to grab margaritas up the road like old times instead?" She looks hopeful. Too hopeful to turn down.

"Yes to drinking. No on the margaritas. Yes on beer. *Light* beer," I say, rolling my eyes, wanting a solid lager, but settling for the lighter brew. "Let me shower. I'll be ready in twenty."

"You're on. In the meantime, maybe I'll make myself useful and try to get rid of one of these bags. Just knock when you're ready."

"Will do."

Wonder if I should talk to her about Reese when I return? Get a woman's perspective on this whole mess, but I think that conversation is best left over margaritas and beer.

A man is only so strong. With images of Reese in that little leather skirt and see-through shirt taunting me, I give in. It's been years since I got off to her, probably since I was *with* her, until last night and here I am hours later doing it again. The shower has steamed up the bathroom and I take my dick in hand. Resting one arm against the tiles, I press my forehead against it and close my eyes.

Her ass.

Tight leather.

Great tits.

Gripping harder, I pump faster.

Lips.

Tongue.

Blue eyes that remember everything we once were.

Fucking chemistry, drawing me right back to her. Together, we aced that class. No one could ever deny our connection—sexual or otherwise.

I haven't allowed myself to think about her in a long time for good reason. Nothing good would come of it. Yet here I am coming from the mere sight of her and it feels pretty damn good. So maybe something good can come of it.

My hand covers my face when I step outside. My lame attempt to hide the smile shining has failed. I can't help it. What I thought might be a bad thing has turned around. Maybe Reese coming back into my life is meant to be. Definitely meant to be.

She looked good at Spago.

Really good.

Even better at the beach—natural and beautiful.

A singsong voice breaks into my memory lane reverie, "I recognize that expression."

My head bolts up and I see Holli standing there on her top step. I don't bother hiding my goofy-ass expression from her. She sees right through me anyway. But I suddenly feel shy about it, not embarrassed, but like I've just had a secret revealed and I'm not talking about the action in the shower. Because yeah, I don't care if she knows about that, but her seeing that I might be wearing a silly smile over a girl, now that's embarrassing. "Look away, woman!" I tease, hiding my face from her.

She laughs as she tugs at my hands. "No hiding from me." When I lower my hands, she says, "She must be some girl."

"She is."

As we walk down the path, she asks, "Do I get to hear about her?"

"I have a feeling I don't have a choice in the matter."

"Eh, you always have a choice with me." She nudges me in the hip. "But if you want to share, I'm all ears."

"Beers, my dear. I need booze for this conversation."

Holding up her wallet, she shakes it. "I'm buying."

We're sat at our regular table, the one by the window where we emptied many a pint over the years. We've eaten half the chips and the salsa is gone. Mainly because Holli doesn't dip. She scoops... or shovels from what I've witnessed. I stopped trying to get salsa by the second chip. "Do they not feed you in that mansion in the hills?"

She almost spits out her food when she breaks down laughing. Tears enter her eyes as she covers her mouth. When she catches a breath, she takes a mouthful of her margarita. "I've been on a diet."

"You don't need to starve yourself. Just eat healthy and enjoy the good things in life."

"Like salsa?"

"Yes, like salsa."

"What witchcraft do they put in this salsa that makes it taste so good? Chipotle pepper? Is that chipotle?"

I stare at her and laugh, mocking her. "You're a mess."

"And surprisingly you're not. So tell me about this girl that has you grinning for reasons I know I'll regret asking about, but I'm going to anyway. Tell me everything."

"That's just it. There's not much to tell." I can't even lie to myself. I feel that ridiculous grin returning. "How about the truth?"

"That's what I'm hoping for."

"There's too much to tell of the past to share and not enough of the present. Yet."

A genuine smile appears, and she says, "I like the sound of that 'yet,' but I want more."

I'd love to distract with another drink, but I can't afford to have it and she would see through it. "I'm not sure what to say about her."

"Give me something honest."

"I want a woman I can probably never have. I want a woman that has come back into my life and flipped it upside down. I want a woman that it hurts to think about much less mention."

"Wow. That's a lot of wants."

"If I could have just one of them with her, I'd take it. How's that for honesty?"

"Pretty damn honest." She smiles. "And so damn endearing. Stop being so loveable, okay?"

"I'll take loveable."

"Good, because it's all you're getting from me today. I can't have you going around thinking you're a knight in shining armor or anything."

"Nope," I say, chuckling. "Wouldn't want any damsels in distress thinking that."

"Oh, and maybe next time I see you that *yet* will be gone and you'll have some bow chicka wow wow to share."

Wagging my finger at her, I say, "You, Mrs. Outlaw, are a dirty girl."

Matching my wags, her eyebrows go up and down. "So I'm told." She slaps her palms down and starts to stand. "I need to get back. Those papers aren't gonna file themselves, and I promised I'd be home by three."

"Don't you have someone who can help you with that?"

"I do, but we've been working overtime for months. With our deadlines met and projects done, everyone has this week off. I'm going old school like in the beginning and running the company myself this week. It's like our Christmas since we had to work through that."

I toss down fifty before she has a chance. "I've got this."

"Awww. You always were too good to me. Thank you."

"You're welcome."

When we get back home, I give that girl a big hug. "It was good seeing you. You're welcome to come visit your place any time you want."

She giggles while hugging me back. "Thanks. I'll keep that in mind." Just before she goes inside, she adds, "You know, Danny, this girl looks good on you."

"I keep trying to tell her that, but she's not falling for it yet."

"I have no doubt she will." She waves and goes inside.

I'm not home an hour when I get a text from Jody, Mark's assistant.

Jody: *Free at five?*

I smile.

Me: *You asking me out?*

Jody: *Ha! Mark is requesting your humble presence.*

Me: *There's nothing humble about my presence.*

Jody: *This is true. Grace us with it anyway.*

Me: *What's in it for me?*

Jody: *A big paycheck.*

Me: *I'll be there. Will you?*

Jody: *LOL. I thought so. And yes, I'm stuck here. Forever here at Mark's disposal.*

Me: *You just sweetened the pot.*

Jody: *Stop flirting with me. You're making me blush.*

Me: *I like flirting with you. Can I bring you something? Coffee? Tea?*

Jody: **rolls eyes* And yes, a grande mocha latte with coconut milk and a sprinkle of cinnamon.*

Me: *And here you thought I was the un-humble. You're lucky you're so awesome.*

Jody: *Actually, you're the lucky one I'm so awesome. Haha Ack! Mark is calling me. See you at 5, ya big flirt.*

Me: *See you at 5 with your mocha yada latte yada whatever else was in there, Ms. High Maintenance. *winks**

I set my phone down on the couch and sit forward staring at ESPN on the large screen in front of me. I watch a goal replay three times before I notice the time.

Clicking off the TV, I grab my wallet from the counter and head out.

CHAPTER 11

THE ELEVATOR DOORS open and Jody greets me with a smile. I hand her the paper coffee cup. "Grande mocha latte with coconut milk and a sprinkle of cinnamon, as you requested."

"You're the best. Thanks, Danny. You ready to face the dragon?" she asks as we walk toward the glass doors leading us inside. She rushes to open it wide before I can open it for her.

We round the corner and I follow her through The Pit, saying hi to the few agents working late. "Don't let the dimples fool you. I'm ready to *slay* the dragon." I send a smile over to the new girl stationed at a desk near the conference room.

"Don't even think about it." Jody says, "I'm betting she won't last a month."

"That desk seems to be on quite the rotation." When the blonde smiles back, I add, "I know the rules. No fraternizing with co-workers or clients. Brunettes are more my type anyway." Squeezing her into a side hug to tease.

She laughs. "You're terrible."

"So I hear." I wrap my arm around her shoulders and pull her close. I place a quick kiss on the top of her head. "At least you love me, Jods."

Pushing off, she laughs even harder. We're standing outside Mark's office, so she lowers her voice. "I'm an eternal fan, hot stuff." She walks back to her desk.

"Now why does that sound sarcastic to me?"

She points at Mark's office. "Thank you for the afternoon pick-me-up. Go before you get both of us in trouble."

"Does that mean I'm in trouble? I think I like the lie of the paycheck better. And I'm always available for afternoon pick-me-ups."

She turns her back to me to grab a call, but when she answers she's still laughing causing me to laugh. I knock on the door.

"Come in."

Walking in like I own the place, I joke, "You summoned?"

"Stop flirting with my assistant and shut the door. I need to go over the finalized contract details for Vittori so they can pay us."

"I like getting paid."

"So do I. Signature here." He points to a line. While I sign one page and then the next, he says, "You're in Marfa, Texas. Vittori wants the casual line shot there. The suit line will be shot in New York. The formal line will be shot in Paris. They haven't ruled out Rome."

When I sit down, I set the pen on the desk and get comfortable. "What's the schedule and can I get a haircut." I run my hand through my hair. "It's getting shaggy."

"Let them tell us how they want it cut. I'll send an email over today asking for specific style instructions. We need to knock this shoot out of the ballpark, so I don't want to fuck anything up so close to the job. Marfa is in five days. New York a week after that. I haven't gotten a confirmation on Paris yet. Does this work for you?"

"Yes. Don't I have other jobs already scheduled though?"

"Yes, but one is the week between Marfa and New York, so no conflict. Jody also has a stack of invitations for you to go through. She'll reply and make sure there are no conflicts for any you want to RSVP yes to, so stop by her desk before you leave."

He takes his glasses off and sets them in front of him and finally looks at me. "How are you?"

"I'm fine." He's not usually this serious with me. "What's wrong?"

"Nothing. Just checking. I know you're not used to being home this much. Just making sure you're good with it."

"I like being home. I've been working non-stop for years now." I shrug it off as if nothing's wrong. "Are you worried about my career?"

"No. The opposite. You should have less jobs because of your fees, but you're booking the same as you always have. Just making sure you're up for it, still into it. Are you scouting locations for anyone?"

"No, I had to put that on hold for the work."

He sets down a stack of packets. "Five scripts arrived in the last two weeks. I wanted to scan them first. These three are worth taking a look at."

"When are the auditions?" I ask, taking them in hand.

"That's just it, Danny. Two of these you can have if you want it, acting unseen. The other they want you to do a scene with the lead actress to see if there's chemistry."

"Why are you saying this like it's a bad thing? I've done a million commercials."

"I've been through this transition before."

I sigh. "I know. I've heard this story."

"Brad Lowe was a good guy. Fame can do nasty things to people."

"You think I'm susceptible?"

"No. I think you've always known who you were. Doesn't mean I don't worry. Temptation is a dangerous thing."

"I'm not Brad."

He lightens and sits back looking pleased. "No, you're not. Just remember you're in charge of your future. You don't need movies. You have years left in modeling."

"I like what I'm doing. I'd rather look at photography jobs over acting for now though."

Tapping his fingers on the glass top of his desk, he buddies up. "Tell me the truth. What happened between you and Reese the other night?"

Chuckling, I rock back, the front legs of my chair lifting off the floor. "I told you the truth. Nothing. I made sure she got in safely and left her, fully clothed and passed out." I look out at The Pit through the window that divides us.

"I thought she was holding her liquor fine, but then bam, it seemed to hit her all at once."

"She was always a lightweight," I say mindlessly.

Casual convo just turned serious. The lines streaking through his forehead deepen. "What do you mean, she was always a lightweight?"

Shit!

My eyes dart back to him. "Um." I go blank momentarily before I find the lie I need to tell. "She told me. When we were walking to her room. She said that happens to her."

"Oh. I see." His lines lighten. "For a minute," he says, laughing, "I thought you meant you knew her."

Being honest, I add, "Nope. That's the first time I've met Reese Carmichael, the woman."

"You're talking weird. Are you okay?"

"Yep."

"Does everything have to pop with you? Yes or no will do."

"Yep, you're right."

My plan is working. He's annoyed. I'll get the boot any second.

"Go. I have work to do. I'm sure you have some woman to do."

I laugh while standing up. "You think so highly of me."

"Do you not?"

"For your information, I have no plans tonight. Vargo is in two days, so I'm laying low."

Once again he looks pleased. "Well, this is a surprise. A good surprise. Stay on top of your job. Get some rest and we'll talk soon."

"My body's my temple."

"Okay, you're laying it on a bit thick now. Just look good and let me do the rest."

"Deal. See ya later, boss man."

"Later."

When I close the door, Jody spins around in her chair. "So, are you going to do a movie?"

"I'll look at the scripts. Mark said you have some invitations for me?" I sit down in a vacant chair and roll over to her desk.

"I do. You've got fancy schmancy events to go to. How about I run through them and you can say yes or no and then we'll go through the yeses?"

"Sounds good."

Five yeses and twenty-three nos later, I'm on my way to Luke's. The door is open so I go on in. "Dude, has it started?"

His arm is draped over the back of the couch. He turns over his shoulder. "Nope, five minutes. You're just in time." He drinks beer from a bottle, then says, "Grab a brew. I ordered pizza."

"Fuck you and that pizza." I grab a bottle of Vitamin Water from the fridge.

"What? You dieting, princess?"

"I have a shoot in two days. I can't eat pizza." Walking in, I sit on the other side of the couch and kick off my sneakers and use the coffee table as a footrest.

"The tough life of a model. Guess that means more for me."

"Yeah. Yeah."

"What'd you do today?"

"Met up with Holli."

"So let me guess, you had drinks with her but not me?"

I kick him in the leg. "You jealous?"

"I'm jealous of you. She's still fucking hot. I saw her on some blog the other day."

"Man, don't talk about her. Anyway, you reading the gossip blogs and have the nerve to call me princess?"

"Dude, she was in a bikini."

"Good point. Okay, forgiven."

The game starts and we go quiet because watching a game requires intense concentration. Two minutes in, Luke stands, points at the TV, and yells, "Fuck you! Shit. If this is how the game is gonna go down, I should have bought more beer."

Damn. The opposing team already scored. "Grab me one. I can tell I'm going to need it."

The doorbell rings and he hands me a beer as he goes to answer it. When he returns he sets the pizza on the table in front of us, then hands me a salad. I smile. "Aw bro, you do love me."

"I love you buying rounds of drinks. For you to keep doing that, I need you to keep working. Enjoy your lettuce, princess."

I kick him again. Just 'cuz.

I don't know why we're still watching. Our team has had their ass kicked by halftime and it feels like Luke and I have had ours kicked as well. We're both sunk into the couch on our respective sides, stuffed... well as stuffed as you can be from a plain garden salad with no dressing and chicken. The beer's doing a good job though. "Each one of these bottles is five hundred crunches or two more miles for me to run. Tomorrow is going to suck."

"Are you showing off dresses or shoes this time?"

"Fuck, dude, you don't even want to know."

"Really?" Now his interest looks piqued.

"Jeans and boxers with a Victoria's Secret model that was hired. Lots of bed action. They told me to sex it up, if you get my drift."

"*Fuuuuck,*" he says, shaking his head. "I hate you. I hate you so fucking much right now. How did you get so lucky?"

"Good-looking parents. Ha!" Just then a knock cuts the laughter and we turn as if the door is going to open itself. "You expecting company?"

He gets up to answer it. "Not that I know of." The game comes back on, but the surprise visitor is more interesting than this sad game.

The door is opened, and I hear, "Jane?"

I sit up and angle forward to get a view of the scene that's about to play out.

"Hi," she says to him, but her eyes shift to me. "Hi, Danny."

Raising my hand, I reply, "Hi."

"I'm sorry for interrupting. I can come back another time." She starts to back out of the doorway.

He takes her by the hand, holding her. "No, now's good. We can talk out back."

She nods, and they walk to the back patio. The glass sliding door is closed, cutting off any chance of me eavesdropping. I still can't help but watch as they move around each other, each step a careful dance—close, but not too close.

I look down at my phone, feeling guilty for watching. To see two people who thought they would always be together act so cautiously around each other is hard to watch. The tension is felt from here. Yet when I look up, even I can see how much they care about one another. But something, egos, other people, life or all of the above has gotten in the way, blinded them to what's right in front of them.

I've always liked Jane, but my friend is going to be messed up from this visit. She's not here to make up, which is the only outcome that won't screw him up more than he is now because of her.

She starts crying and Luke rushes to hold her. When she sees me through the glass, she turns to face the other direction. I get up, not wanting to witness this either. It may be him going through it, but it's rubbing the rawness that Reese left behind.

I go into the kitchen and lean against the counter to give them complete privacy. They come inside and walk to the front door. When they leave, I go back into the living room and turn the volume of the game back up.

Luke returns a few minutes later. I'm not a girl so I don't pepper him with questions the second he sits down. I let him be. Not wanting those same questions thrown back at me. A commercial is muted, and he says, "She said she's been thinking about me."

Turning to him, I don't add my own commentary, his own thoughts are probably adding enough color to not want to add to that confusion. He turns to me and adds, "I still love her."

I nod.

"She said she had to tell me she'd been thinking about me. Do you think she was feeling things out? How I felt for her?"

"That makes sense."

"Does that make me her fallback?"

"No. It means you both got off track. Maybe you'll get back on, back to where you're supposed to be."

The game comes back on and the volume is loud again, the

conversation over. We're guys. We're great like that.

The TV goes silent again. "Would you take Reese back?"

So I'm wrong. We're two women sitting around talking about our exes I guess. "Fuck. Why are you saying her name?"

"I'm serious, Danny. Would you?"

I drop my head into my hands, frustrated by more than just his question. "I don't know. I've been questioning myself lately. She looked good, but do I know her anymore? I don't know anything about her life in New York other than where she works. That's not you and Jane. Don't compare."

"I think we're kind of in the same boat here. Whether you want to believe it or not."

"Here's what I don't want. I don't want to think about it. It's all I've been thinking about—"

"See?" He reaches toward me. "Here's your oar. Get to paddling."

"We're not in the same boat. You've been broken up for more than a year but have kept in touch. Reese and I haven't."

He starts paddling with an imaginary oar. "Until now, which conveniently you haven't told me about. How'd it go the other night?"

"It sucked. Reese looked incredible. She's smart and funny and when she drinks, she gets all adorable and stuff."

He grins some righteous smile he's pulled out of his ass to taunt me with. "Adorable, dude, really?"

I shake my head at myself. "I'm done for. She's gonna destroy me twice."

"Or maybe this time... maybe this time it works out."

"Speak for yourself and turn the game back on. Enough of this emotional feely stuff."

He chugs his beer. "You know I'm right."

I reach for the remote but he turns the volume back up so I sit back, arms crossed, irritated, and stare at the TV.

"Danny likes Reeeeese," he sings.

I peg a pillow at his head and jump down on him. We end up in a heap on the floor wrestling until I have him pinned face down with his arm behind his back. "Stop it. No more Reese talk. Got it."

"Got it."

"Admit you want Jane."

"I want Jane."

I stand pushing off my knees. "Then go after your girl."

He tosses the pillow back at me, but I deflect sending it back at him. When I turn the volume back up, our team scores. Perfect timing. Fist-pumping already, we stand and throw in a chest bump to get rid of the earlier talk about our feelings.

After taking a long swig from the bottle, he says, "Did you notice that you said her name three times? No cringing. No hesitation. Just said it like it was second nature?"

Glaring at him, I want to tell him to shut the fuck up, but the smile that's growing across my face prevents me. So I just enjoy that her name feels so comfortable on my tongue again.

"Maybe there's hope for us both, Dan Man."

"Maybe," I reply, thinking four extra miles tomorrow will be worth the two beers tonight.

CHAPTER 12

Reese

KEATON IS STANDING at the bar cart in his corner office with his back to me. My heart is pounding in my chest. When he turns around, the ice in his scotch rattles against the glass. "Why are you so upset?"

"You gave this account to me."

"*Gave*. That's the operative word, Reese."

"I earned this account. I earned it by having the best concept with *my* ideas, and winning Vittori over. Why are you doing this?"

"It's dinner with one of *my* clients. I don't see the problem."

"You're my boss. How does that look if I can't handle a simple dinner meeting? I just traveled with the man for the last two weeks. I think I can handle dinner."

"Boss? I used to be more." He sighs, but I'm numb to his disappointment in me at this stage.

I walk to the window and stare out. The view is one of the best in the city. The view of Central Park from his home rivals it. I give in like I always do, knowing he's going to do as he pleases. "Whatever."

"What was that?"

When I turn to face him again, I don't let my eyes meet his. Instead I stare at the Windsor knot at his neck wanting to tighten it. "This is going nowhere," I say grabbing my purse from the chair. "I'll see you at eight."

"See you at eight, sweetheart."

I hated how condescending he was when he called me that while we were dating, but now that we're not, I want to throat punch him. I grit my teeth instead, and say, "With bells on." I don't slam the door per se, but my emotions are heard loudly through the empty office.

Dinner is tense between Keaton and me. I'm hoping Vinnie doesn't notice, but as I discovered in LA, he's quite observant. Keaton doesn't like him. He doesn't fit the mold of what Keaton would choose for a friend. Another reason we wouldn't have worked out. Keaton asks, "How has working with Reese been?"

Vinnie smiles when he looks at me, but some of the joy is lost when he faces Keaton. "She's impressive. Not only does she speak French but she charms everyone she meets. I'm quite taken with her. If you're not careful I might try to steal her away from Klein Advertising."

Keaton's eyes dart to mine before he responds, "She's very loyal to my family. I'm sure there's nothing that could sway her away."

Vinnie sets his glass of wine down after taking a sip, and cuts into his steak. "I'm sure I can think of something."

I clear my throat. "Can we please stop talking about me like I'm not sitting right here?"

Keaton reaches over and rests his hand on the back of my chair. Completely inappropriate, but he knows I can't argue with him in front of clients... or anyone. I hate being the center of attention, especially when it involves drama.

"Sorry," Keaton says with a fake frown of remorse. "I feel so lucky to have you onboard. I'm willing to fight for you."

"This isn't a battle. No one's at war." I touch Vinnie's hand. "Thank you. I've been missing you after having a few days away."

His other hand covers mine. "It was a grand adventure, but now the fun really begins. The dates are set?"

"Yes, for all but Paris. Let me know when you decide if Rome is still part of the vision. Then I'll finalize the dates for Europe."

"What about Mr. Weston?"

The wine thickens as I swallow. Avoiding Keaton's intense stare, I look to the friendlier face of the two. "What about Mr. Weston?"

"Have we found him a suitable mate?"

I almost spew my drink across the table. Instead I start hacking up a lung, my throat burning as I struggle to catch my breath. Keaton takes any opportunity he's given and jumps into action, wrapping himself around me while clapping my back.

Basically making it worse and extremely awkward. I fight the urge to hit him back, but catch my breath and tell him to stop, reassuring him until he sits back down and all the eyes in the restaurant are off me.

Vinnie is laughing too hard to be of any use. I roll my eyes when he asks, "Was it something I said?"

I glare.

"Are we talking about the model?" Keaton asks, seeming confused.

Vinnie responds before I can, "Yes. He's absolutely purr-worthy, and our little Reese scored with him. Right, Reese?"

Keaton is glancing between us. "What do you mean Reese scored with him?"

Holding my breath, I wait for him to answer and pray he says the right thing. "Excuse me. I meant scored him. She closed the deal."

I quickly add to that, "He signed on to the project."

Vinnie adds, "As for his colleague in the campaign, we need to finalize our choice. I'm going to go through the last three contenders' portfolios tomorrow. I'll let you know who I think will turn up the heat for the photos with our leading man."

Keaton scans the room. "Where's our waitress? I need another drink."

"Maybe it will be quicker for you to go to the bar," I suggest, wanting some time with Vinnie.

"Great idea. Come with me. I want to discuss something."

"I think I should stay with our guest."

"Eh," he says, waving Vinnie off, "he'll be fine."

Vinnie says, "Go ahead. I'll use the restroom."

I stand, pushing out my chair and set my napkin on the table. Weaving between the tables to reach the bar, I'm in shock over Keaton's behavior, so my sarcasm seeps out. "Haven't you had enough to drink tonight? Maybe you should go home."

"I want you back, Reese."

Backing away from his probing hand, I remark, "Your wants are no longer my concern."

"Didn't anyone ever tell you that you're your own worst enemy?"

"I never stuck around long enough."

He laughs, but he's not amused. "Truer words never spoken."

"I'm not having this conversation here."

"You never want to have this conversation, but I'm tired of waiting."

"I'm not a possession you control anymore. So you'd be wise to back off and set your sights elsewhere."

"My eyes are set right here. You will not make me look the fool. I let you postpone the wedding, but it's time you get back in line with what's happening."

"I didn't postpone the wedding. The wedding was never going to happen. Hell, the engagement never even happened. But really, Keaton, why do you want someone who doesn't want you?" I laugh, but I find nothing funny about this situation.

The back of his hand slides down my bare arm. "We can be great again, like we once were. If you'd only open your eyes to the possibility of a reconciliation."

"The only thing I will reconcile is that you're a cheater and a liar."

"I treated you very well when we were together."

"Whether together or not together, you rarely thought about me or what I wanted."

Rubbing his temples in frustration, he says, "I don't want to go over this again."

"Good. Neither do I. We should get back to our client."

"I want you to come home with me tonight. Let's finish this. Leave the past in the past and move forward together."

"Fool me once, shame on you. Fool me twic—"

His lips press to mine. The shock stiffens my body and I push back. "How dare you kiss me!" I look around, panicked. "What if Vittori sees us?"

"Then he'll see how much I care for you. Come home with me, Reese."

I'm disgusted by not only the kiss, but also the assumption on his part that he could get away with it. "When hell freezes over." I start to leave, but my wrist is grabbed.

He leans in and whispers, "You should watch what you say to me, *Ms.* Carmichael." To anyone else here, we look like an affectionate couple, but by the way he's squeezing my wrist and by how he's gritting his teeth, there's no love exchanged. "You only have this job because I was generous enough to give it to you. If you lose me, you'll lose everything, including that fancy apartment you're so proud of."

How did I ever see him for anything other than the despicable human he is? I yank my wrist away, trying desperately to not make a scene, but I have to say something. "For someone who claims he wants me back, your threats speak louder than any of the bouquets you've sent me."

Vinnie's eyes catch mine. I lower my gaze, ashamed for him to see anything that might reveal how vulnerable I really am. I swallow hard and raise my chin as I walk back to the table.

Vinnie stands while I sit. "He's an asshole."

"I agree," I say under my breath when Keaton approaches with another drink in hand.

Vinnie reads the situation for what it is and gives me a reprieve by redirecting Keaton. "Will you be joining us on any of the shoots, Mr. Klein?"

"No, no. I leave that to the professionals who work under me."

"Yes, you must be too busy for that kind of thing," Vinnie says, taking a jab.

Fortunately Keaton's had enough to drink to not notice. When the check arrives, I take it and pay for it... with my business card. *Ha!*

When we're standing on the street, a cab is hailed for us and we insist Keaton take it despite his protests that I share it with him. "It's all good. I'll make sure Mr. Vittori gets home safely." He can't argue with me in front of Vinnie, so it all works out.

As soon as we're alone, he loops his arm with mine, and starts dragging me down the street. "Finally, we get our girls' night out. Time to party."

"Where are we going?"

"To a bar down the street and then clubbing. You up for a fun time?"

"More than ever."

With pretty pink Cosmos in front of us, he sheds the famous Italian designer act and my Vinnie is back. "What happened between you and Model Danny? Tell me everything and do not leave out any details."

"Nothing happened."

"I gave you the last day of our trip and nothing happened. That's very disappointing, Candy."

I lean forward and hug him. "I missed you, Vinnie."

He takes a few sips of his cocktail and then sticks out his bottom lip. "Really? Nothing happened?"

After a few large guzzles of my drink, I find the courage to share what I've wanted to since it happened. "He asked me to lunch."

"And?"

"And he took me to the beach. He had box lunches and a blanket. We talked and ate."

He faux faints without leaving his barstool. "That is so damn dreamy, girl."

"I know, right?"

"The boy likes you."

"*The boy* is not a boy anymore. He's quite the man. And that *man* likes many women. You've seen the rags."

With a swoony sigh introducing his words, he replies, "You're right. He is no boy. Did I mention the fireworks between you two?"

"You did. I get it. I appreciate you playing matchmaker for me, but believe me, my life is a mess. I can't afford to fall for anyone, much less someone like Danny Weston again."

"Again?"

Damn. Oops. Backpedalling, I try to cover, "I didn't mean again. I meant him. Just him. Whatever." I start drinking my cocktail and don't stop until the glass is empty.

"You've said a few things like tha—"

"Bartender?" I hail him like I'm hailing a cab, doing anything to distract Vinnie from finishing his train of thought.

When the bartender comes over, he leans both hands on the wood in front of me. Wearing a white shirt with the sleeves rolled up, exposing a detailed tattoo or two of something I'd like to get a better look at, a gray pinstriped vest, clean-shaven with his dark hair slicked back. He asks, "What can I get you, beautiful?"

I giggle because, yeah, he thinks I'm beautiful. "Another round of Cosmos please."

"Coming right up."

Vinnie's eyes are glued to the bartender's backside, but I elbow him as if he hadn't noticed. We both keep our attention right where it should be. Vinnie leans over, and whispers, "I want him."

"Haha. He's gorgeous."

"I want him to walk for my spring show." He looks me in the eyes, dead serious. "Get him for me, Reese. Pretty please." He's like a child begging for an ice cream, and completely adorable.

"I don't think I'm your girl for that, but I can talk to him for you if you'd like?"

"I'd like. I'd like very much."

He turns around and sets the drinks in front of us. "Drinks are on me, but only on one condition."

My bottom lip is tugged under my teeth in anticipation of what that one condition might be. I sip the drink, intrigued. "And what might that be?"

He sets a pen and white bar napkin in front of me. "You give me your number."

"What if I'm not single?"

"No ring. That means if you're not married, you're single."

"I might have a boyfriend."

"He should've taken the next step then. His loss."

Taking another sip, I set the glass down again and grab the pen while pulling the napkin closer. "You're very sure of yourself."

"I don't believe in wasting time."

After I write my number down and push it back to him, he studies it before his eyes come back to mine. "Nice to meet you, Reese. I'm Leo."

Vinnie stands on the foot rail of his barstool and reaches forward to shake his hand. "Hello."

Laughing, I signal to him. "And this is my friend..." I look to Vinnie, not sure how I should introduce him. Vittori is so well-known, an over-the-top icon in the fashion circles, but tonight he's Vinnie. He's in a tailored suit. His hair is styled, but not in his signature bouffant.

He understands my debate, so he helps out. "Vinnie. I'm Vinnie, Leo. It's very nice to meet you."

"You too. So just a night out?" Leo asks us.

"Yes, we're catching up."

"Oh, how long since you've seen each other?"

Vinnie and I exchange glances and laugh. "Five days." But I try to help explain our silliness. "We had just spent two weeks traveling together, so I've become partial to him and missed him."

"Awww, Candy, you're bringing a tear to my eye."

Leo looks perplexed. "Candy?"

"Just a nickname he has for me."

"I look forward to hearing more about how you earned it." He scans the bar and the impatient patrons trying to get his attention. When he looks back at us, he leans forward and says, "I'm going to call you and ask you out. I hope you say yes. I'd like to get to know you better."

He's not looking for an answer and his confidence is completely sexy. He walks away and helps other customers. Even though we stay here for another forty-five minutes I never see him get a number, or hear him using the same line he used on me. All the reasons are there for me to feel special—attention, complimentary drinks, handsome face, great build. I should be over the moon about him showing interest. I should be popping my imaginary collar, but that's when it hits me. Danny used to do that in college. The memory takes me right back to him. As I sip the last of my drink, I wonder if he's the reason I'm not into Leo. Everything about Leo is appealing and yet, nothing. Even with the short time we've spent together, Danny's starting to feel a lot like a new habit. It will be interesting to find out if he's a good or bad one to form.

Standing by the bar, I leave a large bill because free drinks means bigger tips. I wave goodbye, but he's busy. Vinnie and I start making our way toward the exit, but I'm grabbed and when I spin around, Leo is there. He kisses my cheek. "I'll see you soon, Reese."

I stand there a second, surprised by his assertiveness. He apparently doesn't waste time, but goes after what he wants. If only I could do the same. *Danny.* The only man who ever made me giddy comes to mind.

Vinnie coos, "Bye, Leo."

"Bye, Vinnie." He laughs and returns to the bar.

Vinnie jumps giddily. "Man, he's amazing. And yet, so different from Model Danny. Where should we go? We have so much to still talk about."

"You're relentless and wearing me down. I'm getting tired."

"C'mon, Candy. We'll go to my apartment. I have a hot tub."

CHAPTER 13

Reese

I HAVE NO idea how I get myself into these situations, but I somehow do. Less than an hour later, I'm sitting in a hot tub, dressed only in my panties, on Vinnie's rooftop deck.

We have champagne and a beautiful star-filled night. Resting my head back, I'm staring into the dark blue yonder, when Vinnie says pouting, "You didn't get Leo's number. He only got yours. I want him, Candy, and you failed me."

"To walk the runway for you or for you personally?"

"Both," he says sassily.

Laughing, I reassure him, "Don't worry. We know where he works. But I'm sure he'll call and then I'll get his number for you."

"Well, aren't you little Miss Confident tonight?"

"Yes, when it comes to him. It's obvious he was interested or he wouldn't have chased me down. Anyway, men are easy to read."

"Except when it comes to Model Danny," he retorts.

"Touché. You let me drink too much. You know I can't handle my booze."

"I know, which is why I got this bottle of champagne out."

I laugh, but then I'm speaking before I can stop myself, "Can I tell you a secret?" The bubbles must be going to my head.

Vinnie is sitting across from me. Fortunately, he's wearing a bathing suit. "You can tell me anything, Candy. My lips are sealed, a vault of steel."

"I know Danny Weston."

"Yes. I know. I was there when you met him."

Lifting my head up, I look at him and swallow hard, afraid I'm making a bad decision by telling him this secret. This is the only secret I've ever been good at keeping. It's by far the most personal and breaks me little by little when I think about it, so I don't think about it. I've buried it. Until two months ago. "No, I know him know him."

Excitedly, he bolts upright and points at me, the water splashing me in the process. "I knew it. I knew you had sex with him."

"No, not that. I didn't." An image of the first time we were ever together, the first time we had sex, flashes. "Well I did, but it's not what you think."

His disappointment is palpable as he relaxes back and fills his champagne glass. "So you didn't have sex in LA?"

"I didn't. But I need to talk to someone and I know I can trust you."

"Of course you can. Now spill your darkest secret and I'll share some of mine, but that's for another night because I have a closet of doozies."

Vinnie makes me smile, something I've become quite addicted to. It had been too long since I had felt so happy around someone. "Danny and I dated in college."

Champagne covers my face and chest as my hands go out to protect myself. "Oh my God!"

When the champagne spray stops, I open my eyes only to be

met with Vinnie's wide as a saucer eyes. "You used to date Model Danny?"

It doesn't sound so much like a question but a reaction, a very strong, shocked reaction. Nevertheless, he's staring at me waiting for an answer. "I did." I start sweating, feeling a bead roll down my spine. "Has the water gotten hotter?"

"No." He checks the temperature gauge. "I think it's your conscience."

"Most likely." I suddenly regret saying anything. This was best left buried, but now I'm stuck in the middle of my past that feels a lot like quicksand, burying me instead.

"Are you going to make me drag this out of you?"

Sighing because it's too late to take back the confession, I say, "We dated in college. I thought we would get married one day."

"That's a pretty serious relationship."

"Yes, I thought so too, but it didn't work out." *Annnnnnd* scene. Maybe he'll get that there is no more to tell.

"No. No, the story doesn't just end like that. I need more. Like how long did you date? How did you meet? How big is he? And how did it end?"

"How big is he? You just slipped that right in there, didn't you?"

"No, but he slipped it in... or was it too big to slip in?"

With both hands, a full on splash assault begins. "Ew."

"There's nothing *ew* about Model Danny."

Lowering my weapons, I reach for my champagne thinking I'm going to need a lot more to get through this conversation without full-blown mortification setting in. "No kidding." I finish half the glass and hold it out for a top off. As he fills my glass, I decide it's too late. I opened this can of worms. So I need to let all those worms out, free them so to speak. "We met at a party when we were juniors in Nebraska."

"Nebraska? Why is that so hot?"

"I have no idea." I sit back, letting my legs float in front of me. With my elbows propped on the sides I let it all out. "We saw each other across the room..."

I knew who he was. Everyone on campus knew who Danny Weston was. He's tall, handsome, funny. I didn't know this firsthand, of course, but I'd heard people talking about him. One time in the library at a table behind the one I had my books spread all over while I researched a biology paper due the next day, I over heard a girl say, "He's the best sex I ever had."

Her friend remarks, "For you, that's saying something."

I laugh, but quickly cover my mouth so they don't think I'm laughing from their conversation. I lamely point at the book in front of me and mumble something about tree frogs being hilarious. They either don't hear me or don't care because they keep talking, but lower their voices. "He's big, like really big."

"How big?" her friend asks excitedly. It gets quiet and then she adds, "Whoa?"

Hand gestures. She's making hand gestures. And because I'm curious, my head whips around to see the first girl holding her hands apart. Catching me, she makes a snide comment, "Excuse you. This is a private conversation."

"Sorry," I reply, my face heated, mortification covering it. But as I stare straight ahead, I blush for very different reasons. The very thought...

Vinnie is awestruck. "Oh my Mary!" He holds his hands apart, matching mine. I see his Adam's apple bob and he licks his lips. "That's like a good f—"

"I know! Believe me. I know." I take a large sip of champagne. *God, do I know.*

"How long were you together?"

Searching for answers amongst the stars, I say, "Two years. It just kind of fizzled out."

"There was no fizzling from what I saw in LA. It was full sizzle."

"Sizzle. No fizzle." I snort-laugh.

And then again, the bubbles are tickling my throat.

"Honey, you might be done for tonight. As much as I want all the answers to the millions of questions about your sex-dezvous with that hunk of a man, you need water and bed."

"I'm fine. More than fine, fine like Daniel Big Earl Weston."

"Earl? That's a boner killer."

"Killer is right. He was called Big Earl for a reason." I try to wink but it's like a double wink. I'm too toasty for winking anyway, so I go back to the very fond memories I have of Big Earl. "My va-j never stood a chance." Standing up, with my arms in the air, I yell, "Hello New York City! Wooooohooooo!"

"You have spectacular titties, but you do realize you're topless, right?"

"I don't even care." I do a little footwork to music that's only playing in my head.

Vinnie stands up and takes me by the hips. "Yep, time for bed. C'mon. Get down from there before you wipe out, Candy girl." I sit on the edge and swing my legs out. He climbs out behind me as I walk to the edge to look over, but he comes up behind me, wraps a towel around my back, and redirects me back toward the apartment. "This way."

"You're sleeping here."

I follow him down the stark white hall, which seems to be in contrast to everything Vittori the designer stands for. He leads me into a bedroom that is solid purple. Purple everything. Even the numbers on the alarm clock are purple. I don't know whether to lie on the bed or run for my life. "It's very purple-y."

"It's Vittori purple."

I lie on the bed with the towel still wrapped around me while he messes about the room. With my eyes closed, I slip one foot onto the floor and rest my arm on my forehead. All the lightheartedness has left my heart. "I loved him. I loved him so much."

He sits next to me, kisses my arm, and drops a pair of pajamas on my stomach. "I can tell he loved you too." The lamp next to me is turned off and I watch him at the door. He stops. "Put on the jammies, go to sleep, and get some rest."

I do what I've done every night since I walked away ten years ago. I try to block out the memories, wipe the tears away, and fall asleep. But the night of his first confession haunts my dreams...

That night in bed, I watch Danny sleep. The snow falls outside on this cold winter's night, but I can feel the ice forming inside. I've been naïve. I hadn't thought about him kissing other women while "working." I hadn't considered what else he might have to do for a job besides model clothes. But now I do. Now it is all I can think about.

I let the kiss go, not asking anymore questions about it. I don't want to know anymore. My heart won't be able to handle it. I trust him. I trust in us.

It is only work.

A job.

Nothing more.

I close my eyes and imagine the most beautiful woman in the world kissing my boyfriend—a blonde beauty opposite of me in so many ways, so beautiful that I lose him.

Gulping down the image, I open my eyes again and watch him as tears blur my vision. Change is coming and if I try to stop it, I become the bad guy. If I accept it, what will we become?

I've never been patient. I didn't get to where I am by sitting around and hoping for things to happen in life. I go after them. Everything from the university I attend to my scholarships. The only thing that came easily to me was Danny and now he's slipping away into the unknown, and I hate the unknown.

My fingers dance over his shoulder light enough not to wake him. Leaning forward, I kiss him there. I love having him home, but I'm already wondering when he'll leave me again.

Christmas passes and Danny doesn't go home with me. I remain at my parents' home until I decide to return to school on New Year's Eve. Tired of being alone, I ring in the New Year with my friends at a local bar. Danny had left a message that he wouldn't make it back to me in time for the traditional kiss. Who needs one anyway? I drink another shot thinking about how he was stuck in New York City, probably with a hot blonde model to help him ring in the New Year instead.

Standing in the middle of the bar, in the middle of the revelers, I'm alone. At 12:01 a.m. I go back to my dorm. Not his. His place is his, and being there makes me feel lonelier. The smell of him and his cologne is fading and I can't bear to find out if it's gone. Something that had given me comfort now makes me sad.

Fortunately, my roommate is staying with her boyfriend tonight, so I have the place to myself.

The second message he leaves comes before I have a chance to catch the call. I reach for the phone, but he's gone. I listen to the voicemail, but my heart has already turned cold on the whole celebration. By two a.m. I've cried enough that exhaustion sets in and sleep comes easier.

I stir before dawn and turn, right into his arms. Without

opening my eyes, I snuggle closer, his scent easing the pain from
my body. "You're late."

"I'm here now."

MY OUTFIT IS sexy. From the second I laid eyes on it, I had to have it. I was more than willing to pay the inflated prices for the designer duds once I tried it on. I wouldn't even need alterations, so I'd save there. It was stunning and made me feel more so last night when I wore it for the first time.

At eight thirty in the morning getting out of a cab in front of my apartment building wearing it while everyone leaving for work is wearing suits and Chanel, I don't feel so stunning anymore. I feel cheap. I just wish it were for the reasons they're all concocting in their heads while I walk into the lobby shamefully.

I wave to the doorman, feeling like he's judging me all the way to the elevator when I'm sure he barely notices me among the morning crowd. The elevator door opens on my floor and I slip off the heels and walk barefoot to my apartment. As soon as it's unlocked, I slip inside and lock it behind me. When I turn around, I scream, covering my mouth.

I don't give Keaton a chance to speak. "Fuck! You scared me."

He stands from the barstool and comes toward me. "Swearing is classless. You're better than that, Reese."

"What are you doing here?"

"I came over last night." He holds up the key I gave him back when we were happy, or I stupidly thought we were happy. I'm sure he was already fucking around on the side. "I wanted to apologize for the restaurant. I felt bad. I don't like who I've become lately. I miss you. You gave me balance.

You made me happy."

"You wouldn't know it by what you said last night." I walk into my bedroom, knowing he's not leaving until he says what he came here to say. I've learned this lesson the hard way.

"That's what I mean," he says, following me. "I don't want to talk to you like that. I don't want to treat you like that."

I set my shoes on the shelf and unzip the dress and let it slip down. He appears in the door of my closet and I jump again. Covering myself with my hands, I warn, "Stop sneaking up on me and turn around."

"I just loved you so much. I still love you." He's leaning against the wall just outside the closet, and with my robe in hand I stop to listen to what has turned into a plea. There's something different in his voice, something more than he usually gives away. *Real emotions?* "I want to be with you." As soon as I walk out bundled in my robe, he says, "I want to marry you, Reese. I'm a better man because of you."

Besides the shock of his confession, my heart softens under his desperation, so I try to be honest, but kind. "Keaton, we're not meant to be together. I'm sorry, but we're not." I go back into the living room and open the door. "I understand you're hurting right now, but I was hurting back then. I'm proof you will heal. You will get over me."

"I'm not getting over you. I won't. I can't."

"You need to." I open the door wider. "And you need to leave now."

He leans against the island, not looking like he's leaving anytime soon. "Were you with someone last night? You came home looking like you've been fucked. Did you let some guy treat you like that?"

"I thought swearing was classless?"

"So are you by your appearance this morning."

And here we go. This is where it turns ugly, but I keep my voice even, knowing if I yell it will only escalate. "Then there's nothing keeping you here."

Standing up, he crosses his arms. "Why are you so stubborn? Fine, you had sex with someone else. I don't care. But I want you to see how good we are together."

"We're not together, Keaton."

"Then let me show you how good we can be again."

This conversation reminds me of Danny, which I'm pretty sure wasn't intended. "I'm too tired to have this conversation. Please. I'm exhausted. Please leave." Holding out my hand, I add, "And leave my key."

He walks past me. "I think I'll hold on to it a little longer."

"Just make this easy and don't make me change the locks."

"You're going to see how good we are. We're not just good on paper. We can be good together in life. We are a perfect match, Reese."

I take offense to that statement though it wasn't meant as an insult.

"We like the same things."

"No, I never liked the ballet. You did and you only liked it for the business being conducted before the curtain went up."

"Okay, tennis. We played that all the time."

"Because I wanted to bond with you. But you made that impossible because of your need to belittle me in front of your so-called friends at the club."

His shoulders slump in defeat. "I took you to see that country singer." He points at me accusingly. "And that was just for you because I think he sucks."

"You did. I will give you that, but it was hard to hear him sing through your constant complaining." *Worst night ever.*

He doesn't take kindly to my remark. "Look, Reese. I've been good to you. More than generous with my wealth—"

"I never cared about your money. I know all the women in your life circle you like sharks, but they can have it all. I'd rather have something real, like a—"

"Like a yacht? You've got it. I'll buy one today and name it The Reese."

Shaking my head, I realize… or more like remember, that speaking to him in any terms that he doesn't understand, such as love, devotion, passion, none of it computes with him. Three of the many reasons why I think he's still single at thirty-eight. Emotions don't register. In his world, money talks, and when it does, he always listens. Something he never did with me. The one thing my mom always told me to look for in a partner. She's passed and it's as if I've forgotten the life lessons she left me with.

No more. Refusing to be belittled by him, to be intimidated and manipulated by his lies, I open the door wider. *Hint, hint.* "I'm going to sleep, so again, I'm asking nicely. Please leave."

That desperation from earlier is back in his tone. "I'll go, but you need to know that I will protect what's mine."

"I'm not yours." I never was, I add silently, not wanting to fight with him.

His back is to me as he walks down the hall to the elevator. "I'll see you on Monday, bright and early."

I slam the door closed even though I know it won't give me the same satisfaction it used to. *Shoot!* I didn't get my key. Beyond being physically tired, I'm now emotionally drained. I'll get a reference from the doorman next time I'm down there for a locksmith. Pulling my robe tighter around me, I get a large glass of water and retrieve my phone from my purse. The decision has already been made—binge-watching a cop drama series will commence as I spend the day recovering. Maybe they'll teach me how to hide a body in Manhattan.

Two episodes in, my phone buzzes with a new text. When I pick it up, I notice I've missed several. All from Danny.

CHAPTER 14

"YOU WERE NEVER reluctant before, Danny. Kiss me." Laylah—twenty-eight, blond, green eyes, face perfectly symmetrical with cat eyes and best known for her killer body and walking for Victoria's Secret—is pinned against the wall, my arms trapping her between and all I can think about is what Reese has been doing and hoping she's not been doing anyone at all.

Is it too hopeful, too soon to want that?

Maybe.

Probably.

Definitely.

I kiss Laylah's neck like the photographer has been demanding. Laylah's breath covers my ear as the clicking of the camera is heard—quick, several per second. Her hands run down my side under the intricately-designed smoking jacket I'm wearing and I angle my shoulders so the camera gets a clear shot of the watch against the silk pajama bottoms. She pushes the jacket back to show off my abs while we try to appear intimate.

"Tilt your hips forward, Laylah," the photographer says. "Yes, just like that. Danny, flash the face of the watch toward me."

I turn my arm, but my shoulder remains tension filled.

She whispers, "Relax, Danny."

The photographer suggests, "Maybe change places."

I swirl Laylah around and try to get into her. It's not working, so I fake it. An hour later, I'm leaning against a brick wall outside staring at my phone. Maybe I shouldn't have texted Reese the other day...

Me: *I have a question about the shoot.*

Me: *I lied. I don't have any questions. I've just been thinking about you.*

Me: *The problem is I can't stop thinking about you.*

I can't even blame alcohol for sending those during a late-night texting session. Maybe the wheatgrass was going to my head, making me see things too clearly. Sometimes it's easier to hide behind the façade than face reality. The liquid cleanse I did for two days touted clarity. I'm seeing it as a bad side effect as regret sets in.

Reese hasn't replied. I must have scared her. *I definitely scared her.* But damn, I'm not over-confident about us. She's gotten under my skin. I imagined what would happen if we ran into each other a thousand times or more over the years. Then it happened and it didn't play out anything like I expected. I never expected to still feel so much for her the second I saw her. I foolishly thought some anger that had lingered over the years would surface, the hurt I felt revealed in an acquired immunity to her beauty, her quick wit, and stubbornness.

Nope. That didn't happen.

The exact opposite did.

I still have feelings for her—whether new or reminiscent of long ago, I have no idea. They're there though because I can't get the woman off my mind.

Her independence is sexy. The way she looks at me drawing

me in, capturing my heart just like she did before.

The photographer's assistant tosses the cigarette to the alley and grounds it in. "We should get back. One more setup to do."

I watch him walk inside, then check my phone one more time. Nothing.

Giving my best James Dean, I hold the sports coat by the lapels to show off the $15k gold watch I'm modeling while tilting my head back to show some good jaw. The camera clicks as the shutter opens and closes in rapid succession. Laylah is watching in the distance as her makeup is removed since she's wrapped. I avoid that direction. She's gorgeous, just not Reese gorgeous.

I'm booked because I'm not affected. I believe in my work and let my emotions show, so I work the inner turmoil that's building and let it show.

The photographer eats it up. "More, Danny. Yes, brooding. Dangerous. Give it to me. Just like that. Yes. That's it. Hate the camera. Love the camera. You just fucked the camera and now want nothing to do with me. Make it about the camera. Give it to me and flash the watch."

A pro at giving up everything during a shoot, I have no idea what he's talking about so I do it my way and watch him practically orgasm as he watches me through the lens.

BYPASSING THE TRAY of champagne flutes, I grab a beer from the bar when we walk into the party. We fit in here. In a trendy home in the Hollywood Hills we're just another group of models. Photographers, designers, and artists dot the landscape, immersed as deeply as we are into the fashion world.

From 2Xist to Abercrombie & Fitch male models, this party is filled with my competition. I don't stress. I've got experience over youth. And I've never heard any complaints about my abs.

I don't pretend people don't recognize me, that I'm not a big deal. It may not seem like it, but our industry is small and everyone knows everyone or you've heard the rumors. I gave up my chosen path of my degree for one that sidetracked me. Luckily it paid off. Big time. I'm one of the exceptions. I've broken through beyond face recognition. I have *name* recognition— Fame. Being an exception, I've earned a level of respect.

I live with few regrets, though I often wonder how my life would be different if I had chosen to use my bachelor's degree in Geography. I'd be married. For sure. I'd probably have a couple kids. Plural. *Wow. Wonder if Reese still wants kids?*

"There's a free couch over there," Laylah says, walking in next to me. She doesn't mind the added attention. She never did. It doesn't hurt the photographer to be seen with us either. I toss my jacket on the leather couch as I sit down. The Vargo photographer sits next to me, his assistant and Laylah across from us.

His assistant points to the food out by the pool. Pretending to be hungry, I excuse myself before any conversations keep me here.

The sleeve of my shirt is tugged. Laylah smiles, and for a minute I see that girl from Ontario again, the one who showed up knock-kneed and nervous eight years ago. "You're coming back, right?"

I reassure her, "I'll be back."

She smiles and sits back on the couch, one long leg crossing over the next. I head outside. The view of LA is awesome from here. Lights appear to glitter, making the city magical again. Most people are inside the house and I find it strange that the view, this view in particular, is taken for granted, but I appreciate the solitude.

My phone buzzes with a text.

I pull the phone from my pocket and smile. It's from Reese. I don't even care what the text says. That I heard from her at all feels like a victory. That in itself is a win.

Swiping the screen, the full message appears.

Reese: *I can't stop thinking about you either.*

My smile grows. Instantly, my fingers are on the keyboard ready to text back, but I stop, wondering if I should. Or should I wait? *I hate games and here I am playing one.* Reese is a delicate operation. One false move and we're set back ten years when she walked away from everything we had.

In the middle of the master debate I'm having, I receive another message from her.

Reese: *Looking forward to seeing you again.*

We have Marfa in a few days. Seeing your ex-girlfriend in the middle of West Texas—isn't that how all great stories... all great *love* stories, start?

"What are you smiling about?" Laylah sidles up to me, empty glass in hand. When I look at her, she keeps her eyes steady on me. "You've had something on your mind. All day."

"Someone," I volunteer.

Her eyes widen in surprise, but a small smile appears too. "Someone?" She turns her gaze to the distance and her mood turns melancholy. "Relationships don't bode well in our business. Even less of a chance if you're a model on top. We've both been around long enough to know this."

Turning back to the lights of Los Angeles, I want to say I met someone who would be worth reevaluating my long-term career goals. I want to share the ridiculous details of how Reese makes me feel alive and yet, vulnerable and exposed. But I don't because she's not someone I just met and I don't want to get into a past that's better to keep to myself for a while longer.

"Danny?"

Then I think of the woman Reese has become, and no matter how I feel I might know her, I'm not sure I do, and the implications that come with that, make me hesitate answering. I shake it off and run my hand through my hair, loosening the stiffly moussed strands. "It's warm tonight."

She gets the hint that I'm not going to give up anything, but warns, "Don't let a temporary distraction ruin the empire you're building, the legacy you've built. I learned that lesson the hard way. Don't put yourself through the heartache. I'm going to eat. I'm starving." Laylah leaves me with that advice... or is it a warning?

I flip the phone in my palm over and over wanting to read the messages from Reese again, the ones that make me smile and give away my secret. I don't. I tuck my phone into my pocket and go to the bar to refresh my drink.

An hour is enough to know I can't be here. I don't want to party; I want to sit in a dark bar and lose myself in someone else's life for a while. Luke picks me up and we drive to a dive in Hollywood. I've never seen a celebrity in here, though I've heard rumblings about "this one time Matt Damon and Ben Affleck" shared a pitcher here.

The vinyl booths are ripped, smoke has infiltrated the red velvet wallpaper, though cigarettes were banned in bars a few years back. It's dark, the only natural light seeping in through an octagon window carved into the front door. The bartender doesn't greet us. That would be a waste of his time as he cleans thick pint glasses and lines them up along the bar. This is why I like it. There are absolutely no pretenses. Nobody here gives a shit about me, my problems, or anybody else's.

Luke gets a pitcher and comes back to the booth by the jukebox we've taken ownership of. While he pours, I complain,

"That's too much head."

He glares at me, so I correct my statement, realizing how I set myself up. "Learn to pour a beer. Give me that." I take the empty glass and fill it myself.

"So, let's go back to the fact that you left a party full of hot models to come drink with me?"

"Aren't you lucky?"

"But why again?" This is lost on him. He thinks like everyone else: I lead a life of luxury, fast cars, and sexy women. Okay, he's right there, but he knows me better. He knows *me*. Period. No one at that party does.

"She's vexing me."

"Okay, Commodus, you're not Joaquin Phoenix and this isn't Gladiator. So nothing should be 'vexing' you."

"If only this was a Ridley Scott movie. We could fight evil. Victory and the woman would be ours."

"And then you die at the end. I'm more of a Gus Van Sant guy myself, and since when did you have girl trouble?"

"Once. But it's made its way back around."

He's shaking his head at me. There's not much he can say and I sound like I'm whining, so I drink my beer, then call to the bartender, "Can you turn up the TV?"

The pitcher is empty and we have a second half-full one in front of us. The channel is changed to a kung fu movie from the seventies, so I get up to check out the jukebox. Flipping through the old albums loaded on there, Guns N' Roses, Metallica, or The Rolling Stones would be great. I need music that drowns out my thoughts. Instead I have music from the fifties like Sam Cooke to The Carpenters of the seventies. I've already stuck my money in, so I pick Aaron Neville's "Tell It Like It Is," knowing nothing on that jukebox is going to make me forget about Reese.

When I sit back down, Luke is judging. "Really, dude?"

"Whatever." I'm judging myself too. Feeling defensive, I do what any good friend would do. I throw it back at him. "Talk to Jane?"

He bites. Hook, line, and sinker. "No. Do you think I should?"

"I don't think I'm in any position to give advice right now."

"I almost called her. I just kept thinking what if she was just having momentary doubts. She went home to him, so how much can she really be thinking about me?"

"I think you call her out on her shit." He looks stunned by my harsh reaction, but I shrug. "Sorry, man, but she told you all that and then went back to him. Is she fucking with you, leaving you dangling out here until she wants you?"

"Fuck, you don't have to lay it out so blatantly. Haven't you heard of 'breaking it' to someone lightly?"

"Sorry. I just have a lot on my mind. I don't even know if Reese is dating someone. What if she is?"

He double snaps his fingers in front of my face. "Hey! Focus. We're talking about me. We'll get to you next."

I laugh, because I can't not laugh at him. He's ridiculous. I take a deep breath and pretend to be serious. "Okay, let's talk this through because that's what two dudes do. They talk through all their girl problems." I side-eye him.

"Your sarcasm isn't appreciated."

"Actually, it's appreciated quite often. But seriously, let's go through the pros and cons."

He nods, eager to work out this riddle. "Pro. We were together for eight years."

"Con. You never sealed the deal. Why not?"

"I don't remember anymore." He leans his head down on his hand, the thought weighing him down. "Little things that didn't matter."

"Pro. You've been broken up over a year or more now, and no

one has managed to replace her."

"That's a big pro," he adds. "Con. She's in a relationship. She lives with him. That's pretty damn serious."

"Pro. She lives with another guy and she still came to see you."

"Pro. She lives with another guy and I don't care. I would do anything to have one more day, one more chance to show her I'm the better man."

I smile. C'mon, I'm not heartless. The poor sap is tugging at my heartstrings. "What are you waiting for then?"

"A sign."

I thump him on the head. "Will that work?"

"Fuck. That hurt," he complains. I laugh, because he knows he won't get me. I'm too quick, even after drinking. "Watch your back," he threatens, but is laughing.

His phone is on the table, so I push it toward him. "What can you lose at this point?"

"Nothing. I already lost the only thing that mattered."

"I know the feeling."

"It's our time, Dan Man. We're not getting younger or more attractive. It's now or never."

"Speak for yourself." I pop my collar. Braggy move, I know.

He pushes my phone toward me. "Stop wasting time on the ones that don't matter. Spend it on the one that does."

Fuck it, I'm typing.

Me: *Three days. You're all mine. See you in Marfa.*

I could stress that I'll freak her out being that direct, but like I said, fuck it. She doesn't keep me waiting. I take that as a good sign. I'm just glad she can't see what an imbecile I look like right now with this big goofy grin taking up prime real estate on my face.

Reese: *See you in Marfa, Danny.*

CHAPTER 15

THE DESERT IS hot. Not exactly a newsflash but just wanted to get that off my chest, along with my shirt. I leave it on since I'm in public representing Vittori and being paid. I'm classy like that. But if it gets any hotter, all bets are off.

The driver shows up and thank God he has the air conditioning jacked up when I get inside.

Marfa is in the middle of nowhere West Texas. I did some research and other than the Prada installation and the Chinati Foundation, there's not much else to see. As we drive into town I'm told we're taking the scenic route and pass Ballroom, another hotspot of featured artists. We head down the main street and are dropped off at Hotel Paisano. The landmark hotel harkens to its roots from the 1930s—Spanish influences and historic tiles. I pass through the hall and pass an ode to the days when the cast of *Giant* stayed here—James Dean, Elizabeth Taylor, and Rock Hudson photos hang proudly.

In the lobby, I see Reese standing at the large window overlooking the courtyard. She's on the phone, too lost in a conversation to notice me. I sit in the leather wingback chair behind her and wait. I'm not trying to eavesdrop but the distress in her voice draws me in to listen, and I narrow my eyes on the tile floor taking on her tension.

She says, "I'll be back in two days." A heavy sigh is released. "I'm not having this conversation over the phone. You can't force—" She's cut off and as I sit there, I realize she's angry, sparking my own anger on her behalf. The asshat on the other end of the line has upset her. When he or she stops talking, she adds, "You need to do what you need to do, Keaton." *Keaton? Who is this dick?* "I'm not stopping you. I'm not holding you back. You're holding yourself back. Don't wait for me because I'm not going to be there."

I clear my throat. When she whips around and finds me sitting there, her face heats and she panics. "I need to go. Vittori's here." She hangs up and tries to recover by asking, "When did you sneak in? I was hoping to greet you."

"No sneaking." I stand, my body moving closer to hers. She falters, her breath deepening and I want to kiss her. I don't, but I want to. "I walked in and saw you."

"Did you have a nice drive in?"

Keeping it conversational, I reply, "I did. Did you?"

A slow smile spreads across her face and she blushes, I hope for me, this time. "I did." She pauses, her body relaxing as she sighs happily. "It's good to see you, Danny."

Now I kiss her. Taking my time, I lean closer, giving her ample warning that I'm coming in. Taking her by the arms, her hands hold me tentatively, but she stays. I kiss her cheek slowly, appreciatively, wishing it were her lips. I take a deep breath and press my cheek to hers. With my eyes closed it's as if we were never apart, as if we didn't let ten years escape us. This is what I've been missing. Reese. *My Reese.*

Soon. Not now, but right then I make her a silent promise to kiss her mouth the way she deserves to be kissed. Reverently. By how her hands are squeezing me she makes me a promise in return that it's not out of the realm for her to reciprocate. Even when my lips leave her skin, she remains there with her eyes closed. I stare at her, amazed by her beauty. When her eyes open, her hands slowly return her sides and that just feels wrong.

A shrill of excitement from behind me makes me jump. "Model Danny is here!"

Vittori is coming down the stairs in all his fervor. Decked out in purple from head to toe, I'm sure West Texas has never seen the likes of him. On second thought, this place is an art community so maybe they have.

Hurrying toward me, I'm not sure if he's coming in for a hug or a handshake. I prepare for either.

Hug, it is.

He's lucky I like him. Not like that, dirty bird.

Reese is too busy to help a fella out. I pat his back before putting a foot or two between us. "Good to see you."

"Is this place not divine in the most unaffected way? I love its non-New York City vibe."

"It definitely is nothing like Manhattan. When did you arrive?"

Reese says, "We got in around lunch. Enough time to settle in and refresh." She looks at my suitcase. "They don't have a bellhop. And no elevator."

Vittori adds, "No room service or spa either."

"That's okay. I can carry my suitcase and I guess we can rough it together," I reply sarcastically with a chuckle.

Reese holds a brass key for me. "You're in room 223. The James Dean room. I thought it was fitting."

"More than you know." I take the key and try the same look from the Vargo shoot on her, but she doesn't react so I stop, which is probably for the best. "We have dinner reservations at six. Is that too soon? We're starving, so we thought we'd eat early, then go explore."

"That works for me."

"Claudia is upstairs sleeping. She might join us. She's undecided."

Another woman that will only pale in comparison to the woman standing in front of me.

Reese says, "She says you know each other?" She poses the statement as a question and I briefly wonder if that's jealousy I hear in her voice.

"We've met a few times."

"Oh." Her tone falls as if she wants to ask more, but doesn't.

Vittori's phone rings and he takes it outside, leaving us alone. I look at Reese. "Guess I should take this upstairs."

"Yeah. Good idea." She's all business, the mention of Claudia, souring her. "If you need anything, I'll be down the hall from you in room 233 and you have my cell, so feel free to use it."

"Okay." I swallow harder than I want. There's no way she didn't notice. I just lay it out to ease her mind. I want the Reese I had before business Reese showed up. "I never slept with her. I've truly only met her at parties. Nothing more."

Her hands go up. "Oh, no. No. You don't have to explain anything to me. That's your business, Danny."

Taking her flailing hands, I still them between us. "I want to explain. I want you to know my business, Reese."

When the tension leaves her and her fingers curl around mine, she lowers her voice and says, "I shouldn't want to know."

"I feel the same way about you."

She takes a step back, stepping away from the cliff that's between us before she falls... before either of us falls. "I can't," she says, her voice shaking, "please. I can't. Not again. My heart can't handle it." She walks away, heading for the stairs.

"Reese?"

She stops, keeping her back to me. With her hand reaching for the wall, bracing herself, her voice is barely heard when she answers, "Yes?"

The desk attendant is watching me as I make a heartfelt plea to the one woman who severed it ten years earlier. "I missed you." *I loved you.*

She remains silent and I'm tempted to go to her, but I resist, knowing she needs the time to herself. "Me too," she replies glancing back, and then continuing up the stairs, disappearing. I'm left with a suitcase at my feet and an audience.

With the awkwardness swarming the lobby, the attendant looks down, suddenly busy with the registry log in front of her. I squeeze the keychain in my hand and grab my suitcase. "Room 223?"

"Up the stairs, sir."

"Thank you."

My room is at the top of the stairs and around the railing. There's about an inch gap at the bottom and light peeks out from inside the room. I unlock the door and take my luggage inside. The hotel is old and the doors seem antique like the furniture. The door stays open until I close it. There are no automatic close or locks here. I sit on the bed and then lie back with my arms under my head. Staring at the ceiling, the day starts sinking in and my body relaxes on the mattress.

A light knock on the door breaks the silence. "Come in."

Vittori walks in and shuts the door as if we're breaking some imaginary rules. I sit up. He walks with purpose to the balcony. Opening the door, he slips out, inspects the view, then looks back in. "James Dean had a bad view."

"Doubt it was the same view back then."

"True." He flops onto his stomach at the bottom of the bed.

I sit up, putting my back against the pillows propped against the headboard. I'm not sure if I need to remind him he's not my type or if he's always this playful with people he barely knows. "Whoa there, big guy."

He rolls onto his back dramatically. "Why are you and Reese fighting this so much?"

"Fighting what?" I ask, curious to what he knows.

His hands are in the air, waving around. "There was so much sexual tension in that lobby I almost put on a condom so I didn't get knocked up."

"That's not exactly how condoms work."

He flips onto his stomach and props his chin on his hands. "Pfft. You know what I mean, Model Danny."

"I know every major fashion house designer and I have to say, you are one of a kind, Designer Vittori."

Amusement sparks in his eyes. "Call me, Vinnie. My friends do, and Model Danny, I've decided we're friends."

"And how did you come to that conclusion?"

"Because Reese likes you, and if she likes someone, I know I will."

"Doesn't seem like she does."

"She just feels too much."

"Too much?"

"Too much for you. I see how she looks at you, but she doesn't know what to do with all those emotions. I thought about making her a purse for them, so they'd be easier to carry around."

I smile because this man is nuts, but his heart is in the right place. "And what changed your mind?"

"I decided it was better for her to deal with them, with you, instead of hiding them away, even in a designer, custom-made bag."

"Should you be telling me this?" I chuckle that I've found an ally in the form a purple-loving fashion designer. "Don't get me wrong. I like having this insider's perspective, but would she want you sharing her secrets?"

He stands as if he can't sit still any longer, his zeal is too powerful to contain. "She's fearless and creative, intelligent, and has great titties. But she's also guarded to the point of closing herself off."

"Okay, slow up here. You've seen her tits?"

He waves me off. "Of course. Half of New York has, but that's beside the point."

"How can *that* be beside the point? That seems like the main point in this discussion," I say, bothered by the direction this chat has taken. *Half of New York? What the fuck?*

"Model Danny, focus. The point I'm trying to make is that she's protective of her heart."

"Why?"

"Why is anyone protective of their heart?"

"Because they've been hurt."

"Gooooooal!"

I overlook the crazy and do as he told me. I focus on the point, wanting more information. "Who hurt her?"

His gaze lands on me and he seems to be debating, then he says, "She was in a bad relationship. She got out of it."

Is he talking about me and Reese or her and someone else? I probe deeper. "In New York?"

His eyes brows arch. "Yes. Where else? Nebraska?" He's throws that out there like he's joking, but my instincts make me think he's not.

Now I level my eyes on him. "Nebraska? What do you know about Nebraska?"

"I know it's the home of the Cornhuskers. Well, I didn't know that, but I looked it up when Reese said she went to school there."

I don't say anything, fearing anything I do will incriminate us. But he's good. Very good. He challenges me with his own silence.

Ending the standoff, I ask, "They have a great football team. Do you watch college sports?"

"No, though I've always appreciated a tight end."

Laughing, I say, "So you do follow football."

"Not at all, but I've picked up a few key things. Things like offensive, defensive, tackle, you and Reese used to date, sidelined, Super Bowl—"

"Whoa, whoa, whoa! Back up."

"To Tackle?"

"After that."

"Sidelined?"

"Before that?"

"You and Reese used to date?"

"Touchdown. What do you know about that?"

"About touchdowns? Nothing. About you and Reese, not enough," he says, eager for more. "Why don't you fill me in?"

I'm not sure what to say. She told him. She told him about us. Doesn't that go against what we were doing, keeping our past a secret so it didn't affect our present? "I need a minute." Standing and going to the balcony, I open the door and stand outside on the recently replaced wood flooring. I lean on the railing, unsure what to think or how to process that he knows and I had no say in the matter.

His voice is calmer, more cautious when he says, "I want what's best for her."

I turn around and through the open door, I ask, "And you think I'm best for her?"

"I think you're better than her last boyfriend."

"That's not exactly a compliment, especially since I don't

know anything about her ex." Though I like that it sounds like there's not a current boyfriend in the picture.

When he walks to the door, I step back inside the room just as he says, "I should leave something for her to share when she's ready, but I see how she looks at you. What I don't know is why you guys broke up back then and I'll leave that for now. But you've got two days to make her remember why you guys worked."

"So this is a setup, a matchmaking scheme?"

"No, Model Danny. This is serendipity."

"This isn't a game. This is our life. And how do you know if I'm willing to play along?"

Opening the door, he steps out, but stays to say, "Because I see how you look at her."

CHAPTER 16

BEYOND THE COMMENT about her tits, and I'm left wondering what I'm supposed to do now. I sit on the edge of the bed, but it's the last thing I want to do. I get up and shut the balcony door and grab the key ring as I walk out of the room.

I march toward room 233, but stop when Claudia comes out of her room. She sees me and smiles. "Danny, hi." After locking her door she comes toward me. "How are you?" We exchange a cheek kiss greeting.

"I'm good. How are you?"

"So good. This is a great gig, huh?"

"It's great."

"I'm so relieved," she says, wrapping her arms around my neck, "that I'm working with you. It's always been a dream and it's good to have a friend here with me."

"Yeah, it's good to have a familiar face to work with," I reply. Over her shoulder Reese steps out of her room and sees us. Of course she does with her perfect timing.

I drop my arms from Claudia and she releases me. "Let's go get a drink. I heard there's a bar in the restaurant downstairs."

Reese goes back into her room and shuts the door. Claudia is looking at me, hopeful. "I can meet you in a few minutes."

Her expression falls when I don't respond right away. "Whatever it is can wait. C'mon." Taking me by the arm, her hands are vice-like grips. "I refuse to take a no for an answer. I'll buy the first round."

Talking to Reese with Claudia hanging around is impossible, so I acquiesce. "All right."

"Yay." She starts talking again, but I look back at room 233, not hearing anything she's been saying. I just nod and agree and that gets me by.

I don't know how much time has passed, but I've only stomached one iced tea when Reese and Vinnie walk into the restaurant. Claudia jumps up and hugs Vinnie. "I'm so happy to be here. The concept is amazing. I can't wait to see the finished product."

My eyes meet Reese's, but she looks away. "I think our table is ready."

She's wearing dark, tight jeans with boots, and a black tank top. It's casual, nothing like she wore in LA, but she looks sexy as fuck. I follow her to the table. Claudia and Vinnie are still talking shop back at the bar. When we sit down, I say, "You look beautiful as always."

In disbelief, she says, "Oh God. I'm sure I look a complete mess after the traveling."

"It's the truth, Reese."

That comment finally catches her attention. Before the others join us, she whispers, "I was never good with compliments. Thank you." Leaning over, she lowers her voice even more. "Before they come over, I just want to tell you that I understand we live very different lives. It's none of my business what you do in your free time. Just don't let it compromise the shoot. I've worked very hard to make it happen."

When her eyes go back to Claudia, I understand what she's really saying, so I say, "If my intentions aren't clear, I'll be more direct."

"What are your intentions?"

"I told you before. To make you miss me when we're not together."

"Dann—"

"I'm famished," Claudia announces as she takes the seat across from Reese, between Vinnie and me.

Reese glances at me, then says, "Me too."

My appetite is gone though I continue to peruse the menu. The waitress takes our drink orders while my anxiety grows. I don't want to be here. There's no way I'll be able to sit through dinner and pretend nothing is wrong when everything is so fucking screwed up. I want to be alone with her to figure out where we stand. All patience is lost when I'm with her. My mind muddled under her scent and beauty, her restraint and poker face. I want us to be together... *shit*. Damn Luke and his girly feely shit the other night, dragging all this up. I'm losing my shit and that never happens. Not since I lost her. *Fuck*. When the waitress returns with a round of waters, I'm standing. "Go ahead and order without me."

Everyone is staring at me, but I only look to one set of eyes. Reese asks, "Are you coming back?"

"I just remembered I have a call with my agent. I don't want to hold you up. I know you're hungry. If I don't return I'll catch up with you guys later."

I walk away before the lie becomes more complicated. Walking through the door that leads to the hotel, I go to the fireplace. She's got me all fucked up already and then Vittori lays that other bullshit on me, making it worse. This is ridiculous. I've only felt this twisted over one woman and it's the same one doing it to me again.

Listing a million pros out for Luke to spur him into taking action, taking a chance, and going after Jane has not done anything for my motivation. I fucking suck.

"Danny?"

I look behind me and see Reese standing there in her beautiful perfection. All the anger and hurt I've felt for years boils to the surface, transforming inside. There's a million cons crossing my mind, but my body acts on the instinct of one pro—kiss her.

She says, "I wanted to check—"

My lips cover hers, cutting her words off. While holding her face to mine, I expect her to pull back, maybe even slap me, but she doesn't.

She does the opposite.

When she takes me by the shoulders and lifts up, her breath becomes mine and I take it, inhaling her deep within. My tongue meets hers and our bodies come together.

But then she's gone and I'm left fumbling. Her back is against the wall and she's breathing hard. With her hand on her chest, she says, "I can't. I can't do this." The expression on her face wavers between horror and embarrassment before she's leaving, hurrying out the entrance toward the stairs.

And then I'm running.

I stop her at the top of the steps by taking the stairs by three and blocking her. "Don't run away from me. Not again, Reese."

With her hands pressing to my chest, keeping me at arm's length, tears fill her eyes. "What is happening?"

"What do you mean?"

She looks down as her arms fall to her sides and her gaze goes to the floor. When she looks back up at me, she's exasperated and walks around me. Standing at the top, she grips the railing tightly. "*Us? This?* This wasn't planned, but here I am swept right back up in you. How is that possible?"

"Because we never had closure." I cover the last few steps dividing us and cover her hand with mine. "And all of this was planned. You put that plan in motion when you suggested me for the campaign. You made this happen. You brought us together as if you expected a different outcome than what you've gotten."

"My feelings for you weren't planned."

"Tell me, Reese. What do you feel for me?"

"Home. You feel like home to me."

A tear falls down her cheek, but I kiss it away before it can fall any farther. "You taste like home," I whisper against the side of her mouth. She turns and our lips meet again. Her fingers weave into my hair as my hands slide around her waist. I take the final step and spin her around, walking her backward until we reach my door. With her back against the wall, I unlock my door, our lips part, and I step inside. We stand with the threshold dividing us. "Don't you see, Reese, we were always good together."

"Until the end, Danny. Then we were bad. So bad. *You* were bad for me."

Her words hit like a shot to the chest and I jerk in reaction. Blue eyes on my brown as she waits for the comeback she expects, the comeback she wants. But I can't give her anything, except my hand. I'll tourniquet my emotional wounds when I'm alone. With all of my strength, my heart on the line, I hold my hand out for her and wait to see if she accepts it.

Her body shudders as traitorous emotions expose her true feelings, and tears fall steadily. She can't fight this anymore than I can despite the valiant effort. "This won't give us closure, Danny."

"This is not our end. This is a new beginning."

Pulling her slowly to me by her delicate hands, her head is

against my chest. Standing behind a locked door, I wrap my arms around her, rubbing her back to ease the heartache and struggle she's going through, the same struggle I'm battling. Our feet move together, both of us content to dance to a song that's never heard, but played in our hearts for years. At one time, she was the one I came home to and she's the song my soul continues to sing. It's the song of our love. It's... us. In her arms, *I'm home again.*

The simplest of acts—a kiss to my chest, a kiss to the top of her head—and we both know. We both feel it. I so desperately want to see her blue eyes shining, to pick up where we left off ten years before. Since that's not rational, I turn her chin toward me. When her beautiful eyes meet mine, I see the girl I fell in love with now a woman with that same passion flickering inside. "You could destroy me, Reese Carmichael."

Her smile is soft, empathetic. "I don't want to destroy you."

"Then what do you want?"

"A second chance to right my mistakes."

"I'll give you whatever you want," I whisper, and lean down to kiss the side of her mouth. "Just tell me what that is."

"I want you."

"You've had me all along."

She smiles, leaning her forehead on me. I rub her back and ask, "What's so funny?"

"I screwed up."

"I'll forgive you if you tell me why."

"Not back then..." She looks up. "Actually, yes, I screwed up back then, but I also screwed up thinking I could see you and not feel anything."

Brushing the back of my hand over her cheek, I say, "There's too much history between us to ignore."

"I was fooling myself."

"Are you in there, Danny?" Claudia's voice penetrates the door and we both turn in that direction.

I hold a finger over my lips. "Shhh."

Reese—doe-eyed, just-kissed pink lips—all aimed at me. I kiss her instead of stopping like we should, picking up exactly where we left off. A little moan from her coats my throat as I cup her face.

Claudia is persistent. "Danny? Open up, it's just me."

Reese pulls back this time and teases me as she whispers, "Yeah, Danny, it's just *her*."

I shoot her a look, and whisper, "I see things haven't changed as much as I thought."

"I wasn't any good at this back then. I'm not any better now."

"Good at what?"

Closing her eyes quickly, she shakes her head. She's even quieter this time. "I've never been good watching you with other women, even for your work, especially with your work."

"You don't have to be jealous of Claudia." As her admission runs through my head I ask, "You were jealous back then?"

Annoyance flashes in her eyes, but I'm not sure if she's irritated with herself or me. "I hated that I was, but I was. You know that."

"You didn't have to be. I promise you. You don't have to be now either," I say quietly, taking her hand. "We'll figure this out together."

When her head tilts away, I hate that I can't see her full face, her eyes, her expressive eyes. The pink lips of her mouth are in a line and all I want is to see her smile again. "That's just it. We can't." Those communicative eyes plead to mine. "We're not allowed to date. Not only does it go against your contract, but your company policy. As for me, I can't give my bosses any ammo to fire me. I need my job. I have responsibilities."

Models don't get much respect. I'm used to that. But why does it sting when I hear that from Reese? Narrowing my eyes, I sit on the bed as we distance ourselves emotionally and physically, something our practice has led us to master. "*Ouch!* I have bills to pay. I have my own set of responsibilities."

She crosses her arms across her chest as she leans against the door. "I know you do. I'm not cutting you down by telling you about my situation. It's either win or lose for me. So, although I know you have your own set of responsibilities, you can afford to pick and choose your jobs. I can't just fly off because I have a whim when I wake up on a Thursday and need a vacation. I don't have that luxury."

I could argue, but I can tell it's pointless right now. The door might be closed, but it's obvious that mentally she's already got one foot out. So I sit, listening and watching her defend herself, her actions, her digs at me.

"You're right. I have choices that most don't. I've worked hard to create that opportunity in an industry where it's possible." I walk toward her. Reaching around, I unlock the bolt, then take the knob in hand. "I may not work a nine-to-five. I may not have to take a job or work for a few months if I don't want to. But nothing I do is on a whim or done carelessly. I've been degraded in ways you'll never believe, so when it comes to my money and how my face or my body sells a product, I earn every penny I make." I open the door, bumping it into her foot.

She steps to the side, but her eyes are still on me. "I didn't mean you don't earn your money." I move out of the way, letting her exit. She steps out into the hall. "Danny, I'm sorry."

Whether she meant it or not, hearing her disparage my responsibilities, when she knows how hard I've worked to achieve what I have—how much I have always wanted this—it's just too much. I feel fucking raw. *She doesn't want me.* And even if she did, she's right regarding the contracts. We can't start anything while under the terms. *Fuck!*

My eyes meet Claudia's and Reese turns to see her standing behind her. Embarrassment shades her face when she looks back.

Playing games has never interested me, especially when it comes to Reese. I know she's not heartless, but that comment hurts my pride. I'm too irate to talk this out. Even though I hate what I'm about to do, I do it anyway. "Claudia, want to get a drink? I heard about a bar just a short drive from here."

Anger flashes in Reese's eyes that still glisten from the tears that recently filled them, but she doesn't put up a fight. "If you'll excuse me. I'm going to find Vittori."

Claudia says, "Let him know I'll be keeping Danny company."

Reese smiles, but there's nothing friendly about it. "Will do."

I lock my door and Claudia adds, "I'm ready if you are."

Reese looks up one last time before she disappears down the stairs. I turn to Claudia, and reply, "I'm ready."

CHAPTER 17

I DON'T DRINK the day before a photo shoot. *One of the golden rules that has kept me on top of the modeling world.*

Until tonight.

Reese has me all twisted inside. It's fucked up to feel this way.

We've got a few beers in us when Claudia lights up. Blowing the smoke into the air, she has her attention set on me. "What's the story with you and the ad woman back there?"

"No story."

Laughing, she leans her elbows on the table. "There's definitely a story there, but if you want to forget about it, then I'm your girl."

"You'll help me forget?"

"Damn straight." She takes another long drag. She's pretty in that too perfect kind of way. I can appreciate the uniqueness of her wide-set eyes and reed-like body. Her confidence is sexy in a blatant expression of sexuality. Reese's sexy is understated and undeniable—her body, her mind, her words, the way she moves her lips when she speaks of something she's passionate about. Everything. All of her. Sexy.

Spinning my bottle between my fingers, I ask, "I thought you had a boyfriend, so how are you going to help me forget?"

"We're fluid."

"I have no idea what that means."

I sit forward and she sits back. "It means we go where life takes us, experiencing life, and the adventures as they come."

"I call that going with the flow." I throw in a hang loose hand sign.

"You're so old school, Danny."

Nodding, I chuckle. "I might have to agree with you." I stand to get more beers when Claudia speaks under her breath. "Your girlfriend's here."

I follow her stare. Vinnie and Reese are walking in, Vinnie smiling. Reese not. While approaching, he asks, "Can we join you?"

Claudia scoots her chair to the side. "Yeah. Danny was getting another round, but I can get it if you want something."

He waves her off. "Oh, no. No. I'll buy. I want to ask their sommelier what he recommends to go with tumbleweeds." Looking around, he says, "This place is just so desert charming."

We laugh, and I say, "I think this is as fancy as Marfa gets." Checking out the bartender, I direct him to sit down so he doesn't humiliate himself by asking for a wine connoisseur in the middle of nowhere. "Earlier the bartender said it was the sommelier's night off."

Pouting, he sits down dramatically, throwing his arms up in surrender. "Fine. I'll have what you're having."

Reese and I lock eyes. She says, "Bourbon please. On the rocks with a slice of orange on the side."

I head to the bar, hands tucked in my pockets not sure how this night is going to go. It's either going to be amazing or disastrous. fifty-fifty chance of going either way.

Vinnie joins me at the bar, propping his foot up on the foot rail as if he'll somehow blend in despite the head-to-toe purple he's wearing. "I'm thinking we need the bottle." He slaps black plastic on the counter, the credit card hitting with a crack. "I guess it didn't go well?"

"What?" I'm kind of impressed in his ability to read us so well.

His head rolls on his neck to turn to me. "No need to play dumb with me, Model Danny. I'm on your side."

"You're not on Reese's side?"

"See, that's what you don't understand. We're all on the same side." He leaves me with his words of wisdom, rejoining the ladies.

I hate when I'm blinded by my emotions. The dust cloud in my head clears; I look back at Reese. It's so obvious now. He's right, but so is she. We can't be together. That would go against everything I signed. It would go against what I promised Mark. Reese Carmichael is off limits. For her sake and mine.

In the meantime, I can still admire how damn sexy she is, even when she's mad at me. Maybe even more when she's mad. The thought amuses. The problem with enjoying an inside joke is that people start to think you're crazy. That makes me laugh louder, finding it too funny to stop myself.

Naturally, that's when the bartender finally comes over to take my order. I take the bottle, the tab, and glasses to the table. I sit across from Reese, crammed between Claudia and Vinnie. The ice clatters when bourbon is poured over it. Once we have a drink, we raise them meeting in the middle. Vinnie toasts, "To great photo shoots."

We all repeat, "To great photo shoots."

I finish my drink in one long swallow. The others sip. Staring at Reese, I silently will her to look me in the eyes. I miss having her look at me, look at me like I matter.

When she finally does, she says, "How did your shoot go the other day?"

"Well."

"Who was the client?"

"Vargo."

"Ahh."

That's it. That's all she says. I honestly don't understand what we're doing, so I ask her, moving on from the boring topic of what company I was working with. "What keeps you in New York?"

She about spits her bourbon out, but doesn't. That's my girl. When the shock disappears, she replies, "My life."

"What if you had the chance to travel without worrying about your life in Manhattan?"

Thoughtfully pondering, she doesn't rush to answer. When she does, she says, "I would take the money and reinvest in a world trip. I want an espresso in Italy and croissants in Paris. Chocolates in Belgium, and strudel in Germany. I sound like such a foodie, but really it's just an excuse to eat all the bad stuff." She laughs and it's carefree, the bourbon sinking in, lowering her guard. "Where would you go and what would you eat?"

Claudia eyes her cynically, then lights another cigarette. "I don't eat."

Oh shit!

Reese pops an eyebrow, the challenge accepted. "You have to eat. To survive," she says and I expect sarcasm to be dripping, but it's not. She's completely serious with Claudia.

"You're right, but I don't eat the kind of stuff *you* eat. I snack on water-based foods."

Reese snorts and Vinnie reacts by laughing nervously. I'm used to the strange eating habits of models and what they'll do to stay thin, but I'm still cringing inside despite outwardly enjoying this more-than-entertaining conversation. It's heading into confrontation territory. Claudia has her claws out, but the ball is in Reese's court.

Reese's pupils zero in and the look on her face I'm all too familiar with. Here it comes...

"And when you say water-based, is that like cigarettes and alcohol? And what food groups do tobacco and booze fall under anyway?"

I stand abruptly, my chair wobbling back before the feet land loudly back on the stone beneath our feet. "Reese, let's dance."

Her head whips to the side where a few couples have taken to the makeshift dance floor in front of a small stage. "I don't know how to country dance."

I'm before her with my hand out, palm up. "It's been a few years, but I'll lead."

Accepting the invitation, she stands. The dance floor is empty as the song changes when we make our way to the middle. A sign of her unease slips into place when her bottom lip is squeezed under the pressure of her top teeth. With stiff upper arms, our bodies align, remembering their position from years before. When she looks up, she says, "It's been a few years since we've danced together. I think I've forgotten how to do this."

A few notes of our heart song plays in my head drowning out our earlier argument. I'm holding her again, and she's willingly following. Leading, I step forward and she steps back, her body remembering. "Let me remind you how good we were together." We continue to move, our pace in sync.

"You say that as if we're not talking about the two-step."

Pulling her closer, our bodies pressed together, my hand sliding to the curve of her waist, my head tilted down, hers tilted up, her cheek pressed to mine, I say, "I'm not."

She feels it. I can tell by the way her body moves against mine, a comfort found in the closeness. "Danny, why do you say such things?"

When the song changes we continue to sway to the music, my grip holding her here with me. Though from the grip she has on me, I'm thinking she intends to stay as much I want her to. "Why do you try to deny it?"

She leans back to look at me. "I haven't. That's the problem. We're not in a position to act on temptations."

It's my turn to take a step back. "Temptation? We're more than that and you know it. I have a feeling you knew exactly how this would play out when you pitched me in that meeting. What were you trying to get from this reunion?"

"I'm not going to lie to you. I had no motives, not conscious ones, but I've been curious. That's only natural. You've never thought of me?"

"I can't say I haven't, but I tried damn hard not to."

"Why is that?"

Dropping my hands, I'm ready for another drink. I stand there vulnerable to emotions I had buried. Emotions that make me feel raw inside. I hate it. "Because it was too painful to think of you at all." I leave her in the middle of the dance floor. I never liked the two-step anyway.

Vinnie is by himself when I take my seat. "Where's Claudia?"

"Bathroom."

"How long has she been gone?"

"Just a few minutes." He doesn't seem alarmed so I pour myself a drink and sit back to drown the feelings Reese summoned. When Reese returns, I top up her glass, figuring she'll need it as much as I do.

She asks, "Where's Claudia?"

"Bathroom," Vinnie replies. He looks over his shoulder toward the bathrooms. "Maybe you should check on her."

"Why?" she asks.

"Because everyone seems so concerned about her absence."

I sit back, listening to the exchange and am about to go check on her myself when Reese rises. "I'll do it."

She's gone long enough for me to keep checking the hall that leads to the bathrooms every half minute. When they finally come back, at least five minutes has passed.

Claudia takes her seat again, and she nods like nothing is new in the world.

I look to Reese for an unspoken question to what happened, but Claudia asks, "I heard they have shuffleboard. Come play with me, Danny?"

Again, my eyes flash to Reese, who looks pissed but is managing to hold it in. I stand up, not to spite Reese, but to be there for Claudia. Something's changed in her mood and I want to make sure she's all right.

Walking with her away from the table, I don't look back, fighting my instincts. Just inside an old addition to the structure, a long shuffleboard table stands. Claudia detours to the bar for change and I'm left to dust the surface. She returns with change and starts the machine. Standing at the opposite ends of the table, we wing it since neither of us really knows how to play. After the first game, I catch a glimpse of Reese. She's sitting on the table with her feet propped up on a chair. Her back is to us as she talks animatedly to Vinnie. He's all smiles and laughter in return. A crappy feeling comes over me. It's been a while, but I recognize it. *Shit!*

I'm jealous.

I shouldn't be over Vinnie, but I am. Is this how she felt seeing me in magazines, on commercials? Is this the legacy I left her with from our relationship? The memories of what she held on to? No fucking wonder she left. This sucks. I want her to talk to me like that—so freely, so happy. It's exhausting to constantly be under the microscope of our circumstance. I want his freedom with her. I want a fresh start... with her.

Claudia is quiet. I'd almost venture to say contemplative. She wins, and while setting up for another round, I ask, "What's going on with you?"

"Nothing," Claudia replies, badass defensive attitude intact.

Staring into her eyes, her pupils are dilated, the darkness overtaking the green. I debate if I should call her out on it or let it go. Because of her mood, I feel the need to talk to her about it. "You've got to get clean."

"I am clean."

"You know what I mean. The drugs give the illusion of happiness, but when you really look at yourself on them, you've lost the joy inside."

"You don't know me, Danny. I take them to cope with this life."

"You have an amazing life—a boyfriend who cares about you, a great career. You've broken through that barrier most models crack under. Don't throw it away."

She laughs. "Men age and they're called distinguished. Women are called hags. There's no hope for me, so I'll take something that gets me through this when I need to."

A well of hopelessness lives deep in her damaged parts. I've seen it in others, but not this close. She needs help. Maybe I can. "And you need to?" I keep talking while she shrugs unapologetically, "I think you like to distract yourself from what's really going on."

"I don't like to think about it." Her sadness permeates the desert air. "My agent says my career is winding down and I should consider going to school. Everything is bullshit, Danny." She puts her arms out wide. "An illusion of glamour and money."

"Your mind is playing tricks on you because of the drugs."

"Well, it's a fabulous fucking trick," she says perking up. "Want to join me?"

"I prefer reality."

"I bet I could get your girlfriend to join me."

Too close. I feel a growl rumble through my chest. There's something in her eyes that's sinister and my guard goes up. My words come out more protective than casual. "Leave her out of this. She talks a big game, but she doesn't mean anything by it."

"Touchy touchy." She starts to walk away, but stops and adds, "Have you ever destroyed a hotel room, fucked someone in a public bathroom, done coke just because you want to? Just live— wildly and in the moment? Been authentic?"

I pause, not comfortable with the conversation. "Living an illusion isn't being authentic, Claudia. It's being pretentious."

"This illusion is so much prettier than my reality." She pats my chest and returns to the table. I overhear her say, "Light it up, bitches. Let's get this party started." Claudia takes the bottle and tilts it back, downing more than a shot.

I take it away and set it on the table. "We have the shoot tomorrow. Maybe we should go."

Reese's glass is empty and she leans back, staring at me. "It just got fun."

"Don't be a party pooper, Model Danny," Vinnie says, adding to the obnoxiousness.

I double-check the bottle. Yep, there's barely any left. "Did you guys down this while we were gone?"

Reese laughs and pokes me. "Maybe. I'll buy you a drink."

She gets up and brushes against me as she passes. I'm quick and stop her from leaving. "I'm good. I think we should go though."

Claudia gets up and dances behind Vinnie.

Reese throws her arms into the air. "I love to dance."

Did I just walk into a twilight zone? What the fuck is going on with everyone? "I think the desert air is messing with you."

She laughs. "You're right. This clean air is making me loopy."

"I need to get you out of here before you do something dumb."

"I've already done enough dumb for a lifetime." Her finger touches my temple and she slowly drags it down around my jaw and taps me on the chin. With a little lick of her lips, she then smiles just for me. Something erotic, something brave, maybe that's freedom seen in her eyes before she says, "Now I want to have some fun."

For her sake, she's lucky we're not alone or I'd be all over her and that goddamn tempting tongue.

A weathered cowboy with a large chip sitting squarely on his shoulder under his wide-brimmed hat approaches just as I reach for her belt loop and tug her closer. Vinnie does a low wolf whistle, eyeing the cowboy and I cross my arms, standing my ground, as he looks Reese over. As if I'm not even there, he asks her, "Wanna dance?"

"I love dancing," she replies, her finger now getting caught in my belt loop. Her body language is crystal clear to me, and should be to him. "Sorry, but my dance card is already full."

"C'mon, little lady, let me take you for a spin."

He remains there, the crystal not so clear I guess. So I stand, and say, "She said no."

Looking her over again and giving me an eat-shit grin, he offers her his hand. "Just one dance."

He doesn't like no for an answer, and I'm not going to argue with him because I don't like wasting my time. "Time to go, Reese."

Besides no, he doesn't take kindly to strangers either. "You run along now and leave the grownups to party."

Reese leans against my chest, one arm around me the other resting on my chest. She looks up and smiles at me—this time seductive and insinuating. As my arms wrap around her, she says, "Thanks for the offer, but I'm leaving with him."

Grumbling is heard when he mutters, "Lucky bastard." He walks away with no further complaint.

Reese says, "You hear that, ya lucky bastard?"

I laugh for many reasons, but mainly because she's so cute right now. Squeezing her a little tighter, I repeat, "I am a lucky bastard. The luckiest."

CHAPTER 18

CLAUDIA IS ON a mission to self-destruct with a shot of tequila in one hand and Vinnie eating out of the other as she tells him fables of her model's life. I'm done drinking for the night. I don't want to feel like shit tomorrow and want to savor tonight. "You ready?" I ask Reese.

"I am," she says, and gives her farewells. I set the keys in front of Vinnie and whisper, "The hotel is only a few blocks away. We'll walk. Don't let Claudia drive back. Okay?"

"Okay. Goodnight, Model Danny."

I nod toward the exit and we go. The six or so blocks back don't feel like enough time alone with Reese, but I'll take what I can get. The fresh air will also do us both some good.

Not wanting to waste a second, I ask, "Who was your rebound?"

Bumping into me, she says, "You might be." When her laughter rings out, including a snort, I know I should have stopped her from having that last shot. But I'm too blindsided by what she actually said to worry about her snorting or how much she drank. Instead the words "you might be" are ping-ponging around my brain and I'm tempted to get her more truth serum, aka tequila.

We can't.

I know this, I remind myself.

We know this.

She's a damn flirt. A damn, temptingly gorgeous flirt.

It's in the new Illustrious handbook and stated clearly in the last contract. But when she twirls, all her worries gone from her body, I'm close to breaking that contract and every promise I made Mark.

I catch up to her and we cross the street together. "You shouldn't drink. You're gonna get yourself in trouble."

She looks hopeful. "Would that trouble include you? Because I'm all for getting into trouble with you."

I think I've opened Pandora's box, or maybe revealed Victoria's secret. *Sexy girl.* "You say that as if you'd follow through when we both know you won't."

She moves in front of me, making me stop. With her hands on my stomach, small little movements tell me she's taking advantage of the situation and enjoying the feel of my eight-pack. "Is that a challenge, Danny boy?"

Sighing, she's exasperated in the most adorable way. She's trying so hard to get me to play along, and I'm tempted. I can play with the best of them. Just not with her. This time it's too close to my heart. She's too close to my heart and a huge part of my history. I take hold of her wrists and drag them down until she's about to touch me where I really want her hands, then stop and remove them altogether. "I'll lose to you, Reese. Every time— whether intentional or not. So this isn't me challenging you. This is me recognizing the situation for what it is."

With a flourish, she turns and starts walking again. I stay behind her, thinking she might need the time to think like I do.

Or not...

"Remember that time we almost got arrested for having sex in the car?" she asks, her smile back in place.

"I do. I remember being handcuffed while wearing only my boxers."

"You looked hot if that makes a difference."

Chuckling, I say, "Sure, that makes all the difference."

"Well, I did talk him into freeing you and you never did pay me back."

"I remember very distinctly paying you back about four times over that night." As if cued to do so, I wink.

"No, not that. Although that was a very fun night."

She's light on her feet, her happiness abounding with each step. So much like the girl I once knew. The girl I fell head over heels for. An ache grows in my chest. Along with the good memories, others take away from the happiness we once shared together. I don't say anything. I'm not in the mood to relive them tonight or to argue. I just want to enjoy this star-filled night in the middle of nowhere and this moment in time with a woman I've fallen for all over again. But we can't go there. *Yet.*

I indulge her this time. "I pay all my debts. What did I promise you?"

"You promised to recreate the first night we met."

It's the poorest of excuses, but I voice it anyway, "Life got in the way."

"A lot got in the way." She's much more reflective this time, the bounce gone from her step.

We walk the next block in silence. The hotel is up ahead and I find my pace slowing. I'm not ready for tonight to end. I'm not wanting for it to end like this either. I grab her, surprising her, and duck into an abandoned storefront, an alcove housing a locked glass front door and no witnesses around. "Reese."

She smiles, knocking me a little off balance by its sincerity, the trust seen so clearly with the street lights sparkling in her eyes. "Yes?"

Her lips are left parted and I find them distracting, everything I planned to say to her now gone, completely vanished from my mind. "Don't look at me like that, okay?"

"Like what?" she asks, her smile growing, a giggle punctuating it.

"Like I'm a good guy."

"Ooh, are we quoting movies? I love this game. Um, let me think. I've got the next line. You're not a bad guy."

"I don't even know what you're talking abou—"

"Wait, that's not how the movie goes."

"I'm not quoting a movie."

"Oh! I thought you were quoting *Twilight*."

"I've never seen *Twilight*."

"It's a really good movie. You should watch it."

"Huh?" I shake my head, wondering where I went wrong with this conversation. I wave my hands as if I can erase all of this and start over. "Listen to me. I'm no good for you. It didn't work when we were young. Why would it work now? It won't. But I'm so damn attracted to you—I have all these feelings—new and old. Seeing you smile and laugh, being with you..." I look away, but like every other time, I can't stay away for long. "I'm going to kiss you. Again."

"Okay," she says, the smile gone, the sincerity remaining.

Her back presses against the window as she's bracing herself, and I lean in. This time I look at her lips, so pink, her breath coming out harsher than seconds before. So ready for me. Her eyes drop closed and mine follow as our lips touch. Gentle pressure becoming firmer. I rest one hand on the glass above her head and with the other I touch her cheek. A small moan is shared when our tongues touch.

I need to stop, so I back away. "I can't do this. I can't stop with you if this goes any further."

"Danny," she says, tentatively stepping closer to me, "I know we have reasons enough to not do this, but being here with you, dancing back there, kissing you earlier... I have no willpower when it comes to you. I never did."

"You did once. When it mattered the most, you found the willpower." I spent years mourning the loss of us.

Watching her, she gazes down to the ground between us. *She looks hurt.* "There's so much to still discuss, all the reasons we didn't work back then. I have questions just like you do, but not tonight. Tonight, can we leave that in the past and forget about everyone else?"

"If you could, what would you do?"

She moves against me, chest to chest, her hand sliding to the back of my neck. "I'd kiss you and more." Kissing me, I hold her just where she is.

It's where I like her most, right up against me. When we stop, I say, "I'd like more with you."

"I would too. Just tonight. Nothing else matters." She takes my hand and says, "It's my turn to lead."

While walking back to the hotel, she asks, "What turns you on?"

I like when she's forward. I reply, "When the camera is turned off."

Her quick glance makes me feel exposed, but it's good to feel this way because I feel like the walls between us are coming down.

With a flash of a smirk of her own, she says, "I'll keep that in mind."

By the time we reach the hotel, the sexual tension between us heightens, the possibility of what's about to happen turning me on. She holds my hand the rest of the way, her fingers tightly woven with mine. Stopping twice to kiss, we come close to "almost" getting arrested again, so we hurry through the courtyard, and straight through the lobby.

We make it to the top of the stairs, right outside my hotel room before we break down and give in to temptation.

I kiss her—hard. I kiss her so she knows there's no one else I'd rather kiss. When our bodies come together, I feel the nudge between my knees, her softness wedging against my hardness. My back is against the wall, the plaster shaking when I slam against it.

Meandering hands roll over the muscles of my shoulders and into the hair at the top of my neck. I take the time to appreciate the ebb and flow of the curve of her waist. Our tongues frenzy and I spin, trapping her between the door and me.

Tongues delve deeper, fueling desire. My mouth goes to her ear and I lick the outer shell, then whisper, "I want you, Reese."

"I want you, so much."

She closes her eyes and softens against me. I kiss her neck and work my way to the side causing her to moan. The warm kisses are replaced by cool air and goose bumps cover her arms. As a shiver runs the course of her body, she squirms, and lifts just enough to capture my lips with hers.

In one swift move, she's lifted, her legs wrapping around my middle. Our kisses deepen as I walk in and to the side of the bed while she tugs my shirt off. Setting her down, I stand there a moment, watching her as she scoots to the middle. When she looks back at me, she asks, "Are you joining me?"

It's the best invitation I've had in years. It's also the only one I've wanted even longer. "Absolutely."

She eyes me and says, "You're known for your six pack, but clearly I see eight. Good Lord, that's hot. Come here and let me lick you."

I laugh as I toe my shoes off in a hurry. She slips her shirt over her head and tosses it carelessly to the end of the bed. I take down my pants and slip off my socks. She's seen me a million times in my underwear at this stage, so we forgo the foreplay of undressing and just get naked.

"Good gracious," she exclaims, looking at what I'm packing. "My memory failed me in this area."

My cock definitely likes the attention, and I harden even more. "Mine didn't, but you've gotten even sexier if that's possible." Her nipples—pink and pert for me.

Just as I'm about to climb onto the bed, she asks, "Do you have protection?"

I nod, a little too eagerly, so I try to seem less like a geek getting laid for the first time and more like the magazine referred to me—Sexiest Man Alive. I shrug for added good measure. "I've got two condoms."

"Only two?"

Now that makes me smirk. I give her the full thing, no holds barred. She sighs happily and lies back. I grab the condoms and get on the bed. We were frenzied before, but now, now I want to take my time with her, getting reacquainted with her fully.

I lean down and kiss her stomach while kneading her breasts. Lifting, I move up her body and kiss her breasts, appreciating each one with my tongue. Her fingers weave into my hair and she tightens, the hair tugging on my scalp, and urging me on. I look up and she says, "Up here."

"As you command." I make sure to slide my body against her as I move up until I'm positioned above her. "God, you're beautiful."

Her eyes close, the compliment seeming too much as I grind between her legs. My erection is slick and I'm so close to thrusting into her that I struggle to stop, but I do. Lowering, I kiss her quickly and roll to the side to put a condom on before returning to the same position. This time I press against where I really want to be. She takes my face between her hands, and says, "I've missed you."

That does me in completely. This is how I want those three words uttered, her gorgeous eyes on me, looking into mine. I close my eyes and push all the way in. I stop, my breath caught somewhere in my heart.

Seconds tick, as we lie bonded together once again. Her hands are on my face, cradled in her warmth. When I open my eyes, she reminds me to, "Breathe." She always took my breath away and with the reminder I push in, her breath pushed out in the sexiest fucking chant that was ever uttered, "Danny. Danny. Danny."

I kiss her because I can't resist her dark pink lips, and when her mouth opens, the gesture makes me crave more. So I pull out and push in. "This. Feels so good."

"So good."

Resting on my forearms, I kiss her again, and again. I kiss her until my kisses are the only ones she'll remember. We make love and when she pushes against me, I roll onto my back and let her take charge. With her hands pressed against my chest, her body rocking on top of me, and her hair loose, I try to memorize everything—every feeling, every sensation and breath that escapes her. "I've missed you, Reese," I say, touching her body freely, something I've wanted to do since we reunited.

Her nails start to dig in, her head falling back, but her fingers lift suddenly and she grabs my wrists for something to hold on to as she falls into bliss. Her body hugging mine, heat flooding around me, and the sound of her falling apart drags my own orgasm out of me. I grab her hips, keeping her in place as we ride them out.

She lies down next to me, facing me, staring into my eyes as I do the same to her. It hits me. These are the eyes I should have been staring into for the last ten years. Although I'm sure she's just tired, when she looks down, my heart begins to ache. "Reese."

She looks back up and I see passion and desire, but I also see warmth and comfort. I see the home I should have had. I look away briefly, her loving gaze making me want to tell her all the things I'm feeling. I get up and dispose of the condom.

She speaks just as I come out of the bathroom, "We can't tell anyone."

"For now."

"Maybe forever." She rolls to her back and stares at the ceiling and I don't like the loss. "This was a one-time thing. It would cause a lot of problems and I would lose my job."

I climb in bed and face her again. "Look at me."

She glances.

"No, Reese. *Look*. At me."

When she rolls back to face me, she does as I asked.

"We can pretend this never happened. We can pretend we're strangers with no past. We can pretend we don't mean anything to each other to the rest of the world. But when we're alone, I'm not going to pretend I don't care about you. I can't pretend I don't have feelings for you, or have real feelings based on a history that was never resolved. I won't." I *can't*.

Her eyes fall closed and she moves closer, then rolls over so I can hold her. I do. I always will. I pull her snug against me and close my eyes too, liking the time we do have, and not wanting to worry about what we don't.

She whispers, "Okay. I won't."

I smile but it's hidden in the back of her hair. We have tonight, and for now, that's enough. I'm content to find a lustful escape into a peaceful slumber as a warm, pliable body molds to mine and the hour closes in on one a.m.

CHAPTER 19

THE PHOTOGRAPHER GOES to the large umbrella to change out his lens. The crew arrived late the night before. The photographer, Bryker, flew in with the team hired out of LA, including Becs handling wardrobe, a makeup artist, and an assistant.

Claudia is escorted back to the makeshift makeup and wardrobe setup on the side of the building that's shadowed around the corner. I go to stand under another large umbrella where Vinnie is seated in a director's chair.

Without looking at me, he says, "The photos are amazing. How are you feeling?"

"They feel right, a good vibe, sexy, all that you said you wanted."

Reese comes from around the corner, pulling a wheeled cooler behind her.

"I saw how much chemistry you two have together." I'm thinking he's not talking about the photo shoot anymore. "When you were dancing, fireworks."

Bingo. "The explosive kind," I reply. "Every time I remind her how good we were, she reminds me why we weren't."

"Then keep trying."

"You're a hopeless romantic, Vinnie. It's not gonna happen. She's too determined to play by the rules while I'm willing to break them."

"Again, I shouldn't tell you this, but it's something I've witnessed, not something she's told me, so I feel I can share it." He leans closer and whispers, "When I see her with her ex, she doesn't react to him like she does you. I struggle to see the attraction that ever existed between them."

"How have you seen them together if they're broken up?"

"He's her boss. We've had dinner together and he was there for her pitch meetings."

I glance over at her kind of surprised she would date her boss. "Huh? Interesting."

"That's just it. They aren't interesting at all. There's nothing— no spark, no fire, *no fireworks* between them. Not like with you."

"We've got the convenience of ten years dulling the edges of our break up."

"Why *did* you break up, Danny?"

"Good question. When you find out, let me know." I walk away to get a bottle of water before we continue with the next set because the desert is damn hot. This might be the first time I've been thankful for modeling swimsuits and underwear. Standing next to the cooler, I down half the bottle in one go. "Thanks for bringing these."

Reese grabs a bottle for herself. "It's hot."

"Thanks. That's why we're paid the big bucks."

She laughs. "I meant the weather, but it applies for the photo shoot too."

Chuckling, I add, "My bad."

"No. You guys are anything but bad. You look great together in your model perfection."

When she sits on top of the cooler, I move around to block the sun for her. "You underestimate the power of connection. It runs deeper than skin surface."

"You two have it all. The connection, the chemistry, the look—it's all working today. These photos will be amazing."

Kneeling down in front of her, her gaze follows me. "You say that, but you've not modeled."

She snorts in amusement, and I have to say, I find that noise pretty damn adorable. Nodding toward the chair that was just moved off set to the side, I say, "C'mere. Come with me."

I like that she doesn't question what I'm up to or why, she just follows. She trusts me. Smiling, I sit in the chair and pat my right leg. "Sit down."

"What?" She looks over her shoulder to see if anyone's watching us. No one is.

When she turns back, I say, "I want you to straddle me, Reese."

"I can't do that," she says incredulously. "How would that look?"

"Are you asking how I feel? Or how it will look to others? Because honestly, I don't give a fuck how it looks to others, and I can't imagine a better view than you on top of me again."

A sly smile begins, the right, then the left of her lips sliding up. When I see her blush, I've gotten just the reaction I was looking for. Even better, she lifts her dress up on the sides and slips onto my lap, my middle between her legs, my cock at the apex of her thighs. Her hands find my shoulders and I take hold of her hips. "Close your eyes."

She does, the smile drifting away.

I move between her legs so she can feel how hard she makes me. "You feel that?"

She nods.

"*She* was topless on top of me, wearing the smallest of panties." Her eyes open as I finish. "And I never got turned on, not once with her." The grin from last night, the one drunk on lust appears on her pretty face. The minutest of moves on her part causes my eyes to momentarily close from that same lust-filled sensation. "You affect me like no other." I slip my hand down over the bunched material of her dress and then under it, skipping right to the good part.

She's wet.

Through her panties.

For me.

Over Reese's shoulder, I see the photographer testing the light. He looks our way, but pays no attention and moves on. Nimbly, two of my fingers bypass the lace edging and slip under the silk. She was never one for cheap lingerie—another checkmark in the pro column.

Her skin is soft. I rub and her mouth drops open as she struggles to keep her eyes open. "We can't do this, Danny."

"We're already doing it and no one is watching."

Her lids flutter down when I slide into her slickness.

"I want to kiss you."

"This isn't about kissing. It's about connection and showing you the difference." I move inside her, slowly. "How do you feel?"

Her hand moves down over her breasts and lower, until it's on top of mine, the one making love to her. "I ache." She takes my free hand, flattening my palm on her, and drags it over her stomach and up to her chest. "And in here."

With her heart beating beneath my palm and her body on the verge of pulsing, our gazes meet. "That ache you feel is for me, baby. *Only me.* Like I ache for you. *Only you.*"

"Damn you, Danny Weston." Her eyes close, her back arching, her body tremors, her head falling back.

Like she wanted minutes before, I want now. I want to kiss her little moans away. I want to lick her neck like I did last night. I want to make love to her. I want to fuck her. I want everything with her. I want forever. Not just stolen moments.

Her chest is rising and falling, each breath inhaled deep into her chest, and slowly exhaled. She looks at me. Her thunder, the fight, the opinion of the others that she worries so much about— it's all gone, replaced by a relaxed satisfaction. Running her hands over my shoulders, she lets them rest on either side of my neck, the gesture probably more loving, more gentle than she's aware of.

Bryker ducks under his tent. The tension that's now missing from her body has leached into mine. I move my hand out from under her skirt and pull it down. "We should go back."

"Okay." She stands up, her body unsteady at first. I hold her by the elbow and she leans against me. "You make me do very bad things, Danny."

While trying not to alarm her, I realize what we just shared was reckless. Everything in my gut tells me I shouldn't have put her in that position, literally and figuratively. She's wanting to talk, to touch as much as we can without being noticed. What she doesn't realize is that we've been noticed.

Not only noticed, but most likely stalked by a long-lens camera.

As she adjusts her skirt, I look down at what I felt when I was under her. *She's marked me.* In any other circumstance, I'd wear her passion on my underwear as a badge of fucking honor... underneath my pants. But when said underwear is the star of the photo shoot, I need to get a new pair. "C'mon. I need to change." I rearrange my hard-as-fuck dick, then take her by the elbow to hopefully block anyone from seeing the damage we've done.

Looking down, she giggles. I roll my eyes. "Yeah. Yeah. Laugh it up, baby. Laugh it up."

I catch her eyes on me. The first time I called her baby on purpose. That last time it slipped, flowing naturally. She doesn't say anything, but as her fingertips drag over the top of the weeds, I see her smile—one not meant for me, but for her. Her happiness blankets me like the sunshine. I look away, leaving her with her inner peace.

We wordlessly part, going our separate ways. Claudia is sipping a diet cola through a straw while having her makeup touched up. I try to hide the "mess" and slip past to a rack of clothes. "Becs?" I whisper from behind her as she hangs a freshly-steamed collared shirt.

She turns. "Where have you been? We need to get you ready." She doesn't even give me a chance to speak before grabbing the shirt and a new pair of boxer briefs from on top of her sewing kit. "Here. Change."

When she gets a real look at me, one eyebrow rises in surprise and she turns around. "I hope you're not keeping that weapon loaded for me. Did I mention I started dating a craft service chef who works for Warner Brothers?"

Turning away from her, I laugh and swap out the underwear. "You didn't mention that, but good to know, and about time."

"About time on the boyfriend or that he's a craft service chef?" she teases.

"Haha."

I look for a place to throw away the underwear I was wearing with Reese, though I'm slightly, and sickly, tempted to hold on to them. Then I wise up. If they were hers, that would be a different story. When I don't find a place to dispose of them, I start to stash them in one of the sneakers I wore here to deal with later.

Becs asks, "What are you doing?" She reaches down and snatches the underwear before I can stop her. She's now waving them around dramatically. "You know I have to log these in for expenses, then I can trash them. Now get going. I know they're waiting for you guys."

Turning, I want to escape before she notices anything... you know, different about them compared to when I got them an hour ago.

"Danny?"

With my back to her, I reply, "Yes?"

"Next time, kiss her."

Glancing back, I nod. Her cat-that-ate-the-canary smile evokes my own. "Okay."

She doesn't torture me. That's not her style. She just gets back to work straightening the clothes rack, and as always, covertly covering my back—not just with clothes.

I round the corner and find Reese sitting next to Vinnie under the far umbrella. She has a cold bottle of water pressed to her cheek. I chuckle. She's not the only one heated, and although it's hot under this Texas sun, that's bearable compared to what I feel for her right now.

I'm going to take Becs's advice and kiss that woman as soon as I get the opportunity.

Bryker meets me on the next set—a bed with crumpled sheets. Bryker points to the mattress, and directs, "I want her sitting here and you standing facing her. I want her eyelevel with your abs. She's going to be tugging the briefs down. I want you looking into her eyes. Work it from there. Do what you would do naturally. Start in that position, then move onto the bed from there."

"All right."

Glimpsing Reese out of the corner of my eye, she gets up, standing in front of Vinnie, putting her back to me. When I look over there, they're talking, but I can't hear what they're saying, but it looks serious. Claudia joins Bryker and me just as Reese disappears around the building. When my eyes meet Vinnie's, he's not smiling. He's not upset either. He's too damn hard to read, so I try to focus on my job instead of worrying about what's going on with Reese. I need to do my job.

It's show time.

We get in the instructed position. Claudia has a black bra and matching panties. After checking that Bryker is ready, she runs her hands over my abs. The shirt is unbuttoned and a subtle breeze blows the ends. I keep my eyes on her though I'm tempted to look around for Reese to see if she's returned. I'm sensing she hasn't.

I try to clear my head and get into the photo shoot, but it's a struggle. The wrong hands are on me. The wrong eye color. The wrong lips are licked. All wrong. *Fuck!*

"You're tense," she says.

Taking a deep breath, I shake it off when I exhale. "I'm good. Let's do this."

Ten minutes feels like hours. I shift down just to mix it up. Bryker calls out, "Do what you were doing on the chair. That was sexy."

The mental freak out happening in my head eclipses my logical side and I'm about to ask him what he saw, but Claudia pulls on my shirt as she scoots on the bed, and says, "I was sitting like this and you were leaning over me."

Ohhhh! That.

I position my hand over her shoulder mimicking the earlier shoot. But Bryker says, "Not what you did with Claudia."

If a record had been playing, this would be the part when the needle skids across the album and the room goes silent. But there isn't a record playing, not even a CD to set the mood. So I'm stuck between the confusion on Claudia's face and the hope on Bryker's face.

He adds, "What's the hold up? We're losing daylight."

Claudia says my name. My glare shifts from the mattress to her. "What?"

"What's wrong?"

What's wrong? I push off the bed, narrowly missing Claudia in my rush to Bryker. Standing a good six to eight inches taller than him, I can't be face to face so I tilt my head to the side and look him straight in the eyes. "What do you think you saw?"

"I saw what you wanted me to see." He doesn't back down, even though I've made it fucking clear he should.

"It's not what you think, so forget you ever saw anything."

"It looked intense."

"I was showing her how to model."

He smiles out the side of his mouth. It's distorted, untrustworthy. "Okay," he placates.

Unfortunately, I'm not left with a lot of choice here. I can't risk the campaign and we're losing the light. "Okay," I repeat, mine more threatening than his convincing.

I'm returning to the bed as he says, "Sure, Danny. Whatever you say."

I lock eyes on his. "I don't care what you *think* you saw. You didn't. Now drop it before I walk."

"And here I thought you were invincible. The ultimate male model playboy, but it seems you have an Achilles heel like the rest of us. Ours just don't go by the same name."

"For your sake, you better hope I don't find yours." He's smart enough not to further the discussion, so I return to the bed.

Claudia doesn't look shocked or surprised by the scene, but expressions aren't her strong suit when modeling. She was just gifted with a pretty face and knows her angles.

Vinnie is standing nearby watching this go down, so I need to get the shots he's paying me for. Redirecting my attention to Claudia, we get down to business.

CHAPTER 20

Reese
Ten Years Earlier

HE LIED. DANNY lied to me. As I stare at the proof in my hands, I look up and stare out the library window. Why would he lie about something so easily found out? What are his motives? What are his thoughts? I have no idea what he's thinking anymore. We have been out of sync for a while, but what I thought was a temporary speed bump in our relationship might be turning into a dead end.

I tuck the magazine into the back of my notebook and slam it closed. He should be getting back any minute and I promised I would meet him at his apartment, so I pack up my stuff and take off across campus.

When I walk in, I hear the shower. I drop my bag by the door and head toward the sound of running water. The door to the bathroom is open, but I knock anyway not wanting to startle him.

Pushing the curtain to the side, he peeks out. "Hi."

My heart flutters from his smile as if I'd forgotten how attractive he is. He's gorgeous and I lean against the door as my knees weaken. "Hi."

The curtain opens wider and he invites me in, "Join me."

I'm tempted, but when I look in his eyes, I wonder what lies he'll tell me this time. Pushing off the door, I step back. "I'll wait for you out here." I leave, not wanting him to try and convince me because I will. I'll go to him, as I've missed him so much.

I get a glass of water and wait on the couch. The shower stops and I listen intently as he steps out. Rounding the corner, he stops and looks confused. "Why are you out here?"

With my glass held between both my hands over my lap, I say, "I wanted to give you some privacy."

Chuckling, he says, "I don't need privacy from you. I want the opposite. Remember, what's mine is yours."

"How did the shoot go?"

"Italy was incredible. I can't wait to take you one day. There was this little bar we would hang out at until it closed at three a.m. That bar is hundreds of years old. It was really ama—"

I stand and set my water down on the coffee table, forgetting to use a coaster. Taking the magazine out of my notebook and bag, I walk over and hand it to him. I return to the couch, this time, hugging a pillow to my chest and watching him as he studies the magazine. "You saw the ad?"

"I did."

He tosses it to the coffee table almost hitting the glass. He tightens the towel around him, frustrated, "I should get dressed."

"Probably."

I hold his gaze until he turns with a heavy exhale and goes to his bedroom. I'm not kept waiting long. He reappears minutes later, walking around the corner rubbing his hair with the towel. He tosses it into the bathroom then returns to sit in the chair near me. "You obviously have something on your mind. Should we talk about it?"

"I'm not sure I can talk. I'm mad, but more than that, I'm hurt."

"I'm sorry."

"For what, Danny?"

"Whatever will make this better."

There's something insanely sweet about his sentiment and I understand his desire because I feel the same. This can't be solved that simply. "You lied to me."

"I lied," he says, jumping at the chance to make this go away. "I'm sorry."

"I just wish it was that easy, that straightforward. But it's not. I'm now left wondering what else you've lied to me about."

"Nothing. I swear to you."

"You're saying you've only lied to me that one time?"

"I kissed her. I was new and thought it would be a one-time thing."

"It won't be?"

"No, Reese. It won't."

I wanted him to tell me the truth, but it stings. My mind wanders to what's really happening when he's gone. "Did you kiss someone in Italy?"

"I did," he replies instantly, not even attempting to ease my mind. "And I will again. But I can tell you it's for work, nothing more. I've never kissed anyone off camera other than you since the day we met."

His honesty incites traitorous tears that prick the corners of my eyes. As they fall down my cheeks, he moves closer, sitting on the edge of the coffee table, his knees trapping mine. The spot is cramped, but there's nowhere I'd rather be than right here with him. "I can fight you on this."

"You won't."

"How do you know?"

"Because I know you and you know I'm telling the truth." Picking up the magazine, he holds it between us. "These are photos, professional photos to convince people we're a couple to sell a product. *This* will never be *us*. These photos portray an illusion." He drops the magazine and takes my hands in his. "We're real, Reese. *Real*. They can't touch what we have. They can't manufacture what I feel for you."

My heart is torn between wanting to believe him and what seeing those photos did to my trust. I love him. It's that simple. Leaning my forehead on his shoulder, his hand rubs down my back.

Kissing my head, he adds, "I love you. I need you to believe in what we have."

"Do you?" I whisper.

"More than anything else in my life. I have you. I have someone worth coming home to."

"I'm not sure I'm strong enough to deal with this."

"You are," his voice dropping down. "You're stronger than you realize."

Lifting my head, my gaze follows and lands on his. "I'm strong when we're together. When we're apart, I don't know what to believe."

"Believe in me."

I TAKE THE stairs by two, sprinting down the hall. Knocking, I say, "Reese, open up. It's me."

I knock again.

"Come in."

When I open it, she's standing in a room full of sunshine but with what looks like heartache on her face. I push the door closed as I close the distance between us. Despite her hands starting to come up, I kiss her before the words can be said. Before regrets are spoken. Before history repeats itself.

I kiss her until faith is restored.

I kiss her until she remembers how good we can be.

I kiss her until she believes in me...

Again.

Suddenly things change and she's now kissing me.

Restoring my faith.

Reminding me how good we are together.

Believing in me.

Again.

Her hands are on my shoulders, and she's stretching to kiss me. I bend and lift her into my arms. Her legs wrap around me and I move her to the bed, slowly lowering her onto her back while staying right where I want to be.

The dress she's wearing gives me access to run my hands down her outer thigh while I press my erection against her. She squirms and maneuvers around, settling on top of me. She's breathing hard, her hair is a mess, and her lips are red from uninhibited kisses. Her palms hold me down when all I want to do is drag her under me and kiss her again.

The smile that shines through the sunlight flooding the room is one free of deep concern. It's the lightest one I've seen since... just since. She asks, "What are we doing? We said one time."

Grabbing her by the hips, I move up, letting her settle back down, as I come up face to face. "We're not the one time kind of love, baby."

She kisses me, then runs her fingertip over my lips. "What kind of love are we?"

"We're the insatiable kind, the kind that stays long after the other is gone, the type you can deny, but you can never stop feeling. Not ever."

Wrapping her arms around me, she hugs me and I hold her just as tight while sitting all the way up.

With lips to my ear, she whispers, "Make love to me."

"I don't have to make. We already feel it."

"You love me?"

"I never stopped."

Tears fill her eyes and her hands touch my face. Her breath is but a feather-light whisper against my lips when she says, "You silly, foolish man." Her lips meet mine and our tongues engage, a slow dance beginning. Our bodies slide together until I'm on my back again. She slips off the bed. With the light haloing her body, she takes her clothes off.

The evening is lazy, like we have our whole lives to spend in this bed. We both know better, but it feels good to pretend. Just for a little while.

The rest of the world fades away. Our bodies each other's.

No beginning.

No end.

Only one.

Us together.

Reese rests on top of me. Naked. Baring her soul without even realizing it. She sleeps in such peace. I rub the back of her head, wanting her to feel that peace for as long as she can. I'll take the burden that we face when she wakes up and carry it for both of us.

Through the windows—gray, coral, and yellow have replaced the bright blue. While the sun sets outside, I try my damnedest to set my feelings for this woman aside. She said it's only a one-time thing. Although I can argue we broke her rule the second time we had sex. By the third, I rest my case.

We'll leave Marfa in the morning, return to our respective coasts, and right back into our regularly scheduled lives. Apart. As if the last few days don't matter. As if what happened between us never existed. This is what she wants, what she needs from me. I have to be strong. I can't let these few days get in my head and twist my reality.

I close my eyes, still my hands, and try to find some of that peace Reese has found.

LAUGHTER FROM DOWN the hall infiltrates the room where darkness has conquered. A streetlight in the distance, on the other side of the glass, teases us with shadows. My chest feels empty—inside and out, knowing this is it.

Despite wanting to remain in the darkness, in an ignorance of bliss, I open my eyes. Turning my head, Reese lies next to me, her eyes open, a wet line on her cheek streaking to the pillow. I roll to the side and wipe it away. Leaning forward, I kiss her where it was, as if that could clear the pain as easily as it was for me to wipe it away.

I do what I hate doing, but have to. I lie. "It's going to be okay."

In my eyes, she sees beyond the lie. With her hand resting over my heart, she feels the truth. But she doesn't say anything. She just nods and closes her eyes. Her cheek replaces her hand and I wrap my arm around her.

I WAKE UP with the sun, but the light gives me no warmth.

Running my hand over her side of the bed, the sheets are cold. I'm alone. Silence fills the small space where she once filled it with her beauty, where we once filled it with our love. No evidence of her remains.

She's gone.

Images flash through my mind causing my head to pound. Kissing Reese. Making love to her. The intensity of her eyes on me as I moved in and out of her. Her tear-streaked face. The look in her eyes when we knew our time was up.

Sitting up, I rub my eyes and yawn. I get dressed and go back to my room. When I open the door, there's a note on the floor. I pick it up and sit on the corner of the bed to read it.

Danny,
You always were a good liar.

I laugh, some of the weight looming over my shoulders lifts, and I continue to read.

We may never have New York or
Paris, but we'll always have Marfa.
See you around,
Reese

Holding the note in hand, I fold it closed while staring at the wall. Yes, we'll always have Marfa, but I want more.

Three hours later, I'm sitting on a plane in El Paso, waiting to take off. Becs is next to me reading a magazine. I have my phone on the tray in front of me, my headphones plugged into them. She says, "You should call her, or at least text her."

"What you do know about 'her' when it comes to me?" I ask, a small grin tugging on my lips.

"I have eyes. We all do."

"I might have screwed up."

"With her?" she asks, seeming surprised.

"No. By opening that wound. Um, I mean door."

"Wound. Door. You've got my attention. Which is it? Wound or door?"

"Door," I say, trying to convince her of the story Reese and I concocted back in LA on that first trip.

She shifts, angling toward me, so I try to stop this interrogation before it begins. "Nothing's going on, Becs. Just forget about it."

"From the way Ms. Carmichael looked this morning, she won't be forgetting about it anytime soon." She picks her magazine back up, thumbing through it as if what she just said is meaningless when it means everything.

"You saw her?"

"I did. Bryker, Vittori, and Reese were checking out and heading to the airport together."

She stops, so I encourage, "Go on."

"I was drinking my coffee in the sitting room off the lobby. I had a clear view of them. She was laughing, carefree. I might venture to say happy. She looked relaxed considering the hour. Maybe this was a mini vacation for her. You know what a rat race Manhattan is."

Becs reads me too well. "Or maybe a certain hot male model spent the night making her forget about that rat race."

I turn back to staring at my phone on the tray.

Her elbow nudges me on the armrest. When I look at her, she says, "I won't tell anyone, Danny. I can't be bought and I don't sell out my friends. I consider you a friend. I hope you know that."

Real friends are hard to come by. In this business someone's always looking for how to use you in one way or another to further his or her career. So when I give my trust, it's because the person has proven trustworthy on more than one occasion. Becs has never used me or been anything but honest with me. "Thank you. I consider you a friend as well."

She giggles and says, "Now that we're established friends, she was glowing. Noticeably different in the way she moved with such ease and laughed so lightly." Listening to her describing Reese, I imagine her in my head, and hope I made her feel that way. "Vittori even commented on the difference."

"What did he say?"

"I didn't hear the first part, but when Bryker left for the car, Vittori told her she looked, and I quote, 'happy.' And then he added, 'and freshly fucked,' end quote."

I don't say anything, but my grin grows.

She adds, "Our secret, but if I had to give a description to the police, I might use those same three words for her." She laughs quietly and opens the magazine back to the page where she left off, not expecting me to confirm or deny. Becs leaves me sitting there in the knowledge that Reese left feeling much like I feel now. With no regrets.

CHAPTER 21

MY PHONE RINGS and I answer while walking onto my patio. "Hello?"

"Are you still scouting or do you want the week off before you head to New York?" Mark often forgets the basics in human interaction.

"Yes, my trip went great. The client is pleased with the photos and I still have the next gig in New York lined up. Thank you for asking."

He chuckles. "I have a shit ton of work to do. Sorry about that. I heard from the ad agency. As you know, they are happy. Which makes Vittori happy, and in turn, makes me happy. Now about the other job. I have two offers to work with you. I know you put location scouting aside to focus on modeling when work picked back up, but we haven't talked about your return to it or photography job offers. Do you want to stop by the office and go over the offers?"

"Are they worth considering?"

"I think so."

"How about lunch on you?"

"Deal. Let Jody know time and place."

"Got it."

After showering and getting ready for the day, I head downtown. I stop in a shop down on Melrose. They're holding a suit for me. It was sent by Vittori that I'm supposed to wear to a benefit tonight. I try it on for fit. It's been tailored to a T. I might have to take this with me to New York.

In the car, driving to the restaurant, Luke calls. I answer, "What up?"

"What do you have going on tonight?"

"A charity event."

"Got a date?"

"Why? You offering?"

"Fuck no. I'm meeting some girls at a club tonight. I need a wingman."

"It's funny how I'm paid millions and am the current Sexiest Man on the Planet title holder and *I'm* the wingman."

"Some need more help than others."

I joke, "I'm thinking about getting that title engraved on my tombstone."

"You're so full of yourself. You need to come spend time with the little people and gain some perspective back."

"Sounds like a solid plan. I'm game."

"Two girls. Are you looking?"

"Not really."

"I take it all went well with Reese?"

"I plead the fifth."

"No pleading shit with your best friend. You two hooked up?"

I don't bother answering. He carries on anyway. "So you're up for tonight, say eleven?"

"I can meet earlier. The event starts at six. I'll be done by nine."

"Meet me at Hud's at nine thirty."

"Later, dude."

The valet takes my car as soon as I park at the restaurant. Walking in, I see Mark and Jods at a table by the far window. I lean down and kiss Jods on the cheek. "Always lovely to see you."

"You too."

I reach over and shake hands with Mark. "Not lovely to see me?" he jokes.

"Ravishing," I say, sitting down.

We place our orders before we dive into business. Jods hands me a file while Mark starts going over each offer, listing the pros and cons of continuing to scout. "You're a name now, Danny. This is just a bonus. So if you don't love doing this, spend your time more wisely and focus on the modeling."

I read over the offers, mainly the dollar figures. "They're good money."

"They're good money for people who aren't named Danny Weston. You make ten times that in a day."

"I'm not attached to location scouting. It was just a way to branch out a few years ago. The photography I enjoy and I'm good at. I know how to get the best from models, but I think right now it's more a hobby than something I want to focus on for money." I close the file. "I say no to all three."

"I'll let them know. I think this is wise for your career right now. You're at the top of your game and from here, it's the stratosphere."

"Top of my game makes me think I can only go downhill from here."

"No, that's not what it means. It means we choose our next steps carefully. How are you feeling about acting?"

Shaking my head, I instantly reply, "Not that keen."

"As I mentioned in my office, you don't have to audition for some of the roles. Easy gigs."

"I don't need easy gigs. I'm working a lot as it is."

"What about the future?"

"We can talk then. Right now, I'm not feeling it."

Mark smiles. "Good. I think that's wise. As for Vittori. How's that going?"

"Well. I leave in two days for New York, then we're off to Paris two days after that."

"So you sure you want to eat that burger?"

Tilting my head, I'm annoyed and hope me giving him the evil eye gets the job done.

He blows me off. "Do you have to take your shirt off? Jody?"

Looking through her binder, she runs a finger down her meticulous notes. Stopping three-fourths of the page down, she taps it. "You might," she says, looking up sympathetically. "There's a clause that says you might. It's better to err on the safe side."

With the best timing ever, my burger is delivered. This calls for another evil glare in Mark's direction. I push the plate away, and before the waitress leaves, I ask, "Can I get the burger to go and order grilled chicken lightly seasoned with a side of in-season veggies sautéed in light canola or vegetable oil, no butter?"

She smiles, picking up the burger. "Of course. I'll put that order in now."

Jody is about to dig into her salad, but looks like she feels bad. "Sorry."

Mark says, "I'm not. This burger is damn good. You hitting the gym after lunch?"

"I guess I have to. I have a benefit to attend tonight."

"Ah yes. Make us proud," he adds, wiping his mouth.

I respond silently with my middle finger expressing how I feel about watching him eat what I'm craving. He's lucky I like him so much, and he gets me the good gigs or I'd walk out on his ass right now.

Damn lucky.

"DANNY?"

"Over here."

"Look here. Look here!"

"Danny Weston?'

"Right here."

Angling left, I keep my smile minimal. That works best on the red carpet in photos. *Unaffected.* Even if I am, I pull it off like this is just another day in the life. I turn to face forward, tucking my hand in my pocket and raising my chin. This angle is always a good one in a well-fitted suit. Shows the lines down my body and highlights my height. With both hands in my pockets, I give the paparazzi to the right a new expression, a slight smirk and steely gaze before being directed to move to the next spot for photos.

The paps think they know what they want. They don't. I do. I give them what they don't even realize they need until I deliver it. And then they devour it—eating out of my hand.

I stop on the X marked out on the carpet and repeat the last stop.

Once I'm inside I head straight for the bar. "Bourbon on the rocks."

The drink is set down and I leave a tip. "Thanks." Turning to face the room, it's filling up. I see a few familiar faces but no one who inspires me to cross the room. I'm fucking starving, but don't see anything on the buffet I can eat before this photo shoot. My mind wanders while staring out one of the large windows. I should take a jog in the morning. I can't drink too much tonight. I need sleep, but I definitely need at least one to take the edge off.

Since leaving Marfa, I've been off my game. I've wanted to text Reese a thousand times, but I'm starting to think she wants the time apart to figure out what's happening in her life *and* with us.

Chuckling to myself, I find it funny that I assume I have this all figured out. All I know is that Reese Carmichael has made me reconsider my dating habits. I also don't want to eat crow with Luke. I've told him to go after the girl, so I can't sit idly by and let her walk away again. But I'm more confused than ever. Despite what Becs said about Reese's mood after spending the night with me, I'm reminded of her closing sentiments.

We may never have New York or Paris, but we'll always have Marfa.

"Hello."

I follow the melodic voice and look beside me. A woman, beautiful blonde with her hair up—classically styled, black dress, not too revealing and pretty. Hazel eyes lit up by the bright day before us, and a confidence that comes with a comfort in herself. I'm guessing she's in her late twenties, but you never know in this town the way Botox flows like champagne. "Hello," I greet her. "I'm Danny Wes—"

"Weston." She glances down embarrassed. "Please don't consider me a stalker. Oh, maybe I am." She laughs. "I was hoping to meet you tonight."

Turning toward the attractive woman, I ask amused, "Were you now?"

She whispers, "My father is a philanthropist. This cause is personal for him, so he wanted it to be perfect, and of course raise a lot of money."

"I left a donation check at the door."

"Oh his behalf, I thank you. I must confess that I requested the invitation be sent to you."

I'm intrigued. "And why is that?"

"I can't imagine my reasons are much different from any other admirer."

"You're an admirer?"

"I feel silly admitting this to you. I'm a not-so-secret admirer, I suppose, since I've outed myself."

"So my not-so-secret admirer knows me and my name, and yet, I know nothing about you other than you have great taste in men." I chuckle. She laughs, then sips her champagne.

She offers her hand and I take it. "I'm Anna Collins."

"Very nice to meet you, Anna Collins." No ring. Eyes on mine. "For a stalker, I don't think you're living up to the reputation."

"How's that?"

"You're much too restrained." I tease, "I don't think you even swooned since meeting me."

That makes her laugh again. "Well, maybe I'm not a stalker after all, but it is very nice to meet you." She finishes her drink. "And I've been swooning on the inside."

"If I wasn't enjoying your company so much, I might be offended by your lies."

"No lie, but it does take a lot to make me swoon."

"Well, I'm here if you need smelling salts."

"Ahh, you make the ladies swoon and then help revive them. You're quite the man, Mr. Weston, but I guess I knew that already. What I didn't expect is how charming you'd be."

Smiling, I say, "I think I might be undeserving of all the compliments."

"I read how active you are with different charities, and I was impressed. You're handsome and generous with your time *and* money. I never get star-struck, but you seemed to do it to me."

"My apologies," I retort playfully. I take another sip of my bourbon. "So you invited me just to meet me?"

"No, but selfishly I benefit. As does the charity."

I lean against a column, my attention on her instead of the view outside. "I'm happy to be of service, Ms. Collins."

Taking a step back, she seems to blush under my gaze. "I've taken too much of your time with my ramblings over a small infatuation. I should go and mingle." Her hand waves toward the room behind her. "It's been a pleasure, Mr. Weston, to meet you."

"The pleasure is all mine, Ms. Collins."

Looking back out the window, I finish my drink. A tap on the shoulder gets my attention. I smile when I see her.

Anna says, "Sorry for bothering you again, but I was wondering if you were seeing anyone?"

An eyebrow is raised from her boldness, but I can't stop the smile. "If you want me to be honest, then I would have to say my current relationship status is complicated."

Exhaled disappointment is expressed. "Well, it was worth a try."

"I appreciate the interest," I say, and because I hate letting people down, I add, "If the situation was different—"

"It's fine. And thank you. Maybe another time things will be less... complicated."

"Maybe."

I watch her walk away this time, wondering if I'm making a mistake. I'm pretty confident the mistake I made was letting Reese get away ten years ago. I take my phone and decide to text her, consequences be damned.

Me: *I miss the way you smell.*

Shrugging, I make no apologies for the heavy-hitting message. Just as I'm tucking my phone away, it buzzes. Flipping the screen on, there's a message from Reese.

Reese: *You smelled me?*

Smiling, I type: *And more. I also miss the taste of you.*

Reese: *Danny…*

Me: *Reese…*

Reese: *We shouldn't do this.*

Me: *We should.*

Reese: *We can't.*

Me: *We can. Tell me what you miss about me.*

Staring down at my screen, I wait, but nothing comes. When the screen goes black, I sigh and go back to the bar for another drink. Right as I'm about to order, the screen lights up. Stepping off to the side, I turn my back to the crowd for privacy.

Reese: *I miss you tasting and smelling me. I miss the way you taste and smell. I miss the way your scent lingers on my skin and hate that when I showered it was gone. I miss so much I shouldn't.*

Me: *There is nothing wrong with the way you feel. I feel it too. This isn't wrong. We're not wrong.*

Reese: *I could lose my job.*

Me: *It wouldn't be a job worth having then.*

Reese: *Says the millionaire.*

Me: *I can't make you any promises when you won't believe in us.*

Reese: *Believing in us equates into risking my career. I can't give up everything I've worked for on the unknown.*

Me: *I'm not the unknown. You know me better than anyone. Like I know you better than anyone else.*

Reese: *You never lacked confidence.*

Me: *It's what attracted you to me in the first place.*

Reese: *Actually, that was your ass. You always did have a great ass, you sexy bastard.*

Chuckling, I'm reminded how good we were together. So good. I just need to keep reminding her.

Me: *Yours isn't so shabby itself.*

Reese: *I guess I have to settle for "isn't so shabby" compared to your great ass.*

Me: *You have a fantastic ass, but I don't want the compliment going to your head.*

Reese: *Good point. Your ego is big enough for the both of us.*

Me: *Truth be told, I could spend hours telling you how amazing your ass is, but I have a feeling you won't believe me.*

Reese: *I might have to take you up on those hours. Maybe when you're in NYC.*

I mentally fist-pump. *Score!*

Me: *I'm going to hold you to that.*

Reese: *I like being held by you. Almost as much as I like your ass.*

Me: *You always were an ass girl.*

Reese: *You're telling me.*

Ha!

Me: *It's a date.*

Reese: *Don't get ahead of yourself. I said hours.*

Me: *That's all I need.*

Reese: *So cocky.*

Me: *Speaking of...*

Reese: *On that note, see you Monday, Danny.*

Me: *I look forward to it.*

CHAPTER 22

HUD'S IS PACKED. Luke is sitting like the king of the castle in the corner. I sit down.

"How'd you score this table?"

"I dropped your name."

"Naturally. Where are your girls?"

"Bathroom."

"Ah. So who are they and what are we drinking?"

"Crystal and Yvette. Pharmaceutical reps in town for a convention."

"How'd you meet them and why don't I have a drink yet?"

"I've ordered already."

The waitress arrives with a tray of martinis. I shoot Luke a look and shake my head in disgust. "Okay, 007, you're obviously trying to impress these women. Hook me up with the details before they get back."

Luke hands the waitress his card to keep the tab open. When we're alone again, he leans over the edge of the table and says, "I need a date in a few weeks."

"What's in a few weeks? And since when did you have

trouble finding dates?"

"I appreciate the support."

"You're welcome," I say, rolling my eyes. "Get on with it."

"There's a wedding, a co-worker's. The thing is, my co-worker is marrying this jackass that's friends with Jane's loser boyfriend."

Sitting back, the picture is clear. "Ahhh, so you'll see Jane there, but you don't want to be dateless."

"I don't want to look like a loser."

"You're playing this all wrong, my friend."

He drinks half his martini, then sets it down, nervously messing with the napkin. "Tell me, old wise one."

"I don't appreciate the old cracks. And I'm only three years older than you."

"Fuck, Danny, get on with it. The girls will be back soon."

"If you walk into that wedding with some girl you just met, you're just proving once again that you aren't the commitment type. You're also sending a non-verbal message that you're fine without her. When, let's face it, you're a mess, even after all this time without her."

"Shit. So I should call off this whole operation?"

Nodding, I reply, "If you want Jane back. You need to end this. And what happened to Josie?"

"Janet. Eh, she wanted to get more serious than I did."

Everything about him shouts commitment-phobe tonight. "You sure you want Jane back?"

"I'm sure. Life is easier with her."

Now he's got me leaning forward, feeling the need to dig into this deeper. "Love is not about life being easier. Love is life being better during the hard times." He's staring at me. "I've said too much, right?"

"Oh, Dan Man. You're a goner."

Two women approach from the side and I think my jaw drops open. Oh, no.

"Hi," a redhead with big green eyes and a sprinkling of freckles across her nose. "You must be Danny?"

Standing up, I say, "I am. You are?"

"Crystal. And this is my friend Yvette."

Fuck! The other woman is gorgeous too. When she speaks, I hear a French accent. "You're French, Yvette?"

"Oui. I am."

"I've spent a lot of time there." I hold the chair out for her.

She sits and looks up at me. "I'd love to hear about it."

Luke helps Crystal and returns to his seat. Over drinks that I wouldn't drink for anyone other than these women, we talk about their jobs, France, and the convention they're attending. Crystal googles me. Everyone gets a good laugh, I'm thinking at my expense until Yvette's hand slides up my thigh under the table.

At another point in my life, in a time when Reese Carmichael had not re-entered my life—and I still wasn't thinking about the text conversation I had earlier—I'd let Yvette's hand run the course and find out what I'd have in store for her.

Instead, I cover her hand with mine, and trying not to embarrass her, I whisper, "You're beautiful, but I'm seeing someone."

Her hand pulls back like she's been burned. Most women don't care, I've discovered, when I say that. Yvette. She's different. She's humiliated, which is exactly opposite of how I wanted her to feel. "I'm sorry," I add as if that will take away the rejection.

"I'm sorry. I was not acting myself, but thought I was in LA and I should... it's stupid. I'm sorry."

"It's not stupid. And if this were a few weeks ago, I'd have a very different reaction. So please. No apologies."

She nods, not able to make eye contact. I stand, needing to get fresh air. "Please excuse me. I'll be back."

Luke excuses himself as well. When he catches up to me, I remind him, "We're not chicks, dude. We don't do the bathroom in groups."

"I need a cigarette."

"You don't smoke."

We walk out the back door to the patio. He asks, "Why did I stop again?"

"Because it's bad for your health." I lean against a wood wall, wishing he hadn't followed me out here. I'm irritated at him. And myself. "Dude, go back inside."

"Why did you leave?"

"Why did you fucking set me up?"

"What? Why are you mad?"

"I'm mad because you know how I feel about Reese, then dangle one of the hottest women I've ever seen in front of me like a fucking carrot and expect me not to bite."

The stress that resided in the lines across his forehead lighten and he laughs. "So that's what this is about? You're tempted? Let me ask you, Danny. What happened in Texas that has you so closed off to what seems like a sure thing—a beautiful and sexy sure thing to be exact?"

I nod, not willing to give away everything that easily.

Standing next to me, with his head against the wall, he doesn't seem so sure of his sure thing either. "I can't do it."

"By it, I take it you mean you can't do Crystal?"

"Yup."

"You understand Jane is still fucking the prick, right?"

"*Ouch!* Whose side are you on anyway?"

I push off the wall and face him. "Yours. I'm always on your fucking side, Luke, but this shit has gone on long enough. Go after her or don't, but make up your fucking mind and don't drag me into your attempt at getting revenge. I'm gonna tell you the truth here, brother. Jane's keeping you at an arm's length, not letting you closer, not cutting you loose. Just stuck in the middle. You're going to have to make the hard decision. Figure out what the hell you want and then go after it."

He stands up, looking me in the eyes. "I could say the same fucking thing to you, *brother*. The difference is Jane may be struggling to figure out what she wants, but I know what I want. That's a hell of lot more than what you're doing."

"I had sex with Reese. Twice in Texas. So don't come preaching to me that I'm not doing anything. But unlike your situation, our situation can cost her a job. Besides that, I've made myself clear on how I'm feeling for her, *to her*. And that's all that matters. Have you told Jane how you feel?"

He looks away.

"I didn't think so, so you have nothing on the line to lose. Take Crystal, Yvette, Janet, or whoever else you're fucking around with while waiting for Jane, parade them in front of her and see how she reacts." I hate fighting with him and I can tell he's torn up over it too. "I say this as your friend. Those girls in there are hot, but they're not Reese and they aren't Jane." I pat him on the shoulder. "Go home, my friend. Go home alone and figure this shit out. Give my goodbyes to the girls. I'm out of here."

"C'mon, Danny. Don't go."

I wave over my shoulder as I push through the gate to the parking lot. My Jeep is parked at the far side of the lot, but I don't hurry toward it. I need the air to think. My situation with Reese is fucked up because we fucked up a long time ago. He's right. I don't take my own advice much, but I've laid my heart on the line for her. Whether she picks it up remains to be seen.

I WALK INTO Illustrious to check in one last time before I head out of LA. My feet come to an abrupt halt when I see one of the last people I expect to see—my biggest competitor sitting across from *my* agent. Irritated, I detour to Jody's desk. "He's in a meeting with Sebastian Lassiter?"

Glancing over her shoulder, she nods. "Yeah, Mark's been trying to sweeten the pot to get him to come work with Illustrious."

"And here I thought the day was going pretty damn well."

She spins in her chair to face me and lowers her voice. "I know you don't like hi—"

"He's a rich kid who couldn't give a shit about modeling."

"He sure is raking in the jobs for someone who doesn't give a shit."

With my hand on her shoulder, I warn, "Don't be fooled by the good looks, they're only surface deep, like his sincerity."

"Good to know."

I stare at him through the glass. He stares right back, the cocky fucker. When he grins, I'm left perplexed on why his day rate is so high. "Maybe I'm bias, but he caused a lot of problems for one of my good friends."

Mess with Johnny Outlaw. He can take care of himself. Mess with Holli, and he's got Johnny *and* me to deal with. He's just lucky his ass got kicked when it did, or I would have been the one kicking it. And I would have broken more than his nose. The fucker. I cross my arms over my chest and face her. "Are you serious about him signing with Illustrious?"

"Yes. Mark found out that Sebastian recently left his agent. He switched up his whole team from his manager, agent, and PR. He claims he doesn't like the direction of his reputation in the media."

"Interesting." I glance back once more. He's still got that smarmy-ass smirk on his face. *Fucker's challenging me.* "Keep me in the loop."

"I will. Here's your itinerary. Have a good trip and check in when you get back."

"Take care, Jods." With Mark in with Lassiter, I've lost my desire to meet with him. I can't deal with Lassiter today, so it's best I leave now before I get even more riled up.

When I get home, I put on shorts and my running shoes and hit the pavement hard. One mile in, I'm soaked with sweat and still just as frustrated about everything. By the fifth mile I find a bench and sit, trying to recover from pushing myself. The problem is I can't outrun Reese in my head. I can block out almost everything, everything except for Reese. She's ingrained in my brain and I want to see her and finally have that talk.

I pull out my phone.

No more texts.

It's time to call her.

The phone rings once, twice, three times before it goes to voicemail.

"You've reached the voicemail of Reese Carmichael. Please leave your name and number after the beep. Thank you and have a great day."

Beeeeeep.

"Reese, it's me, Danny. If you get a chance, call me back. Thanks." My mind is made up. I pack my phone away and head back home.

I'm going to be on the first flight to New York tomorrow morning.

Oh, who am I kidding? The first flight is never gonna happen.

I like sleep too much, so maybe the third or fourth flight but definitely on a flight by one or two in the afternoon. At the latest, by three.

CHAPTER 23

Reese

THE ELEVATOR DOORS close before Keaton can catch up to me. I release a heavy breath that had been stalled in my chest. Everyone behind me has their head down or they're staring up at the tiles of the ceiling. I'm so glad no one can read my mind. I'd be fired for sure if they could. But no one else made a move to hold the doors open as he came running toward it either. Very interesting. Maybe he's not as popular as he likes to think.

What did I ever see in him?

I shake my head, beating myself up over that bad decision. Bad on so many levels.

Almost as bad as walking away from Danny. Just young, dumb, not in a good place mentally. Now I'm older and don't have those excuses. I'm just dumb, but with crow's feet that I can't seem to get rid of no matter what expensive cream I try.

Outside on the sidewalk, I find a bus bench, slip on my Jack Purcells, and start off for my apartment—twenty-one blocks. Keaton always hated these sneakers. It makes me like them more. He hated this walk more. After two times, he started taking his car and meeting me there. I hate the gym so this is my compromise to stay fit. Eventually I gave up the battle and rode in the car with him though. I was tired of being pressured. Our relationship was always good when he was getting his way.

My social life was lost once he started getting his way. I should have seen the signs. Beyond him being my boss, the isolation I felt should have sent up more red flags than it did. I can do this life without him, without anyone.

I can stand strong on my own.

Vinnie—he's kind of my knight in purple armor. I trust him. I'm not sure if I should, but I feel I can. And he loves Danny, for good reason.

The fifty texts I get each week from Vinnie telling me to screw it all and to screw Danny instead, are funny. He makes many valid points. I guess I should tell him I've already screwed him a few times already.

Danny is so handsome. He's ridiculously charming. Smart. He reads me like no one else. He knows me even better. Even after all these years, he knows my soul almost as well as I do. He's real with me. And I'm my most true self with him.

The real me.

He accepts me flaws and all. Without him, I wouldn't be where I am in my career. He was my biggest support back then. He still might be now as well.

When I round the corner and look up, I smile seeing a familiar gorgeous face. Leaning against my building—flowers in hand. Casual clothes look anything but casual on such an incredible body. A gray beanie and sunglasses protect his identity from everyone, but me.

Mine.

As I get closer I see the scruff his jaw is working. It's just enough that if used in the right way, I'll remember the feel of it for days after when I cross my legs.

My pace slows though all I want to do is run to him, have his arms wrap around me, and kiss him.

He doesn't hold back. Pushing off, he smiles then rushes toward me. When we reach each other, he does what I'm not brave enough to do—he puts his heart on the line and wraps his arms around me and kisses me.

And then I throw my heart into the ring and kiss him just as deeply right back. Because it's *him*. Danny. *Mine*. His lips on mine.

Flowers at my back as he holds me the way I remember him holding me in Marfa. *I missed this. I missed him.* I thought his texts were nice fillers, but as our tongues caress again, I realize texts will never be a substitute for the real thing.

Our breaths—like our kisses—are exchanged. When air becomes scarce we reluctantly part. His beautiful brown eyes stare into mine and if I'm not careful I might fall under his spell and throw more than my heart into the ring. I might be willing to throw everything I've worked for away over those puddles of caramel love.

"You're here," I say, dumbly, because yeah, he makes me lose my better senses.

"I'm here, for you." He pops the flowers in front of me. "I brought you flowers."

Smiling, I take the bright red Gerberas from him. "They're beautiful. You didn't have to bring me flowers."

"I wanted to bring you flowers. They always made you smile."

"They still do. Thank you." Not wanting to have this conversation on the street, I ask him up. We walk inside the lobby and wait together for the elevator in silence. My doorman greets us, but leaves us be.

Danny bumps my hand with his and looks down. When I look up at him, he smiles gently at me. My face heats. We step into the elevator, keeping a respective distance until the door closes. He's on me—my back against the wall, his mouth on my neck, his breath warming my collarbone, his words pure lust in my ear. "I missed you. I missed being inside you. I want you, Reese."

The doors open and he steps back. I take his hand and lead him into the hall. "Is that why you're here, Danny? You missed my body?"

"No. It's just one of a million things I missed about you. I'm just struggling to voice those when your body elicits such a fervent response from mine."

My thoughts get lost under my own impassioned desires for him. I unlock the door and set the flowers and my bag down on the table. When he's inside, I lock the door behind him and lean against it, gripping the knob to hold me in place. My heart's racing in my chest, my breath deep with want, my thoughts in turmoil over what to do while I stare at the back of his head. Do I put the brakes on or go? He turns and his eyes meet mine.

Go.

Go.

Go!

I push off and run to him, jumping into his arms. My legs wrap around his middle, my arms are around his neck. Our mouths clash together as my back is slammed against the wall. His pelvis tilts and I moan. Through my pants and his jeans, our desire is felt—hard against soft. I need more, the need for him consuming me. "The bedroom," the words stagger out between kisses, my desperation is heard. "That way. Go. Danny."

His hold under my ass is firm. I feel secure in his arms and relax as he carries me into the other room. Pressing me against the wall just inside the door, he pulls back, and says, "I'm going to fuck you against this wall before I leave New York." He spins me around, takes me to the bed, and sets me down. "But this time I want you to think of me every time you get into this bed." He pulls his shirt over his head and drops it to the floor, the beanie coming off with it. His hair is a complete fucking mess and as if it was possible, he's even hotter. "Get naked, Reese."

The command in the deep timbre of his voice is felt between my legs and I take off my clothes. He pulls two condoms from his pocket and tosses them on the bed next to me. "You came prepared."

"I came prepared to make you come."

My thighs clench from his words and I move up the bed. With my head resting on a pillow, I run my hands over the comforter as I spread my arms wide, letting my legs follow. "Don't let me keep you."

"Damn, woman. You're gonna be my undoing."

"Only if I'm doing it right." My voice is suddenly huskier, befitting this conversation and the thickness of the sexual tension filling the room.

He kneels at the base of the bed, taking hold of my ankles. "I have no doubt you'll do me right." My head hits the mattress as he pulls me until my knees are bent over his shoulders. "But I'll go first."

The scruff I mentioned earlier... *Oh yes!* Hail to the scruff. I'm a believer. My eyes drop closed and my back arches as he scrapes the inside of my thighs, his lips taking possession of my pussy like it was his all along.

Maybe it always was... like other beating parts of my body.

My thoughts become quicksand, slipping under as my body tightens. Running my nails lightly up his neck and into his hair, I take hold, and fist. His hands are on my stomach, my breasts, my hips. He's consuming me, his body owning all of mine, making me fall to pieces beneath him.

When he moves, my thighs squeeze together, trapping his

head between them as my body reacts to the sensitivity in my post-orgasmic euphoria. Hands slip between my legs and he spreads them apart then looks up.

I shrug, and though I'm a little tired, I smile, feeling so good, almost too good. "Sorry."

He chuckles as he kisses the inside of both of my thighs and then slowly removes my legs one at a time from his shoulders. I move up the bed and he takes a condom from on top of the covers as he moves up.

Coming down, he holds his body above me, only allowing access to his lips through a kiss, restraining himself, until he's not. His eyes are set on mine and he says, "I'm going to make love to you."

"Okay," I reply breathlessly, craving his heat to cover me.

"After I fuck you, Reese."

My eyes widen and my mouth opens. "Okay." Only one word is needed.

He drops down on me as he takes control of my mouth, holding my jaw in place as he covers me with intense kisses. His body throbs, moving in ways that summon mine to match his rhythm.

With the orgasm he conquered coating his lips and tongue, I don't think, I taste and feel, the act dirty and raw, visceral, and real. Danny doesn't hold back. This is me and him, him and me in our most natural state. I refuse to feel ashamed for enjoying the intimacy of sharing ourselves this way.

Sitting up, he flips me over so I'm face down. Excitement is stirred inside me and I like feeling vulnerable to his needs, to his demands. I like giving him what he wants and craves from me. "You're so beautiful," he says, the condom wrapper heard right after.

Looking at him, he strokes himself a few times and then rolls the condom down his proud length. I turn back around just as his leg comes over mine, his cock rubbing against my ass. Both of his hands slink under my body, grazing over my breasts and sliding down until they're holding my hips, and he lifts me up. I prop up on my elbows and his hands run over my backside and lower. Two fingers are dragged over my pussy and up until they're on my lower back and one disappears.

A quick smack to my ass surprises me, my head jolting around. "Are we playing?"

"Do you want me to?" he asks, positioning himself at my entrance, the tip of his cock teasing. The sweet pressure makes me want to seat myself solidly on his lap, but his hold of my hips gives him the final say.

"I want you to fuck me like you promised."

He slams forward, bringing my body to meet his in one fast motion. My head drops down, the weight too much to hold up under the power of each thrust. His fingers wrap over my shoulders for leverage and he keeps his promise.

Our bodies are slick with sweat and the sound of them hitting together is vulgar, animalistic, and so fucking sexy. He slides his hands around and grabs my breasts, squeezing as he fucks. They go lower over my belly. His thrusts slow as he weaves his pelvis behind me, hitting me deeper while one of his hands incites my clit. "Don't stop, Danny."

"I won't, baby. I want you to come so hard for me."

"God, so close." I lift up onto my hands just as the twisting in my middle unravels, taking me with it. My whole body trembles and he continues to move, making it last longer.

My arms shake, weakening under the pleasure just as his orgasm hits him. "Fuck, Reese!"

He curls around me and I lie down, my head to the side, my hair stuck to my face. Maneuvering to the side I'm facing, he takes the condom off and disposes of it somewhere I don't see. Danny lies in front of me. He reaches up and lifts the hair from my face, placing it so I have a clear view. With the gentlest of touches, he rests his hand over my heated cheek. I look at him through my sated state and smile. "Welcome to New York."

"I'd say so. Best greeting I've had in a long time."

I can't stop the quickened beat of my heart hearing those words. I love that it's his best greeting, of course, and how could I not know that after feeling his passion. *Twice.* Yes, I feel good. Best I've felt in forever.

Since we have been apart for ten years. I'm not sure I really want to go there, but I can't help but wonder how many greetings he has had like that, and unfortunately my mouth speaks before I can stop myself. "How many greetings have you had since... since me?"

"Do we really want to sully the incredible time we just had with things that don't matter?" He runs the back of his fingers over my cheek and down my neck. "Let's just be two people getting to know each other."

"I'd ask this of anyone I would sleep with." The tips of my fingers glide over his chest. I'm liking the light covering of chest hair.

"I don't want you mad at me. I still owe you a lovemaking."

"I won't get mad. I promise."

Rolling onto his back, he rests his forearm on his head. "I don't know, Reese. You sure you want to talk about this?"

"Is it that bad?"

"I don't know what it is. I'm not one of those guys who keep a running tally, makes notches on bedposts, or any of that. If I had to guess, it's probably over seventy since you."

I swallow that down, then repeat more for myself, "Seventy?"

He sits up and leans over me as I roll onto my back.

"See what you're doing?"

"I'm not judging. I'm not mad. I'm digesting."

"Shit. I should have lied. I knew it."

"No," I say, looking at him and reassuring him. "I'm glad you didn't lie. I don't deal well with liars. I'm glad you were honest, even more so because you were worried about me." I scoot closer so I'm tucked into his warmth. He wraps an arm over me and his head drops behind mine onto a pillow. With a loud exhale I'm thinking he doesn't believe I'm not mad. "Don't stress. For real. It's okay. I mean that's like seven women a year for the last ten years. When it's broken down like that, it's not that many and you are a supermodel, so it could be a lot worse."

"Two things: Did you just call me a supermodel? Secondly, did you just break down my sex life over the last ten years? 'Cuz when you put it like that, I feel like I've really slacked."

Laughing, I nudge him with my elbow. "You did not slack. I'm just not going to freak out over something I can't control. You were a free man and could do as you pleased. And I assume you don't like being called a supermodel?"

I turn in his arms so I'm looking up at him. He kisses me, then says, "Just doesn't really fit what I'm doing and I associate that term more with women, but it's technically correct, so it is what it is."

"I'm sorry." I rub his neck. "I won't use it if you don't like it." Lifting up, he also leans down and we kiss again. Moving a little so I can get a better look at his face, I ask, "You didn't ask me my magic number. You're not curious?"

"I know you've been with other men. I'm not naïve enough to lie to myself, but I don't need any visuals or details. I'm fine living in ignorance when it comes to your life after me."

If I'm not mistaken I think I've hit on another sensitive subject. Taking his face in my hands, I move my pelvis to the side to meet his, and whisper, "What was that about a lovemaking?"

The right side of his mouth lifts into a sexy smirk, but it's replaced with his lips on mine. And round two begins.

CHAPTER 24

Reese

WE TALK.

We laugh.

We make love. Again.

We fall asleep by nine and wake up famished at midnight—for food this time.

Danny Weston is irresistible.

Yes, he's hot. Yes, he's famous. Yes, his body is perfection. But he's also adorable and so funny. I haven't had this much fun in forever. He says, "Okay, this time, lie down." He pats the marble counter. "Naked."

I laugh. "Why do I have to be naked on a cold marble countertop?"

Holding a bowl he just retrieved from the fridge, he says, as if it's the most obvious answer in the world, "Because I want to eat these berries from your body."

"I should really tell you no every now and then."

"But you can't and I love that about you."

After pulling my panties off, I press my bare body against him. He's still in the knit boxers that cover way more of his body than I like. "What else do you love about me?"

Any other guy would turn serious, but not Danny. He rolls with the punches, another characteristic of his I've always admired. He doesn't let life bring him down. "I like that you ate the cake at dinner when no other woman in Spago would dare smell a dessert, much less eat it."

"That was some damn good cake."

"Looked like it. You know what else I love?"

"What?"

"I love that when you laugh, like tonight, it's real, from the heart, or the gut more like it. You're not doing it to humor me. You're laughing for you."

Charmer! "Fine, Romeo. You win. I'll get on the cold marble just for you."

"Yes!" He fist-pumps. In one swift motion, he lifts me and props me up on the counter.

I sit straight up, pushing up with my hands. "Holy shit, it's cold." Swinging my legs around, I get into the crab crawl position. "Help a girl out, why don't ya? Get me that towel. Chop chop," I tease. "It's freezing up here."

He reaches around and grabs the dishtowel hanging from the oven handle. He lays it flat and I sit. It's still cold, but bearable. "I hope you're hungry."

"Starving." He places berries in particular places on my body, admiring his work as he goes along.

"Is that the big dipper?"

"Good eye." He takes the berry tip of the big dipper and pops it in his mouth.

I try not to move too much, but I very carefully rest my head on my arm, giving me a better view of this incredibly sexy man eating off me. I'm not shy around him. Not guarded. I'm relaxed in a way I haven't been in a long time. I'm comfortable in being me, being naked, being exposed—body and soul to him like no one else before... not even him. Reveling in this ease of our relationship, I decide now is a good time to ask him a few things I've been curious about since I came home. "You really flew in a day early just to see me?"

He plucks a berry from my belly button and pops it in his mouth. With the smirkiest of smirks, he replies, "I did."

"Did you have to wait long?"

"No, not long." The smirk transforms into a genuine smile, one that makes my thighs squeeze together in response, and a few berries go rolling off. "Oops." I laugh making the rest of them scramble into the lines of my body, sending some to the floor, and a few onto the counter.

He ducks quickly to the floor to grab the runaways and I sit up stretching to get the few that escaped across the slick marble. While reaching as far as I can to get the last one, I hear it.

Shit.

But I'm too slow to stop it. The brass bolt on the door clunks, the front door knob turns, and Keaton walks in. I freeze in horror. He's stunned in place just inside the doorframe. I gasp. The berries fall from my hand and I cover myself in shock. *And* shame—something I've always felt around him.

Danny stands and before I can scream, I'm swooped from the counter and behind him with one arm wrapped around me, shielding me from my ex.

Keaton breaks the silent standoff we seem to be having. "Reese! What are you doing?"

"What are you doing, Keaton?" I ask, peeking around Danny's shoulder. "You have no right to walk into my apartment without my permission."

"I was stopping by to check on you."

"It's after midnight, Keaton. What the hell?"

Danny cuts in. "Hold up. Who the fuck are you?"

"Who the *fuck* are you? And what are you doing with my girlfriend?"

Danny's arm returns to his side, my body cold without him. He glances back at me. His tone is firm when he says, "Get dressed." He hands me the dishtowel because there is nothing else to cover me with.

Pushing down the unsettling feelings overwhelming my insides, I take it out on the ex. "Leave, Keaton. I mean it."

His eyes are set on Danny, his gaze locked. "This is *the model.*" Instead of leaving, he moves closer, his accusatory tone becoming threatening. "You're that fucking model."

"What's it to you?" Danny throws back.

"What's it to *me*? Everything. That's *my* girlfriend you're fucking around with. Vittori is *my* client." He laughs. "You are so fucked. I am going to ruin you."

Danny leans his hands on the marble. Only minutes before, I had sat there in complete bliss. "Let me tell *you* something. You can't fucking ruin anything for me. I've got a reputation that far exceeds one job. And as for Vittori, fire me, but he'll just hire me direct and bypass the middleman. And lastly, and I want you to listen good and hard. Reese isn't *your* girlfriend and I wasn't fucking *around* with her. I was fucking her. Get it straight, asshole."

Keaton's hands are fisting, his face red with anger. I've never seen him like this and a million scary thoughts of the revenge he's going to attempt run through my head. With the towel tucked under my elbows, I raise my hands in a cautionary manner in hopes of calming him. "Please, Keaton. Please just leave. We can talk tomorrow. You've been wanting to talk. I'll do it. I'll meet you and we can talk."

Danny's breath is heavy, the sound filling my ears. His

disapproval is heard when he says, "Go to the bedroom, Reese."

"This isn't worth a fight. You have a shoot tomorrow." Turning to Keaton, I plead, "We can't risk losing this campaign. Vittori spent a fortune on the last shoot and we'll lose even more if Danny can't make this shoot. Please. Just leave. We will talk tomorrow. I promise."

"You heard her. Leave," Danny snarls. "This is your last warning before I call the cops and have you removed."

Dread sinks to the bottom of my stomach as Keaton laughs again, purposely pushing all of Danny's buttons. "I've got news for you, pretty boy." He holds up a key. "I come and go as I please."

Needing this to end before this confrontation gets violent, I screw my lack of dress and walk to the door with the dishtowel over the front of my body. I open the door wider. "I want you to leave right now or I will call the cops. You have no right to use that key." I hold my hand out. "Give it to me."

He turns to me, looking up and down my body with disgust. "We're going to talk in the morning." When he slams the key in my hand, the teeth dig into my skin. I wince, but hold back showing the pain I experience.

As soon as he walks out, I shut the door and lock all three bolts and add the chain. Danny has gone to the bedroom. He's sitting on the end of the mattress with his head in his hands when I walk in. Giving him space, I take my robe and slip it on, then lean against the wall. "Do you want to talk about it?" I ask, keeping my voice quiet.

"I don't know. Do I? Do I want to know what that was about out there?"

"I think you know."

He stands up and grabs his jeans from the floor. "Yeah, I know." He starts putting them on and I want to stop him. I'm just not sure I have a right to. He reaches for his shirt and his beanie, snatching them from where they landed in our sexual frenzy to get them off earlier. "I'm gonna go."

"I'd like you to stay." I tuck my hands behind my back, restraining myself from running to him and begging him to stay here with me when that's all I want to do.

His eyes reach me and I'm pinned to the spot where I stand. "I don't know anything about your life. You haven't given me anything except what I've found out because I overheard a phone conversation, and now I'm stuck in what looks like a fight between a boyfriend and girlfriend."

"Keaton and I are not together, Danny. I wouldn't have been with you if we were."

"Then what the fuck was that about? He has a key and apparently uses it when he pleases."

"I've tried to get it back from him. He wouldn't before, but I got it now."

"You got it because I was about to pummel him." He's frustrated pulling the beanie onto his head. He walks past me. "I don't want to fight with him. I haven't been in a fistfight in years, but I'll tell you I was close. Very fucking close. But I don't give a shit about him. I care about you and I don't want to fight with you either."

"Let's not then." I follow him back into the kitchen. Berries are all over the counter, a reminder of how good it was a short time ago.

He turns toward me, his back to the door. "If I stay, we will. I need to cool down and I can't in here, not with you."

"What are you saying, Danny? Are you mad at me?"

"Blindsided. I don't know what's going on and I'm upset. So yes, I'm mad at you."

"You have no right to be mad at me. I didn't ask him to come over."

"I need time to sort through this so I don't take it out on you. I'm being honest with you so I don't make it worse. If I stay, it will get worse."

My heart is pounding in pain and I feel betrayed. Why did I drop my guard for him? "Honest? Now you're honest with me? Wow," I say, my pride making me snarky.

"What does that mean?"

"You know what that means. You weren't honest with me back when we were together, but now you spout off about how important honesty is to you?" I scoff. "Well, I'm glad you've grown a conscience."

A look of disbelief crosses his face. "I'm leaving, that's something you should be familiar with."

"Screw you!"

He turns and unlocks the bolts I thought were protecting us from the outside world. It seems maybe we need protection from each other. He opens the door and keeping his back to me, he says, "I'll see you at the shoot."

The door closes and with full fury I pound against it with both of my fists. I turn my back on it and slide down, closing my eyes as I bring my knees to my chest. I wish I could stop the tears, but there's this place deep inside that only Danny Weston can reach and he just ripped it open.

Again.

CHAPTER 25

Reese

SLEEP DOESN'T COME. I sit near the window I paid so proudly for a year ago, but the view has lost its luster. Sitting here feeling his loss reminds me of the last time I lost Danny...

My bags are packed, suitcase by the door, backpack at my feet. It took me days to get everything in order, all leading up to today. I push the play button once more to listen to the voicemail message Danny sent yesterday when I was out.

"I'm coming home tomorrow. We need to talk. Be at the apartment at six. See you soon."

No I miss you. No I love you. Just we need to talk.

Modeling has taken over his life, and my life has become a side effect to the life he left behind. I knew we'd go through a change, transitioning from seeing each other all day, every day, to every few days or even a week. But I could have never predicted the last year we struggled through. Or maybe it was only me who's been struggling.

I haven't seen him in over a month. Paris, Milan, Rome. Everywhere but here for five weeks. He doesn't even know I found a job in New York City. Our time on the phone is too limited to mention such things going on in my life when his life is so exciting. So big. Mine feels small in comparison. I feel small—small time, small town, a part of a small past. His small past.

I really thought I'd get to tell him face to face. Been desperate to see his reaction, his pride. His anything *for me. Missed calls, out-of-sync schedules, and unpredictable email service all add to the list of obstacles keeping us apart. The leading factor is Danny becoming an overnight sensation in the modeling world. That boy next-door meets the sexy alpha male are names he's often called. My hands fist and I tamp my annoyance that I could have told them that. But my thoughts don't matter. I don't matter in that world, his world.*

I grab the stack of magazines from the dining table and drop them one by one on the coffee table in front of me. Each one taunting me with an ad of him and some model or models that all look too cozy for my comfort.

If that were me cozying up to male models, he would not be happy. He would not be okay seeing other men touching me.

I'm bitter. Life here has become unbearable. They took him, the man I love, and made him a star. The magazines can't get enough of him. The designers all want him, but so do I. So much. I miss him. I miss the way we used to hang out all night and talk. I miss his arms around me. I miss going to bed with him and waking up to him kissing my breasts, rousing me from sleep.

There's no doubt he'll be packing his stuff soon enough and moving away. I'm the only thing holding him to Nebraska. It's time I let him go. I'm tired of feeling second best to a career. I'm tired of the tabloids, and seeing him at the center of it all. I'm tired of seeing him with other women.

And then the message came while I was at the library.

We need to talk... We need to talk... We need to talk...

I don't care about his job. I care about him, but he's lost who he was and now he's willing to lose me. Dump. Me.

Our friends, my family, everyone tells me I have to let him go so he can pursue his dream. While my dream of getting married, having kids, and career are sidelined. We're on two different paths going in two different directions. I'll get moved to New York and give him my address as soon as I have one. Maybe with me pursuing my career things will be better. Maybe he'll find me interesting again.

My breath comes rapidly and shortens. How am I doing this? How am I leaving the only man I've ever loved? With the last bit of strength I have, I stand taller and lock the door. He needs to see what it's like to be lonely. He needs to understand how much he's hurt me. This will wake him up. He'll miss me. He'll miss me I just know it. I pray that we can work through this again. With me in Manhattan, the stars have aligned if we can work it out.

So a year after his career took off, I stand in the doorway, saying goodbye to our... his place forever with his, "We need to talk" ringing in my ears. I say goodbye to this lonely place and leave, just like he left me behind.

I can't lose him again. By five a.m., I get dressed for work and by six I'm out the door. I decide I'd rather lose myself in my job than sit here losing myself to the hurt I'm feeling.

Walking through the lobby, the overnight doorman, Dave, is leaving his shift, so we walk together. "You worked all night again?"

He says, "Ralph's still sick. I worked half his shift and mine. It's not a party building so I got a few naps in. But don't worry, the doors were locked."

"That's good."

"Don't tell the boss."

I laugh. "I won't."

I know he's only making casual conversation, like the weather, but when he says, "That was mighty nice of your friend to visit yesterday."

"Yes, it was," I reply, not wanting more tears to surface before I even reach the street.

"Judging by how long he waited and those flowers, I'd say you have quite the admirer."

I stop walking just before we reach the door. "The flowers were very nice, but out of curiosity, how long did he wait?"

"I didn't time him or anything," he says, shrugging, "but it was a good three hours. At least."

"Three hours?" Danny's words come back to me—*No, not long.* "Wow, that is a long time. I didn't know."

"I just thought he deserved the credit." He walks out, holding the door for me. "Have a good day, Ms. Carmichael."

"Thanks, Dave, and call me Reese."

"Yes, ma'am."

"Have a good day."

I remain on the street, and when I look where I'm standing, it was here. Right here. Twelve hours ago, this is where Danny changed our course. This is where he made me see what was right in front of me in Nebraska, what I knew in Marfa. He made me realize that he's been the missing piece to making my heart whole again. The tears come as I pull my phone from my purse. The screen lights up as I open it. I call Danny, praying he'll answer.

My heart starts hurting even more when the third ring chimes. By the fourth, his voicemail kicks in along with regret. So much regret. I should have never let him leave. Under any other circumstances, I would hang up. But this time, this time for him, I'll swallow my pride and pain and leave a message for him to call me. After I hang up, I stay there as if my feet don't want to leave the good in the past.

That's what I've been doing all along. With Danny. With our relationship. The bad is so easy to remember, the good forgotten in the memories. But there was so much good. We were good. Standing there I realize I barely remember the bad anymore and yet, I've held it against him. *Why?*

I stare at my phone, hoping it rings. I assume he's sleeping, somehow able to when I couldn't. A small comfort comes over me. He'll have clearer thoughts. He'll see *me* more clearly and want to come back, come back to me and just... just be together again.

When I look up I realize I know where he is booked to stay this trip. My arm flies into the air to hail a cab. At this hour, it's easy to get one. I direct the driver to Ninth Avenue in the Meatpacking District. With my phone still in my hand, I lean back as I run everything I want to say to him on rotation so I can cover everything needed.

I pay the driver and head in through the revolving doors. It's still early, not even 6:45. The lobby is empty of guests and only one person is behind the counter. With a broad smile, she says, "Welcome to the Gansevoort. Checking in?"

"No, I'm here to see a guest. Danny Weston." My fingers begin tapping on the counter as I lean against it anxiously. "Can you call him for me?"

Her smile falls. "We don't normally disturb our guests at this hour. Is Mr. Weston expecting you?"

"No, but I need to speak with him right away please." I throw the please in with a slight plea, but nothing is going to get her to make that call. I can tell by how tight her lips have become as she types on her keyboard.

"I'm sorry. His room is set to do not disturb." She puts a pad of paper and pen down on the counter and slides it toward me.

"Would you like to leave a message?"

"Can I wait here?" I ask, pointing to the seating area by the window.

"Yes."

I walk over and sit down, setting the phone on the coffee table in front of me and stare at it.

One hour...

Two hours...

He waited three.

I'm willing to wait longer, but my phone rings and I jump, startled by the sound. *Keaton.* I gulp down my disappointment and brace myself for this conversation. It's one I need to have and as I start thinking about it, it's one I should probably have before having one with Danny.

"Hello?"

"Get to the office, Reese."

"Don't talk to me like that."

"As your boss, I can talk to you however I want to."

"I'm working from home today."

"You're fucking him at home today, forgetting that your job is waiting for you to start your day. Or do you not care about your job anymore?"

"You know I care, Keaton. I care more than you'll ever give me credit for."

"That's not true. I gave you Vittori, which is the same as giving you credit. Now get to the office. We need to talk."

Swallowing becomes hard as I give him more than he deserves. "I said I would and we can." Looking around the lobby that's much busier and getting louder, I say, "I'll meet you in your office in an hour."

"Forty-five minutes, Reese. Don't be late."

He feels more powerful by taking fifteen minutes off the hour like that but I'm not in the mood to argue. I'm sure I'll be doing plenty of that in forty-five minutes.

I stand up and throw my purse over my shoulder. Walking around the rotating door just as a man enters the other side and pushes, I look up. *Danny.* The door stops trapping us both on opposite sides with no way to exit. He moves his finger in the air to show me he's going to push us around. When the opening is to the sidewalk, I walk out and look back, but he's gotten out in the lobby.

My shoulders drop as he puts his hand out to stay, and then comes out the other door, skipping the revolving one.

Before he can say anything, I blurt, "I'm sorry."

He looks surprised.

I continue, "I'm sorry for everything. For my ex showing up, really sorry for that. For not sharing more of my life with you. For making you feel that you're not as important as my career when it scares me how you already are, and always were. I'm sorry for not calling you in the last ten years, and I'm more sorry for not meeting you that day. I could have given you a million reasons why I didn't back then, but today... today I stand before you not able to remember any that were worth losing you, and regretting them anyway."

"Reese, stop." His tone is somber.

And just like that my hope plummets.

He doesn't want me anymore.

Stepping forward, he takes my hand. My heart beats painfully in my chest. "Reese, you don't have to apologize for the past or the in-between. That's exactly what it is—the past. We can't change it. But last night, I don't get into fights. I don't date other men's girlfriends or wives despite what the tabloids say about me."

"I'm not dating him."

"I know. I know because you told me." His grip tightens and

he pulls me closer. "I want you to tell me everything about you. I want us to know each other like we used to."

Tears prick my eyes for different reasons this time. "You do?"

"I do." He wipes my tears just as they fall. "I want you to know the real me, the me now." Chuckling, he says, "I may be an ass for all you know."

"You may be an ass after I get to know you too."

His laughter draws out mine as we joke, skirting around the deeper emotions we're feeling for each other. I drop my head against his chest and wrap my arms around him. I feel his strength as he holds me just as tightly. A kiss is placed on top of my head and I close my eyes, inhaling him.

Deep down I know he was already there, inside my heart all along. "I'm sorry for last night."

"Just so you know, I was willing to kick his ass for you."

With a smile on my face, I whisper, "I know. But just so you know, I was willing to kick his ass for you too."

I feel his chest moving. The feel of his happiness makes me happy. When I look up, he says, "I'm sorry for leaving last night."

"I understand."

He lifts my chin so I look up again. "I mean it, Reese. I shouldn't have left. I don't want to justify it, but I was angry—at *him*, at you, and at myself. I knew I'd take it out on you if I didn't leave. That's the last thing I wanted to do because I know you didn't have anything to do with him being there."

I back up so we can talk face to face. "Look, Danny, we left things unfinished ten years ago, but I feel the connection I always had with you. I think you feel the same—"

"I do."

Needing to touch him again, to feel his warmth envelop me, I curve my fingers around his. "When I'm with you, I feel like my old self, the person I wish I was."

"Who are you?"

"I'm someone who lost their way."

His fingers tighten around mine. "Find your way back to me."

"I'm trying." The clock is ticking. I adjust my purse, and say, "I want to, so badly, but I need to close some doors before opening this one. Out of respect for you, and for myself."

He looks curious, but doesn't ask. He knows. When he hugs me again, he knows. "Come back to me."

"I promise. As soon as I can get away." I pull back and start trying to leave when all I want to do is stay. Job and career be damned. I never had anything worth giving it up for before now. "Bye, Danny."

"I'll be waiting for you. I'm in room 1455."

He stays there on the sidewalk—smile on his face, hands in pockets, looking perfectly edible. I give one last little wave and hail a cab.

STANDING OUTSIDE KEATON'S office with two minutes to spare. I wait three and then knock. This little joy makes me smile.

When I hear him tell me to come in, I open the door and walk in feeling a renewed confidence in myself. I walk to the desk and when he tents his fingers in contemplation, I start in, "We are no longer a couple. You will not treat me as if I am, as if you have any right to know anything about me personally. You don't. You are my employer, nothing more."

"Sit down, Reese," he says, getting comfortable in his large leather chair.

When I sit, he adds, "As your employer, I own your ass from eight to five. Anytime you're on site representing one of my accounts, I own you. If you're with clients on my dime, I own you. Taking the expense report you submitted yesterday into account, I apparently own you more than two hundred hours a month."

I don't like where this is going. A sickening clots my veins listening to him stake any claim he can over me. "That's all you have. Nothing more. No more, Keaton."

"That's all I need. We're done here. Shut the door after you leave."

Staring at him, his attention is back on his monitor as if I'm not still here. I get up and head to the door without another word, not because I agree with him, but because I can't be bothered with him. I'll spend this week sending out my résumé.

When I get to my desk, there's a pile of envelopes on top. They have all been opened, so I pull the heavy cardstock out and read the first one.

Keaton Klein and guest are cordially invited...

I drop it and open the next one.

And then the next.

They're all the same. Scooping up the pile of invitations, I then carry them back to his office. This time I don't give him the courtesy of knocking before I enter. I drop them on his desk and shake my head. "You can't force me to go on dates with you. You can't use business to win me back or to spend time with me."

"Can't I?"

"You're an asshole."

"I'm busy, sweetheart. If you have business to discuss I'm all ears. The rest of this garbage is boring me."

"I won't go," I state, crossing my arms over my chest.

"Get your dancing shoes on. I hear tonight's gala will have a large dance floor and live band."

"I'm not going, Keaton. I've got no business there so that makes it null and void."

He stands, leaning his hands on the desk dividing us. "Let me tell you a little bit about null and void. Your plaything is in breach of contract, so all bets are off and we will fight a more civilized battle through our lawyers." He picks up a file and drops it in front of me. "Make sure to read the fine print. Especially the part about him not fraternizing with anyone employed by Klein Advertising. Not to mention your personal violation of our code of conduct."

My anger gets the best of me. "I think you're overlooking the fact that you're in violation as well. I guess I should file a report with HR."

"Klein has never disallowed employees to date each other. We just ask that it doesn't affect the performance of your job."

"Cut the bullshit, Keaton. What are you saying?"

He looks pleased with himself as he takes the file back. "I'm saying you'll stop seeing the model immediately. As for work, you will not see him unless another member our team or Vittori's team is with you."

"I recognize a threat even when it's delivered with a smile, so what's the or?"

"Or we sue him for breach of contract. So how rich is your pretty boy?"

"This is a personal vendetta. Keep the focus on me and my job performance—"

"Don't worry. I'll be keeping a close eye on your *job* performance. Now if you'll excuse me, I have a conference call with my lawyers."

"You're the biggest mistake I ever made, Keaton." As soon as I say it I know it's a lie. I know what my biggest mistake is and I refuse to make it twice.

"That's fine. You can hate me all you want, but as long as you're employed here, you'll respect me and our code of conduct." He looks down, dismissing me by waving me off.

I hate him. I do. So much. I walk to the door, but before I can open the door, I hear, "Reese?"

Stopping, I slowly turn around. With my hand on my hip, I wait for him to speak. He says, "Wear the Louboutins. They were always my favorite."

The bastard. "You bought those for the whore you were fucking on the side. You always bought me Manolos." He's a despicable man, and if I wasn't already so angry at him, the sting from finding out he was cheating on me would cause my blood to boil. He humiliated me with a Louboutin-wearing whore who he paraded to the ballet while taking me to the opera the next night. New York societal circles are small. I turn on my Pradas and he's smart enough to let that lie. When I exit his office, I shut the door and exhale an anxious breath. I walk with purpose back to my desk, his warning and the invitation playing on a loop.

Even with the threats toward my job, my career, my life in general, I can think of only one thing... or one person to be precise.

Danny.

CHAPTER 26

AS SOON AS I get back to the room, I get out of my clothes and take a hot shower. A night of sex and a morning of walking around the city aren't doing me any favors.

My skin feels raw from last night. It's a feeling I've missed, and one that takes my mind back to another time in life.

Reese.

I climb into bed naked. Call it wishful thinking, but after making up with Reese, my bets are on a sure thing. I want to be ready when she comes over.

Closing my eyes, I feel content, another sensation I haven't felt since being with her. I just never recognized it until now. Even in the dark of this hotel room, I smile, the emotion too strong to stop myself. I exhale, long and hard, the crazy of the last twenty-four hours released and I fall asleep shortly after.

HOPING FOR MORE sleep, my eyes remain closed. Muscles tired.

Head groggy. The room is black from the window coverings, so I have no concept of how much time has passed. Sporting wood, my cock is even confused to the hour. Rubbing it to calm it down, I realize this will only make matters harder. *Like steel.* Especially when the brunette with blue eyes comes to mind.

I throw the covers off and go take a piss. I'm about to climb back in bed when I catch a glimpse of the clock. 5:03. I struggle to register if it's a.m. or p.m. When I do, I grab my phone off the nightstand and sit on the edge of the bed. Fuck! p.m.

There are plenty of missed texts, a batch of new emails, but no missed calls. *Where is Reese?* I thought I'd hear from her, but it's almost dinnertime and I haven't. I call her, worried. When she doesn't answer, I leave a message, "Gimme a call when you get this."

Needing to get up before my days and nights are completely screwed up, I shift and open the blinds with the remote. Then dig through my suitcase for clean clothes. I pull on jeans, going commando underneath, after putting on a T-shirt. I walk to the window and look around outside. Something's wrong.

Pulling my phone from my back pocket, I text her: *Where are you?*

Trying to not stress about her, I sit down and start going through my emails. But I worry about what's going on. When she left this morning, we were good. More than good. We were solid. We had said things we hadn't said and it felt good to get it off my chest and hear her side. I wanted to tell her more. I wanted to talk about that fateful last night. Leaving me there, knowing I was going to ask her to marry me was not humiliating. It was hurtful. I need to put it to bed by finding out why she stood me up. It's the past that haunts me the most.

I look at the face of my phone again. No response to my text. I grab my hat and slip on my shoes. Before I leave the room, I put on my jacket. Downstairs in the lobby, I call her once more, but it goes to voicemail.

Outside on the sidewalk, I'm not sure where I'm going, but I couldn't sit inside that room any longer. The walls were closing in, the lack of Reese taunting me. I stand where I last saw her, having a good mind to go to her work. But I don't want to make things worse for her. Her job is important and I can respect that. What I can't respect is that douchebag ex. I can only imagine how he's going to lash out at her.

I mean, I don't fully blame him. If I was in his shoes, I'd be angry finding my girlfriend fucking some hot, extremely sexy, eight-pack-abs stud too. But I've never felt that strongly about a woman, except for one. The same one as him. Fuck. What lengths is he willing to go to get her back? Or more specifically, what lengths has he gone to already to get her back?

Shit.

My fingers are flying over the keyboard: *Call me back.*

I start walking, my pace quick considering I don't know where to go. After covering five or so blocks and still no call or text, I take matters into my own hands. The receptionist answers, "Klein Advertising."

"Reese Carmichael."

"I'm sorry, sir, she's gone for the day. I can redirect you to her voicemail."

"What time did she leave?"

"She was working away from the office most of today. She left before lunch to meet with clients. Would you like her voicemail?" She sounds anxious.

When I check my Fitbit, it's 5:56. She's probably trying to leave. "No, thank you." Just as I'm about to hang up, my gut guides me elsewhere and I do something I never do. I drop my name, using it for leverage. "Wait, this is Danny Weston."

I pause to let it sink in.

It's obvious when it does. The anxiety heard earlier disappears, a purr in her tone is heard. "Well hello, Danny Weston. The supermodel?"

I roll my eyes. "Yes."

"How may I assist you?"

"Is Keaton Klein available?"

"No," she answers casually. "He had an event to attend tonight."

"An event?"

"Yes, Klein Advertising is a large contributor to the Colon Cancer Foundation. They're having their annual fundraiser tonight," she replies proudly, then just above a whisper, she gives more than expected, "Ms. Carmichael is scheduled to attend as well. I have a spare ticket if you'd like to go with me as my plus one?"

Tempting. Very tempting if I can see Reese. If she shows. But something I learned a few years back is my name alone opens doors. "Thank you. I have something to do, but I might stop by."

"My name's Amanda."

"Thanks, Amanda."

"You're welcome."

I hang up and sit on a bench nearby. I need to think. This is when I appreciate the time difference between LA and New York. I make a call.

"Mark Warrant's office. This is Jody."

"Jods, this is Danny. I need you to do me a favor."

STANDING JUST INSIDE the doors of the ballroom, I adjust one cufflink, then the other while scanning the opulent surroundings of the historic hotel.

I walk around the back of the room, trying to blend in while I look for Reese. She's gone cell phone silent on me, which is entirely unacceptable. Sticking to the darker outskirts of the gala, I keep my eyes focused. I haven't seen her yet, but I know she's here. I feel it deep inside.

Suddenly feeling like a creeper, I head to the bar and order my standard. With a fresh drink in hand, I work my way out of the crowd and toward the dance floor for a better view. But I stop in my tracks when I see her. It's almost shocking I missed her before—red floor-length gown, slit up the front showing off her incredible legs, black heels, hair up. Her lips are red to match the dress. Her eyes stand out, her smile entrancing.

She amazes me. How she manages to look more beautiful every time I see her is beyond me—bewilders me—but she does. My heart is pounding in my chest from the very sight of her.

My drink is forgotten on a table as I pass, heading straight for her. She's got an audience when I approach. Cutting in, I offer my hand. "May I have this dance?"

The look in her eyes says more than she'll allow her expression to reveal. But it's me and her, and she smiles as she accepts the offer. "I'd love to."

I lead her silently to the middle of the dance floor and take her right hand in mine. It's not the two-step, but I'm a man of many talents. I come replete with many dance moves, including the box step. I think I just won a few points with her. Her smile is contagious, but my heart feels the distance she's keeping. "I'm not going to let you disappear again. Not without a proper chase. Is that what you're wanting? You want me to chase you?"

"Danny, I don't want you to think you have to chase me. You don't. I want to be with you in whatever way I can be."

"In whatever way? Hmm." I look up and quickly gather my thoughts. "So if I chase you, will you believe in my intentions?"

"What are your intentions?"

"I intend to keep you sexually satisfied and blissfully happy."

"That's a tall order."

"Is it?"

"I have no doubt you," she says, clearing her throat right after, "can back up such lofty claims, but our problems never involved your ability to satisfy me sexually." She looks up, the pink from her cheeks fading. "And I'm not playing a cat and mouse game with you."

"Then why did you not come back? Why did I have to track you down at a black-tie affair?"

She smiles lightly. "You do look incredible in that tuxedo."

"Vittori. The new men's line."

"He knows a lot about a man's body. It's a perfect fit."

I refrain from joking around, getting us back on the real topic at hand. "I need answers, Reese."

"He's gifted. What can I say? He knows from hands-on experience?"

"Nice try. I'm not talking about Vinnie."

I stop moving, planting my feet in the middle of the dance floor. "What's going on with us?"

By the way she's looking around, she's worried about eyes and cameras being directed our way. "Please, Danny." She nods ever so slightly. "Let's not talk here."

We walk to the bar and take two glasses of champagne from the table with a large fountain that has the bubbly flowing. Trying to blend into the busy party, we stand off to the side behind a tall table and watch the guests dancing. I don't say anything. She knows what I want answered. I see the Klein Advertising banner across the room and look for the head douche himself.

Reese says, "I need to handle some business."

"Now?"

"No, before..." She finally looks at me, right into my eyes. "Before we can see where this goes."

"It's not *going*. We're already there."

That brings a smile to her face. "I feel lucky to have you back in my life. Please know that."

Dread pits itself at the bottom of my stomach. "This doesn't sound good."

The smile leaves her pretty face. Blue eyes under black lashes look up to me. "Sometimes timing plays a factor—"

"You're not doing this. I'm not going to let you. Something happened since this morning. Please don't hide it from me. Don't keep me out. We can handle it together. Is it your job?" Glancing around, I say, "I assume you didn't lose it since you're here representing them."

"As a representative of the company, that means I'm on work time."

She won't look at me now and I hate it. I follow her gaze and see him standing across the room watching us. I move closer to her, resting my hand on her lower back, but she stiffens under my touch. "He can't touch us, Reese, if we stand together."

She takes a step away, and with sadness filling her tone, she says, "He already has. If you'll excuse me, I need to play my part."

Disappearing from under my hand, she slips around the table and walks across the room to him. I'm inclined to go after her, but she's working and I don't want to cause a scene.

I don't really like champagne, so I leave it there and find a better spot to watch what's planned.

"Hey, cowboy."

Recognizing that voice anywhere, I turn around. I certainly

wasn't answering to cowboy. Nope. "Vinnie. I didn't think you'd make it."

"I changed my mind, hoping for some fireworks."

"I steer clear of drama and you're enjoying the fact that I'm stuck right in the middle of it."

"It's entertaining, but I came to support my girl."

"She's over there."

He frowns. "I'm not sure what's going on, but it's more than meets the eye."

"Good sleuthing there, Sherlock." I move closer, Vinnie staying near.

Reese is talking to two men and the asshole. They're captivated by the woman in red, their full attention on her. I can relate. As I weave through the crowd, her gaze lands on me just over his shoulder. She excuses herself and makes her way back to me. With a devious smile she approaches. "Every woman in this room has their eyes on you, Mr. Weston."

"And I only have eyes for you, Ms. Carmichael."

She covertly pats me on the ass as she passes. Hugging Vinnie, she says, "I thought you couldn't make it?"

"I came to see you."

Smiling, she hooks her arm with his. "We would have seen each other tomorrow, but I'm happy to see you tonight." They look at me and she gives me a once-over. "By the way, you fight unfair."

He laughs. "I sent in my best weapon."

I cut in, perplexed by the conversation. "Are you two talking about me?"

Reese laughs, her glass now empty, which helps to explain her relaxed demeanor. "We were."

Holding her arms out, Vinnie looks her up and down. "This dress is pure perfection on you, Candy."

"I feel beautiful in it. Thank you for letting me borrow it."

"It's yours, darling, as if it was made with you in mind all along."

Reese glances in my direction, then replies, "I'm honored. Thank you again."

Vinnie says, "I want to see how it moves. Maybe Mr. Weston will take the lady for a spin."

Before I happily oblige, she says, "We already danced. Unfortunately I have more business to tend to, so I must leave for tonight."

"Reese?" I call her before she leaves again. Getting as close to her as I can while "appearing" appropriate, I say, "We just made promises to not lie, to share our lives, this morning. What's going on?"

Standing by my side, she looks around, keeping a smile on her face, she touches my hand between us. "Things are complicated." I turn to face her. That way she has to look at me when she continues. "Let me handle something that's come up."

"You can't tell me?"

She shakes my hand, appearances in play. "I'm doing everything for us."

"Let me help."

"Trust in me, Danny." She releases my hand and turns. "I'll tell you everything soon. Until then, we can't be seen together. I'll call you later."

Standing with Vinnie, we watch her walk away. When I look at him, he says, "I know her boss has something to do with this."

"What do you know about him?"

"Enough." He sighs heavily and I feel much the same way. "Let her do what she needs to do. If there's anything I've learned about Reese Carmichael, it's that she's very capable."

"He's pulled rank on her."

"He's pulled something." He pats my shoulder. "Pay no mind. I know her real feelings."

"Are you talking about him or me?"

"Both." He laughs and goes to the bar.

CHAPTER 27

DANNY

I TAKE THE tux off. I'd been hoping she'd be the one taking it off, but Reese hasn't called, or come over. I can't relax until I know she's okay, until she's back with me. I hang it up and put it in the bag. Wardrobe will be picking it up to use for the Paris shoot.

Sitting in the chair, I know I need to get some sleep but my daylong nap has thrown me off. Not good for the photo shoot in the morning. Makeup will be working overtime.

Thirty more minutes pass and I'm too anxious to sit still, so I get dressed and head to the hotel gym to run off this excess energy. With my headphones in, I cover two and a half miles when a pretty woman in a red dress enters my line of sight. I decrease my speed from seven to three, letting my heart rate regulate back to its normal beat. Pulling out my headphones, I look at her. She's beautiful even when I'm frustrated with her.

Reese says, "It's almost one in the morning. What are you doing in here?"

"I couldn't sleep."

"Let's go upstairs. Maybe we can together."

"Is that why you came over?" My jaw tenses as betrayal starts eating away at me. "To sleep?"

"I came over to explain."

I lower the speed again so I'm walking slowly. She's leaning on the treadmill, looking up at me. "Explain what? Why you blew me off today? Why I had to find you at that event tonight bogged down in half-stories and alluding to more than you could say?" Hitting the button, I roll off the back of the treadmill and land on my feet. I take the towel in my hands and scrub over my face and head, wiping away the sweat.

"I spoke with Keaton this morning."

Nodding, it becomes clear. He used his power to sway her back to his side. I walk to the water fountain and drink, waiting for her to drop the bomb. When she doesn't, I look back at her. She comes closer, close enough to touch me, and as if she can't resist, she does despite the possibility of getting my sweat on her fancy dress. "You have it all figured out in your head, don't you? Have you no faith in me at all?"

"I did once. I got hurt."

"I got hurt too, but I'm trying not to fall back into that trap and hold the past against you."

"And what trap is that? Not one I set." My voice rises as does my anger, all the irritation I just ran off comes rushing back.

Her voice remains impressively calm under the circumstances. "Can we go upstairs and talk about this instead of having it play out in a smelly gym?"

Waving my hand toward the door, I say, "After you."

She walks by and I'm tempted to grab her, to touch her, to take her against the mirrored wall, making her watch as I fuck her and this irritation out of my system for good. I reach for her, but drop my arm back down, knowing that won't solve anything. Looking up, I see the camera in the corner of the room aimed at us. Fuck. Lowering my head, I follow her back to the room.

The door shuts and locks automatically. She takes off her shoes and I go straight to the bathroom and turn on the shower. I kick off my shoes and strip down. She appears in the doorway and leans against it the frame. "I'm not with him, if that's what you're thinking."

"I don't know what to think."

"But I have obligations I have to fulfill."

"To Klein Advertising or to him?"

"The lines are blurred."

"That's what I was afraid of, and yet, you ask me to have faith in you."

"I still do. Faith and trust that I want what you want."

"I want to."

She walks to the counter, turning her back to the mirror to face me. One by one she starts taking pins out of her hair. "I'm yours, Danny. You own my heart." Little by little, strands come tumbling down over her shoulders. I should get in the shower. I really should, but I don't. I'm mesmerized by the brunette beauty who has turned her back to me, asking for help. "Will you unzip me?"

My fingers find the small zipper and I slide it down her back. As the two sides go slack, her skin is revealed. I glance up at her reflection in the mirror. Her eyes are down as she moves her hair to the side. It comes down to either trusting her or not. I lean in and kiss her exposed skin. I'm choosing to trust the woman who could easily destroy me. *Again.* Reese moans softly letting her head loll to the side, whether subconsciously or on purpose, she gives me more access.

I take advantage of the opportunity and lick her neck, then blow, making her shiver. "Danny." Her hands come around to hold on to me. But I want the dress off, so I move back just enough for it to pool at her feet.

She steps out and I tilt my head to get a new perspective. Everything about her entices me, makes me want her more each day. "I've given you my heart. With that, comes my faith and trust."

Turning around under my watchful gaze, she slips her panties down and takes her bra off. "I've given you the same." Wordlessly, she comes to me. Taking my shirt by the hem, she lifts while I bend over and she removes it. Her hands run down my body, a slight sheen from sweat, but she doesn't blink twice. Rubbing over my cock, I cover her hand, and then take off my shorts. "Please never doubt how I feel about you. I did what I did tonight for us."

Our bodies bare before each other, I drag the tips of my fingers over her breasts. "What did you do? Tell me."

My cock is hard as I stand there. I want to slide so slowly inside her then fuck her fast and hard. I want to make her feel how much she makes me want her. But I'm patient, so I let her answer first. She replies through labored breaths, "I have to play his game."

"Why?" I whisper as I take her earlobe between my teeth and just breathe.

Her nipples are hard, her body squirming. She closes her eyes as if in pain, squeezing them shut. When she reopens them, she says, "Because he'll ruin you if I don't."

"No one can ruin me. No one but you, baby."

I take her wrists in hand and our bodies gravitate closer. "Make love to me, Danny." The plea is guttural, a desire driven from hunger and erotic pleasure, not matching the sweet words.

My grip on her wrists tightens as I try to fight my own desire for her. I release her and back away to the counter.

She looks surprised, not happy. "What? Why did you let go?"

"Because I didn't think I could."

"You were testing yourself? What? To see if you could resist me?" The water pours down in the shower and I wonder if I should either get in or turn it off, but I stay where I am despite the debate. She looks confused. "You want to let me go?"

"No," I say, "I want you to let *him* go."

"I have."

Shaking my head, I look down. "I want to be with you, Reese. I want you so much. I want you in ways I should probably go to church and confess my sinful thoughts."

"You're not Catholic."

"That's my point. I think it's lust that draws me to you, but then you're asleep in my arms with no makeup and you look like an angel. You've got me all fucked up, but when you say you have to play *his* games, I come to my senses."

"Why?"

"Because you don't have to play his games, you're choosing to."

"I have a mortgage. I have bills."

Frustration creeps in again and I shake my head. "I have money, but the one thing I've realized is it won't bring you happiness. You have to find that for yourself."

"I found you."

"No, you just finally called me back." I turn my back on her and look down, resting my hands on the countertop.

I'm poked. Once. Twice before turning around. She says, "Listen to me. I'm here. I'm here when he threatened me. I'm here because of you. So believe me or don't believe me. That's up to you, but I know why I'm here and you're not going to twist my words."

She walks to the door but stops before she leaves. "I know you're used to having your way, but this time, you're going to have to trust that everything I'm doing is for us. You said I have your heart, faith, and trust. Now prove it."

"You're asking me to let that asshole control your life when I don't even want him near you."

Coming back to me, she places her hands gently on my chest as if she's scared of the outcome. "I'm asking you to let me handle this. We have the photo shoot tomorrow and then we're off to Paris tomorrow night. He will be a distant memory and after this campaign we'll be together."

Taking her by the waist, I hold her there, not wanting to ever let her go again. "That's asking a lot."

"I'll make it worth your while. I promise."

"I would be crazy to let this guy come within fifty yards of you."

"Vittori is the culmination of everything I've worked so hard for. I started as an intern and have worked my way up through the most reputable agencies in New York. I have to lead this team to the best campaign possible. Then I'll have options. Right now, I've got nothing. He holds all the cards."

Reese is smart and sinfully sexy. As Vinnie said earlier, she is more than capable and much more resourceful than him. But I need to know she won't back down, that if she's going to do this on her own that she'll stand her ground. I always admired her strength—particularly her strength to not back down from me—so I need to trust in that now. I don't doubt her, but I sure as fuck don't trust *him*.

"If he holds all the cards, you're underestimating what *he's* capable of. I'm flying blind to what's even happening and you're asking me not to help. It's like sending you into battle without any armor. Let me be your armor, Reese."

Guilt seems to plague her, but she stays steady on her mission. "I'm sorry. Not this time. Okay?"

"Just don't tell me to stay here and look pretty," I say, quirking an eyebrow.

Her laughter is full, carrying beyond the two of us. It's music to my ears. "I won't. I promise. Though you are ver—"

"Eh! Nope. Don't say it," I tease, and then sigh. "So you're doing this, aren't you?"

"I have to."

"Then I'll let you make this mistake and hopefully learn from it. But no matter what, I'll be here however you need me."

For us. It's so fucking frustrating she feels she has to do this on her own. Especially when it's regarding us, but I'll let her do what she feels so strongly about and be here waiting. Looking her over, she really is too damn sexy when she's so determined.

As if reading my mind, she says, "I want to have sex, and I want you to make me forget about tonight. I want to be blissfully unaware of everything, except for right now, here with you."

I'm already smirking. *How can I not when I have temptation in its truest form begging me to fuck her?* It's a hard job... like rock-hard, but I can handle it.

"Sit up here." I lift her up and place her on the counter. "I'll be right back. Be ready for me."

After turning off the water, I slip out and go for a condom from my suitcase. When I return, she has her arms wrapped around her legs, giving me a peek of her sexy pussy. "Open for me."

She spreads her legs and waits for further instruction. "Put your hands behind you." She does. After stroking myself while eyeing her incredible tits, I rip open the package and put the condom on.

Her back is curved, pushing them forward, and I run my hand over her sensitive nipples. "You know how sexy you are?"

"No," she says, the reply jagged. "Tell me."

"I'll show you, but brace yourself." Just as she firms her palms against the counter, I slam forward, holding her by her hips as I thrust in and out several times, hard and fast.

Her warmth draws my eyes to close, the fuse inside sparking to life. I won't last, not with her, not like this. I'm getting close to release when she says, "Stop. Danny, stop."

My whole body is alert to the sound of her voice and I stop. Worried, I back up but keep my hands on her. "Are you okay? Did I hurt you?"

Each breath sends her chest rising and falling to a rapid beating heart. "No, this feels good. It's too much and not enough." Her hands cover her tits, teasing herself and me. "I want to see you. I need to see your eyes on me, on mine."

Her pleasure is mine. Touching her cheek, I let my hand drift down and I smile. "I want to watch you come." My fingers slip between her legs and I find that spot that makes her purr. "Keep your eyes on mine."

She looks up, pupils wide as she takes me in. Her hands are holding me to the spot, her back to the mirror. I build her up again, tightening the coil that I want to watch unravel. I run my thumb over her bottom lip, wetting it. Then I kiss her as small circles increase in intensity and her moans are swallowed. When she starts holding on to me, I lean back and our eyes meet again— passion, addiction, obsession reside in the clarity of her deep blues and I don't want her just to physically feel how strongly I feel for her, but to see it. "I've always loved you."

The back of her head hits the mirror, her eyes close, and her mouth opens. "Oh God, Danny." She shivers as the force of ecstasy takes over her body.

"Look at me, baby."

I can see her struggle, but when her eyes open and meet mine, I don't relent until I see her body coming down.

Sitting upright, she kisses my neck and whispers, "I want you inside me."

I'm there. Positioned, and then I'm inside her heat, thrusting, racing toward that fiery descent. The embers of her orgasm burn me, bringing mine forth. It's fast, too fast. I drop my head next to hers and give in, not caring about anything but the feeling exploding inside, filling me, and igniting every cell in my body. She's done me in and I shudder inside her. My breath is harsh, but her hand on the back of my neck is gentle as she strokes my sensitive skin.

This is what I've been missing.

This is what gives me peace.

This. Is. Love.

CHAPTER 28

WE LIE IN bed, only our hands bridging the gap between us. I stare up at the ceiling though I can't see anything in the dark room. Not even her. The discretion allows me to think about everything that is happening, about everything that has happened.

I can hear her breathing and I want to smother her with my body and emotions, covering her until she only breathes me. She says, "You should sleep. You have the photo shoot in the morning."

"You do too."

I can't see her smile in the dark, but I hear it in her tone when she says, "But I'm not on camera."

"You could be."

"Thank you," she whispers and I can bet she doesn't believe me. Her hand squeezes mine. "This has to be perfect. There is no room for okay. We need amazing to happen. Promise me you'll give me amazing no matter what they ask of you."

The undertone of the conversation is weighted with little information. I still don't know what she's up to, but I can overlook that because I know she's choosing me. "I'll give you amazing,

Reese." I yawn, and her body rolls toward mine. I put my arm under her and bring her closer. A yawn of her own follows and then my world disappears, exchanged for dreams and memories from the past that have been long-since buried.

CLAUDIA STANDS ON a large venting hood, her pale pink dress blowing behind her as she stares at me. My hands are firm on the short brick wall that surrounds the roof where we're shooting. The black suit and shirt I've been styled in works for this gray day. I look off at the Empire State Building in the distance, then slowly turn back to Claudia.

The clicking of Bryker's camera is heard above the noise twenty stories down on the streets of Manhattan. Walking to her, I keep my eyes on the woman in the dress who appears to be floating as the sheer skirt blows wide around her. I'm feeling it, so I hope the camera captures the élan vital of what we're trying to evoke.

Claudia reaches forward for me and as I take her hands I try to stay focused on her and not on the woman off to the side who just showed up, three hours after me. Taking Claudia by the waist, I twirl her in the air and then bring her down until we're face to face, our eyes locked.

Bryker directs, "Kiss her."

Our eyes close as our lips come together. I'm careful of our angles, acutely aware of where the camera is as the photographer shifts around us. Holding Claudia in place, I'm careful to not mess her hair and give the camera the best angle of my jaw, keeping my promise to Reese—giving her photo-shoot perfection. Just as she requested.

Bryker's telling us to make love to the camera, to make love to each other, use the eyes, kiss her lips, drop our shoulder, angle toward him, away from him, spin her around, move the dress, show the suit—do what feels natural.

I glance over and send a glare on that one. I know what he wants. He wants what every photographer wants—to capture the moment in its rawest form—to find love, lust, realness in the subjects. These subjects—Claudia and I—aren't in love. Our job is to manufacture those emotions through silence and our bodies, our eyes, our passion, to play pretend and trick the viewer's eye.

But passion for my job and "getting the shot" are no match for the real thing. I look at Reese, sneaking a peek as I turn us around. She's not watching. She still struggles because I'm too good at my job, convinced what she sees before her is real.

This is where faith and trust come into play, something I'm being forced to embrace since she won't let me know how she's "handling" her ex.

Bryker calls out, "That's a wrap for this location. Pack up."

Claudia walks to wardrobe, and I detour to Reese. "Morning."

"Morning. You left early. You must be tired."

"I've had two espressos."

She reaches forward, a comfort in the action, but stops and holds her hands in front of her. "We must be careful."

"We're heading to the apartment. Are you coming?"

"No. I have two meetings with other clients."

I lean in to kiss her, but catch myself, understanding her struggle just seconds earlier. "You're on the flight tonight?"

"Yes. Do you need anything?"

"Only you."

A broad smile brightens my day. "You've got me, Danny. You had me all along."

"I've wasted many years then."

"We both did." She puts more space between us. "The photos are going to look amazing. The chemistry is undeniable."

"Don't believe everything you see."

"I'll keep that in mind, but for now, I need to go."

Perfect timing, as if planned to not have to watch anymore. I get it. I don't know how I'd feel about watching her and another guy. Yeah, I do. It'd fucking suck. "I'll see you later." I head over to Becs.

Quietly, Reese says, "Hey, Danny?"

Turning around, I say, "Hey, Reese."

Her smile is genuine, the girl seen within the woman standing before me. She says, "Last night," she glances to the right, and then back to me, "you were incredible."

"I'm hoping for a repeat in Paris."

That sends the blood rushing to her cheeks and she shies away, leaving before anybody else notices. But I notice and that's all that matters. The beautiful blue-eyed girl is mine. Again.

I strip off the jacket, starting on the shirt as soon as I reach wardrobe. I get down to my boxers before I step behind the makeshift dressing room. Claudia is pulling a T-shirt over her head sans bra while I pull off the Vittori underwear and pull on my jeans. She yawns. "I'm so fucking tired today. I can't sleep for shit in Manhattan. I never did like this city."

"Is it the city or the partying that kept you up?"

With a trilling laugh, she taps her chin. "You might have a point there."

That's when I see it. "Wipe your nose."

The residue is barely seen, but it's there. She rubs her nose on her shirt. "All clear?"

"All clear. You didn't have that while shooting did you?"

"No." She reaches down and flashes open her purse. The vial looks empty for the most part. I'm glad she's out.

"Do you need it to work?"

"I need it to survive."

I pull on my shirt and grab my jacket from the top of the screen. "When did it get that bad?"

"The first time I tried it."

"When was that?" I ask, though I should probably let it go.

"I was sixteen, and on a shoot in Italy. The photographer wanted to 'help' get me in the mood."

Trying to keep things casual, I start to feel sick as I bend down and put on my socks and shoes. "What happened?" I ask because there is always more to a story that starts like that. I've heard it a hundred times—models get taken advantage of all the time. They're young, desperate to hit it big. I imagine modeling is a lot like acting in that way, both professions full of people who want to be the next star, the next one "discovered."

I stand in front of her, both of us fully dressed behind a screen in the middle of Manhattan on a cloudy day. She lowers her voice and says, "I took the drugs and gave him what he wanted."

Our eyes meet, a desperate sadness in hers that never seems to dissipate. I'm hesitant to say more, but do it anyway. "The photos turned out?"

"We never took any pictures. At least none for the campaign I was shooting."

My stomach rolls. "He raped you?"

"He would say I agreed."

"What would you say?"

"I don't say anything at all."

There's something so vulnerable about her, despite the hard and edgy that got her to the level she's at. But beneath the surface is something youthful and naïve. This woman has a damaged side that will never heal. She's stunted in an action that formed who she is now.

I hug her.

She hugs me back.

There's nothing sexual, no ulterior motives, no judgment. Just two people who are trying to survive in the middle of the chaos that's raised them.

Becs asks, "You guys ready? The crew is packed."

I wait for Claudia to answer. "Yes." She walks by me as if the conversation we just had never happened. She leaves the roof and hopefully a little of her pain behind.

When I come out, Becs folds the portable dressing screens. I take them from her, she grabs her rack, and we leave like the rest.

In the back of the Suburban, Becs says, "She's very pretty."

Turning my attention from the passing people outside the vehicle to the one next to me, I agree. "Claudia nailed it this morning."

"I wasn't talking about Claudia."

Smiling, I reply, "I should have known."

"Any update or are you going to keep me in suspense forever?"

I lower my voice so the driver and the makeup artist don't hear me. "What would you like to know?"

"I'm a romantic at heart. Tell me everything."

I chuckle. "I should probably leave out some of the sordid details. I could be arrested in at least two states if word got out."

"Damn, those are the best details. *Do not* leave those out."

I sound more serious than intended, but maybe that's because my heart is speaking for me. "I'm in deep."

A soft, but proud smile enters her expression. Leaning over, she wraps an arm around me. "Awwww, you'll be okay. It's just new right now. Once you get off set and spend quality time together I would wager that this is the one."

"Why do you say that?"

"From watching the two of you." She sits back on her side of the seat and reflects. "There's something about the way you move when you're together, as if your bodies can't stand the distance. I see her when you're not looking. I see you when she's not watching you. You're one in the same. I'm afraid when it comes to your stubbornness as well."

"I'm not stubborn, Becs."

"You're set in your ways and that way isn't working for you anymore. You need to be honest with yourself and Reese. The rest of us don't matter."

"I've been honest with her. She knows how I feel. She's just caught up in the side effects of dating me." I drop my head back. "I don't want to lose her again, but I don't know how to hold on to her either."

"Love doesn't need to be held. It's in our veins, flowing through us like blood. It's essential to our makeup. So don't let your need to hold something tangible make you miss what's inside."

"Stop being so damn insightful," I tease.

"Eh, it's a gift."

I lean over and kiss her on the head. "You're a gift."

When she looks at me, her eyes are wide. "That's the same as calling me awesome, right?"

"Better than awesome. See? I'm not so stubborn."

With a roll of her eyes, we're back to being playful. The emotions Reese and I are feeling for each other will stay tucked away until we deal with it later. I have a good three hours work ahead of me and need to get in the right frame of mind. Then later, we have that seven-hour flight to Paris to get through. How I'm supposed to be near her for that long and not touch her, not kiss or make love to her? That is going to be the longest seven hours of my life.

CHAPTER 29

THE PHOTO SHOOT had such promise.

But as I look at Reese's ex, and current boss, lying on the ground in front of me, I realized it the second he walked in. None of us stood a chance.

Forty minutes earlier

"LOOK AT ME, Danny," Bryker directs. "I want intense. I want lust. I want power. I want controlled."

I stare straight into the camera. My jaw tenses as I hold my breath to give him all that he asked for and more. When I release, I look down and then back up. The camera hasn't moved, but I do, shifting to give him something new. He backs away, going for a wide angle. King of the world, endless three-sixty views of Manhattan backs me as I sit back in the desk chair. Claudia comes around and with her hands on my shoulders, she massages. The boss-and-secretary scene plays out until she stops to pose.

"This is good. Danny, look out over your playground. You own this city. Devour the views, then Claudia." I turn my back to the lens, only my head and arms in view as I stare ahead. Claudia faces the camera, then directs her attention to me. I grab her, pulling her into my lap. Her legs go up as I spin back around, the scene playful until I see Reese and her ex standing in the doorway of the room. He has his arms crossed as he glares at me disapprovingly.

Worry creases Reese's face, her bottom lip tucked under her top teeth. I turn my gaze back to Claudia when she cups my jaw and redirects me. "Look at me, Danny," she whispers, "only me."

Taking my hand, she runs it over her bare leg and higher under the hem of her skirt. "Only me," she repeats seductively.

I lick my lips and even though I want to look at Reese—want to touch Reese this way—I redirect the wants onto the model I'm paid to desire. She leans in and kisses me. My eyes close to block Reese out, but the blackness behind my lids are filled with images of her—her face as she looks back at me while I fuck her, the way her lip gets tugged under and released the moment she comes, her eyes as they take me in while taking me into her mouth.

Fuck!

My eyes flash open. Claudia is staring at me, and asks, "Where'd you go?"

I stand abruptly, setting her on her feet. "I need five."

Bryker sways his arm in the air. "Everyone take five."

I head right for Reese, keeping my eyes locked on hers. She does the minutest of headshakes and I walk right past and head to wardrobe, which is set up in the other room.

Becs questions, "Danny?"

I keep moving out the door, needing air, the apartment air is stale in my lungs. At the elevators, I punch the lobby button. When the doors open, I rush to the back and turn around. Reese is there. She steps inside and pushes the button to close the doors.

As soon as they do, she's against me, chest to chest. Her hands are running through the back of my hair as I hold her by the shoulders, kissing her. Kissing her so hard, as if she might be taken away. The floors tick by and we don't waste a second. I grab her perfect tits in my hands and squeeze, causing her to moan into my mouth.

The lobby floor dings and we fly to opposite sides of the elevator car. Our breathing matches each other's—erratic and heavy. Her lips are parted and swollen from my lips. *My fucking lips*. I own hers. That fucker can go fuck himself if he thinks he's ever going to touch her again.

She walks out and I follow in silence, both of us headed to the front doors of the lobby. It's been raining since we've been upstairs, the ground wet. A few umbrellas still above heads as the sidewalk remains crowded in spite of the foul weather.

Reese stops and I stand beside her. She says, "Don't."

"What?"

"You know what. Don't do what you're doing. If I can see it, the camera can read it."

I turn to her. "What am I doing, Reese?"

"You're imagining the worst."

"I'm imagining your life before me."

"Keaton and I broke up over a year ago. He wasn't like this, like how he is now. He wasn't possessive."

"I am."

"It's not the same. He's become obsessive. He lost me. I'm only a prize to him now."

"You broke up with him?"

"I did. I think I'm the first, so he's not handling it well."

"If it's been over a year, why does he think he still has a chance?"

She moves back out of the pedestrian traffic, under the cover of the large forest-green awning that fronts the entrance to the building. "He doesn't. Trust me."

"You throw trust around as if it will make this turmoil I feel inside go away, but don't you see I do trust you? But that fucker—no way will I ever trust him."

My declaration brings a smile to her face. "I feel the same way." She checks her watch. I take a deep breath. Actually, the few moments with Reese *are* my deep breath. My calm. "We should get back. As they say, time is money."

Riding up the elevator, we stand next to each other, our eyes on the other. There isn't a frenzied make-out session. The early crazed kissing came from an uncertainty that needed to be claimed. I've claimed her and she's claimed me. Our feelings established.

The elevator doors open on the forty-second floor and I come face to face with him. He has the nerve to call Reese over to him. "I've been wondering where you went. We're going to be late for our meeting." His eyes hit me, and he says, "We have private business to discuss, so you should probably put on more *makeup* and get primped to get your picture taken."

Reese asks, "What business?"

He whispers in her ear, his hand wrapped around her shoulders as if he has a right to hold her, much less touch her. She moves out from under his arm and keeps walking. "Have you forgotten already? You're on Klein time. I was thinking we could grab drinks down in the Village. I know how you like it down there with that eclectic crowd."

Waving him off, she says, "Go ahead. I have things to do here."

"What would be the point of me going alone?" he asks, following her around. "And what business do you have here?"

The three of us enter the office again, my hands fisted at my side while the pestering gnat circles Reese. Bryker is walking with the light meter when he sees me. "Stand right here, Danny. I think this will be a good shot without washing you out from the sunlight coming in."

Keaton mocks me. "Yes, Danny, do as you're told and let's get this shoot wrapped. I have a date that seems to refuse to leave until this shoot is finished."

Poke.

He nudges Reese who's not laughing, and says, "Funny, right? Seems he wants to pla—"

"Shut up, Keaton," she cuts him off.

Becs appears uncomfortable and Bryker attempts to ignore the tension building off set. Claudia sets her phone down and looks up.

While I stand where Bryker wants me, I watch as Keaton takes Reese by the arm. "It's time to go."

Jerking free, she warns him, "Don't tell me what to do."

"Somebody has to."

When he takes her by the arm again, I say, "Let her go."

All eyes in the room turn to me, but my eyes stay right where they need to be—on her.

"What did you just to say to me?"

My gaze shifts to her right. "Don't touch her again."

"Jealousy is an ugly look and considering your looks are all you've got to offer, I suggest you watch your threats." Surprising Reese, he wraps his arm around her waist.

While she wriggles free, I'm already in motion before I have a chance to think this through. The thing is—while I watch him fall to the ground—I don't regret punching him. I only regret that I didn't do it sooner.

Gasps fill the room, one of them Reese's as she holds her

hands over her mouth. When our eyes meet over the sniveling, bloody-nosed man lying between us, an understanding is shared through that look. I see beyond the blue and into her soul. It's not about him. Everything we feel for each other is only about us. Us alone. He doesn't matter, and that's when I feel it. She loves me.

I smile 'cuz I love her too. Then I'm knocked down, falling head over feet—literally. I slam to the floor, landing on my ass. No the fuck he didn't. I'm back on my feet before he can blink. One more fast swing connects, sending him down for the count.

He holds his face, wailing, "You are so fucking dead. You'll pay for this, pretty boy!"

"That's fine," I reply. "It was worth it."

He gets to his knees, still threatening as loudly as he can. "I'm going to sue your ass. I'll see you in court, motherfucker."

Reese stands in shock, as does Becs. Becs rushes to my aide. "Are you okay? That looked like a nasty fall. You came this close," she says, holding her fingers two inches apart, "from hitting your head on the desk."

Brushing her off, I tell her, "I'm fine."

Claudia stands from the leather chair on the other side of the desk, looking bored. "Are we shooting anymore or what?"

We all stare at her. Bryker says, "I think I got all we need."

She replies, "Good. Today's my day to eat and I'm starving."

Reese's dramatic sigh can be heard as she rolls her eyes. "Can I please buy you a burger?"

Claudia looks at her. "I don't eat meat. But I'll take a bowl of peas."

The asshole stands in a huff. "Peas? What the fuck? Are you people insane? Why is no one helping me? Get me a fucking icepack."

Becs makes a move to the door. "I have one in my first aid kits. Come with me. Danny, I'll bring one back for your hand."

As soon as they're out of the room, I laugh. Reese smiles. Bryker just shakes his head.

Then *he* comes back in, and demands, "Reese! Let's go."

I watch her shoulders slump as she debates. She looks at me but knows how I feel about his demand, yet she still insists, "I'll handle it."

Knowing she needs my support more than my judgment, I nod, but I'm still pissed. "What about the flight to Paris?"

"Be on it. I'll talk to Vinnie and explain, but we're moving forward with this campaign whether Klein Advertising is involved or not."

I watch her walk away, hating the dread that fills me. I know I need to let her go, to handle this on her own, but it doesn't take away the twisting in my gut knowing she's going to see him. I wouldn't give him the courtesy of even telling him I quit if I was in her shoes. But that's not Reese and I respect that about her.

Becs comes to the door and hooks her finger. "Come on, let's get you out of that suit and hope there's no blood on it."

I'M STANDING AT the entrance to the airplane, anxiously waiting. There's been no sign of Reese and she hasn't called or answered her phone. I got one text telling me to go to Paris even if she doesn't make the flight.

"Sir," the flight attendant taps me and says, "we need you to board. This is the final boarding call."

I look down at the text once more: *I'll see you in Paris. I promise.*

I board per her wish and settle into the first class seat. Just as I power off my phone, a flurry of commotion happens at the entrance to the plane. I look up to see Reese coming toward me. She flops down in the seat next to me and tucks a large purse under the seat. She's radiant. Wild hair, bright eyes, casual clothes. She says, "I quit."

I look at her in shock. And awe. My pride in her taking over my tone. "You did?"

"I did." She's nodding and exuberantly giddy.

"What about your responsibilities?"

"I'm seeing this campaign through. We're going to get the shots we need and then... I don't know. I have some savings. Not much, but some. I'll come back and find a new job."

Taking her hand in mine, I lean back. "And you did this for?"

"For me. For us. For my soul. God, I feel so good right now." She looks at me with a new hope I haven't been privy to since we laid eyes on each other in that first meeting back in LA. "What a weight lifted."

But beneath the relief she's feeling, the high she's riding, I start to wonder how she's going to feel when she comes down. "What happened?"

"I told him. I told him everything."

"Be more specific, Reese." I try to keep the sternness out of my voice, but through her hope, I can't help but think I'm going to be the reason she loses it.

The flight attendant makes us pause. I order water and Reese orders wine. She turns to me, and laughs. "You should have seen the look on his face, Danny. You would have been so proud of me."

"I was already proud of you. Now please tell me what happened."

"I went back to the office and told him how I really feel about him. Then I told him I'll finish this campaign and gave my two-weeks' notice."

It would be easy to get swept up in her delight, but my instincts regarding a man like Keaton Klein are usually spot-on. With dread entering my stomach, I ask, "How did he react to that?"

"I don't even care anymore. He's controlled me for too long. I felt I had no options, no outs. I bought my apartment because I had that job and security. But over time I realized he wasn't going to just let me go. It didn't even matter that he didn't want me. I was just this thing he didn't want anyone else to have either."

"If he wants you, he's not going to let you go that easily."

"He doesn't have a choice. Once I realized I could sell the apartment, I saw that I have options. I don't want to be tied down by stuff when I can be living a fuller life. I don't need that job. I can find another." She touches her chest. "I have control of my life again. Danny, we can be together. I can live anywhere. We should be celebrating. Isn't this what you wanted?"

"I want all that. I want you to be happy. I never want him around you again—"

"I'm not going to be after this campaign and that makes me happy. Being here with you makes me happy. A future full of possibilities scares the shit out of me, but I'm happy because I need to be scared. I need to be challenged again. I need to start living my dream."

"What do you dream of?"

"I dream of you."

"You don't have to dream of me. I'm right here. I'm yours already. I always was." Leaning over the armrest, I kiss her on the forehead and hold her hand a little tighter. "I love you."

"I love you, too. So much."

Sitting back when the attendant returns with our drinks, I can't ignore my gut. This is gonna blow back in our faces. If there's one thing I learned about her ex, it's that he's not afraid of the low blow. The fucking weasel.

CHAPTER 30

Reese

"WE'RE MAKING OUR descent."

I open my eyes to find Danny rubbing my leg gently to wake me. I stir, feeling groggy. "I only meant to close my eyes for a minute."

"Being a badass heartbreaker takes energy."

His smile warms me so I reach up and adjust the air vent above my head, hoping to cool down before he notices. Massaging my temples eases the pain in my head, a headache forming.

He asks, "How are you feeling?" I hear the trepidation in his voice.

"I'm fine," I reply resting my hand on his thigh, wanting to touch him more, but knowing now is not quite the right time. *Later. Most definitely later.* "Why do you sound so worried? Everything with the shoot is still moving forward."

"I'm not worried about me, Reese. I'm worried about you."

"Why?"

"Because I think you acted spontaneously last night."

"I thought you'd be happy? He's out of our life now."

"His firm is still in charge of this shoot. And Klein doesn't seem like the type of guy to let it go. I shouldn't have hit him. Twice. But he provoked me. I just hate that I lost my temper at all. He's not worth it."

"He was demeaning, Danny."

He chuckles. "I'm not naïve. I know how people feel about models. They only look at the surface. No pun intended. But I take my job seriously, and it's given me a life I couldn't otherwise experience or afford. But more than that, I respect everyone who's a part of this industry. I've met a lot of great people because of modeling. So when he demeans me, he's demeaning all of them. And that's why I hit him. Twice."

"It was hot."

"What?" He looks my way smiling.

"You hitting him. It was hot. And the hotness doesn't come from the fact it was *him* you hit. It was the way the suit was taut around your biceps and how your eyes were set on him. He didn't stand a chance against you. Reminded me of college."

"Of all the things I've tried to remind you of, that wasn't meant to be one of them. I'm getting too old for that shit. I'm supposed to be maturing."

"Oh, you've matured," I say, sliding my hand higher up his leg. "Yes, indeed."

"Are you drunk?"

"No," I answer, wondering why he asked that. "Why?"

His eyes are narrowed, but his lips are amused. "You're just so... not like you."

"Is that a bad thing?"

"No. It's a good thing. And you're like you, but not like the Reese you put on for work. The business you."

"The business me?" Now I'm squinting my eyes, puzzled. "I didn't know I was putting on anything. You make it sound like I'm not fun. I'm fun. Tons o' fun."

Pointing, he laughs. "That. See? Right there. Tons o' fun. What is that?"

"I don't know. Just popped in my head and I said it."

"That's what I mean. Usually you don't say anything unless it's carefully crafted and then presented with caution and care."

"I don't craft what I say." *Wait, do I?* Damn, he might be right. I think I might actually craft what I say. "Not much anyway."

He smiles and takes my hand that has been very touchy feely. "You're making me hard. Unless you plan to follow through right the fuck here in first class, let's hold off."

Why is it so hot when he swears from sexual frustration and sexual release? Just everything sexual. It's even hotter when he's swearing. "I'm willing to follow through *right the fuck* here. If you want me to."

"Drugs?"

I hit him, and as he laughs blocking the second hit, I say, "No, I'm not on drugs either. Geez, you make me sound awful."

Lifting the armrest up, he then wraps his arm around me and pulls me as close as he can. "I don't mean it like that at all. I find you incredibly sexy whether you're in business mode or not, so don't take it the wrong way. I've only gotten glimpses of the carefree Reese since seeing each other again. I got *her* in Marfa."

The memories of Marfa make me smile. "You did." I sit up as the plane touches down. "I'm happy. I feel more alive with that noose no longer around my neck."

"For the record, Reese, I like every side that smiles." With that million-dollar smile of his own, he says, "And if the offer for the *right the fuck here* is still open, I'm game."

The plane comes to a stop at our gate and I shrug, feigning indifference. "I'm afraid the offer's expired."

Leaning over, he puts his lips against my ear, and whispers, "I'll take a rain check." He leaves me with a kiss to my neck and sits back in his chair like that didn't send a surge of sex-tricity throughout my entire body. It did. *It sooo did.*

At baggage claim, because our closeness has become obvious to everyone—Bryker, Becs, Claudia—we don't bother hiding our feelings any longer. Danny takes hold of my hand while we're waiting for our luggage to come down the belt. I glance at him, but don't pull my hand away. Instead, I squeeze it, holding his just as tight.

Forty-five minutes later, Danny stands with the others in the lobby of our hotel in Paris while I settle the rooms. After giving keys to Bryker, Becs, and Claudia, they leave, and I say, "I just saved the company money."

"How's that?"

"We're staying together. You're stuck with me now."

"I can't think of anyone I'd rather be stuck with than you."

"You say the sweetest things, Mr. Weston," I reply, shaking my derriere for him as I walk to the elevators.

"Speaking of amazing asses—"

"We weren't speaking of asses."

"We are now, and yours is the best. Shake it for me, baby."

I do. I shake my ass with sass just because he asked. It's not the same ass I had in college so I'm glad he likes it so much, and I'm happy to indulge his wish.

Upon entering the room, I release a deep breath, the weight of everything gone from my shoulders, and my heart. It feels good to be free. It feels great to be with Danny. I flop down on the bed and close my eyes. "I slept, but I'm so tired."

"We should stay awake to get on the current time."

I roll onto my side and prop my head up on my hand. Watching him move around the room, I smile as he puts our suitcases together by the wardrobe. I decide to tease, though it's really a tease wrapped in truth. "You're too good-looking. You know that?"

"I've been told."

I'm reaching for the pillow to throw at him but he lands next to me and traps my arms above my head before I have a chance. "You want to play?" I know he means a pillow fight, maybe tickling, being silly, but there's this undertone that speaks directly to my lower half, causing my hips to seek out his. He hovers over me and there is no fight. I want him. I just do. From his body to his charm, his jaw to his jokes, his abs to his sincerity—everything about this man turns me into a sex fiend. But more than the physical, our hearts speak the same language. "You make me feel, Danny."

"Feel what?" he whispers, kissing my shoulder.

"Everything, all at once."

A kiss is placed on my neck. "Is it too much?"

"Always too much... and never enough." My eyes drop closed and I murmur, "Never enough." How did I live without this? How did I live without *him*? For years after I left, I thought I saw him. A man on the street. A dark-haired guy in line at the grocery store. I thought he would come. But it seems our heartache morphed into stubbornness or forgetfulness. His life was exciting, his fame growing. He moved on without me being a part of it. I looked at the magazines. I looked at him online. My life was a stark boring contrast to the glamorous world he lived in. I worked my ass off for years for the simplest praise, for measly pay raises, to build a name for myself in advertising.

Ironically, our lives have been so intrinsically connected, but our love disjointed, pushed to the bottom of our priorities. *Buried.* I buried myself in work so the pain and tears wouldn't bury me. Living in a state of perpetual denial, I denied us and the memories that haunted me. I closed my heart to that part of my soul and moved to New York.

My achievements were hollow until Vittori allowed me to venture into the past, to remember, to allow that opening. How did I survive without his arms around me, without him? What was once hollow is now overflowing with feelings—happiness, love, peace. Lying in his arms, I realize how foolish it had been to think I could ever be without him. There is no *me* without *him* and by how he's looking at me, there's no him without me.

He was the missing piece of my soul.

He'll be forever in my heart.

He's forever mine.

And I his.

His lips meet mine in a turn of passion, my breast kneaded as my breath is stolen. There's no need for foreplay. Our hips clashing unbridled, needing more, craving the feel of him completing me again.

My shirt is tugged up and my bra down. His mouth covers one of my nipples, lavishing me with his tongue, making me moan. Reaching down, I tug at his belt and win the battle before tackling the button and zipper. A shadow scraps across my breast as his chin grazes me, spiriting my desires to the surface. "Danny," I whisper, too weak under this sexual spell to summon more.

He's freed, commando under his pants. My hand wraps around his length—soft skin over hard muscle. *Hard for me.* My body relaxes for his, under the influence of how much we turn each other on.

My jeans are unbuttoned just as quickly, the zipper lowered. His hand is in my pants before I can catch my breath. Pillow talk turns dirty. "You're so wet for me. You want me inside you?"

"So much."

His lips are at my ear. Strong fingers begin working me over just where I want him most. "Do you like me fucking you with my fingers like this?"

"Yes. That. So much." My head tilts back, my mind going fuzzy in the sensations.

But then he stops, and asks, "Or do you want me to fuck you properly?"

I just want to come. God. *So much.* Too much. Too much of everything with this man. A breath steadies my mind, allowing me to think. "How do you want to fuck me?"

"From behind."

If I weren't lying down already, I'd surely collapse under his certainty. "I want that."

The right side of his mouth slides up. On anyone else, the half-grin would come off as sinister, conniving, or devious. On Danny, it makes me not only want to rip his clothes off and mine, but burn them so we stay naked like this forever. "I want that," I repeat for no reason than I must be losing my senses again. He does that to me.

"So to be clear. You want me to fuck you from behind?"

"Good Lord." My bottom lip is bit. "Why is that so hot?"

"What?"

"You talking to me like that."

His eyes are set on mine. His voice is steady and assured. "Everyone else treats you like you're breakable. I treat you how you like to be treated—fuckable."

"Danny, fuck me. I don't even care with what. I just need you inside me."

He chuckles.

Inhaling a deep breath in protest, I do not approve of the lack of him touching me.

Sliding off the bed, he strips off the rest of his clothes before turning his attention back to me. Taking off first my flats, and then my jeans, he watches me while I take off my shirt and bra. My breathing is harder than I like, but I don't feel self-conscience in front of him. Not when he's standing there looking at me like I'm the air he needs to breathe, the food that sustains him, the water that keeps him alive. He looks at me like no man other than him has ever looked at me. I'm pinned to the bed under his scorching gaze and my heart pounds in my chest, beating for him as I wait.

The suspense is making me squirm as he centers himself on top of me. The weight of his body is sweet pressure, mine adapting to keep him exactly where he is. He asks, "Do we need condoms?" His question doesn't make me think of the lives we lived apart. Like most would think. He's genuine. His question is just as protective of me as it is him, if not even more so.

"I trust you," I reply. "Do you trust me?"

"I do," he says, and kisses me. "I trust you." Readjusting his body, his lips part as I reach up running the tips of my fingers over the rough growth covering his jaw.

Spreading my legs, he takes over the space unapologetically. My hands glide over his muscular shoulders and I hold on knowing our connection is going to intensify. Before he has a chance to move, I say, "Go slow."

With a smirk, he replies, "I thought you wanted fast."

"I meant with us."

Understanding sparks in his eyes. He pushes my hair back then holds my face. "I'll go as fast or slow as you want, baby. I'll let you lead."

His eyes are too intense, his feelings long escaped into emotion. Looking away, I focus on the space between our chests. "Stop being so perfect."

"It comes naturally."

"That's what worries me."

"Reese, look at me."

"I can't."

"You can." When I finally look up, I'm met with his melting browns—clear, shining, and seductive. "I'm not perfect. Don't fool yourself. But what I am is sure that we're good together. We always were."

"Then why didn't we make it the first time?"

"We weren't ready."

"Ready for what?" I wait with bated breath.

"Ready for forever."

Ready for forever.

I lower my eyes, the impact of his words striking me in the heart.

Ready for our forever.

God, how I love this man. I take his face in my hands, lifting up until our lips meet. His plush. Mine determined. His patient. Mine rushing. We're balanced in the simplest of pleasures. When we part, I sigh contented. With our lips still touching, I say, "I'm going to turn over."

His body leaves mine and I maneuver onto my stomach. "I'm yours, Danny. My body is yours. Now fuck me like you promised."

Just like every other time, he takes his time, running his fingers over my back, writing messages I can't interpret. Until now.

I.

Love.

You.

Goose bumps scatter across my skin, my soul bared to his, an exposure that only happens when our hearts are honest. My eyes drop closed. *I love you, too.* A squiggly line leads his hands to part and go to my ribs and lower. He rises up, bringing my hips with him. His chest is pressed against me and his tongue finds my spine. Slowly, oh so slowly, he tortures by teasing, leaving a wet trail until he reaches my lower back. With his thumbs circling the divots, I arch. Hands tighten as his tongue finds the top of my crack. "I'm going to go down on you." He gives me fair warning.

He's fast. His head slips between my legs, his back on the mattress. "Lower."

I lower myself onto his masterful mouth, but he pulls me farther and holds me in place. Resting the top of my head on the pillow beneath me, I open my mouth needing air. I use one of my hands to touch him however I can—his hair, his ear, his jaw, and then his neck. When I move back to the jaw, I can feel the strength as he opens and closes, sucking me into his world, into his mouth.

As if called to do so, my hips start gyrating and he ends up right where he needs to be. "Right there. God, yes, Danny."

He replies through a lustful moan as if he can't get enough of me and despite my valiant efforts to hold on longer, I succumb to his talented mouth. As soon as the tremors cease firing through my body, Danny's up and positioned. "Fuck," he says, when the tip of his cock touches the wet warmth at the apex of my thighs. "You're so hot, baby."

"I'm burning alive, you make me feel so good."

His cock eases in, his patience gone. "You're on fucking fire."

I exhale as he replaces the air that once filled my body with his own. Inhaling him into me, I find peace in the middle of ecstasy. "Oh God!" I shake, another orgasm hitting hard.

He moves faster, his breath covering my back as our bodies slide together. Each thrust punctuated with a definitive grunt that comes from deep within his chest. A chant of persuasion rolls off his tongue, "I love you, Reese, beautiful Reese."

Then he's coming and with no barriers between us, my body reacts to the pulsing. I fist the sheets beneath us and let go, falling like we both already have, all over again.

CHAPTER 31

Reese

THE SHOOT IS perfection, just like I hoped. I may have quit, but my job is officially done once we wrap. One more setup outside tomorrow and I'm free from Klein Advertising and Keaton forever. He won't be able to argue that I wasn't fantastic at my job. Not with the Vittori campaign on my résumé.

Fingers crossed he doesn't actually send someone to fuck things up like he threatened. I'll just keep an eye out just in case.

Leaning against the wall behind a large fan, I watch as Danny and Claudia stand in formal attire against a picturesque window highlighting the Eiffel Tower in the background. They're pretending to be what Danny and I are, in love. I have no doubt in my heart or head anymore.

He was always the one.

I just naïvely detoured from the right path. So seeing them now, I can tell the difference. I see it in his body, in the way he looks at her, in the way he touches her. It's not the same as when he's with me. He's sexy, even with her, and the camera will never notice the difference in their relationship. But I will. *I do.*

I smile, and he glances over, catching me, sending a small

smile my way that's not seen on his mouth, but in his eyes. He's so handsome, even more so in the tuxedo they tailored to fit him. When Bryker calls for the end of today's shoot, I meet Danny at the water cooler. "Hi," I say, much like a schoolgirl speaking to her crush. I shrug knowing I'm ridiculous, but I don't care. I'm in love and he makes me feel giddy.

His eyebrow quirks up amused. "Hi there yourself, pretty." He gets me a cup of water before filling his own. When he stands up, he asks, "You're awful smiley today. It's good to see."

"It's good to feel this happy."

"Last night, it was good."

"It was." I giggle again as if cued by Pavlov training just from the mere mention of last night.

He tucks some hair behind my ear and kisses my cheek. Then he whispers, "Wait until you find out what I have in store for you tonight."

I lick my lips and gulp hard.

A knock at the door draws the crew's attention. "Hold that thought." I scurry away, even though I was enjoying that spot against him in the corner. Wondering what's on the other side of this door, I pray it's not a spy Keaton sent. When I open the door, a Frenchman—tall and dark hair, with thin lips so tight one would think he was sucking on a lemon—asks in a thick accent, "Daniel Weston?"

Danny comes to the door and the man hands him an envelope. "I've been asked to hand deliver this letter to you and to tell you on behalf of the sender that you have been served."

"What?" Danny asks, looking as confused as I feel.

"My apologies, sir. I am merely repeating what I was told to say. Have a good day."

"Fuck." Danny's eyes land on mine before he turns back and opens the letter.

My heart stops in my chest. My breath comes up short, trapped in my throat while he silently reads.

His head lowers, his eyes close, and he sighs. When I reach over to touch his wrist, he looks up, and says, "It will be all right. Don't worry."

Nodding seems to be the only thing I can do, my breath still caught in a lump, but I can hear the lie underneath his steady tone, I can see it written on his face. He's upset and all he can think about is making sure I don't worry. He walks away and all the air escapes before I take a deep inhale. I give him a minute although that's the last thing I want to do.

The windows are the only space that seems to give any privacy though all of Paris is just beyond the glass. As he stares out the window, I stand there dumbfounded watching him while he pulls out his phone and makes a call.

Keaton promised revenge and he delivered, twelve fold. If he can't hurt me, he'll hurt Danny, the only man I've ever truly loved and now I've caused him heartache and probably more.

I start walking, stepping over extension cords, and around a director's chair. I go to Danny as quietly as I can, needing to be there for him, for us. For me. Out of the corner of Danny's eyes, he sees me but turns to face back to the windows. "It's me," he whispers into the receiver. "Call me as soon as you get this message." When he hangs up, he turns around. "I need to call my lawyer."

One more tentative step forward and I say, "I'm sorry."

"For what?"

"He said we were in breach of contract. He more than hinted that he would do this, but I didn't take him seriously. I disregarded the threat." I step forward, pleading with my hands on his chest. "I'm sorry, Danny. I didn't believe him, but I should have."

His hands cover mine, and the tension in his jaw releases. "It's not your fault." He sighs. "We can deny it, but I don't I want to. It would be like denying a piece of my soul. I've done that for too long. I'll fight him."

"I don't want to cause you any pain. I'm so sorry. I can fix this. I can."

He stares into my eyes, disbelief turning to anger. "You're not going back to him if that's what you're thinking. I said I can fight this and I will. I have a good lawyer and a pit bull of an agent." Referring to the few people on the set, he says, "And they won't give us up."

"I can handle this quietly. Just give me a chance."

"You may have quit a job, but this could cost you your career."

"I don't think he really wants to hurt me—professionally or personally."

"He's hurting you by going after me. Nothing is beneath him to try to get you back. It's a ploy. Don't play into it."

"I'd rather it cost me my career than lose you... again."

He hugs me, his hands around my head, holding me to his chest. "You may cost me a pretty penny, but you're not going to lose me."

We found out how much this lawsuit was going to cost later that night—fifteen million dollars if we fight it. Either way, we walk away the losers.

Danny hangs up the call with his lawyer and says, "Whoever said love doesn't cost a thing lied."

"I want to laugh, but I can't." I lie on the bed while he stands at the balcony with the doors wide open. I don't think he hears me, so I call to him, "Danny?" When he doesn't respond again, I go to him. Touching his shoulders, I can feel how tense they are.

He turns just enough to see me behind him. "I'm fucked, Reese."

That's not the Danny I know. His tone is all wrong, not fitting the man who seems to always look on the sunny side. His resignation hurts my heart. Leaning my forehead against his back, I close my eyes. "I'll do whatever you need me to do."

"My lawyer said we have two options."

I move onto the balcony next to him. His hands grip the railing so tight his knuckles are whitening. "What are they?"

"I can fight it but most likely I'll lose since, well, we've breached the contract. Fighting it in court means we try to find a sympathetic jury who believes love is stronger than a contract. But legally, the contract is the final word with the judge."

Not good. "And the other option?"

He won't look at me. My stomach rolls when he turns away and lowers his voice. "We walk away until the term of the contract expires."

No. "That's six months to a year. Maybe longer." *I won't do it for even a day.* "The expiration of those clauses were based on us working together—"

"And the ads being public, apparently, not just shooting the ads."

"No."

"Yes, Reese." When his gaze hits me it's harsher, more troubled than I've ever seen. "My lawyer has gone over the contracts twice looking for a loophole. Klein isn't new to this. They know how to word these things. I signed it. Hell, you fucking signed it."

The clause flashes through my head. I've been in a Danny daze and forgot my better judgment at the bedroom door. *Shit.* "I'm sorry."

"I don't want you to be sorry. I just…" He walks inside and sits on the end of the bed.

"I knew better. I knew what I was signing and," I say, looking away from him pained I've brought this on him. "I shouldn't have crossed that li—"

He holds a hand out to me and says, "C'mere."

I walk to him. Standing in front of him, I add, "I don't want you to hate me. I don't want to lose you."

He leans back, inviting me to straddle him. Running my fingers through the hair around his ears, I wait for him to talk. Taking hold of my hips, he tries to give me a smile but it's not really there. The worry runs deep. "I want to be with you. I don't want to lose you, not for six months and definitely not for a year. We've lost ten already. I don't want to wait to start a life with you. Do you want to be with me? Right here, right now, do you want to be with me?"

My eyes fill with tears threatening to fall. "That's all I've wanted for what feels like my whole life."

Sitting up, he drags me closer. He kisses my chin and whispers, "Say it again. For me."

"You're all I've wanted my whole life."

Our lips meet in a gentle caress while his hands slide up my back. The kiss deepens, darkens, as something else possesses it. A need. A craving. A conquest. He turns me over on the mattress, my back flat as he moves on top, his body urging mine to join his rhythm.

We kiss, but soon the frenzy slows, an ominous cloud hovering above the bed. His forehead is rested against mine, one small kiss placed on my lips before he moves to the side of me. I snuggle against him.

Lying there with our hearts exposed, our emotions raw, I feel outside my body, a feeling I was temporarily distracted from when he came back into my life. I don't want to live in the dark anymore. Not when I have so much light back in my life. I refuse to let go. I will fight. I will fight for us, for this second chance.

Emotional exhaustion leads to sleep, and I give in.

Awakened in the middle of the night by ringing, Danny sits up startled. He grabs his phone and answers rashly, "What?"

I sit up and lean against the headboard watching him, trying to give him privacy, but his temper has a rippling effect. He responds, "I can't do it... I won't." His anger gets the best of him, and he gets out of bed. "That makes no sense. Who'll believe us?" The moonlight highlights each sculpted muscle on his bare body as he stands looking out through the closed French doors. "Give me time to think. I'll call you in the morning." When he hangs up, he looks over at me. I'm pinned by his gaze; unable to read the most readable eyes I've ever seen. He's hiding something from me, protecting me.

I can feel it.

Wrapping my arms around my legs, I rest my chin on my knees. "What's wrong?"

Walking to the bathroom, he says, "Get some rest. We still have the shoot tomorrow."

"Danny, tell me what's wrong?"

He stops in the doorway with his back to me, and says, "Go back to sleep, Reese."

Swinging my legs off the bed, I don't reach the door before it shuts. I open it and my eyes meet his in the reflection of the mirror. His palms rest heavy on the marble counter, and he asks, "Were you always this feisty?"

"No. I learned that lesson the hard way."

"What lesson did you learn?"

"That I need to stay and fight for what I want."

"It's like history repeating itself. But this time, we may not have a choice."

I move to the counter, ducking under his arm and sandwiching myself between the marble and him. "What does that mean?"

With just a breath between us, he replies, "The collective advisement is for me not to see you again."

His words punch me in the gut. My arm covers my stomach and I ask, "By your lawyer?"

"Yes."

"Why?"

"Because it's fifteen million dollars, not including legal fees."

A harsh breath escapes when I'm sucker-punched by the reality that he might not fight for me. Leaning back, I need perspective and being this close makes me lose it. "What are you saying? I thought you were going to fight?"

"You said you didn't want me to."

"I want you to, Danny. Of course I do. I'm a woman. I want you to fight for me. I just don't want you to lose your money or your life doing it. I could never live with that guilt. You'd never look at me the same."

His expression softens and he steps back. With a sly grin on his face, he says, "I'm going to be very upfront with you, Reese. I've got money in the bank and endorsements that will earn out over the next few years. I would give anything to be with you, but if something were to happen..." His hand waves down his body. "This is my reality. My job is based on my face, my body." Looking away briefly I can see how much this troubles him. "I couldn't take care of you. Not how I'd want to. I don't have a career that will support me for a lifetime without saving my money now. My agent, my lawyer, and my financial advisor all tell me not to fight this and to settle out of court."

"If you settle, how much will it cost you?"

"Seven."

"Seven million dollars?" I try to process how fucked up this really is, that our love has caused a lawsuit.

The silence is broken when he says, "If this was two years from now, I'd be more comfortable with the savings. A plan is in place to grow the money and I'll have those endorsements paid out. But right now... I want to buy us a house one day and the real estate market in LA is insane." Taking my hands in his, he looks right into my eyes. "I will give it up for you, Reese. For this second chance." He touches my cheek. "I lost you once. I won't lose you again."

"You won't lose me if you don't fight this. But I can't sit by and let you take this hit all on your own."

"It's my situation to handle." I watch as he walks back into the bedroom and climbs into bed.

I'm right behind him. When I climb into bed, he immediately pulls me close though I feel terrible I've caused him this much trouble. "I'm sor—"

"Don't say it again. I don't blame you. I'm not innocent in this. You didn't cause this anymore than I did."

With my head against his chest, I listen to his heart beating strong. "I'm to blame for Keaton."

He's quiet. When I look up, his eyes are closed. "Sleep, pretty. We'll deal with it in the daylight." I close my eyes, and he kisses my head. "We always have tomorrow."

Do we?

I've been given a chance at the life I've always wanted, and now it's being taken away. My heartbeats are faint, the thought of losing him, again, devastating. When he reassures so kindly, I only have one thought...

Do we have tomorrow together?

CHAPTER 32

TOMORROW.

Tomorrow.

Tomorrow.

Will we have a tomorrow? I remember the last time I foolishly thought I'd have a lifetime of tomorrows with Reese.

Ten Years Ago

TAKING THE STAIRS by two, my hand is on my pocket, making sure the box doesn't fall out of my coat. The door is locked. I hate that I'm an hour late, but I can't control flight delays due to bad weather.

Unlocking the front door, I barge in excited to see my girl. "Reese, I'm home." Silence returns my greeting. "Reese?" I shut the door behind me. Something's off, but I can't place it. "You here?" I scan the room as I walk through the living room into the bedroom.

When I enter, I stand in the doorway. "Reese?" It's clear she's not here. I check my watch again. Damn. I hope she's not pissed that I'm late. She knows how flaky flights can be. It's not the first time I've been delayed or even had a flight cancelled altogether. She's always understood in the past. I don't know why she'd be mad this time.

That's when I see it, or should I say don't see it... her stuff. I walk into the room and straight to the closet. Opening it wide, her stuff—it's gone. Turning behind me, the room is empty.

Of personality, of life, of love.

The room is how it was before I met her.

I dash into the bathroom. The counter is cleared, the drawers that held her toiletries now empty, the medicine cabinet left bare. Shit! I grab my phone from my pocket but find the ring instead. Going into the living room, I sit on the couch and set the ring, box lid hinged open, in front of me on the coffee table. I dial her number as I stare at the ring.

On the fourth ring I go to voicemail. "Reese, it's me. I'm home. Where are you? Call me. I want to see you. We need to talk." When I hang up, I set my phone down next to the box. That's when I notice the magazines on the table beneath it. I slide them out and look. Me. Ads I've done. Why are they here? I look back at the diamond ring sparkling from the light coming in through the open blinds.

My eyes close as my head drops into my hands. Fuck. Looking at the magazines, almost all of them are of me and another model—female models. And not just from photo shoots. I always left the parties alone, but I know photos can be deceiving.

Damn it, Reese. I call her again. When the voicemail tone sounds, I say, "Reese, please call me back. I don't know what's going on, but you're not here and I want to see you. So badly. I need to see you. Please. Call me back. I love you."

I sit there with the phone set on top of a stack of magazines. Staring at the diamond in the middle of the black velvet box as the sun sets outside the window, the stripes from the blinds drift across the wall until it's dark—inside and out.

She hasn't called. Still on Paris time, my eyes grow heavy as I stare at the two-carat princess cut sparkler I picked out just for her. Saving a percentage from my paychecks for this ring, I wanted her to have the best, the prettiest. The ring reminds me of her. Shutting the lid, I don't want to see it anymore.

Checking my phone just in case it somehow miraculously rang and I didn't hear it, I'm still lost on what is happening. I get up, shove the ring and my phone in my coat pockets and take off. As soon as I get in my car, I start it but I don't back out. I'm not sure where to go. Our closest friends have graduated and moved away. Reese has a part-time job on campus. I decide that's my only hope.

I stand in front of the alumni house, but logically I know it's not open at this hour. It's just gone eight at night. I knock on the door anyway, hoping what deep down I know is true is not happening, hoping she just got caught up in work and missed our date. I'm standing there knocking, praying her clothes, her stuff, that her being gone is all just a misunderstanding that can be cleared up.

No answer.

Not just the door, but for all my other questions as well.

Getting back into my Jeep, I sit there, staring at the empty parking lot, not knowing what to do, where to go, what to think. I thought we were happy...

I was happy.

My phone rings and I jump to answer, scrambling to pull it from my pocket. "Hello? Reese?"

"Danny Weston?"

My body deflates in disappointment when I hear an unfamiliar male voice on the other end. "Yes," I answer.

"This is a reminder call that you have two movies overdue. I'm sorry, but we're going to be charging your credit card on file unless you return them."

"Charge it." I hang up.

I start the car, and crank up the heat. Nebraska is so damn cold. While I drive back to the apartment, it starts snowing. First snow of the season. "Fuck you, Mother Nature."

My hands slam down on the steering wheel, my heart icing over like the road I'm on. I walk back into the apartment and check my messages. There are no new ones. I grab the box and am about to rip it from the wall, but I can't. I can't risk missing a call from her.

I try calling her twice more before I tuck the ring into my drawer, hiding it under some boxers. I climb into bed and flick on the TV. Hours pass and I have no idea what's been on or even what's on TV now. I turn it off just after midnight and stare at the ceiling while snow falls outside, tormenting me and our tradition.

The next day I have no choice. I drive the three hours back to her hometown. Her dad stands in front of me explaining that his daughter has moved to New York, lectures me that if I had loved her, I would know this. The door is shut in my face. I don't know how long I stand there, but it's long enough for Reese's mother to reopen it and step out. "Danny, I'm sorry."

"Give her time."

"She's hurt."

"She doesn't want to hold you back."

"She's been so lonely."

"She tried to get ahold of you, but there was no way."

"She'll come around."

I don't hear the rest, my head pounding while I have it confirmed. Everything I truly loved has gone away. Give her time... She's been lonely? I was so lonely. I may have been surrounded by people while working, but not the one person who made me whole. I missed her every fucking day.

Stumbling back to my car, I lean against it, not able to comprehend what I just heard, my heart refusing to accept that Reese left. Left. Me.

I need to get away from here, from the memories, from this life, and this fucking snow. When I get in my car, I figure out what I have to do. The trip is long, the mileage racking up. I stop for gas, for food, and the occasional coffee to keep me awake, but I keep driving until I see the sign—Welcome to California.

Walking into the Los Angeles Illustrious offices the following Monday, I don't give myself time to change my mind.

The receptionist smiles and I ask for Mark Warrant. I'm led to his desk in The Pit. He pulls a chair up and I sit in the small space. "I need work. As much work as you can fill my weeks with."

"What about Nebraska? As I said before, it would be easier if you were in New York or even LA."

"I'm here now. Can you get me more work?"

He smiles. "I can get you a lot of work. Are you sure you're ready for the commitment?"

Commitment...

"I'm ready."

Shaking my hand, he says, "Get ready, Danny Weston. I'm about to make you famous."

Present Day

I SPENT EXTRA time in makeup. The stress of the last few days has engraved tired lines into my face. Standing next to the vintage Aston Martin, I look away from the camera. Claudia is sitting in the car, her expression matching mine with different troubles on her mind.

A Papillon barks at my feet. I bend down and pick it up, careful not to mess the expensive midnight-black Vittori suit I'm wearing. I let the dog lick my face and hear Claudia laugh as she lifts her sunglasses and stands up. Leaning across the seats, she pets the small dog. It's a moment captured for future use. Even I know it's gold to get something "natural" on camera.

When I set the dog down, it runs to its handler, leaving Claudia looking into my eyes. When I lower mine, she mimics and I offer her a hand. Her dress is long and she's slow as she moves it with her and sits down in the passenger's seat. I get in the car and pretend to start it.

We're told to look back and give a farewell. When we do, I see Reese on the phone behind Becs. I fulfill my role and Bryker finally yells, "That's it. Last shot." He hands his camera to his assistant and claps his hands together. "Thank you. It's going to be a stunning campaign."

I face forward and exhale a long breath. Claudia stays next to me, staring ahead, lost in her thoughts. I reach over and take her hand. When she looks at me, I say, "You were good."

A smile not often seen tempts her mouth. "You were good. We were good. I think it will be very successful."

Nodding, I put my hands on the steering wheel. "Where do you head next?"

"Nowhere."

"Home?"

She laughs. "Where is that again? It's been awhile."

Relating, I chuckle. She gets out of the car and shuts the door. "I'm glad I know you, Danny."

Scooting up on top of the door, my smile fades, her sentiment catching me off guard. "I'm glad I know you, too, Claudia."

This time she nods, and then picks up the skirt of the dress so it doesn't drag and walks to Becs.

Reese joins me car side, and says, "Vinnie is going to love these shots."

"I hope so." I'm not sure what else to say. I'm aggravated because I'm not even sure what to do around her, or what I *can* do. I get out of the car and mumble, "I should return this suit."

"Don't do this. Please."

The tremble in her voice hits deep, gutting me. "Reese, don't make this harder than it is already."

Taking a step closer, she touches me cautiously on the arm. "You're shutting down on me."

I am.

"I'm not."

The sky blue in her eyes clouds over, and this time, she lets me walk away. The gravel crunches under my leather shoes, but the raging in my ears from the lie I just told overpowers it. Becs sees me coming.

My devastation.

My resolve.

She's quiet as she stands behind me and helps me remove the suit jacket. I loosen the tie, but it's caught. After she hangs the jacket on the rack, she comes around and helps me. "I've got it." As her nimble fingers slip it neatly through the knot and she pulls it from around my neck, she stops in front of me. "You can talk to me."

"I know."

"Trust me, you do not want me to sing "That's What Friends Are For" to you. I'm a God-awful singer. Spare us both the trouble and talk to me, Danny."

My eyes burn, so I squeeze them shut. "I can't."

"You should. You need to talk to someone and if you can't talk to Reese, talk to me. I'll help however I can."

Getting my emotions in check, my specialty after all the years I've modeled, I put on a smile—it might not be my million-dollar one, but it's at least a 10K one—for her. "I'm paying the price for making a deal with the devil."

She knows me too well to let the charade of my expressions cover the words I'm saying. Like I hoped. Focusing on the real issue, she asks, "And who's the devil?"

"Klein Advertising."

"Ahh," she says, seeming to understand. "So it's true? You were served for breach of contract?"

I unbutton my shirt and hand it to her. "I was served for letting her leave ten years ago. I'm just paying the price now."

"Are you? Are you going to pay the price?"

"*I* want to. My legal team says no."

"Well, you're the one who makes the final decision. How much is love worth to you?"

"That's not fair, Becs."

"You know what's not fair? Turning your back on someone who loves you as much as she does."

I follow her gaze straight to Reese who is back on the phone and pacing behind the car. It's clear she's upset. Her hands are swinging around making her point to someone who can't see them. Her head is down as she talks intently.

"I'm not turning my back on her. I need to figure out the best

320

way to handle this."

"Are you talking about the lawsuit or Reese Carmichael?"

I strip down my pants, not even caring I'm not behind the screen. I need to get the fuck out of here. I warn, "Careful."

"No, I'm not going to be careful. We're friends, remember? So I can tell you when you're screwing up." She snatches the pants from me and throws my jeans at me. "You're screwing up, Danny."

Holding the jeans against my chest, I stare at her. "What has gotten into you?"

Her irritation lessens and she says, "That woman is ready to give up her life for you. Can you say the same?"

"I have to consider all the options." The words come rushing out. "I picked her once and she left." *Shit.* To throw her off my heart's pain gushing out through the open wound, I think fast and let my wallet speak instead. "It's a lot of fucking money."

"You picked her once?"

Fuck. Of course, she sees. She is a woman. They don't miss anything. I pull my jeans on and slip on my socks. "Yeah," I mutter. "I was ready to give it all up for her. And she left me."

Becs is there, her hands rubbing my arm in consolation. "Oh, Danny. I'm sorry. I'm not trying to make things worse. I'm trying to make you see what you have. The second chance you've been given." I look over at Reese. She's hung up and talking to Bryker. When I turn back, Becs asks, "Money gives us security but it doesn't keep the bed next to us warm." She walks away, leaving me with flashes of holding Reese all night and how good that felt, how good she feels in my arms.

The sheets are warm when we're together. It occurs to me that it's never been about hating cold sheets. It's always been about the sheets being warmed by the right woman, by someone who turns my life upside down and then rights it again.

I look back at Reese. She glances my way but looks away just as quickly. That woman. That woman right there.

She's my someone.

Reese is my someone.

I shove my sneakers on and grab Becs into a tight hug. "Thank you."

She says, "For what?"

"For making me see it's never been about the sheets." I kiss her cheek and do a one-eighty.

With purpose, I go to her, walking past Bryker and Claudia, and head straight for Reese, who's separated herself from the group and is back on the phone. She sees me and turns her back. But I move around and bend down so I'm eye level with her. "Hang up the phone."

Her pretty little face scowls and places her hand over her ear. "I'm sorry. Can you repeat that? I'm getting interference."

"Hang up the phone, Reese."

She squints at me in warning and points at the phone, mouthing, "This is an important call."

I take the phone from her hands and tell whoever's on the other end, "Reese will call you back." I end the call and toss the phone into the grass nearby.

"What the hell are you doi—"

Grabbing her by the waist, my lips are on hers. Her shock relents and her body softens against me, her hands are on my back, pulling me closer. Her lips become insistent as she lifts up on her toes and wraps her arms around my neck. I pick her up and spin us around. Her feet go into the air behind her as she holds on as tight as she can. When I set her down, we pull back, both breathless.

I'm met with a smile made of pure sunshine, filled with beauty. "I don't care about the money. I only care about you."

"I care about you, too. So much."

Reaching up again, the relief I see in her eyes assures me I've done the right thing. The hurt I saw earlier broke me. *But this?* This beautiful, happy woman in my arms? This is right. This is what I am fighting for. And fight I will.

She plants her lips on mine and I know I'm home.

This time when we part, I share my whole heart. "I want you to be a part of my life. A big part. I want you to warm the bed with me. I want you to be my someone. I want you to be mine."

"I'm all yours."

This time my smile grows and I grab her into a tight embrace. "I love you, Reese," I say as if I can't keep my feelings bottled up any longer.

As if the sun couldn't shine any brighter, her smile blooms. "I love you, Danny Weston."

CHAPTER 33

Reese

SITTING AT A table in the back of a bistro next to the hotel, I can't take my eyes off him—my handsome "someone." Danny and I are on our second bottle of a recommended French red when we hear, "There they are."

When we look toward the entrance there's a spectacular commotion of purple. "Vinnie," I say, standing up and running into his arms. "You're here."

"I am," he says, whispering in my ear. "How are you, Candy girl?"

I take his hand and look him in the eyes. "Ridiculously happy."

"Happy looks great on you." We walk back to the table. Danny stands, and Vinnie asks, "How's our favorite model?"

Danny reaches out to shake hands but Vinnie makes a face and they hug. Danny rolls his eyes as Vinnie embraces him around the middle, but he laughs. "It's good to see you too." When Danny tries to break the embrace, Vinnie remains latched on. "Okay. Okay. Back it up there."

We laugh together. It's light and carefree, feeling so good.

After we sit, Danny asks, "What brings you to Paris?"

"I came to check on my favorite dynamic duo." He picks up my wine and drinks half before speaking. "I also wanted to check on my store here and to see how the shoot went. It's good to check on an investment." Looking at me, he asks, "How did it go?"

"Better than we could envision."

"I received some preview shots. They are better than we planned. I'm thinking Vogue and Elle for the New York and Paris shots. GQ for the Marfa photos. Thoughts?"

"I think they're perfect for those magazines. I was also thinking a collage that moves for the commercial. Bryker said he took enough to make that happen."

"Interesting. I'd like to see that." He turns to Danny. "How do you feel it went?"

"The locations were amazing. The clothes were incredible. I loved being a part of it."

He takes a sliver of Brie from the tray in front of us, and as he wiggles it back and forth, he says, "Let's be frank here. I heard about the breach of contract. I'm here. How can I help?"

Danny says, "I don't think there's anything you can do. Thank you though."

"What are you going to do?" He pops the Brie in his mouth.

"I'm going to pay. I'm not willing to sit in a court of law under oath and lie about how I feel about Reese."

Vinnie's smile is contagious. He takes my hand and kisses it. "I love a good romance and yours is one of my favorites. I saw that connection the first time you guys met. But I guess that was because it wasn't a first meeting but a reunion. So romantic."

"I couldn't have made a better match for my Candy than you, Model Danny."

Danny chuckles. "I'm glad you approve, Designer Vittori."

Vinnie stands and claps his hands together again. "We must

celebrate. Why don't we go get you two hitched?" His eyes are wide with expectation and hope.

"What?" I take the word out of Danny's mouth.

Vinnie nods. "So that's a yes?"

"No," we reply in unison.

Standing up, I say, "Slow your horses. We just got back together. I think we're enjoying right where we are."

Danny adds, "For now," and drops money on the table.

I'm drawn to him when he stands, surprised by his response. His hand warms my lower back, and he shrugs. "I'm not opposed to marriage. I never was."

I lean against him. "You just made my heart flutter."

Vinnie says, "You both just made my heart flutter. We should celebrate your togetherness with a wedding."

My evil eye works and Vinnie backs off. "Fine. Can't blame me for trying. Think how romantic that would be. Just the three of us and a candlelit service."

Danny ushers me forward. "Come on. I know a great bar around the corner." His phone rings and he stops, his hand disappearing from my back.

I turn back when I realize he's stopped. "Vinnie. Wait for Danny."

Danny turns his back to us and plugs the opposite ear of the one with the phone pressed to it. I overhear him ask, "Where are you? What room? I'll be right there." He hangs the phone up and comes toward us with purpose. "We need to get back to the hotel."

"What is it?"

"Claudia." As soon as we're on the sidewalk, he takes off running to the hotel next door.

Vinnie and I run after him. He's disappeared up the stairs, and we rush to the elevator. I'll never be able to run those stairs in the heels I'm wearing. "I know her room number."

The door is open when we reach her room, the large latch from the inside, swung out. I push it open slowly and walk in. I find Danny on the bathroom floor holding Claudia. Her head is tucked against his chest and her mascara has run down her face from crying. Her hair is a mess, and when I look around, several prescription bottles are in the sink. I try to stifle my gasp, but I don't think it works. Danny looks up and shakes his head just enough for me to get the message. I back out of the bathroom, tugging Vinnie's sleeve as I go.

In her room, we sit on the side of the bed. He whispers, "She's alive and they're talking. That's a good sign."

Nodding, I watch the bathroom door for any sign of them coming out. Danny's deep voice carries even when he's trying to be quiet. "You're going to be okay. I'm here for you."

My memories drag me back to the time he was leaving me for a job, back when we were together years ago...

The tears keep coming and my body is racked with sobs. I can't do it. I can't watch him walk out that door again. I was going to marry someone who wanted to study maps, travel during work hours, not gone weeks at a time. Danny's degree came with those guarantees. Modeling came with none. "I don't want to be alone anymore, Danny. Please stay."

"I've taken the job. I can't back out on them at the last minute. It's one week. I'll be back before you notice I'm gone."

He's convinced himself that this is normal. Maybe this is our new normal. I hate change. I hate him being gone even more. "You're not even using the degree you just spent four years earning."

Rolling onto his back, he drapes his arm over his eyes. "Please don't do this. I can't back out now."

"I'm sorry if my emotions inconvenience you," I snap.

Turning to face me again, he says, "I love every one of your emotions. Even the ones currently angry at me. I understand. I miss you too, but I want to earn money for us, for our future."

"You've been home three days in the last two months. This doesn't feel like a relationship. This feels like an affair. An affair you're having on your job."

"Reese, it will be okay. You'll be okay. We'll be okay."

He leans in and kisses my shoulder. "We are going to be okay. Let's just get through this. I'm sure it's just the busy season for modeling or something. This won't be my life. You're my life."

"Promise me. One week and then you're home for at least a week."

A gentle smile that wins me over every time it appears. "I promise you."

...He broke that promise. And in the end, for what? Money he earned that he's going to have to give away now if we want to be together? *The only life he's known, he's willing to sacrifice for me.* My eyes tear up.

Vinnie brings me in for a side hug. "Don't cry. She sounds like she's going to be fine."

"It's just that man. He's too much. Too good."

"You're good. That's why you two work."

"Thank you." I rest my head on his shoulder.

In the quiet room, I hear Claudia say, "He broke up with me so he could date a girl who works at Hot Topic."

"He doesn't deserve you. He's just cleared the way so you can find the man you're meant to be with."

She laughs and that's a great sign. "Let's hope. I have terrible luck with men."

"Those bad boys will wreck your heart every time."

"Sucks because I always liked Hot Topic. Now where am I

going to get my Funko Pops?"

They laugh, their tones much lighter. I hear shuffling coming from the bathroom, and Danny say, "Let's get you something to eat. I think you need something more than water-based foods tonight."

"Me too. I might take your girlfriend up on that burger."

Danny says, "I think she'd like that."

I laugh under my breath, and stand up.

Just as they walk out, Danny takes her and hugs her. I hear him whisper, "You're not just beautiful on the outside. You're beautiful on the inside too. Don't let some jerk ever dull that beauty again. Or I'm going to kick his ass and I fucking hate getting in fights." When they part, he winks at her, and adds, "Takes me out of the game if I mess up this pretty face of mine."

Claudia pushes him in the chest. "You're ridiculous."

"You're not the first to tell me that but it's usually followed by –ly handsome. I'll settle for the shortened version though."

When Claudia is done rolling her eyes, she turns to me, and teasingly asks, "How do you put up with him?"

"He's the easy part. It's his ego that is impossible." After sharing a laugh as a group, I see her tears are dried and a smile lingers on her face. I hug her and she hugs me. I'm thankful she had someone to call who she trusted. She's not a threat. She's Danny's friend, and that makes her mine.

Vinnie coos, "Look at my girls." Claudia and I laugh as Vinnie holds his hands in front of him, feeling the love. Then his irritation shows. "Your ex is a loser with a capital L. This is the best thing that could happen to you. Mark my words."

Claudia replies, "Let's hope."

She looks at me, and I ask, "So, about that burger? Room service?"

It's amazing what you can get at any hour, even in Paris, if you flash the big cash. The four of us have shared our dinners, laughs, and stories while sprawled out in Vinnie's large suite. It's been an unexpected ending to an eventful day, but it's been good. Relaxing, and I haven't felt truly relaxed since Marfa.

Watching Danny, I wonder if every night with him will always be this easy, this... wonderful. I'm betting seven million it is.

Vinnie stands and starts swooshing toward the door. "I need my beauty sleep and we still have lots to discuss in the morning with the campaign." Looking at the clock, he corrects, "Lunch. Since it's two in the morning, let's just meet for lunch instead."

"Call me when you wake up and let me know what time you want to meet," I say.

After goodbyes full of hugs, love, and smiles, Danny and I go back to our room.

I brush my teeth and get ready to go to sleep, and then we swap places. I'm exhausted—the day draining, both emotionally and physically. While I lie in bed, I think about the journey we've taken. The bad has been dragged up because of unhealed wounds. But lying here, I take a freeing breath, releasing all the bad history and breathe in the future that awaits us.

Danny climbs into bed next to me and immediately molds his body to mine. "With a grin like that on your face, you have me curious what you're thinking about."

Taking his hand, I hold it to my chest, loving the feel of his arm around me. "Not thinking. Feeling. I feel my heart beating for the first time in years. Like really feel it. I feel alive and full of hope." Lifting my hair up, he kisses the back of my neck. I whisper, "You're the only one who ever broke my heart. You're also the only one who could piece it back together until it was whole and beating again."

"I'm sorry I broke it. If I could change how things played out, I would."

"So would I. If we would have had improved email or even Skype back then, we could have kept in touch better than we did."

"It killed me some nights when I couldn't call you, just to hear your voice again. Damn phone cards never did work well in other countries."

"No matter what, you still deserved better than how I left."

"You had a job to start—"

Turning in his arms so I can face him, I say, "No job was worth losing you over. I lost myself without you and thought you had found yourself without me."

"You were wrong. I never had a life without you. For years, I've been searching for something that I stupidly thought I could replace."

With a light laugh, I rest my hand on his neck. "You were wrong."

"I have no doubt that you're the stronger and braver of the two of us." He smiles so gently that I can't help but return it.

The passion, the determination that builds inside, I can't hold back any longer. "I'll fight for us this time. Whatever it takes, I'll do it."

He kisses me softly. Then with our foreheads pressed together, he says, "Thank you for showing me the way back."

"I didn't show you. Your heart led you. Straight back to mine."

"You'll always be home to me."

We don't make love. We don't fuck. We hold one another and whisper gratitude for each other. *You'll always be home to me.* His words comfort me until my eyelids grow heavy and I fall asleep.

LUNCH WITH VINNIE is fabulous, just like him. He can't be more pleased with the photo shoots and I can't wait to see how the campaign turns out. When we return to the hotel, Claudia is checking out. Her flight is earlier than ours. She runs over and hugs me, and I hug her because I have a soft spot for her now that I've gotten to know her better.

With her suitcase in hand, she hugs Vinnie and tells him she'll see him in New York. She's about to go, but makes sure to tell me, "I think you and Danny are an amazing couple. Hold on tight to each other."

"I intend to."

"He's special, and not just because he's a supermodel." She laughs. "Don't tell Danny I called him that. I know how much he hates it."

"I won't," I reply, grinning. "Good luck, Claudia, and safe travels."

"Bye. Oh, and thanks for the burger last night. It was amazing. I've not felt this good in years, but maybe that's not from the food, but the company."

Vinnie blows her a kiss and turns to me. "I'll pay the buyout fee."

My jaw drops open. When I gather myself back from the shock, I say, "What? No way. You can't do that."

"That money is nothing to me, but everything to you. I can't stand the thought of you and Model Danny fighting for your love through the court system. That would be so retro, late 80s/early 90s courtroom drama-ish. Oooh, maybe Chris Hemsworth can play Danny in the movie."

"Slow down there. Let's hope this never sees a day in the courtroom or we'll really be screwed."

"The offer stands, and now I'm leaning toward the other Hemsworth, Liam, for Danny's role. But it would be a shame to cover up his blue eyes with contacts. Oooh, maybe Josh Duhamel. He's ridiculously dreamy."

I hug him, so grateful to have this man in my life. "Thank you for everything, including making me smile. I can't accept your money though. I'm working on something and hopefully it pans out."

"I'm intrigued."

"More details on that soon, but for now, we should get ready to leave. Our flights are in three hours."

"Yes, real quick though, and this is important." I stand before him waiting to hear what he has to say. "Who will play *you* and *me* in the movie adaptation?"

"My dear Vinnie, please never change."

He wraps his arm around my shoulders. "I'm doing my best to stay the same, but the world is a changing, my sweet Candy girl."

CHAPTER 34

Reese

IN THE MIDDLE of Charles de Gaulle airport, I try not to cry and be the ridiculous lovesick woman who can't manage a proper goodbye without snot-sobbing. It's silly. I'll see him soon. But not soon enough. Like in the next ten minutes, or hour, or day like I want. Standing before my past and my forever, I never realized they were one in the same. Until now.

"Don't forget me," I say, throwing myself into his arms once more and holding on like Claudia told me to.

"I never have."

I smile, though it's small, it still counts because he's the one who made me smile. After one more kiss, I say, "I love you."

"Don't look so sad when you say it. Love should only be spoken from a happy heart."

"I'm more happy than I appear. I'll just miss you."

With his finger under my chin, he lifts my head up. "Always hold your chin high and look on the sunny side." He grabs me, tightly clinging to me as I did him a minute earlier. "I'll miss you, baby."

Purple-encased hands and arms envelop us both. "I'll miss

you too, my favorite dynamic duo."

Both Danny I stay where we are, but slide one arm each around Vinnie. "Come on, don't be sad. Reese will be right next to you the whole time."

Vinnie sniffles. "But what about you? When do I get to be with you, Model Danny?"

Danny's arms go into the air. "Everybody good? I'm good."

Vinnie flings himself at him. "Hug me."

With a shaking head, Danny looks at me. I frown at him, and mouth, "Hug him."

He does, making me smile. I see his lips tugging upward despite his best efforts to stop them... until Vinnie turns his head to catch my eyes. From wrapped around Danny's torso, Vinnie spreads his hands apart, and gobsmacked says, "Oh my Mary! Candy, you were so right about him. Lucky girl!"

As soon as he realizes what Vinnie means, he steps back. "Okay. Okay. That's enough. We all have flights to catch."

Laughing, I step up, kiss him on the lips, and step back again, keeping it casual like we see each other every day. Putting the vibe out into the universe that this is what I want with him. To kiss him like I'll see him in an hour and for it come true.

I adjust my bag on my shoulder and give him a little wave goodbye. "See you soon."

"See you soon," he says, keeping it casual for me, and maybe for himself.

Turning around, I start walking away because it will gut me to watch him. But I can't resist and look back, just once. There's more distance between us than I expected and I realize he walked away at the same time, probably for the same reasons.

I thought it couldn't get worse. Leaving Danny to go back to New York was plenty painful. Dealing with a lawsuit that cost him millions because of me, is awful. The guilt levels me to the ground.

But when I sit down in first class and ask for a magazine to read, and the flight attendant gives you a selection, one featuring a photo of you mid-orgasm on the cover, suddenly the money even seems minor. Grabbing the tabloid from her hands, I search for the date. Today. That means it's been on newsstands in America for a few days. My heart sinks, as if it could go any lower, as I stare at the little photo on the top right corner of Danny and me in Marfa.

Desert.

Chair.

Me straddling Danny.

Head back.

Mouth open.

Fuck.

Bryker. The traitor.

"Oh God." I cover my mouth in horror as I stare at the eye-catching headline—***The Model and The Mistress.***

Vinnie looks over. "What?"

I point, unable to speak.

"Huh? *Ohhhhhh.*" He grabs the magazine from me and flips it open to the feature inside. "There are four more photos."

"Oh God." I cover my eyes now, mortified.

"Wow, these look great. Have you ever considered going into porn? You really are pretty when you come."

"We must never speak of this again." I grab the magazine from him and whack him on the arm.

"That will be hard to do when it's national news. See how hot he looks. God, his eyes are so intense, so... virile."

The back of my head hits the seat and I close my eyes. "Danny is going to flip out."

"Danny should be giving copies to everyone he knows and create a Facebook account for them. Or, even better, make an Instagram account. I'll stalk you there. These photos are incredible. How much do you want for them? I could sell a million dollars worth of perfume by just Photoshopping a bottle right there in the corner."

"Vinnie, I'm not kidding."

"Neither am I. This is nothing. It's a corner with a leading headline on a trashy rag. Everyone knows these magazines make shit up."

My phone rings. When I pick it up from my lap, I see Danny's face, a pic I took of him shirtless back in Marfa and saved as my screensaver. "Hi."

"Reese, have you been to the newsstand today?"

"No." I swallow hard. "Why?"

He pauses. "Your flight's about to leave. Do you have Wi-Fi on your plane?"

"Yes."

"I'm sending you a photo. A magazine cover. You might want to email your lawyers while you're in the air. I know you're about to take off, but contact me if you can. Don't stress. We'll handle this together."

"I've just seen the photos. There was a copy of the magazine on my flight. I have to go, but I'll email you as soon as I'm in the air."

"Okay. I love you."

No matter what's happening in our lives—chaos or peace, I will always smile when he says that to me. "I love you, too. Be safe."

"I will. We'll talk soon."

I pay for the Internet service offered, and we email several times over the course of the flight, but by the time Vinnie and I land back in New York, I'm not stressed, I'm not freaking out. I'm not even worried. I'm filled with a whole lot of I don't care. Vinnie is right. These photos are hot and make me feel sexy. If that makes me slutty in some people's eyes, I think I can deal with it.

In the car ride, I look at the magazine again. Vinnie made us stop so he could buy a stack. I stopped arguing with him when I realized he was still going to do it whether I protested or not. They are really sexy and I need to wear that dress more. It's very flattering through a stalker's lens. "You really think I'm pretty when I come?"

Vinnie bursts out laughing. "The prettiest." He pulls an envelope from his satchel and hands it to me. "Speaking of pretty, I have a pretty offer for you. I hope you consider it."

I open the envelope, pull the Vittori letterhead out, and start reading. Shocked, I stare at the letter. "You're offering me a job?" It took me years to finally land a large account, and Vittori no less—one of the biggest brands in the world. I love Vinnie. My life is better with him in it. Now I have a chance to make my career better. Klein has beaten me down mentally for years, but I was doing what I was told I had to—serving my time, so to be given this opportunity... My happiness lumps in my throat.

"Not just any job. Marketing Director. I need one. You need a job. It works out."

"Vinnie," I say, tears threatening, "I'm so touched. I can't believe you want to hire me."

"You're the best person for the job and I think you're a creative genius. This campaign has gone so smoothly and I enjoyed it. I haven't had this much fun in years. My line is inspired by the colors of the desert, the grays of the city, and the blues of Paris. I've already started sketching and I think this may be my best line yet. I owe that all to you, Candy girl."

"You don't owe me a job and I don't want to take advantage

of our friendship."

"You're not. You're the most qualified candidate I could wish for."

Wiping the corner of my eye when a tear slips, I tilt my head back to keep any more from falling. I'm not sure Vinnie understands how much his confidence in me means. *Vittori*. I could be working for Vittori.

The car comes to a stop outside his building and the sadness from our looming goodbye builds in my chest.

"Just read the offer over and get back to me when things calm down with the lawsuit, which by the way, I'm still willing to cover the payout, if you want."

"No. I can't take that much money. We're working it out, but thank you. From the bottom of my heart for the offer, but mostly for your friendship." We hug just as the door opens. "Oh, I forgot to tell you. Remember Leo, the bartender?"

His eyebrows waggle. "Do I ever."

"We talked when I was in Paris. I have his number and he's definitely interested in walking the runway for you. He's new to this, so I said you'd be happy to give him some pointers."

"Have I told you how much I love you?"

"No, but by looking at the salary you're offering me, I'd say you love me a lot."

He laughs. "It's true. I do." As he's getting out of the car, he says, "Thank you for your friendship as well, Reese." With no over-the-top hand gestures or facial expressions, I can tell he speaks from the heart.

THE NEXT MORNING I talk to Danny when he finally gets home.

"The photos are out there. We've already decided to pay the settlement, so they won't work against us now in the case. We're admitting what we did from the get-go."

My reasoning makes him pause, needing time to process it. "You're okay that they printed them?"

"No. I think we should sue the magazine for printing them and Bryker for selling them, but I don't want to stress about this. I'd rather let our lawyers handle it so we can focus on our future."

His smile is heard through his words. "I'm liking this new Reese. That's so easygoing of you. Well, the non-suing part. What changed your mind?"

"You've changed my mind, about everything. You've been right all along. I'm choosing to look on the sunny side of life. It's much warmer there."

"Yes, it is." I hear him exhale, relieved. "I know we're supposed to see each other in six days, but how do you feel about coming out here sooner?"

Practically swooning, I ask, "You miss me?"

"All day long and don't even get me started on the night."

"I ALMOST LIKE us being apart just so we can have reunions like this," Danny says, lying on his back with me lying on top of him.

"Me too."

His fingers slide into my hair and down my back before they work their way back up. "I like us together more."

"Me too." I sit up and carefully maneuver to the side of him on top of the dining room table, snuggling into the nook of his arm. "This table is hard. Wanna move to the couch?"

"How about a shower? The party started an hour ago."

"It's LA. Everyone's fashionably late here."

He gets off the table and scoops me up into his arms. "Glad you've adapted to the local customs." He attacks my neck with kisses, nips, and licks. While I'm kicking and giggling, he says, "That means we've got time for another round in the shower."

My laughter stops when my eyes meet his. *Oh!* My heart starts thudding in my chest from the intensity revealed in the caramel centers of his eyes. The man's insatiable. Fortunately for him, I feel the same.

I kiss his forehead and his temple, lower against the scruff of his jaw, even lower to his neck. His breath deepens as his skin heats beneath my lips.

He carries me into the bathroom and asks, "Against the mirror or in the shower?"

"Shower."

Setting me down on the rug, he steps into the large shower stall and turns on both showerheads. The body jets start after a push of the button and the water falls from the large panel above that makes me feel as if we've gotten caught in the rain.

When the waters warm, he opens the door and invites me in. The glass door fogs behind me as I watch the fog creep up the other glass wall. Danny's in the middle of it all gloriously wet, his eyes on me, water glistening over his body.

My fingertips glide from his shoulders down over his chest, maneuvering over each hard muscle of his stomach, then lower. I take hold of his erection, the skin smooth over his hardness. Long strokes with both hands, from base to tip, cause him to drop his head back, his eyes closing. A moan is heard from deep within his chest.

"What do you want me to do, Danny? Anything, for you."

He looks at me with a grin on his face, one that shares what he feels inside—ardor, devotion, respect His hand covers my cheek, and he replies, "You think I'm going to say some crazy position or maybe even come inside your throat. But if you ask me what I want most, my answer will always be the same—you, to be inside you. You're too temporary to me. You're a tent that is temporary and can be easily undone." Taking my face between his hands, he kisses me with such deep affection, that my knees slightly give. "You're my Taj Mahal. You're my home built of love and passion. I look at you and see the grandeur." With a light smile, he says, "You're the book I read when I want to relive the story of us."

From his steady confession of feelings, my knees gather strength and I reach up to kiss him. Then with my own impassioned smile, I say, "You're my Taj Mahal too."

"How about being Taj Mahal together?"

"I like that. Very much." One kiss leads to another, and then leads to more. I lower back down and wrap my hand around his length. With a firm hold, I slide against his silken skin.

A rumble in his chest draws my attention and my eyes meet his. "Turn around, baby."

"God I love when you call me that." I turn around and stand with my back to him.

And then the seduction begins.

His hands slide down my arms as his lips drag a trail of kisses across my shoulder. Our fingers entwine and his tongue finds the shell of my ear. I tilt my head to the side, my wet hair falling with it. He licks my neck and behind my ear before he presses his lips to it. Danny takes my hands and slowly brings them above my head, palms flat against the glass. My breath stops, caught in the moment, and he whispers, "You're the most beautiful woman I've ever seen. You're the sexiest woman I've ever kissed. You're the only woman I ever want to be with again."

My exhale turns into quickened breaths as his hands leave mine exactly where he wanted. Taking me by the hips, he pulls me back just enough to angle my backside. "You're so fucking gorgeous, baby."

I feel his cock as he slides against my ass. Although we've never gone there, I'm aroused. I'm not sure if I'm ready for more, like that, but I'm tempted. Pushing back just enough to encourage him for more, his hands tighten over my hipbones and he says, "Patience."

Patient is the last thing I feel. I feel alive, frenzied, and wanton in the worst of sexual ways. I'm a woman on the verge. "I want to feel you inside me."

"You're feeling right now."

"I'm aching right now."

"What are you aching for?"

"You." I struggle to keep my hands in place, my shoulders starting to burn, my body on fire for him. "Please touch me."

He grabs my breasts and squeezes several times before moving two fingers between my legs and running them over my sensitive clit. My body jerks from the contact before I seek it out again.

But he stops and repositions, the tip of his penis, a fan-fucking-tastic pressure where I want him most. I close my eyes, savoring every inch as he much too slowly fills me.

My head pushes against the glass, my arms stretched above, my body taken by the only man who ever made me want to give it to him. Turning my head, my cheek is cooled by the glass as the steam billows around us. The hot water runs down our bodies as he pulls slowly back out and in again.

Torture. He's fucking torturing me. "Please. Faster."

"You sure?"

"God, yes."

"Well since you put it that way." Briskly pulling me back until I'm flush against him, my arms fall down and he says,

"Brace yourself."

My hands press to the glass, tension filling my arms just as he moves me forward and slams back in, controlling my body. I come so close to hitting the glass, but he's careful. Even when he's not.

Each thrust touches me deeper, touches my heart, my soul, and awakens my every muscle. My nerves raw with anticipation, continuing the sensations sparking across my skin that he ignited earlier in the dining room.

His breath cools my skin that the water heats. Grabbing me by the shoulders, I give him leverage to speed his pace, his breathing joining the race. His large hand covers my body and he's pressed against me, his mouth at my ear. "I'll make you feel good, so good, baby." His fingers spread. He puts gentle pressure on my stomach as he moves over it and parts my legs. *So much.* My body feeling everything he gives and yet, craving more. It doesn't take but a few well-calculated circles directly on my clit to have me falling apart beneath him. My moans of pleasure seduce him as he covers my hands, dragging them up the glass until he's thrusting with our own rhythm and falling apart through his owns moans of ecstasy.

His head rests on my shoulder, our hands together in front of us until our breathing calms. He steps away and the hot water covers me instead. Turning around, Danny is leaning against the wall across from me. His sly grin slipping into place. "You're gonna be the death of me, woman."

Cozying up to him, I kiss his chest right over his heart several times. "It will be the sweetest of deaths though."

His arms come around me and he holds me. Kissing the top of my head, he sighs and I feel his body relax. "The best death I could ever wish for."

I duck under the rainfall showerhead and push my hair back.

Catching him watching me, I say, "Don't die on me. I'm gonna hit my sexual prime down the road and I want you to be there."

Chuckling, he joins me. Taking me by the waist, he says, "I wouldn't miss that for anything. I don't want to miss anything with you ever again."

"Love you."

"Love you more."

CHAPTER 35

Reese

SOMETIMES I NAIVELY forget how well known Danny is, especially here in the land of celebrities. When we walk into another celebrity's home, into a party full of famous people, the attention he receives still surprises me. When I look at him, he's my Danny. The same boy from Nebraska that I fell madly in love with is the same man holding my hand. But here, Danny Weston is a name, a brand, a business, and an empire.

Once we get drinks from the bar, he takes me over to meet one of his friends. I've heard a lot about her, from Danny and the media. Her life is lived in a fishbowl, surrounded by gawkers. It must be hard. When I look at Danny, sometimes I can relate.

As we approach the blonde, I feel intimidated. She's prettier than in the photos I've seen, hands down the most beautiful woman in the room. When she sees Danny, her face lights up and she excuses herself before rushing over. My hand is dropped so he can embrace her. If I were still in college, a major red flag of jealousy would fly up. But as soon as they part, he wraps his arm around my back and proudly pulls me to him.

Holli turns to me with a warm and welcoming smile. "I've

heard so much about you, Reese. I'm so glad to finally meet you." My hand comes out and just as I'm about to speak, she adds, "I'm from the south originally, so I'm a hugger." Stepping forward, she hugs me just as tightly as she hugged Danny. Her kindness is contagious so I join in the hug fest and hug her right back.

When we part, I say, "I've heard nothing but wonderful things about you. It's so good to finally meet you as well."

She hooks her arm in mine, and turns to Danny. "I'm stealing her away for a bit. We have lots to talk about."

"Just give me the signal if you need rescuing, pretty, and I'll be there."

"What's the signal?" I tease as we walk away.

Holli gives him a look that shuts him right up. "Ignore him. I'm not going to bite. I'm going to gossip." And there's the hint of mischievousness that puts me at ease. *Thank God.* She *is* human.

We head out back where people are swimming in the lagoon-style pool and lounging in chairs around it. She releases me and as if sharing a secret, she says, "Let's go over here so we can talk."

There's a wooden swing with flowering vines curving over an arbor. When we sit, it gives us a good view of the large backyard. The landscaping gives the feel of a tropical island. I can actually hear birds in the distance. It's a very nice property. We push off just enough for movement but not enough to make us feel like it's an effort. "This is really nice."

"Dalton built the arbor and swing when he came off tour last year."

"Dalton?"

"Sorry. Johnny. Johnny Outlaw. He's Dalton to me."

Ahhh. The rock star. I nod.

"He's into construction." She makes a funny face. "He's always looking for new projects, for something to build. On tour he's so full of adrenaline for months on end that when he comes home, I think he has to ease back into a stationary, quieter life. He builds me something each time to keep himself occupied, to keep his hands busy. This year, he built a tree house at our place in Ojai. It's almost the size of my first apartment in LA." She laughs, then lowers her voice. "And I will never complain. Not only do I get these awesome things he's built, but his body. Mother of Zeus, his arms and body are insane. I mean, he's hot anyway, but Lord almighty, I break a sweat just watching him while he's breaking a sweat."

The red flag disappears altogether. She's not a threat to my relationship. It's clear how much she cares for her Dalton.

"I can only imagine. Sometimes Danny works out on the front patio. It's attached to Danny's spare room. I've been working out of it and I've spent many an hour watching him break a sweat. He's quite the sight."

Laughing together, she says, "My office is that same room."

"I forgot you own the place next door. You're not there very much?"

"I can work from anywhere. Sometimes we're here in LA. Sometimes in Ojai. I stop by my townhome when I need to really concentrate for a deadline. I like being near the beach, hearing the waves in the distance." She pats my leg. "Enough about me. I want to hear about you. I read a little about the lawsuit. I'm sorry."

Downplaying it, I say, "Don't be. We were in clear violation. It sucks to hand over the money, especially to such scum, but it's easier to just pay it so we can move on."

"I agree. Lawsuits suck the life out of you. I've gone through a few. They steal a piece of your happiness away if you let them. Don't let them, Reese. Stay strong."

Sipping my drink, I look around. Holli's done an amazing job of keeping her happiness. It's seen all around and just by looking at her. "Can I ask you something personal?"

"Sure."

"How do you handle the fans and groupies, the women throwing themselves at him, the videos? How do you not get jealous, or do you?"

Laughing to herself, she replies, "I love him and that's part of his life. So I had to make the decision between getting my happily ever after with the man I love or walking away and making do for the rest of my life. I chose love. What will you choose?"

I don't have to think on this and it's not a trick question. "Love. I choose love."

"Then you'll learn to handle it, after a few more freak-outs. Then everything will calm down."

She's being so open so I raise another topic. "Do you mind if I ask you about your business?"

She doesn't get defensive and no walls go up. She smiles and says, "Absolutely. What do you want to know?"

With most women, they'd hold their cards tightly to their chest, afraid of any competition. Not her. She's open and honest. I see why Danny likes her so much. I'm starting to like her just as much. Wonder if she'll be my new best friend? Maybe too soon to bring that up. I inwardly laugh, and then ask, "How did you know you wanted to start a business, that it was the right time?"

"I woke up one day and couldn't shake the idea. I knew I had to pursue it or I'd regret it. Danny tells me you're incredibly creative and quite the advertising guru."

My cheeks heat from hearing Danny's compliment from another person. I look toward the house and see Danny talking to a man close to his size, brown hair, tattoos sneaking out from under his short-sleeved T-shirt. They both have their arms crossed and look everywhere but at each other as they speak. It's quite amusing to watch.

"I'm not a guru, but I've spearheaded some great projects. My friend is a fashion designer and he offered me a job since I quit the last agency. I could work for him direct. The pay is amazing, but I'm thinking I might want to start my own agency. Something small at first. Basically me, but grow it from there. My personal reputation may be shot after the photos of Danny and me were sold, but I can defend my career."

"The photos will blow over, the lawsuit will go away, and everyone will forget about it. But what you do with your ads, that's your portfolio and your work will speak for itself."

"I haven't told Danny yet."

"Why not?"

We stop swinging, and I look back at him again, while the tips of my shoes drag through the grass. "I didn't want to make a rash decision. I wanted this lawsuit behind us before committing to anything. But I know in my heart I can't move back to New York without him and seeing him in LA, this is where he always belonged. He's happy here. His friends are here. This is where he's built his life."

She follows my gaze and smiles. "His life is with you. You do what you need to do. If you need to go to New York, he'll support your decision. He's just that kind of guy." When she stands up, she says, "But I think in your heart, you already know what you want to do. And Reese, there's nothing worse than living a life of regret."

Years of regret cross my mind. "I know a lot about that."

"Then you have your answer. You're ready to start your own business. If I can help in any way, just let me know."

I stand up and take a sip of my drink. Danny nods his head, signaling me to come back to him. Sadly, I've missed him already too. "Should we join them?"

Holli and I head over. Danny wraps his arm around my back.

"Reese, this is Dex. He's the drummer in the band. Dex, this is my girlfriend, Reese."

Hearing him call me his girlfriend fills my soul, seeps into my veins giving me strength. I shake hands with Dex, trying not to make a big deal about my new moniker, but my heart still leaps. I finally reply, "It's nice to meet you."

When I return to Danny's side, Dex says, "I'm working on some songs I want to get back to. I'm going to find Rochelle, then head out." He leans over and kisses Holli on the cheek. "Catch ya laters, Hols."

"Thanks for coming and drive safe." Holli pokes Danny. "Impressive. You got him to say more than five words. For someone who likes to be surrounded by people, he tends to be more introverted at parties."

Danny shrugs. "We were shooting the breeze. Not talking about much. His music."

She smiles. "He likes talking about his music. He's changed a lot over the years. A good change. Or maybe it's just you, Danny. You put everyone at ease."

Leaning my head on Danny, I say, "Back in college, everyone loved him. I've never met anyone who didn't get along with Danny."

The living room behind us falls noticeably quiet and we turn from the sudden change. The rock star himself walks through the party, full of charisma, his presence overtaking all others, except for one—Holli's. She stands confidently next to us, comfortable in her own skin, and asks, "Have you met Johnny Outlaw?"

I hear Danny exhale loudly through is nose and laugh. Okay, so there's history here and the timing couldn't have been planned better. Besides actually starting to sweat from seeing the famous rock star, now I'm nervous I might upset Danny if I get too excited. Plus I don't want to look like a crazy groupie in front of

Holli. But look at him. Oh my God. It's Johnny freaking Outlaw. The Resistance is one of my favorite bands. I stalk with my eyes as he comes around Holli and whispers something in her ear that makes her laugh. She kisses him before turning back to us. "This is Danny's girlfriend, Reese. Reese, Johnny."

He reaches for my hand and I try to stop it from shaking so I don't die from embarrassment. His smile is so kind it's easy to feel comfortable around him. When our hands meet, he leans in, and kisses me on the cheek. "So you're with him, huh?"

I laugh, a little too giddy. "I am."

Danny mutters, "Jesus Christ," making Holli laugh.

She takes Johnny by the arm, and through laughter says, "Is the pissing contest over because I'm sure Reese doesn't appreciate being the prize. Why can't you boys get along?"

Johnny speaks first as he grins at Danny, "We can. Right, old friend? How about I buy you a beer?"

"You've already bought me a bourbon," Danny replies, holding up his glass. "But I'll happily take another."

We move to go inside. Johnny pats Danny's back, and says, "The past is in the past. It's time we all moved on."

Truer words were never spoken.

CHAPTER 36

Reese

ON THE DRIVE home... home. *Danny. My home.* I just spout it out. "I'm turning Vinnie down."

"You are?" Danny asks, surprised.

"It never felt right because of our friendship, and though I love working with him, I want to do a variety of things and different campaigns."

"Are you sure?"

"I am," I say with confidence. "Absolutely positive."

"What do you want to do?"

"I'm going to start my own agency."

"Really? Where?" The concern is heard clearly in the last question.

"What do you think about me staying a little longer, maybe permanently?"

That smile I love so much crosses his lips. "I think that would be amazing." He glances from the road to me. "What do you think about staying with me a little longer, maybe permanently?"

Reaching over, I run my fingertips through the back of his

hair. "I was hoping you'd ask, but I didn't want you to feel pressured."

"Pressured? I've wanted you here since that first day at the Illustrious meeting. So hell yeah, I want you to stay." His hand is on my thigh and he leans closer. I meet him over the gearshift and we kiss. "And I like the idea of your own agency. We can turn the other room into your office if you want."

"You'd do that for me?"

He takes my hand and kisses it. "Don't you know by now, Reese? I would do anything for you."

"And I would do anything for you."

WE WALK INTO the meeting with Mark and Danny's lawyer. We've been told not to say a word. They didn't want me to come, but Danny said if he was basically pleading guilty and paying the bastard, then he was going to "rub it in his fucking face."

I have my own reasons for wanting to be here today.

When we enter the conference room, my eyes meet Keaton's. I'm tempted to turn away from his glower. I can feel his hate burning through me, but I do what Danny always tells me to do. I raise my chin.

We sit down, and while our lawyer goes over the settlement agreement, Keaton continues to stare at me. His limited range of emotions seems to have run out and he's stuck on confusion.

When I glance to my left, Danny is not amused. He takes my hand under the table, and with our fingers woven together, sets them right on the top for everyone to see.

Keaton's eyes dart to Danny, and I hear, just above the silence, "Fuck you."

I squeeze Danny's hand to calm him, but I'm also struggling to stay calm under these circumstances. As soon as our lawyer finishes reading the agreement, Keaton's lawyer sets an addendum down on the table and pushes it across the shiny wood surface so we all can see. There's a lot of fine print, but what stands out is the following line:

By agreeing to this settlement, Daniel Weston, waves his right to see Ms. Reese Carmichael in any professional or social capacity. By doing so, the monies settled will be reduced by $1,000,000.

I'm on my feet, my palms slamming down on the table. "You can't do that!"

Danny's lawyer calls to me. "Ms. Carmichael, I'll handle this. Please sit down." He clears his throat and pushes the addendum back. "This was not a part of the original agreement and we won't accept the addition during this final meeting."

As Keaton's lawyer checks a text message that vibrated his phone, Keaton sits back, smug in his chair, his fingers forming a temple in front of him.

I say, "You won't win, Keaton."

"I already have, sweetheart. Either way, I win. That's what you get for fucking the help."

My feet barely touch the ground as I fly forward to slap him. Danny catches me and pulls me back. "Now you've gone and pissed her off. Good luck, asshole," he warns, with his own wry smirk in place.

He makes me want to spit when he says, "I can handle her."

Through my blinding rage, I manage to reach down and find the reason I'm here. I slap a check down on the table and push it toward his lawyer. Keaton and his lawyer both lean forward to get a closer look. I say, "You'll never separate us. You can't keep us apart. It's a lot of money, but I'd pay it again to be with him."

A check for seven million dollars is between Keaton and us. Danny turns to me, and whispers, "Where did you get that money?"

"I sold my apartment. There was a bidding war, a quick sale, and a cash offer. The deal was too good to pass up, and I cashed out my investments and 401k, so don't worry, the check is good."

Danny stares at me, then says, "I'm not worried if you're good for the money. You didn't have to do all that. Keep your money. I don't want you to pay, Reese. I want to pay and I'm prepared to."

"I'm prepared to pay, too." The whole transaction of selling my sought after apartment in a trendy part of Manhattan took less than two weeks. With money in hand, I'm willing to give it all up for this second chance.

Keaton interrupts, "What the fuck, Reese? Are you seriously fighting over who's going to pay me the money *he* owes me for breaching the contract?"

I hate the sound of his voice. Turning toward Danny, I kiss him. Because we've paid our dues for the *crime* we committed and I don't want to spend another second dealing with this.

With my back to Keaton's side of the table, the other lawyer clears his throat this time. When I look back, Keaton is standing in front of the windows with his back to us. His lawyer pushes the check back to me. "We won't be collecting it. Mr. Klein has decided to drop the charge and forget this happened."

"And why is that?" Danny's lawyer asks.

Keaton turns, a mixture of anger and resolve fills his stance. "Mr. Vittori has agreed to an eleven-million-dollar, one-year deal if we stop the proceedings."

Oh Vinnie. Looking over at Keaton. He feels the victor. He thinks he has won. But this proves what I knew all along. I never mattered to him. All of his claims of love were just deceptions dressed in expensive suits. This was never about love. It was about ownership. *His.* Good riddance, Keaton Klein. Asshole.

I smile. Vinnie may be stuck working with Klein for another year, but you can't beat the sentiment. Looking to Danny, I say, "We're done here. We get to be together and keep the money. Look who wins after all?"

He takes me in his arms and kisses me hard. "Oh baby, we were the winners all along." He stands. "Let's get out of here."

We follow our lawyer out, but Keaton's lawyer calls me, "Ms. Carmichael, against my advice, Mr. Klein has requested to speak with you."

"I have no interest in speaking with Mr. Klein."

Keaton appears in the doorway. "Please, Reese. Just a minute of your time."

Danny's hold on my hand tightens, but there are a few things I'd like to say to Keaton as well. I whisper into Danny's ear, "I'll be all right. This will be quick."

Begrudgingly he nods and walks a few feet away. I walk to the corner, but not back inside the room like I think he wants. When he feels he has sufficient privacy, he asks, "How could you sell? You love that apartment."

"I love him more."

"Give me a break. He's a model. How could *that model* possibly be a better catch than me? I mean... really," he scoffs.

"This is the last time you'll ever disrespect me or my boyfriend."

"What can he give you that I can't?"

Now there's a loaded question if I ever heard one. I love a great setup.

"Happiness. Love. *Real love.* I'm not a puppet he wants to control. His pride doesn't keep him from showing real emotion. He doesn't treat me as an equal. He treats me better. And the sex? Best. Sex. Ever. So you see? He's nothing like you." I turn on my

Louboutin-clad feet. With my hand on my hip, I kick up a stiletto, so he can see the signature-red sole. "Guess what? I bought my own. I think I'll wear these tonight while fucking *that model*."

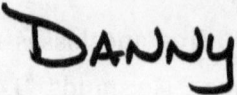

THOSE SEXY FUCKING shoes.

The little devils—tempting me to the dark side of the bedroom where our bed lies waiting for a good romp. But Reese is on the phone with Vinnie thanking him for the bailout. She puts him on speakerphone after he insists. "If I couldn't help you with the money, I had to help however I could. Love should always trump hate. Anyway, Reeses, my little peanut buttercup, you're going to need that money for your agency."

"What happened to Candy Girl?" she asks, laughing, the weight of the world lifted from her shoulders.

"I'm in a chocolate and peanut butter phase."

"Ah. I see."

I shout from across the room. "Thank you, Designer Vittori."

"You're most welcome, Model Danny."

Sinking farther down into the mattress, adrenaline letting go, I get all my sins off my chest. "And by the way, I kept the pants from New York. They fit in all the right places."

"Keep them. I'll never find another model to fill them out anyway."

"I found it impressive that you never measured the inseam and they fit perfectly."

"I've got a good eye for those kind of things. Call it a talent."

Reese starts laughing so hard that she begins to cough. I shake my head. "We'll let this conversation lie where we leave, which is right here. Thanks again."

She finally hangs up the phone after a fit of giggles and goodbyes. Her dress came off an hour ago and she's been walking around in the smallest of panties and bra that covers too much of her amazing chest. *And those heels.* Damn I like those heels on her.

I'm about to call my woman over when my phone rings. I answer it because I know the wedding was tonight. "Hey, Luke, how's the wedding?"

"Terrible."

"Are you still there?"

"Yeah."

"Leave if it's so bad. No one's forcing you to stay if it's torture."

"No, it's not torture. It's terrible because I don't know what to do."

I scratch my head, perplexed. "What's going on?"

"Jane danced with me, but she returned to *him*."

"*Him*, her boyfriend?" I ask.

"Yes."

"Is she coming back?"

"I don't think so. I told her I still loved her. She said thank you and that she had to go back to her date."

"Dude, get out of there. Cut your losses and leave."

"You're right. I need to leave." The reception music is loud in the background, but starts to sound distant, until it's quiet. "Can I come over?"

Reese is bending over while reaching for something in her bag and all I see are two miles of legs, a great ass, and those shoes. I sit up when her legs part oh so slightly, zeroing in on where I want to be most.

"Danny? I'm almost there. It's cool to stop by, right?"

Luke's voice is killing my hard-on. My silent plea is *No!* My verbal response is, "Sure."

"I'll be there in ten."

I sigh when I hang up, torn between being a good friend and struggling that I can't be alone with my woman. She asks, "What's wrong?"

"You dressed like that."

Reaching for the strap on her shoulder, she playfully lifts it teasing me. "If this is a problem, I can take this off."

"Fuck, I want you so fucking badly." I swing my legs off the bed and stand, rubbing my hard-on and willing it down.

"You say that as if I'm not more than willing." Taking her panties down, she adds, "Have I not been clear enough?"

As if my balls don't hate me enough, my voice goes up an octave. "Don't do that. Luke's coming over. And if you take those off, I could give a fuck that my best friend is coming over after having his heart trampled on tonight by his ex."

"Awww. Oh nooo." She pulls her panties up and I whimper. Smiling, she asks, "What happened?"

"Those panties fucking happened."

Tilting her head and with her hand on her hip, she smirks. So fucking sexy. "I meant what happened to Luke."

Oh. "Long story, but he wants to stop by and I don't know, hug it out or something. Once we opened the emotional flood gates, we've been pussies ever since."

"Showing emotion does not make you a pussy, and I thought you liked pussy?"

"Eating. Fucking. Making you come. Making love. Take your pick, but acting like one is not appealing."

She rolls her eyes. "Get rid of that hard-on and I'll get dressed."

As I pull on my jeans, I ask, "You sure it's okay that he stops by?"

Like that's the most ridiculous question ever, she says, "Of course. You're being a good friend. I'm going to take a bath. We can pick up where we left off later tonight."

"With the shoes?"

"That's why I bought them. I'll give you two chatterboxes some privacy." She shakes her ass and walks into the bathroom.

Luke arrives shortly after I get dressed and I grab two beers from the fridge. I hand him one when I answer the door and walk into the living room with him. Sitting down, I get comfortable on the couch. He takes the chair and says, "I can't figure her out."

"I don't think she knows what she wants either."

Taking a long pull from the bottle, he leans back. "Do I give her up?"

"I don't know, man. How do you feel about her?" I finish half the beer as we sink knee-deep into his emotions.

He doesn't hesitate. "I love her."

"There's your answer."

Setting his bottle down, he looks up, and then rubs his hands over his face. "I don't think it's supposed to be this hard."

I follow in the direction he's looking and spot Reese's purse. "If it's meant to be, hard or not, it will be."

"Our timing's off. Our lives out of sync."

"Do you think she'll marry him?"

"I want to say no, but I'm not sure if that's my ego or gut speaking."

I smile. "Probably your ego, knowing you."

"Yeah. Probably."

Standing up, I set the bottle down on the coffee table and open my arms wide.

His face scrunches as he looks at me in mild horror. It's how I feel, so I understand. "What are you doing?"

"We're going to hug it out."

"No. Sit the fuck down."

Holding strong, I say, "Nope. We're going to do this and get it out of the way so we never have to do it again."

"What the hell are you smoking?"

"I'm dead serious. Come on. My arms are getting tired."

He shakes his head. He mutters under his breath. He pretends to leave by walking away. But he returns and hugs me. We hold tight and make sure to pat each other hard on the back before parting. Luke looks confused. "Shit, that actually made me feel a little better. Maybe chicks are onto something."

I laugh. "Whether it made you feel better or not, it made me feel worse. Never again. Agreed?"

Laughing, he nods. "Agreed. And on that note, I'm good."

"So the Jane drama lives on?"

"No. I think it's time for me to move on."

As we walk to the door, I warn, "But no more Jennas, Jackies, or Jennifers."

"Dude, if you take the Jennifers of the world out of play, that won't leave much."

"Eh, I think it will work out." I open the door. "Next time, I want you to meet Reese. It's late and she's taking a bath, so you need to take off so I can take advantage of my naked girlfriend."

He steps out. "Rub it in. Rub it in, man." Backing down to the porch, he says, "I'm not gonna give you a hard time for that. I would be doing the same thing. I'm happy for you, Danny. You deserve to be happy after all this time. Just remember I'm your man when you're casting the best man role."

Chuckling, I say, "You've got it."

"Thanks for the hug," he yells way too loudly. I look around, hoping none of my neighbors hear him.

"Never mention it again."

He's smiling as he walks away. I feel better knowing he feels better. If that makes me a chick, then I guess I'll have to own it. Now back to the previously scheduled program. I lock the door and run into the bathroom to join my girl.

EPILOGUE

REREADING THE TEXT, I smile, happy Jane finally called him. I have no idea what Jane will do, but Reese thinks she'll go back to Luke. Women don't talk to their exes like she has been if she hasn't already *emotionally* left the other guy. I'm pretty sure Reese is speaking from experience. Luke played a good game of pretending he was over her, but it's been obvious he wasn't. Hope still exists. Maybe he'll get his second chance to make things right like I have.

I get up from the couch and go into the bedroom. Those leggings she insists on wearing—the ones she had back in college that drove me nuts, lay on the bed. How pants covered in cats smoking pipes survived our breakup and I didn't, I'll never understand. I guess that's just something I'm going to have to let go. I grab what I came in here for and head out back.

Reese is lying on the back balcony. She's in a very fucking distracting bikini when I go and sit on the chair next to her. I have to mentally make myself stop staring at her fantastic tits and focus on the mission. Trying to act natural, I ask, "Remember how we used to spend the first snow of the year together? No matter where we were, we would find each other?"

"I remember," she says, taking her sunglasses off and smiling at me. "It was our tradition. What made you think of that?"

I shrug nonchalantly. "How about we revive that tradition?"

She laughs her gorgeous laugh. "I'd love to, but I think you've forgotten that we live in Southern California. How do you propose we do it? Take a trip?"

Offering my hand, I stand up. "Come with me." I lead her by the hand through the living room and upstairs. We cut through the room that has become her office and out to the balcony. I open the door and start to walk out but she stops, my body jerking to a halt. Her free hand covers her mouth in surprise.

Despite wanting to give her my million-dollar smile, I'm only capable of a completely cheesy *I-pulled-off-the-greatest-of-grand-gestures* grin. Her eyes are wide in joy. "Come on."

She comes with me this time. We step out onto the terracotta tiles and look up as the snow falls down. "Danny, it's snowing. In Los Angeles. In May." Even though she's barefoot and bikini-clad, Reese runs to the ledge and looks over. The machine is down there, working full time to fight the seventy-degree weather. When she turns back to me, she says, "You did this for me?"

"I do everything for you. Come over here, baby."

She runs and jumps up, her body wrapping around mine, and kisses me, kissing me like this is the last kiss we'll ever share. I kiss her with just as much passion. "I can't believe you did this. It's amazing."

Snowflakes land on her lashes and she shivers. "I guess my timing's off. You're not exactly dressed for the snow."

"Your timing has never been better. I love this so much."

"How about this for timing?" I kneel down on one knee—the left to be precise—and pull the box from my pocket.

Her gasp is loud, both hands now covering her face. I chuckle and pull her hands down gently, until I see her smile, tears filling her eyes. "I want to see your blue eyes when I do this." I thought I'd be nervous, but for some reason—or because of my *someone*—I'm not. Holding her left hand, I rub my thumb over her knuckles. "Ten years ago I let you walk out of my life and didn't fight hard enough to get you back. It's the only regret I've lived with, the only one I didn't think I would ever get a chance to rectify. But here I am, on bended knee before you, silently praying you'll give me the opportunity to make things right, to let me put us back together the way we were always meant to be. Reese Carmichael, will you do me the honor of becoming my wife and partner in this life and for eternity? Will you marry me, pretty?"

I open the black velvet box that was hidden in my drawer under the boxers in the back. The two-carat ring is still as stunning as it was years ago when I bought it in Paris. It's perfect for the stunning woman with shaking hands and tears streaming down her face, standing in the goddamn sexiest bathing suit I've ever seen. For a brief second I think about covering her with my shirt so no one else can see her. But I tame the inner caveman... for now, because I paid a lot of money to make it snow in May. I'm pretty sure she's starting to get cold, but I'm still waiting for her to answer so I can swoop her inside and make love to her to seal the deal.

"You don't know how many times I've dreamed of this moment with you. This is better. You out-dreamed any dream I could have ever had. But I would have said yes even without this, because I have you and you are my dream come true."

"So, that's a yes?"

She's nodding while tears run over her smiling lips. "Yes. A zillion yeses."

I don't waste a second. I scoop her up into my arms and run back inside. Kicking the door shut, I'm quick to the bedroom where that teeny-tiny bikini is off in seconds. I warm her body like I warm her soul—with my body, with my soul.

Six Months Later

I'M EVERYWHERE.

Billboards.

Magazines.

Malls.

Stores.

Bus stops.

Commercials.

Red Carpets.

Airports.

The King of Times Square.

The signs are huge, the ads fill pages, and I'm all over the TV. With the ads out, Mark says I'm back on top, but I say I never left it. Vittori has made me a household name. Well, let's clarify—a household *where I wasn't already a famed* name.

I have my pick of jobs from the modeling world to acting. I can do and have anything, *except* the privacy I once enjoyed. I'm adapting. Reese is doing a good job, though she cracks under the lens of the paparazzi microscope some days and threatens to kidnap me and hide me in Manhattan. She's adorable like that, when she gets all protective and possessive. I don't blame her. I feel the same about her.

I'm just glad she's got Holli to rely on, to vent to, to hang out with. They have a lot in common—ambitious, kind, and funny. But Reese is so much more to me. She knows me, the real me before the fame, and before the money. She knows the present-day me as well, and *still stays*. I chuckle.

I look up at the Illustrious sign as I walk inside. It's always been a source of pride to watch this agency grow into an international success and to know I've been a part of that journey.

Mark is in his office when I arrive. In typical fashion, he doesn't look up, but says, "Good work, Danny."

"Thanks," I reply, sitting down in front of his desk.

"We booked GQ. Sebastian Lassiter has been pushed back a few months." He looks up. "Guess you still got it."

I pop my imaginary collar. It's good to be king.

Mark adds, "And because Mr. Vittori insists on you for his next campaign, the new deal with Vittori closed this morning. He didn't even balk at your new fee."

Vinnie has been very generous with us professionally, to both Reese and me. As for his friendship, the man knows no bounds *or boundaries*. Literally. But it all comes from a good place. We're glad to have him in our corner.

I'll be wearing a Vittori suit for the wedding and Vinnie's designing Reese's dress for the wedding as his gift, in trade, for letting him plan it with her. I'm afraid to see the purple spectacle this will become, but if it makes them happy, it makes me happy.

"We've worked together a long time." Setting his pen down, he says, "I think you have a long career ahead of you and I'm happy I get to share it."

"Me too, man." I reach forward and shake his hand, but

he stands and pulls me in for a hug. We pat each other on the back.

When we stand back, he says, "Jody has the contract for you to sign. Stop at her desk on your way out." And like that, we're back to business.

"Okay. Thanks for everything."

"You're welcome. Now get out of here. I have to close this deal for Sebastian before he flips out over GQ."

Laughing, I say, "Good luck with that one."

"I need it."

I don't even make it to The Pit before I hear Lassiter, for some reason, having enough nerve to talk to me. He says, "That's one smokin' hot girl you've got there."

Stopping, I look back at him. Letting my scowl speak for me, but decide he needs to hear it as well. "That's your one free pass. Say anything about her, even uttering her name will get your ass taken down."

Lassiter doesn't take anything seriously. "So, you don't want me to tell you how I think I'll hire her sexy ass as my up-close-and-personal ad advisor? I'm sure she'll enjoy spending late nights together working on our—"

My fist is flying, but I stop just shy of a half-inch from his jaw. Cocky motherfucker. "Finish what you were saying."

Nervous, he laughs. "I think I'm done."

So close, but I give him the second chance. "Yeah, I thought so." Let's hope he doesn't make that mistake again.

Mark runs out of his office, shouting, "Shit, Danny! He has a job in two days."

"I gave him a warning."

Mark comes between us. "So I guess you're not up for mentoring him?"

I laugh, moving to Jod's desk and crossing my arms. "Thanks, but no thanks. Good luck with that."

"You're lucky I like you or I'd fired you."

Jods hands me the new contract to sign. Ever since the Vittori campaign hit, my asking price just went time and a half. I cock an eyebrow with my signature smirk. "You love me too much."

"I love the money you make me."

I shrug as I walk to the door. "Same thing. See you soon." I take the elevator down and pass the reception desk, sending the security guard a nod. When I push through the double doors and walk under the silver Illustrious letters set atop the modern stainless steel awning, I stop to appreciate the life I've been given, the second chance I've stolen back from destiny.

I live the life many envy, more crave—fame, traveling the world, big paychecks, hot women. But only one thing matters and that's what has me grinning from ear to ear. It may not be my million-dollar smile, but it's worth a billion to me. She's worth more to me.

Reese sits in the driver's seat of the fresh-off-the-showroom-floor dark sapphire convertible Jaguar F-TYPE. I would have called it navy, but that would be an insult to the perfection of this shade of blue. Her engagement present brings out the blue of her gorgeous eyes, which are fixed on me now.

After I hop over the car door and land in the passenger seat, she asks, "How did it go?"

"Good." I won't go into the gory details of almost pummeling that arrogant asshole. I don't want to ruin a perfectly beautiful Southern California day. In the end, Sebastian Lassiter doesn't matter. I got the gig. I got the girl. I've got a damn good life. Winking, I say, "It's good to be me." It's good to be a model on top.

Smiling, Reese shakes her head, and starts the car. "You ready, Romeo?"

Taking her hand in mine, I bring it to my lips and kiss her. "I was born ready, baby."

The End

Keep reading for excerpts from
Dirty Talk **and** *The Resistance* **by S. L. Scott.**

S.L. SCOTT

PROLOGUE

Jane Lewis

SQUEEZING THE STEERING wheel, I blow out the breath I was holding the last few seconds. My heart is racing almost as fast as my car.

This is it.

I'm ignoring my mind, flipping around my hurt feelings, and following my heart. Rolling my window down, I throw caution to the wind.

This feels right.

I've been apart from the other half of my heart for too long, and I'm going to reclaim him.

"I'm going to open your body, embrace your soul, and coax the moon and stars to shine inside."

Words whispered in my ear many years ago make my heart somersault in my chest. My long hair whips around my head, the wind heavy with anticipation as excitement builds deep within.

I park in front of the house he bought post-*us* and rush to the door. Knocking twice, I bounce on my heels waiting for him to answer while trying to peek in through the small side window to see if he's home. I hope he is. My feelings are about to burst free from excitement and I need to share them with him.

The connection we once had was derailed over misunderstandings and hurt feelings. Over the last year, wanting the life I had back, wanting him back, I've broken down and gone to see him. We haven't talked recently, but now is the time to come clean, to tell him how I feel, hoping he feels the same.

Luke Anders is my past, present, and soon to be future all wrapped in a sexy, hard body, and a lady-killer smile. I cannot wait to smother him with deep kisses and late-night snuggles, just like I used to do.

Lifting up, I peek in the window again and huff when I don't see any movement inside. I check the door and when the doorknob turns, I go in. "Luke?"

I get nothing in return, so I walk farther inside and call him again. "Luke?"

My happy bubble deflates as I try to figure out if I stay and wait or if I should go. The space draws me farther in, the calm of the environment, of Luke's life surrounding me, giving me peace. I smile, touching the bannister, running my fingers over the smooth railing.

"I know you."

I look up to find a bleach-blonde woman at the top of the stairs, holding the railing I was just touching like a barricade to the second floor. My heart suddenly feels heavy and blood rushes through my veins, loud in my ears. "I'm looking for Luke," I reply dumbly.

"He's upstairs." She points over her shoulder. "I can get him. He should be out of the shower by now."

The shirt... she's wearing *his* USC shirt. "Did you go to USC?"

"Huh?"

I point and she looks down and tugs on the hem that hits her upper thighs, and laughs. "Oh no. This is Luke's. I borrowed it."

My arm crosses over my stomach as I struggle to keep its contents down. I stare a moment longer before my eyes lower and I notice she has no pants on. Gulping down my hurt feelings, my disappointment, and replacing them with a false pride, I say, "Tell him I stopped by," then turn to leave.

"Jane?"

I freeze. After a deep breath, I turn just enough to look over my shoulder.

"He's happy."

Catching her drift, I ask, "Without me, you mean?"

She leans against the wall, his shirt sliding up her long legs as if she wants me to see just how model-esque she is compared to me. Her eyes stay fixed on me looking way too comfortable in his house. "With me."

My heart crashes and burns into the pit of my stomach and I lower my gaze. "I've changed my mind. You don't need to tell him I stopped by." I beeline for the door.

Just before it shuts, she says, "Tootle-loo," grinding the salt deeper into my open-heart wound.

Running to my car, I jump in and close the door fast, keeping the world and all its pain outside. I back out and when I'm driving away, I make sure not to look back.

My phone rings and I glance at the caller ID. It's not the person I want to hear from, but I answer it anyway, not wanting to feel so alone. "Hi."

"Please come home, Jane. I'm sorry I told people." Lawrence's voice fills the car as it comes out through the speakers.

"You lied to them. We're not engaged."

"You played along."

"I shouldn't have. I was put on the spot. You set me up to

either play along or be embarrassed. I chose to play along to end it."

"I know you love me deep down."

"I care about you, Lawrence, but I'm not in love with you."

"Come home."

"It's not my home."

"It will be if you just give it a chance, if you give me a chance, a real chance this time."

My heart hurts as I enter the freeway. An hour later I'm sitting in front of Lawrence's house looking at the pink flowers he had planted for me.

I always wanted a white picket fence, a house full of kids, and an amazing husband I can't love enough. Two out of three isn't so bad.

Maybe I can be happy with Lawrence, happy like Luke is with that other woman. *"He's happy. With me."* Luke has moved on. He's really not mine anymore. *How could he move on without me? He promised me he'd love me forever.* He lied.

I'm not getting any younger and I want my dreams to come true. Lawrence... loves me. He says he'll give me everything I want and a comfortable life. *Comfortable.* Looks like that's all I will have now.

Luke is no longer mine. He's given his heart away and taken mine in the process.

Who needs a whole heart anyway?

CHAPTER 1

Luke Anders
Ten Months Later

"WHAT IF I touched you right where you want to be touched?" I slide my hand up her thigh, inching her skirt up slowly. Her breath catches, the quiet gasp making me smile. "What if I touched you right where you pretend to be so protective? I know you. I know you like it dirty... maybe even a little rough."

She finds her voice, though it's affected, sexy. "A lot."

"What is that?"

Clearing her throat, she says, "I like it rough. Really rough."

The right side of my mouth curves up, my hand stalling just below the apex of her thighs when my phone buzzes. I release a sigh. Grabbing the phone from my pocket, I sit up and read the text: *Let's get the fuck out of here.* I look back at the black-haired raven I've left squirming on the metal barstool next to me. *Pity.* I'd like to explore exactly how she likes it, but duty calls. Standing up suddenly, I grab my wallet and slap some bills down for the drinks.

"What are you doing?" she demands, desperation lacing her tone as her eyes go wide.

I tuck my wallet back into the inside pocket of my Vittori suit jacket and kiss her on the cheek. Since I'm there, I add with a wink, "I bet we'd be so fucking good together." Straightening upright, I smirk. "My apologies. I hate to run, but unfortunately, I have a prior engagement I can't get out of. Maybe we can pick this up another time. I'll see you around, sweetheart."

She huffs. "You're a playboy bastard, Luke Anders," rolls off her tongue in frustrated anger as she spins back to the bar.

I know. Not turning back, I nod. It's not the first time I've been called a playboy or a bastard. Name-calling doesn't bother me. Not getting laid tonight does.

Pushing open the exit door that leads to the alley, my asshole friends are waiting near the car they've pulled around.

The rusting red door slams shut, the click of the lock heard loudly behind me. The alley is quiet compared to the loud music that blares inside the club. "Fuckers." With my arms out wide, I yell, "What the fuck? Where's the fire? I was closing the deal."

"We were saving you, man. Trust me on that." My best friend is standing in front of the car with his arms crossed over his chest. Danny Weston is one of the best people I know, but right now, he's pissing me the fuck off.

"Saving me from what?"

"Ask Blaise. He has firsthand knowledge."

When I shoot an annoyed look in Blaise's direction, he clams up. With hands up in surrender, he backs away toward the driver's door. "I can't help that the ladies love me." Thus confirming he's already hit that pretty kitty.

I walk to the passenger's side of the car, punching Danny on the arm when I pass him. "Shit, man, just give me a heads-up next time. I wasted some of my best lines on her."

Danny claims the front seat, so I duck into the back seat of a restored 1969 black Gran Torino. Cocky behind the wheel, Blaise takes off before we even have our seatbelts on, and says, "Stop hitting on everyone that takes pity on you then."

"Fuck you. I can get any woman I want. No one's taking pity on me."

Danny breaks into the argument, "You guys really need to find a new hobby."

"One-night stands are plenty entertaining," Blaise retorts, smiling.

Danny puts his arm on the back of the seat and turns toward me. "I'm not going to lecture you—"

"Again," I add.

"Again," he repeats while rolling his eyes. "But we've talked about this a fuck ton of times. She's not Jane and until you figure out what the hell is going on there, or if anything is going on there, these women are all the same—just another disappointment you're going to have in the morning because they're not her."

Blaise verbally steps in, "Damn, dude, why so deep? You're bringing me down."

Danny laughs. I don't. We've been friends for many years now, so Danny knows my game. He knows me well enough to know what I'm doing. Until I sort out this mess with the first woman I ever loved, the rest are just regrets waiting to happen, along with the regrets I can't take back.

But I know him well too. We relate in a way that Blaise doesn't understand, on a level that one day he'd be lucky to experience. No matter what I've been through with Jane, I've loved, hard. I know what it means to love and to be loved. I have no regrets when it comes to Jane, except one: letting her go.

THE HOLLYWOOD HILLS holds many secrets. Behind the closed doors of the pristine homes belies a lifestyle of privilege and sacrifice. The residents may not realize what they've surrendered to be in the position to live in such a prestigious neighborhood, but it's always there lingering in the background—you're only as good as your last—film, hit song, series, novel, screenplay, production, last whatever it is that gained you entrance to LA's elite.

We walk up the driveway to the mansion atop the hill passing a woman who is vaping while on the phone arguing with what sounds like her boyfriend. Danny's over this scene, but he comes for us. I'm not sure if it's to keep us out of trouble or to watch us get shot down. Either way I'm glad he's here. Between his modeling schedule and his relationship, he's rarely in LA anymore or wanting to spend time out.

Blaise walks in first and we follow. The music is loud, and the crowd trendsetting in their attire. We find a bar full of booze before we find anyone we know. After mixing our drinks, we head outside to the pool area. I take the lead when I spot a group of women in short, very tight skirts and heels that make their legs look a mile long.

Actresses or wannabes. Either way, they're hot.

I stop and Blaise runs into my back. "What the hell, Anders? You just made me spill my drink down the front of my shirt."

When I see her, I'm suddenly frozen to the spot—stuck in a history I can't seem to forget.

Danny says, "I think you should talk to her."

I look back at Blaise. "Did you know she would be here?"

He's swiping his hands down his shirt. "Who?"

"Jane," Danny responds for me.

Blaise immediately looks up and over my shoulder. "Where?"

He signals toward the hot tub Jane is standing near, talking to people sitting inside it. "Over there."

His eyes dart from Jane back to me. "I thought it was kind of a given since she lives here."

"What?" I ask, scanning the room. "What do you mean? This is where she and her boyfuck live?"

"He's more than a fuck. He's her fiancé," he corrects. "Wasn't it understood when I invited you?"

What the fuck? Fiancé?

Surely I misheard him, but I'm too numb to voice my questions.

"You never said who the lawyer was." Danny pushes him enough so Blaise understands he just pissed off his friends. "You're an asshole, Blaise. You know that?"

I want to fucking pop Blaise. Before I can say, or do, anything more, I see *him*. *Him*—the man with the smug smile on his face when he sees me. I tell my friends, "I need to get out of here."

It's too late. I know it is. I would look like a pussy if I ran. So I stay. Lawrence Reinstardt—lawyer to the stars, LA bigwig, and fiancé to the one I once thought I was destined to be with. If he wasn't such an arrogant asshole, I might like the guy. But we remain at odds over a woman he takes for granted and one I can't forget.

Capped, bright white teeth. He's older than me by six to eight years maybe, easily mid-thirties or older. Tailored blue shirt with fitted slacks and designer loafers. Sure, he's well dressed, and most women might fall for his blond hair, dark eyes, fake tan, and fat wallet, but I fail to see what Jane sees in him. It's obviously something I can't. He smiles. "Anders. Surprised to see you here."

"I heard Jane was going to dump you publicly and wanted a

front-row seat."

"Ha ha. You're a funny guy." He clicks his tongue and shoots me with his hands, as if they're guns, and we're five years old. "I can see why she chose me," he says with a snarl.

And there it is... the one thing he can hold over me. He has the one *person* he knows I can't have, and he taunts me, riles me, and makes me want to punch his fucking lights out. Just as I make a fast break forward to take him down, Danny throws his arms out to separate us. "Let's remember we're gentlemen here and not do this. It's a party, after all."

My breath isn't harsh. I'm the epitome of calm on the outside, my fury spinning like a tornado deep inside. He shouldn't fear the man that rages loudly. He should fear the one that rages quietly. It would be easy to knock that smug smirk off his face, but I don't need easy. I'm better than that. I'm better than him. I glare at him before backing down and straightening my expensive suit.

When Danny lowers his arms, Lawrence has the nerve to say, "Danny, my friend. So glad you could make it, but I think you should take your buddy and leave."

"First off," Danny starts, "you and I are not friends. Secondly, we're already leaving."

Just as I'm about to take a step, not wanting to be here another second longer, I hear, "Luke."

I know the voice. That same voice whispered my name in varying degrees of emotion from ecstasy to pain, the memories of her tone still emblazoned across my heart like a brand.

Why can't I just forget her and move on?

"Luke?"

When I finally look over my shoulder, my head drops after seeing her. I'm never prepared. Not ever. Her beauty never wanes in my eyes. Never. Maybe it's because of the memories attached to her, but I'm really thinking it's my heart that's still attached. "I don't want any trouble," I say, my voice sounding weaker than I like. "I was just leaving."

She stops a few feet behind me, and says quietly, "It's good to see you."

Lawrence snaps his fingers and when I look at him, his eyes are on my Jane, his tone harsh as he calls her to his side. "Come here, Jane."

I turn to look at her, insulted, offended, and infuriated he would treat her like a dog. Her eyes are on me but they aren't bright like when we were together. The soft smile she's wearing fades when she looks to him.

His demand is harsher this time when he snaps again and points to the ground. "Here. Now. Jane."

I want to fucking throttle him. But by the looks of it, Danny might beat me to the punch. Literally. The back of my hand hits his chest as I try to remain that calm I was bragging about a moment earlier. It's not my place to step in on her relationship, a relationship *she* chose over ours. "Let's go."

Danny acknowledges me, and silently, he takes a step back. Dropping my arm down, I turn to Jane. "It was good to see you." I head for the door, not rushing, though I want to. I walk, wondering where the hell the feisty girl I once knew was. When I look over my shoulder, she turns away from Lawrence and walks back outside, leaving him standing there with his finger still pointing toward the floor.

There she is.

My smile is wide as we leave a place I should have never come to in the first place. When we get back in the car, Blaise doesn't waste time getting us out of there, and I don't waste time telling him what I think about him bringing me here. "Don't ever set me up like that again."

"I didn't set you up. I told you we were going to a party."

"You didn't tell me *whose* party."

"I also didn't know it was Reinstardt who stole your girl."

"He didn't fucking steal her. I let her go." Stupidly.

Danny looks back at me. "You okay?"

"I'll be fine. I always am."

He won't accept that bullshit of an answer, but with Blaise here, he lets it slide. I appreciate not having an audience while my heart shatters, surprised I have enough of it left to be affected.

Danny asks, "Drinks or home?"

"Home for me. I'm done with today."

No one questions or argues. Thank God for one thing going my way.

Later, lying in my bed, the wind blows through the open door, the night getting colder by the hour. The room is dark, the lights out, and the moon hidden by a cloudy sky.

The day started on such a high. One email caused me to call my friends to go out and celebrate. The deal was closed. I'm a producer on a film I know will score on the indie circuit and I can sell to major distributers worldwide. Production begins next week, so work is good. Work is great, in fact. Normally my work takes my mind off everything, especially off *her*.

Not this time.

I'm about to be tested—heart and soul, mind and body. This will determine my future and I have no idea if that future holds the same ending the film does. Somehow I doubt it. Not everyone gets a second chance.

The Resistance

S. L. SCOTT

Prologue

I'M A FUCKING fool.

I'm not even sure how I got into this mess, but I know I need to get myself out of it. I look down at the hand on my thigh inching up higher and my stomach rolls. Squeezing out from between the tight confines of the third row in this van, a girl on each side wanting a piece of me, I fall over the seat into the cargo area and move away from their astonished stares. They're speaking German and I don't know what the fuck they're saying, but I've been in this type of situation enough to know how it will end, if I let it.

Everything has changed... or sometime around my last birthday I changed.

I didn't invite these chicks. Dex did. He'll fuck'em all before the night's through and the bad part is, they'll let him. Thinking they're special, that they'll be the one to tame him. They'll let him do what he wants just to be close to him.

Beyond this set up being predictable at this point, it's really fucking old or I am, probably both. I ignore their taps on my shoulder and them calling my name. I ignore everything to do with them and focus on my phone.

On the inside, I'm freaking the fuck out that I'm sitting in the cargo hold of a huge van in Germany with attractive girls willing to do anything I want them to, but I prefer to look at a photo of a little blonde with hazel eyes. Freaking the fuck out might be an understatement.

I'm a player or was, supposed to be, maybe still am. I don't keep score or anything like that, but I've slept with plenty of women, sometimes more than one at a time. I used to blame my lifestyle, but more recently, I realized I'm the common denominator in the bad relationships I've had.

The car comes to a stop and the driver rushes around to the back to let me out. I stumble while climbing out, and hurry inside away from the sound of my name being called. The girls will be upset when they realize I'm not staying to play, but Dex will be thrilled—more pussy for him.

Cory hops out from the front, and follows me. "Wait up," he says, jogging to catch up.

When we reach the elevators, we look back. Dex is helping the girls out of the vehicle one-by-one. With a cigarette hanging from the corner of his mouth, he's sloppy, already drunk. He never lacks for female companionship. By the way he acts, I don't see the appeal, but I don't think that's why they're hooking up with him anyway.

Cory looks at me and nods once. "What's up? What happened back there?"

The elevator doors open and we step in, pushing the button for our floor. "Over it. Over it all."

"The girl from Vegas?"

"She's not from Vegas, but yeah, I've kind of been thinking about her."

When the brass doors reopen, we walk down the hall to our rooms. Cory and I don't do small talk. We've been friends for years, best friends if I think about it.

"Maybe you should call her," he suggests as we open our doors.

"Maybe I will."

"Night."

"Night," I mumble and shut the door behind me.

1

Holliday Hughes

"Comfort zones are like women. You have to try a few before you find the one that feels right." ~*Johnny Outlaw*

THAT DAMN LIME and coconut song has been playing on a loop in my head, driving me nuts for hours. I make a mental note: Fire Tracy in the morning for subjecting me to that song twenty-thousand times yesterday. She called it inspirational. I call it torture after the first two times.

Rolling over, I look at the time. 4:36 a.m. I have four hours before I need to be on the road. This may be a business trip, but it will still be good to get away for a few days. I need a break. I've been in a bad mood lately. The spa and I have a date I'm really looking forward to. The thought alone relaxes me. I close my eyes and try to get a few more hours of sleep before I need to leave for Las Vegas.

I get two tops.

I tighten my robe at the neck. Just as I open my front door to get the paper, I hear a male voice say, "Hello?"

Peeking through the crack, I hold the door protectively in front of me just in case I need to close and lock it quickly. "Hi."

"I'm your new neighbor. I just moved in last week. I'm Danny."

Curious, I slowly stick my head out to get a better look at this Danny. Strands of my sandy blonde hair fall in front of my eyes, so I tuck it behind my ear and get an eyeful. To my surprise, he's quite handsome and has a big smile. "Oh, um," I say, dragging my hand down the back of my hair, hoping to tame the wild strands. "Hi. I'm Holli. Welcome to the neighborhood."

He nods toward the paper on the bottom of the shared Spanish tiled steps that lead to our townhomes. "I'll get your paper since you're not dressed."

"Thanks." I watch him. He looks like he just got back from a run or workout—a little sweaty, but not gross, in that sexy kind of way. Or maybe Danny's just sexy. He's well built with short, brown hair and when he bends over, I notice his strong legs and arms. Well-defined muscles lead to—*Oh my God!* Not just my face, but my entire body heats from embarrassment. Hoping he doesn't say anything about me checking him out, I turn away and start picking at a piece of peeling stucco near my house number. "Um, so are you settled in, liking your place?"

His chuckling confirms I was busted. But he's a gentleman, so he acts as if it didn't happen. "I like the neighborhood. The place is great," he says. "I like all the space, especially the patio. I'm thinking of having a party to break it in, maybe in a few weeks after I finish unpacking." He hands me the paper and takes two steps back. "You should stop by."

Nodding, I look into his eyes. I think they're brown, lighter than mine, more honey-colored. His offer is friendly, not a come on, which is good since we're neighbors now. "Thanks for the invitation."

Walking back to his door, he steals one more glimpse over his shoulder. "Have a great day. See you around, Holli."

"Yeah, see you around."

I shut the door, paper in hand, and fall against the wood with a smile on my face. One of my golden rules is not to date where I sleep, but I still appreciate that my new hottie neighbor is easy on the eyes. He might know it, but he doesn't seem arrogant.

I lock the door and get ready to leave.

Los Angeles is hot, smoggy, and grey at this hour and I have a feeling it won't be much different a few hours from now. I close the patio door and lock it, double checking for safety. After pulling the drapes closed, I take one last look around to make sure I'm not forgetting anything. I text Tracy and let her know I'm leaving. She doesn't reply, but I'm not surprised. Her boyfriend proposed last night after six years of dating. Being the kind boss and friend I am, I let her out of this trip, so she could spend the weekend with their families to celebrate the engagement.

There are selfish reasons as well for letting her off the hook. I really don't think I can handle hours of sitting in the car with her as she reads bridal magazines and plans every detail of her big day. After too many dud dates in the last couple of months, I'm not in the right frame of mind to plan her happily ever after.

With my garment bag in one hand and my suitcase in the other, I click the button, disarming my car's alarm as I walk to my parking space. I've lived here a couple of years. I wanted a place near the beach that also had space for my office, and I was fortunate enough to find both in this townhome.

A meme I created went viral three years ago this month. Who knew a snarky-mouthed fruit would be the way I make my fortune. I took it though and ran with the brand, building it into a small empire I named Limelight. The company is lean and I keep my costs under control. My fortune has grown by a few million in the last year alone.

I back out onto the street and take the scenic route, one block up to the beach. Driving slowly along with my windows down, I let the sound of the waves and the smell of the ocean center me. At the first stoplight, I take one deep salty air breath, roll the window back up, and leave for Vegas.

An hour into the trip, Tracy calls. I answer, but before I have a chance to speak, she asks, "Can I please tell you all about it again?" Happy laughter punctuates her question.

"Of course. Tell me everything." I'll indulge her wedding fantasies because that's what friends do... and because I have four hours to kill in the car. Listening to her takes my mind off the time and the miles stretching ahead of me as she relives every last detail of the proposal. Fortunately for me, she skims over the engagement sex.

Her excitement is contagious and because I've known her and her fiancé, Adam, for so many years, my happiness exudes. "Congratulations again."

"Thank you for letting me stay home this weekend. You'll be great and don't be nervous. It's just a rah-rah go get'em presentation and cocktail party. The rest of the time is all yours."

"You know how much I hate these kinds of events."

"You don't have to prove anything to anyone. Your company's success speaks for itself."

"Thanks. I'll try to remember that."

"Drive safely and squeeze in some fun."

I laugh. "You know I'll try. Bye." When we hang up, I turn on some music and let the miles drift behind me.

After a stop for gas half-way and a coffee later, I enter the glistening city in the desert. Pulling up to my hotel, I valet my car and take my own luggage to my room after checking in. I like this hotel because of the amenities, but the men aren't bad to look at either—a little edgy, a lot sexy—lucky for this single girl.

I spend a couple of hours checking emails and work on a proposal before I realize the time and need to get ready for the night. It's Vegas, so I mix business with some sexy. I pull on a black fitted skirt that hits mid-thigh, an emerald green silk camisole with spaghetti straps, and a short black jacket. I slip on my favorite new pair of stilettos and after one last check of my makeup and hair, I head out.

The meet and greet isn't long, but I slip out at one point to use the restroom. As I'm walking back toward the ballroom, I'm drawn to a man standing with a group of people nearby. His magnetism captures me. He might just be the best looking man I've ever seen—tall, dark hair, strong jaw leading me up to seductive eyes aimed at me. His head tilts and for a split second in time, everyone else disappears. I break the connection by looking away, everything feeling too intense in the moment. When he laughs, I add that to his ongoing list of great attributes.

When I pass, the feel of his gaze landing heavy on my backside warms my body. With my hand on the door, I pause, wanting to look back so badly. I resist the urge, open the door, and return to the party. The presentation portion of the evening is interesting. Despite that, my thoughts repeatedly drift back to the hot guy in the corridor—fitted jeans, black shirt, leather wristband. *Damn I'm weak to a leather wristband.*

I'm mentally brought back to the presentation when my company is recognized as one to watch. The acknowledgement is nice, and it feels good to be among my peers.

The dinner becomes more of a party as everyone wanders around instead of taking their seats. I'm not hungry and need to psych myself up to mingle. Tracy is awesome in these types of situations. Me, not so much.

The ballroom is dimly lit, I'm guessing to set the ambiance, but since this is business, I can do without the romance. I head straight for the bar just like everyone else—one big cattle call to the liquor to make the rest of the night a little more bearable.

"I usually hate these things," I hear from the guy behind me. When I look over my shoulder, he gives me a half-smile—half-friendly, half-creepy. "But they don't usually have attractive women either."

I roll my eyes while turning my back on him and his cheesy pick-up line.

"I'm sorry. That was bad. I know," he says with a weird nasally laugh.

His breath hits my neck and I jerk back. "Do you mind? Ever hear of personal space?"

"Sorry. You're just really pretty." He shrugs as if that makes everything better. "Your beauty is making me stupid."

"You think?" *Big mistake.*

He actually takes my sarcastic comment as a conversation opener. "Yes, I do. But I can't be the first to be dumbfounded by your beauty."

Standing on my tiptoes to see how many more people are in front of me, I exhale, disappointed by the long line. One person in line would have been too many at this point. "Excuse me," I say and slip out of line. I find the table with my name tag on it, set my purse down, and take off my jacket. This hotel ballroom is crowded and too warm.

Saved by a friendly face, I see Cara, a marketing strategist I know from L.A. Weaving between the tables, I sit down in a chair next to her. With her eyes focused on the paperwork in front of her, I ask, "Working during the party?"

She looks up, smiling when she sees me. Opening her arms, she leans in and hugs me. "Holli, it's so good to see you."

I went with a different company than hers for a campaign a while back and glad she's not holding it against me. "Good to see you again."

"Congratulations on your success. Well deserved."

"I'm not sure if a smartass lime deserves the success it's gotten, but I'll take it."

She taps my leg. "You deserve it. It's funny and quite catchy. Just take the accolades."

"Thanks."

Looking over my shoulder, she leans in and whispers, "I'm skipping out of here early, but I'm meeting a few people for dinner tomorrow. If you're still in Vegas, you should join us."

"I'd love that. Thanks."

She stands up and grabs the papers in front of her. "Fantastic. I'll text you the details tomorrow. I'm so glad we ran into each other."

"Me too. See you tomorrow."

I'm left sitting alone. When I look around the room, like Cara, I'm thinking that skipping out early might be the way to go. If I do, I know Tracy will kick my ass, so I decide to suffer and give this party one last chance. But I definitely need a drink and the line for the bar in here is still way too long.

I head for the doors to buy a drink in one of the many hotel bars—any bar without a line. Guy from the bar line jumps in front of me as I try to exit, startling me. "Hey, hey, hey. You're not leaving already, are you?"

Since my glare and earlier hints didn't work, I reply, "I'll be back, no need to worry yourself."

His head starts bobbing up and down, confidently, and a big Cheshire cat grin covers his face. I start walking again as he keeps talking... again. "Cool. I'll see you later then."

I feel no need to respond to the come on, and will try to avoid him when I return. Following the wide-tiled path through the casino, which reminds me of the Yellow Brick Road, guiding me to what feels like Oz, a bar in all its gloriousness with no lines in site. Inside the darkened room, the sounds of the casino fade away as current hits play overhead. Still on a mission for a cocktail, I step up to the bar and wait.

AVAILABLE BOOKS BY NEW YORK TIMES BESTSELLING AUTHOR

S.L. SCOTT

Talk to Me Series

Sweet Talk

Dirty Talk

Hard to Resist Series

The Resistance

The Reckoning

The Redemption

Welcome to Paradise Series

Good Vibrations

Good Intentions

Good Sensations

Happy Endings

Welcome to Paradise Series Set

From the Inside Out Series

Scorned

Jealousy

Dylan

Austin

From the Inside Out Compilation

Stand Alone Books

Until I Met You

Naturally, Charlie

A Prior Engagement

Lost in Translation

Sleeping with Mr. Sexy

Morning Glory

To keep up to date with her writing and more,
her website is www.slscottauthor.com or to receive her newsletter
with all of her publishing adventures and giveaways, sign up for
her newsletter: http://bit.ly/1pF049r

Join S.L.'s Facebook group here: http://bit.ly/2bq2Tfa

S.L. SCOTT

New York Times and *USA Today* Bestselling Author, S. L. Scott, was always interested in the arts. She grew up painting, writing poetry and short stories, and wiling her days away lost in a good book and the movies.

With a degree in Journalism, she continued her love of the written word by reading American authors like Salinger and Fitzgerald. She was intrigued by their flawed characters living in picture perfect worlds, but could still debate that the worlds those characters lived in were actually the flawed ones. This dynamic of leaving the reader invested in the words, inspired Scott to start writing journeys with emotion while injecting an underlying passion into her own stories.

Living in the capital of Texas with her family, Scott loves traveling and avocados, beaches, and cooking with her kids. She's obsessed with epic romances and loves a good plot twist. She dreams of seeing one of her own books made into a movie one day as well as returning to Europe. Her favorite color is blue, but she likens it more toward the sky than the emotion. Her home is filled with the welcoming symbol of the pineapple and finds surfing a challenge though she likes to think she's a pro.

To keep up to date with her writing and more, her website is www.slscottauthor.com or to receive her newsletter with all of her publishing adventures and giveaways, sign up for her newsletter: http://bit.ly/1pF049r